Praise for T
Amaz

"Two powerless young women must navigate a soul-crushing class system and find the levers of power they wield when they combine their strengths. These women may have been taught to whisper, but when their time comes, they will roar. — Timothy Miller, author of *The Strange Case of Eliza Doolittle*

"Trish MacEnulty has brought Gilded Age New York to life at the start of what I hope will be a long series. A pair of unlikely allies, the seamy underside of New York City, and the even more distasteful underside of high society all come together in a thrilling book that will have you glued to the pages. This is one of the best historical mysteries I've picked up!" — Jo Niederhoff, *San Francisco Book Review*

"A rare fictional perspective of women's historical struggles in a world made intolerable by misogynistic customs, from deeply ingrained sexism and suppression of women to violent gangs, risky abortions, and wealthy criminals who hide under charitable works. MacEnulty's suspenseful, elaborate, and addictive debut historical fiction is highly recommended to fans of historical fiction and readers concerned with equal rights." — Foluso Falaye, *Manhattan Book Review*

"The Whispering Women features two lively female investigators who represent distinct social classes. Richly drawn characters, the vibrant historical setting, and a suspenseful mystery create a strong current that pulls readers into this delightful novel. But it's the women's issues—as relevant today as they were in the early 1900s—that will linger long after the last page." — Donna S. Meredith, *The Southern Literary Review*

"Although Trish MacEnulty's wonderful new novel, *The Whispering Women*, is historical fiction, it couldn't be more timely or relevant. This is an exciting book with so many twists that any description of the action becomes a reveal . . . MacEnulty has presented an accomplished mystery debut."— Michelle Cacho-Negrete, author of *Stealing in America*

The Burning Bride

A Delafield & Malloy Investigation

A novel by

Trish MacEnulty

978-1-7375751-5-3
Published by
Prism Light Press

Manufactured in the United States of America.

For the protestors, advocates,
and rabblerousers —
then and now

And for my daughter

“Your toil made the wealth of the nation. It belongs to you.” — Emma Goldman

“The charm is very complex, as a true charm always is, but the place is very simple, as a place which has taken time to grow always is. It is especially so if the place, like St. Augustine, has had its period of waning as well as waxing, and has gently lapsed from its climax.”

— William Dean Howells
“A Confession of St. Augustine”
1914

Contents

How Quickly They Do Forget

March 13, 1914

By L. Byron
Special to Mother Earth

How quickly the people forget the transgressions of their overlords. Let us take, for example, one John D. Rockefeller, the richest man on Earth and a scourge among humanity. Fourteen years ago — at the turn of the century — he was rightfully despised for his monopolies and his trusts. His company, Standard Oil, was depicted in the papers as an octopus with its tentacles around the halls of government. Today, he's seen as a wise old Solomon (with an eye for the ladies), but the leopard's spots haven't changed.

His son, the great "philanthropist," pretends to be a different sort of man, a man who cares about the poor, who gives and gives and yet somehow never gets any less rich. What does this philanthropist care for the coal miners at the Colorado Fuel & Iron Company, living in tents under the cold glare of machine guns as troops rampage through their encampments — all for wanting a decent wage to feed their families? Make no mistake, John D. Rockefeller, Jr., is to blame for the

Ludlow Massacre yesterday, when the Colorado militia fired on strikers, killing at least 25 people that we know of, including two women and eleven children!

Yet now we see this younger paragon fawned over by sycophant society writers, and I quote: “Mr. and Mrs. John D. Rockefeller, Jr., hosted a dinner at their newly built nine-story mansion on W. 54th St. to celebrate the family’s donation of one million dollars for research into animal medicine. The home is exquisitely decorated with some of the finest modern art from Europe.” I suppose society writer Louisa Delafield thinks it’s fine that children die, shot down in the streets, as long as hogs get their cholera treatment and Mrs. Rockefeller gets her paintings.

I prefer the sentiments of Mother Mary Jenkins, who said in her testimony today, “The laboring man is tired of working to build up millions so that millionaires’ wives may wear diamonds. It is awful when you think of decorating women with diamonds representing the blood of children.”

Chapter 1

Louisa

The problem was she didn't have the right shoes. Louisa had managed to find a splendid lace and chiffon evening gown by French designer Jeanne Hallée at a broker's shop in the garment district. It had been purchased by a Rothschild who had subsequently decided she didn't like the color — a pale blue — so she sent it to a discreet dress broker for resale. The dress was a steal, but looking through her wardrobe, Louisa realized she didn't have shoes to go with it, and the wedding was in an hour. She sank to the floor in despair. The door knocker resounded from downstairs. A moment later she heard footsteps on the stairs followed by a knock on her bedroom door.

"Come in, Ellen," Louisa said. No one besides her assistant and friend, Ellen Malloy, would show up at the front door and be sent immediately upstairs.

Ellen, windblown, her red hair burnished with the late afternoon sunlight streaming through the window, wore her usual sensible cotton frock and toque. She looked at Louisa on the floor in her silk chemise.

"What're ya doing on the floor, girleen?" Ellen asked.

"I have no shoes to wear to Hugh Garrett's wedding," Louisa said, holding up a worn lace-up boot with a broken sole.

"I should think you'd have more important things to worry about than that scoundrel's wedding after what he did to my friend Silvia," Ellen said. Hugh Garrett was Ellen's previous employer, and she would never forgive him for sending a young servant off to have an abortion that killed her. His wealth and status had insulated him from any repercussions.

"I despise him as much as you do, but that 'scoundrel' is still onc of the wealthiest men in the city and therefore I have no choice but to attend the wedding," Louisa said. In spite of her feelings about Hugh Garrett, Louisa's job was to observe and comment on New York society, a job she took seriously, not least because in some ways she was still one of them. She was a Delafield, after all, no matter how meager her bank account.

"Well, I pity the poor girl who marries *him,*" Ellen said and dropped a magazine on the floor beside her. "Take a look at this."

"What is it?"

"An article that slanders you," Ellen said.

Louisa took up the paper and skimmed the article.

"L. Byron? That's rich, isn't it? Does he think this drivel is poetry?" she said. "He calls me a sycophant. That's a big word from such a little mind. And apparently he's not an art lover." She tossed the article aside. "No one reads these anarchist magazines anyway."

She peered into her wardrobe again as if, magically, the perfect pair of shoes would simply appear like Cinderella's glass slippers.

"Anarchists read them, and they're a dangerous lot," Ellen said. She shooed away the ginger cat curled up on cushioned chair, sat down at Louisa's vanity, and took off her hat. The wind had pulled strands of hair out of her bun, which stuck out like red wires.

"They aren't a danger to me," Louisa objected. "Maybe to Rockefeller. There was that attempt on his life recently." She rose from the floor and shut the door to her wardrobe before the cat could leap in it and get trapped inside as had already happened several times. She didn't have time before the wedding to go shopping, and she couldn't bear the humiliation of not looking perfectly put together for Hugh's wedding.

"The older or the younger Rockefeller?" Ellen asked, as she unpinned her hair, brushed it out, and then coiled it into a thick red rope, which she neatly fastened on the back of head.

"The younger, which is ridiculous," Louisa said, taking up the dress she'd laid out on the bed and pulling it over her head.

Ellen came over and buttoned up the back, smoothing the lace overlay so Louisa looked as if she'd just stepped out of a Paris salon. Louisa clasped a pearl necklace around her neck, glad that her mother had held onto it through the days when they struggled so for money. She gazed at herself in the full length mirror and continued, "I can understand why the anarchists hate the elder but Junior is a philanthropist. He's too busy giving away his father's money to oppress anyone."

"Except for the miners," Ellen said.

"Are you one of *them* now?" Louisa asked.

"A miner?" Ellen asked.

"An anarchist."

"I'm not sure," Ellen said with a shrug. "By the way, I'm guessing that Hester has a pair of shoes she could lend you. Her closet overfloweth. Shoes are her one vice."

Relief swept over Louisa. "Do you think so? I could go by her place on the way to the church. Would you ring her first?"

"I will indeed."

"Then we should hurry," Louisa said. "I can't be late to the wedding of the century."

"They're all weddings of the century among your lot," Ellen said.

***

Hester's shoes were a bit too long, but Louisa stuffed cotton in the toes and decided they would have to do. At least they were fashionable. She left Ellen at Hester's Central Park apartment and hurried across the park to the newly built St. Thomas Episcopal Church on Fifth Avenue. She didn't understand the friendship that Ellen had with the wealthy heiress. Ellen had once been a lady's maid. Now she was Louisa's assistant at *The Ledger*. Hester was the daughter of a Pittsburgh industrialist and sister to one of New York's new-money social climbers. Hester herself was a spinster, involved in reform movements, especially women's suffrage, which might explain their common ground, but most wealthy women, even reformers, stuck to their own class.

Louisa reached the church a few minutes before the service began and slipped upstairs to the balcony to sit with the rest of the press. Society writers from *The Times, The Herald, The World, The Sun*, and a few lesser known papers all had front row seats. *The Ledger* didn't have the circulation that the Big Four had, but it had prestige, and because Louisa now had a syndicated column in addition to her local column, she could claim a spot near the top of the pyramid. Dottie Parsons of *The Herald* scooted over and patted the seat next to her. Louisa sat down and thanked her.

"Nice dress," Dottie whispered. "The syndicate must be treating you well."

"Not that well," Louisa responded. "I'll give you the address of a dress broker I know."

"You're a sport," Dottie said. She was a few years older than Louisa — a big-boned blonde with ruddy cheeks. A heavy floral scent wafted from her neck and arms. She wore a rather garish pink dress.

"Anybody interesting here?" Louisa asked, looking down into the sanctuary. The church had only reopened last year after a fire had destroyed the old building in 1905, and the new building in the French High Gothic style was a marvel, reflecting the staggering incomes of the congregation.

"Astors, Vanderbilts, politicians, moguls, and Morgans. The usual," Dottie said. "Say, didn't you grow up with Hugh Garrett? Why aren't you down there among the exalted?"

"Long story," Louisa said. "Suffice to say I am *persona non grata* in the Garrett house." She did not dare a tell a fellow society writer Hugh Garrett's history, that he had actually bid on the opportunity to deflower a captive young woman. Hugh didn't know the young woman in question was Louisa herself. If it weren't for Louisa's publisher, Forrest Calloway, and Ellen, she would have been violated and quite possibly murdered. *The Ledger* had published the whole story under her pen name, "Beatrice Milton," and the article had been a sensation. She could have included Hugh Garrett's name, but didn't because his family had too much money and power and would have destroyed the paper — not to mention they had threatened to send Ellen, who was their servant at the time, to prison on trumped up charges of thievery. So Louisa had made a deal with the devils, and now she would write about this wedding and hope Hugh would be a decent husband. They had been friends as children, and she believed there was still good in him. Perhaps this young woman would be able to revive it.

Louisa jotted down names as quickly as she could. She pulled out her opera glasses so she could include descriptions of the more opulent dresses. Then when everyone was seated, she settled back to enjoy the wedding. Wagner's "Here Comes the Bride" blared from the pipe organ, and Hugh's bride, a wan-looking Minnesota girl without a noteworthy pedigree but with a fortune to match Hugh's own, made her stately march down the long white runner. She wore a Worth wedding dress, dripping with beads, trailing silk and satin, and draped with French lace. Hattie, Hugh's sister, had surreptitiously sent Louisa all the details of the making of the gown. One could feed a small country for a week on what it cost, which is something she would not mention in her story, as she wrote for *The Ledger* and not some anarchist rag like *Mother Earth.* The nerve of that lowly worm of a man. A "sycophant?" She had exposed the failings of the upper class more than once since she'd begun writing her features under her pen name, but no one was supposed to know she and Beatrice Milton were one and the same.

While Louisa entertained her readers with stories of the social lives of society's brightest lights, her alter-ego wrote about things that had more importance. When revelers rang in the year 1914 and the city hummed with the pounding of dancing feet, Beatrice Milton contradicted all the fulsome prognostications of prosperity and progress of the larger newspapers by writing an article about the doubling of New Yorkers without shelter that winter to 30,000 and the growing number of children dying as a result. Some people called it "muckraking" — a term coined by Theodore Roosevelt a scant eight years previous, but writing those articles had given Louisa a sense of deeper purpose. However, after New Year's, the social season went into high gear and Louisa had been kept so busy with balls, soirées, dinners, charity luncheons, and weddings that she had no time for muckraking.

She admonished herself to concentrate on the doings down below. Hugh and his bride were just then exchanging vows. When he kissed her, every woman in the place — even the ladies in the press — caught their breaths. Some of the women wept outright. Louisa was the only one with dry eyes. She had no desire for any of this wedding brouhaha herself. She was happy enough with her clandestine relationship with her publisher, Forrest Calloway. She had the pleasures of marriage with none of the obligations.

The congregants listened to Mendelssohn's triumphant "Wedding March," the traditional exit song, and watched a young woman traipse blithely into the mystery of her future. As Hugh and his bride marched down the aisle together toward the church doors, he raised his eyes and scanned the balcony. Halfway down, his gaze caught on Louisa's face the way a fingernail will snag on a piece of silk. He let a faint smile drift her way. She frowned in return.

Row by row, the congregants solemnly left the church while Louisa tried to decide if she had to attend the reception at Delmonico's.

"Are you going to the reception?" she asked Dottie.

"Of course. I haven't eaten all day. At least with this job we get a good meal once in a while. I wouldn't mind toasting the happy couple with expensive champagne either," Dottie said.

Louisa sympathized. The pay for a society writer was abysmal. Thanks to her syndicated column and "Beatrice's" features, she was no longer relying on social events to get a good meal, but she remembered those lean and hungry days well.

As she and Dottie emerged from the church, Louisa decided she would not go to the reception. Instead, she would spend a quiet night at home re-reading Henry James.

"Enjoy the reception," Louisa said to Dottie. "My readers will have to be satisfied with copious descriptions of the new Mrs. Garrett's dress. They must have worked ten thousand silkworms to death on the train alone."

As they descended the steps, a woman's voice called out, "Louisa Delafield!"

Louisa turned to see who had yelled her name in such a bellicose manner. As she did so, her heel slipped out of Hester's too-large shoe, and she bent down to pull it back on. At that moment, a loud *BANG* shattered the air, followed by a scream. Then more screams. She stood up and saw Dottie behind her with a bright red bloom spreading across the top of her pink satin dress. Slowly Dottie dropped to her knees.

"She's been shot!" someone yelled.

Louisa grasped Dottie under her arms and held her as she slid to the ground. Dottie's expression was one of utter confusion. Louisa laid her down and put a handkerchief on the oozing wound as Dottie whimpered.

"It's just your shoulder, Dottie. You'll be all right," Louisa reassured her, but she wasn't a doctor, and for all she knew Dottie might bleed to death right in front of her. She glanced around to see if the assailant was still there, but all she saw were the horrified faces of the wedding guests.

Chapter 2

Ellen

Louisa hadn't been gone five minutes before Ellen had pulled the bobby pins out of Hester's hair, and Hester's dark tresses cascaded over her shoulders. Next, she unbuttoned Hester's dress, kissing the back of her neck and along her spine as she slowly peeled off Hester's underclothes. When Hester was fully naked, she slipped out of her own dress, and Hester feverishly pulled off Ellen's camisole and her bloomers. She ran her fingers up Ellen's thigh and a tongue over her collarbone. The two women toppled into the bed where they spent the next hour skin-to-skin in a rhythm of crescendo and decrescendo until finally — as night fell — they were satiated.

"Do you think the servants heard us?" Hester asked.

Ellen sighed.

"What does it matter? The servants know everything. Believe me, I was one," she said.

Running her fingers over Ellen's moist skin, Hester said, "You don't have to constantly remind me you were once a servant. I don't like to think of you doing drudgery."

"And why not? It's honest enough work. At least it's not like working in the mines where you can get shot like a dog if you ask for a decent wage," Ellen said.

"That terrible tragedy in Colorado has upset you, hasn't it?"

"I cannot stop thinking of those poor families living in tents all through the brutal winter. Then to be shot down. Women and wee children. Did you know the men work twelve hours a day in those filthy holes? And they only get paid by the pound of coal. So all the other work, the laying of rails and so on, is done for free," Ellen said, sitting up and gesticulating with angry hands. "All the while the Rockefellers are building a nine-story mansion to add to their collection of houses. It's obscene and disgusting. L. Byron may be wrong about Louisa, but he's right about those Rockefellers."

Hester sat up next to her and wrapped her arms around her knees.

"I've never known what it's like to be hungry or without shelter," she said. "In fact, I can have anything I want simply because of the family I was born into. While another woman — no better or worse than I — can be born in a tenement and struggle her whole life for the bare necessities. It baffles me. Last week I met a young woman whose two-year old had just died from diarrhea. She was inconsolable. It left me feeling so helpless."

Hester's pain was etched on her face, and Ellen melted. She knew no one as tender hearted and kind.

"My love, you're anything but helpless," Ellen said, stroking Hester's back. "You take food and medicine to the tenements. You fight for the right of women to vote. You're a saint unlike those selfish gluttons who primp and preen at their balls and parties, each one trying to outdo the other."

"The ones Louisa writes about?" Hester asked, pointedly.

Ellen didn't answer. The fact that Louisa's society column provided Ellen with a job did make her feel a bit of a hypocrite, but the so-called muckraking features more than made up for it and they were the real reason that Louisa had hired her.

She stood up, wrapped a blanket around her shoulders, and walked to the window to stare out at the sprawling expanse of Central Park, so different than the view of an alley from her room in Mrs. Cantor's boarding house. A year ago, she had been a servant in one of the big houses on the other side of the park, and so she'd seen her share of luxury, but this was different. She was a servant then. Now as Hester's lover she was on the other side of the dividing line between the rich and the poor. The shift from Hester's life of privilege back to her own life as a working woman sometimes made Ellen dizzy. She couldn't define her discomfort or explain it to Hester, but there it was. She felt like a thief who had stolen someone else's life.

"You know, Ellen," Hester said. "Many women of wealth and position are ardent reformists. Look at Alva Belmont."

"A little reform here or there is not enough," Ellen said softly, almost as if she were talking to herself. Her thinking had evolved over the last few months. The anarchist papers and magazines had educated her about the disparity in this country. She thought of the lurid displays of wealth by people like the Garrett family with their diamonds and their pearls and their fancy motorcars while a family in the Lower East Side couldn't afford fifty cents for a dozen eggs. "I s'pose it's the blood of the Irish Brotherhood running through my veins that makes me despise these captains of industry."

"You may be right to despise them," Hester said. "But blowing things up as the anarchists do isn't the answer either."

Ah, sweet Hester with her large eyes and wide mouth and her long limbs. Of course she wouldn't understand. Ellen wondered why she'd had to go and fall in love with a woman whose station in life was so far above hers.

A furious pounding on the front door broke her reverie. They looked at each other in alarm. Then Ellen dropped the blanket and reached for her dress.

Chapter 3

Louisa

A maid opened the door to the apartment and Louisa tried to steady her voice.

"Is Miss Malloy still here?" she asked.

"She is, Miss Delafield. Please come in." The maid led her along the hallway and showed her into the parlor. Louisa looked around the room. A baby grand piano occupied a corner, sculptures graced built-in shelves lining one wall, and fine art crowded the other walls. A huge window overlooked Central Park, which was shrouded in darkness. A Tiffany lamp glowed on a table.

Louisa paced back and forth across the Persian rug. She felt a burning sensation in her chest, and kept thinking about the bullet that had been intended for her. If she hadn't bent down, it would have hit her instead. Why, she wondered. Perhaps someone had discovered she was Beatrice Milton and wanted revenge, but that didn't seem plausible. She hadn't written a Beatrice article in two months.

Ellen and Hester entered the room. Ellen's face was flushed and Hester's hair looked hastily pinned back. Louisa at first wondered where they'd been, and then the truth that she should have known all along finally occurred to her. Ellen and Hester were lovers. How had she not guessed this? They'd been constant companions since the women's suffrage march last year, and Ellen never failed to smile when she spoke of Hester.

"Louisa," Ellen exclaimed. "What's happened? Is that blood on your dress?"

Louisa snapped back into the moment.

"Dottie Parsons was shot," Louisa said, "in front of the church." She looked down at the blue silk dress and saw a dark, reddish-brown smear.

"Is she dead?" Hester asked.

"No, thank God. I went with her to the hospital, and the doctor said she would recover," Louisa said, a sudden sense of exhaustion engulfing her.

"Isn't she the society writer for *The Herald*?" Hester asked. "Why would someone want to shoot her?"

"She is. She was standing behind me when I leaned down," Louisa said. "Your shoe may have saved my life."

"I don't understand. How did Hester's shoe save your life?" Ellen tilted her head in confusion as she gazed down at the kid leather shoe. The decorative rhinestone button gleamed in the lamp light.

"My heel came out of it as I turned around and I bent down to fix it."

Ellen still looked blank.

"The bullet was meant for me," Louisa said, the pitch of her voice an octave higher than normal. "She was trying to shoot me, and she hit Dottie instead."

"She?" Hester asked.

"Yes, I heard a woman's voice call my name, and when I turned to see who it was, my foot came out of the shoe, and I bent over to fix it. Then I heard the shot."

"Did you see her?" Ellen asked.

Louisa shook her head. "A few of the guests said they saw a woman, dressed all in black, hurrying away from the scene. Some said she was young. Others said old. She wore a hat with a veil so no one knows."

"But why would someone want to shoot you?" Hester asked.

"I have no idea," Louisa said.

"I do. Anarchists," Ellen said. "That Byron article incited one of them to do this."

"That's ridiculous. It was only one article in a mendacious little magazine," Louisa said.

"Since when do you doubt the power of the press?" Ellen asked, eyebrows arched and hands on her hips.

Louisa had, of course, seen the power of the press. As Beatrice Milton, she'd exposed her share of crime and corruption, but she simply couldn't believe that someone writing for an anarchist rag would have any power at all.

"Come, let's get you home," Ellen said. She turned and thanked Hester for a lovely evening. Louisa was dazed as Ellen led her out the door to the elevator and they descended the ten floors to the street. The doorman flagged a cab for them and they got in.

They were quiet for several minutes as Louisa's galloping heart finally slowed down. She thought of poor Dottie, so stoic in the hospital room, assuring

Louisa that she would be fine. Then she remembered seeing Ellen with her cheeks flushed and Hester with her hair in disarray.

"Ellen, are you and Hester...?" she asked.

The question hung in the air between them.

"I thought you knew," Ellen said after a moment.

"No. No, I didn't," Louisa replied.

"Does it matter to you, Louisa?" Ellen asked.

She puzzled over the question for a moment. Of course, she knew about such things but only in the abstract.

"Do you . . . do you love her?" Louisa asked.

"I do," Ellen answered. "I've loved her since the first time I saw her."

"Then, no, it does not matter to me," Louisa said. "I want you to be happy."

After a long pause, Ellen asked, "And what about you and Mr. Calloway?"

Louisa flushed with embarrassment. She had never discussed this relationship with anyone.

"Forrest is perfect for me," Louisa said. "Any other man would insist on marriage. I saw what marriage did to my mother, and I want no part of that."

"I did not know that," Ellen said.

"When my father was killed, I learned that you can only rely on yourself," Louisa said. "I'd never give up my work for a man. Not without a fortune of my own."

They were silent for the rest of the drive north to Louisa's brownstone in Harlem.

Ellen helped her upstairs and out of her dress while a worried Suzie, the housekeeper, fixed some hot tea. Louisa crawled into bed and thanked Ellen.

Ellen left, and a minute later Suzie came in with tea.

"Did this shooting have something to do with your muckraking?" Suzie asked.

"I don't think so," Louisa said.

"I would feel terrible if it did," Suzie said, putting Louisa's dress away. "Seeing as how I encouraged you."

"You encouraged me to do more with my writing, Suzie, and I'll always be grateful. Now stop cleaning up my room. You're acting like you are my lady's maid," Louisa said with a forced smile. "I'm fine."

"I'm the housekeeper," Suzie said, "and I can't abide clothes all strewn about."

Louisa shook her head helplessly. Suzie had been the only servant to stay with her and her mother after her father's death. She cooked and looked after Louisa's mother and managed the household finances, but Louisa had learned early on to look after herself. Lady's maids were for the wealthy.

When Suzie left, Louisa picked up the cup of tea and noticed her hand shaking. She took a sip and replaced the cup on the table next to her bed beside *Portrait of a Lady,* one of her favorite novels, which she re-read frequently. The character of Henrietta Stackpole had, in fact, inspired her to become a journalist.

She turned off the light and closed her eyes, but as soon as she did, she heard the sound of the shot and saw the bright bloom of blood on Dottie Parson's gown. Dear Dottie had taken a bullet meant for her. She got out of bed, went downstairs, and found her handbag. Inside was Dottie's notebook, which had fallen to the ground after she was shot. Sitting at her grandmother's writing desk, Louisa quickly jotted down a story.

Then she picked up the phone.

"Operator, get me *The Herald,*" she said.

***

Sipping her second cup of coffee at the dining table, Louisa read the story of the shooting of Dottie Parsons in a rival paper. Her mother, Anna, sat at the other end of the table, blissfully unaware of what had happened the night before. Louisa didn't have the heart to tell her that someone had tried to kill her, and fortunately, the papers had missed that detail, portraying the shooting as a random event.

The sound of the door knocker startled her.

"I'll get it," Suzie said.

Returning a moment later, she said, "There's a visitor in the parlor."

"A visitor?" Anna exclaimed. "At this hour? Why, I'm not presentable."

"He's here to speak to Louisa," Suzie clarified.

"Stay here, Mother. I'll take care of it," Louisa said. "Who is it, Suzie?"

"Captain Tunney," Suzie said.

Louisa had worked with Captain Tunney in the past, and she liked him despite his gruffness. He took off his cap when Louisa entered the parlor. He was a burly Irishman with bushy eyebrows, a crown of gray hair, and an enormous mustache. His bright blue eyes constantly scanned and assessed.

"Miss Delafield," he said.

"Hello, Captain," she said. "I already spoke to the police last night."

"May I sit?" he asked.

"Of course. Would you care for coffee?" she asked. He sat, and Suzie brought in a tray with a silver-plated coffee service. Louisa poured cups for both of them.

"Have you received any other threats?" Captain Tunney asked.

"None," Louisa said. "Ellen, my assistant, seems to thinks the anarchists are after me. But why? I'm nobody."

"You aren't nobody. You're a public personage. I read that article wherein one of them disparaged you. Detective Paddy O'Neil brought it to my attention," he said. "For all we know, that could be enough incentive for one of them to shoot you."

"Well, I'm not much of a capitalist," she said and waved at the modestly furnished room — the faded wallpaper, the old out-of-tune upright piano in the corner and the once-grand sofa now faded with oft-mended cushions. Two signs of their former status were her grandmother's Chippendale desk and the large family portrait hanging above the mantel.

"The anarchists are not above shooting a member of the press. Your newspaper is not kind to them," he said.

"I thought your bomb squad had infiltrated their ranks," she said. "Wouldn't you have heard something if they wanted to kill me?"

"Not necessarily, Miss. We managed to get a man in the Italian Bresci Circle, but the Jewish anarchists, the ones from Mother Russia, are a different sort. They're your more intellectual type of loony, and shooting you might qualify as 'Propaganda of the Deed.' You're an easy target."

"What if it's some crazy society woman?" Louisa asked. "Maybe she was offended when I didn't mention her dress in my column."

Tunney brushed his substantial mustache with his fingers.

"Or it might even have been a man dressed as a woman," he said.

"The voice that called my name belonged to a woman, of that I'm sure," Louisa said. "Don't you believe a woman capable of firing a gun?"

"Women are capable of all sorts of mischief," he said. "As you well know."

They were both remembering her abduction a year earlier, which had been arranged by brothel owner Battle Betty.

"What if it's one of Battle Betty's girls?" Louisa asked.

"Could be," Captain Tunney said. "But why now? Betty's dead and her business has been shut down for over a year. No, I'm putting my money on the anarchists. I can put someone on watch here at the house if you like."

"Thank you, but a guard is not necessary," Louisa said as they both rose.

She saw him to the door and then turned to find her mother sitting in her invalid chair in the hallway. By the look of horror on her face, Louisa surmised she had heard everything.

"Oh, Louisa," she said. "I couldn't bear to lose you, too."

Louisa was dumbfounded. Her mother had never been a font of maternal love, and yet her stricken look appeared quite sincere.

"I'll be fine, Mother," Louisa said and bent down to kiss her on the cheek, which only embarrassed both of them.

***

Louisa sat at her desk on the third floor of *The Ledger*, furiously punching the keys of her typewriter as her anger spilled onto the page. L. Byron had had the gall to publish another article, condemning all society writers, claiming they betrayed the laborers who set the type, ran the presses and delivered the finished newspapers. He didn't care if they were all shot.

She didn't know if the shooter was an anarchist, but if it was a war the vile man wanted, she'd give it to him.

She would show him she was unafraid. Finishing the screed with three hashmarks, she pulled the paper from the typewriter carriage and took the stairs to the second floor where the typesetters worked. She wouldn't trust this one to the copy boy.

Instead of going back upstairs, she continued down to the first floor, strode through the revolving door, and left the building. She'd had the foresight to put on her hat with its rolling brim lined with clusters of violets and grab her handbag before leaving her desk. She went directly to the Society of New York Hospital where Dottie Parsons was recuperating. Outside, she bought a bouquet of yellow and white daisies from a street vendor and grabbed an early edition of *The Herald* from a newsy.

Dottie was pale, her shoulder wrapped in white bandages, but otherwise she looked like her old self, brown eyes big and bright.

"I missed my deadline. I've never missed a deadline," Dottie lamented when Louisa sat in the hard wooden chair next to her bed. *The Herald* was paying for Dottie to have a private room, which was generous, considering the pittance they paid her.

"You still haven't, dear," Louisa said. "I found your notebook on the sidewalk after the shooting and wrote up a little something. I called it in last night. Here it is. Your byline and everything." She handed Dottie the paper, open to the society page.

"I meant it when I said you were a sport," Dottie laughed as she skimmed the article.

"It's the least I could do. You took a bullet that was intended for me," Louisa said as she pulled Dottie's notebook from her purse and placed it on the bedside table.

"One for all and all for one," Dottie said.

“I never thought of myself as a Musketeer, but that’s a fine motto,” Louisa said, grateful that Dottie wasn’t blaming her.

“So who was it? One of the anti-suffragists? You have been a bit outspoken lately,” Dottie said. Louisa was amazed that Dottie didn’t seem rattled by the previous day’s events while Louisa struggled to appear calm and unflustered.

“It might have been an anarchist,” Louisa confided.

“An anarchist?”

A knock on the door interrupted them, and Louisa turned to see Forrest Calloway in the doorway with an elegant vase containing the most gorgeous red roses she’d ever seen. He set down the flowers and doffed his hat, filling the room with his presence. Louisa smiled. He never ceased to surprise her.

“Mr. Calloway. Do come in,” Dottie said, obviously delighted. Surely, William Randolph Hearst wouldn’t be stopping by, and so it was doubly surprising that the publisher of a rival paper had come to see her.

“I was so sorry to hear about what happened to you, Miss Parsons,” Forrest said, striding to the other side of her bed. Louisa noticed the expensive gold cuff links peeking out from jacket sleeve. “How are you feeling?”

“I’m a little sore,” she said, “but they’ve given me laudanum and so the pain’s bearable.”

“I had better get back to work,” Louisa said, patting Dottie’s good arm. “I’ll come by tomorrow.”

“I’ll accompany you, Miss Delafield,” Forrest said, before turning to Dottie. “Please send word to me if you need anything, Miss Parsons. In fact, I’ll send my chauffeur to pick you up and take you home as soon as you’re released.”

“That would be lovely, Mr. Calloway,” Dottie said.

"My pleasure." He tipped his hat and followed Louisa. They said not a word until they were out of the hospital and sitting in the back seat of his midnight blue Packard. His clean scent wafted over her, and she slid her hand across the seat so that their fingers touched. Their relationship could never be revealed. He was the publisher of the paper where she worked, after all, and they had to be circumspect in public. Society might turn a blind eye to the peccadilloes of powerful men, but they would utterly destroy a woman in Louisa's position who had the audacity to demand the same freedom.

"That was kind of you," Louisa said.

"It was nothing. Besides, I hoped I would find you."

"Why? Is something wrong?" Louisa asked.

"Louisa, I want you to leave town. This situation is too dangerous. I understand the woman who tried to shoot you is some sort of anarchist."

"Have you been talking to Ellen?"

"I called the paper for you this morning, and she answered. She told me what happened," he said. "I share her concerns."

"Forrest, if it is the anarchists, then that's exactly what they want. To run me out of town, to silence me," she said.

"My dear Louisa," he said, taking her gloved hand in his. "This is not a request. As your employer I insist. You are a valuable asset to my newspaper, and I cannot risk losing you."

"So this is about money?" she teased.

"It's also about love, but my position as your publisher is my only leverage here, so I will use it if you force me to," he said.

"Oh, Forrest. This is silly. Please stop treating me like a child," she said.

"Louisa, please," Forrest begged.

"I know you mean well, but, honestly, I'm not afraid. Besides, where would I go?" she asked. He probably wanted to send her to Newport or Saratoga even though it wasn't summer yet, and there would be absolutely no social scene there to write about for two months.

"Florida," he said.

"Florida?" she asked. Her imagination immediately conjured up mosquitoes the size of house cats. "What's in Florida?"

"Only some of the finest hotels on the Eastern Seaboard, thanks to our friend Henry Flagler," he said. "There's a grand wedding at Flagler's hotel in St. Augustine in a couple of weeks and I'd like you to attend. You can go early and cover the social scene there. I understand it's 'hopping,' as the young people say."

"A wedding? Who is the family? I would have known if anyone was getting married in St. Augustine," she said.

"They aren't New Yorkers. They're a prominent Chicago family. And Daphne Griffin is the only daughter of my good friend, Randall Griffin. I already promised him that you would cover the wedding," he said.

"You promised him? Why?"

"Because Daphne and her husband are planning to settle in New York after the wedding. This will help them enter society. You know how closed off it is here," he said.

She detected a slight trace of bitterness in his voice. For all his money and position, his California background and childhood poverty were an impediment to acceptance into the upper echelons of New York society.

"What aren't you telling me, Forrest?" she asked.

"Daphne is my goddaughter," he said.

"Oh?" He had a goddaughter? She often forgot the twenty-year age difference between the two of them, but he was old enough to be her father.

Truly the last thing she wanted to do was leave New York in March. In a couple of weeks it would be April, and with fewer events to cover, she would have the time to do some investigating of her own. She had planned to find and question one of the men who had swindled her father out of his fortune in 1899. He was finally out of Sing Sing, and maybe he had some clue as to who had murdered her father, once one of the most respected men in New York. She told none of this to Forrest, however.

"Mr. Kimura, would you drop me off at the Ritz-Carlton?" she asked, leaning forward. She turned to Forrest and said, "I still have a job to do, Mr. Calloway. A luncheon to cover and then a fashion show at Wannamaker's."

"Just think about my request please," he said.

Mr. Kimura pulled up in front of The Ritz-Carlton. The slender Japanese man opened the back door for her and helped her out of the motorcar.

"Thank you, Mr. Kimura," she said. He bowed slightly. She'd never known anyone with such dignity. She bent down to look at Forrest in the back seat. "I'll think about it."

Forrest blew her a kiss, and the iceberg of her resolve melted.

***

When Louisa returned home that evening, she walked into the parlor and found Ellen, Suzie, and her mother all staring up at her. She was surprised to see Ellen, who lived in a rooming house nearby, and wondered if she were here on Forrest's behalf to try to convince her to leave.

She sank down onto the sofa.

"Forrest is trying to ship me off to St. Augustine, Florida," she said. "Can you imagine anything more dreadful?"

"St. Augustine?" Suzie sat up straight. "I believe some of my kin moved to Florida and settled near there."

Louisa looked at her incredulously.

"Your family?" she asked.

Suzie pursed her lips and tilted her head. Louisa immediately realized her *faux pas*. Of course, Suzie had family. Somewhere.

"Who did you hear that from, Suzie?" Ellen asked.

Sunlight streamed through the front window and glimmered in Suzie's hazel-brown eyes.

"Colored folk are leaving the South in droves. And whenever I meet someone new at church or at the market I ask where they're from. About two months ago, I met an old woman who lived on the same plantation as me and my granny. She knew my mother and both of my brothers. My mother's dead, but my brothers aren't. She said they moved to Florida, some place called Lincolnville, which I think is near St. Augustine. I'd give anything to go down there and find them."

Louisa's mouth dropped open. It was one thing to acknowledge that Suzie had family, but quite another to imagine her leaving New York to go and find them. Louisa and her mother were Suzie's family now. Those brothers would be strangers.

"Who would look after mother?" Louisa asked.

Suzie bit her lip.

"I will," Ellen said. "You and Suzie can go down to Florida, and I'll take care of your mother. Hester will be happy to help me."

"But you have to work," Louisa said. "I'll need someone in the office in my stead."

"I'll still go into the office every day. You can hire a girl to come in and look after your Ma while I'm at work," Ellen said. "The newspaper will pay for it, won't they? Seeing as they're the ones sending you away."

Louisa looked at her mother.

"Oh, go on," Anna said. "Your old 'Ma' is feeling fine." It was true that since winter was finally slinking away, Anna's color had improved and overall she seemed more robust.

"It seems rash," Louisa said. "And if it is the anarchists who shot at me, I don't want them to think they can scare me away. I've already written a response to that L. Byron fellow." She couldn't let her fear get the best of her.

Ellen shook her head, but said nothing.

"They say it's nice and warm in Florida this time of year," Suzie said.

"I'm sure it is. However, right now I'm off to the Plaza for a tea dance and hat sale. It's a benefit for the Yorkville Social Center Club, which goes to show that we are definitely entering the doldrums of the society season," she said and rose from the sofa.

When all else failed, she always had her work.

"Your father and I went to St. Augustine on our honeymoon," Anna piped up.

Louisa spun around.

"You did?"

"It was so glamorous. We stayed at the Ponce, which was brand new at the time. And we danced at the

Alcazar and swam at the North Shore. Endless parties, operas, and plays," Anna said, gazing up at the family portrait over the fireplace.

Her mother's dreamy smile spoke volumes. Of course, her parents must have been madly in love, her mother a vivacious beauty, and her father a rich romantic who loved poetry. They had seemed ill-matched to Louisa when she was a child, but now she remembered the way her father sometimes gazed at her mother as if she were the only woman in the world. There had been love between them and, she realized, perhaps even passion – at some point.

Ellen pulled on her gloves as she stood. "Hester and I have plans to hear Mrs. Gilman's lecture tonight at the Hotel Astor. She's speaking about 'masculism.' "

Louisa's venture now sounded frivolous. Ellen was going to hear Charlotte Perkins Gilman, a famous writer and feminist. Ellen was a fisherman's daughter with no college education, but her association with Hester and her voracious reading of newspapers and magazines had transformed her in the past year.

"I do admire Mrs. Gilman's fiction," Louisa said, glad the topic had changed. "I'm sure her lecture will be edifying."

Ellen's serious look made Louisa think of a school marm.

"You ought to take Mr. Calloway's suggestion and skedaddle, Louisa," she said.

Louisa sensed that Ellen was miffed and worried about her at the same time.

After Ellen left, Suzie marched out of the room without a glance at Louisa.

Perhaps Louisa had been thoughtless when Suzie said she wanted to see her family. But what a ridiculous idea. She wouldn't even know them after all these years, would she? Louisa looked up at the painting above the fireplace. In it her father sat in a wooden armchair, her mother beside him, a hand resting on his shoulder, while Louisa, who was eight years old at the time, leaned against his other side and gazed steadfastly at the painter with the expression of a child who believed she owned the world. Suzie, of course, was not in the painting, and yet ever since her father's death, Suzie had been their rock. Louisa closed her eyes and put a hand over her throat as she realized she was terrified Suzie might leave them for some long-lost family.

Society Notes

Evening Edition

By Louisa Delafield
March 14, 1914

Our magnificent city, home to approximately five million souls on any given day, is under a dire threat. From all over the world, people flock to our boroughs, our neighborhoods, and our streets. No, the streets are not paved with gold, but there is opportunity here for all. This city opens its arms to the refugee and the adventurer alike. Negro families come here from the South to escape the harsh poverty and indignity so many are subjected to in their homeland. Jewish families flee the pogroms of Russia to find peace and stability here. Italians, Poles, Irish, and Chinese come here to work and give their children a better life.

True, some of our more illustrious families have been here for a century or more. But those families also were leaving behind religious oppression, stagnant societies, crowded European cities where bettering oneself was impossible. Those families scraped livelihoods from the very earth to build this city, street by street, house by house.

New York has something for everyone, but there are those who would deny us the peace and security, which draws so many. I am referring to the anarchists and their violent disruption of our lives. Their hatred for the moneyed class is clouding their vision and poisoning their hearts.

John D. Rockefeller, Sr., and sons, Cornelius Vanderbilt and sons, Jacob Astor and sons, Andrew Carnegie, and Henry Frick — through ingenuity and hard work, these men have amassed enormous wealth. No, they have not always been generous to their workers. They have often been ruthless. I make no excuses for them. However, in this growing and evolving country, let us not discount the enormous public gifts they have bestowed: libraries, grand music halls, hotels, even our train terminals. We would be a poor city indeed without the unparalleled generosity of these families. Let us not forget the charitable works of the wives who have fought for sanitation in the tenements, better conditions for factory workers, and equality for women. These families and their enterprises provide many New Yorkers with livelihoods from domestic workers to the hotel chefs to window cleaners and cab drivers.

Could our society as a whole do better? Certainly. Women should have the right to vote. Unions should be able to peacefully negotiate for better conditions. Corruption should be rooted out of our politics. However, bombs and guns will not further us to a more perfect and just society. The tools of the anarchist are also the tools of the coward. They will only destroy the fabric of our society.

Yesterday an anarchist shot at me, and in her clumsy attempt injured one of my colleagues instead. Apparently, I was targeted because I write for and about society, because I respect and admire those members of society who give back to our country, and because I believe in the value of beauty and art to uplift us all. I will not give in to fear. I will not cease writing because some untalented hack chooses to disparage me. I have faced worse dangers and persevered. I shall do so again.

Chapter 4

Ellen

"Christ on the cross," Ellen said after she read Louisa's column in the evening edition of *The Ledger*.

"Ellen!" Hester said in mock admonishment. They sat, shoulders touching, in the back of a yellow cab on their way to the Astor to hear Charlotte Perkins Gilman's lecture.

"She's playing with fire, she is," Ellen said, unable to believe what she'd just read. "She called him an 'untalented hack.' I'm all moidered here."

"What does that mean?" Hester asked.

"Befuddled. Tied up in knots," Ellen explained. She folded the paper and stuck it in her handbag.

"You have to convince Louisa to leave town for a while," Hester said. "I'm sure she'll listen to reason."

"Louisa overesteems the wealthy and underesteems the poor," Ellen said. "She thinks because the anarchists come from the poor, they can't possibly be that dangerous."

"Well, so far they haven't been particularly successful," Hester said with a shrug.

"Story?" Ellen asked.

"Twenty years ago Emma Goldman's boyfriend tried to kill Henry Frick, who is still very much alive. They recently tried to kill Rockefeller and that didn't work either."

"Those are rich and powerful men. Louisa is neither rich, nor powerful, nor a man," Ellen said.

"Oh, I think Louisa is quite powerful with her pen," Hester said. "Her syndicated column has helped educate women in the hinterlands about contraception and suffrage. Besides, what makes you so sure anarchists tried to shoot her?"

"Because I understand how they feel," Ellen said, quietly. Taking their frustrations out on a society writer was foolish, but she understood the anger. She thought of her *grandda* who had died during the Great Hunger and the rage that marked the following generations.

The cab pulled up to the hotel, a palatial red-brick and granite building, and they got out in front of the canopy where a couple of doorman stood at the ready. A blustery wind raced down the street, nipping at heels, as they hurried inside.

The interior of the building with its shiny brass fixtures, red-coated bellmen and carved ceilings intimidated Ellen. Looking down at her plain, brown cotton frock, she felt woefully underdressed for such airs. Hester, in a smart navy skirt and jacket with an ivory silk blouse, asked the concierge where the lecture would be held, and he directed them past a row of potted trees to the second floor.

They found the lecture hall filled with women: college students, progressive society matrons, wives of lawyers and merchants, and a small group of tight-lipped women dressed like factory workers. A few men sat scattered throughout the audience.

They found two seats and settled down to hear Hester's idol speak. She did not disappoint. Her brown hair was parted in the middle and pinned back into a plain bun. Her nose jutted prominently from her narrow face. She could have looked — should have looked — severe with a nose like that, but there was something gentle and wise in the planes of her cheeks and large brown eyes, which showed an impressive intelligence.

She spoke about the masculine domination of the world and the ills this imbalance had created. Mrs. Gilman did not dismiss all men, giving them credit for their achievements, but she said that, in the end, there was too much "man" in "humanity."

"What are the three worst evils of civilization? They are war, intemperance, and prostitution. Can you question whether any of those are predominantly masculine?" she asked the audience, who responded with nods of agreement and a few chuckles.

After the lecture, a man stood up in the audience. He was short and stocky with thick, jet-black hair and a shovel beard that accented the smile on his face.

"Mrs. Gilman, L. Byron here from *Mother Earth,*" the man said. Ellen's head jerked up at the name. "I hear you preaching to your lovely choir here, but I wonder how do you propose to stop men from going to war? Even now there are whispers and rumors about warmongering in Europe. What can you and your petticoat army do?" he asked.

Ellen reeled from the revelation of his identity. Here was the "untalented hack" whom Louisa had attacked in her paper. A mistake on her part, Ellen thought. He was neither untalented nor a hack, and after seeing him in person, Ellen was more worried than ever.

"I am not a resident of Heaven, Valhalla, or Olympus, Mr. Byron," Mrs. Gilman responded, "or any place where the gods dwell so I'm afraid I cannot stop a war if it comes. But when we women have the vote, when we can work in any profession for which we are suited, when we have all the rights afforded to men, we will change the world for the better."

"And when will that be?" he asked.

"Sooner than you think," she said. Then her expression darkened and she added, looking down at the podium, "but not soon enough." With that pronouncement the lecture ended, and the women began filing out of the room.

"My love," Ellen whispered to Hester. "Please go home without me. There is something I must do. I'll see you tomorrow."

Hester clutched her arm and said, "Wait, Ellen. Tell me."

"I'm going to find out what those anarchists are up to," Ellen said.

Ellen had no more time to explain. She extricated herself from Hester and needled her way through the crowd until she came face to face with Mr. L. Byron.

"Mr. Byron," she said.

"Yes?" he asked. He wasn't dashing, but he possessed a friendly face with a charming expression. This did not reassure her, but still she could be charming herself when she tried. So she smiled, gazing at him with her forthright green eyes, which she knew to be her best feature.

“I admire your writing,” she said. “I’ve been mighty disturbed by that dirty business in Colorado. I believe you’ve put the blame where it rightly belongs.”

“Then you don’t believe I’m an untalented hack?” he said, pointing to the evening edition of *The Ledger*, poking out of her handbag.

A blunder, she thought nervously, but she could honestly answer, “I do not, sir.”

He gazed at her again as if trying to place her in the world.

“You’re not a factory girl, and not nearly submissive enough to be a servant. But you’re not a fashionable lady either. You’re from Ireland and I’d wager by your accent it’s only a year or so since you left,” he said. He looked at her hand and added, “You’re not married either. What sort of creature are you, Miss...?”

“Malloy. Ellen Malloy,” she said and thought quickly. She must tell something close enough to the truth. “I work for a newspaper. *The Gaelic American*. I answer the phone and take stories from stringers, run errands.”

His smile grew.

“*The Gaelic American?* Then you must be on the side of the Irish Republicans, another oppressed people. No wonder you sympathize,” he said.

“I do. In fact, I’d like to help,” she said.

He looked curious.

“How so?” he asked.

“I’m not exactly sure,” she said.

“Sorry. We can’t afford any more help at *Mother Earth*,” he said. “Miss Goldman owes the printers as it is.” He turned away from her to close the conversation, but she stayed him with a hand on his arm.

"Mr. Byron, I'm not looking for a job. I've already got one, but isn't there something I can do? Some way I can contribute to the cause?" she asked.

He said nothing as he seemed to assess her once again. Then he reached a decision.

"Meet me at the Bohemian restaurant in the Village day after tomorrow. Say around one o'clock?" he said. "We'll see what we can find for you."

He turned and walked away. Ellen had no idea where the Bohemian was, but she would find it.

Chapter 5

Louisa

Louisa walked briskly toward the IRT station. She had just reached the corner of her street when a loud *bang* erupted. Her body jolted backward, and she clasped her chest. As echoes reverberated, ringing in her ears, she quickly examined herself. No wounds as far as she could tell. She looked behind her and saw a Model A tooling down the street. It must have backfired. For all her bravado, she realized she was more frightened than she had been letting on.

She steadied herself with a hand on a nearby lamp post, taking deep breaths in an attempt to still her thundering heart. She must not give in. She would wind up a recluse like her mother and then how would they live?

She continued to the train platform and took the Sixth Avenue elevated train to Central Park South. Like other luxury hotels that had popped up in the past decade, the Plaza resembled an enormous French chateau, but it was several stories higher than the others.

Louisa would have preferred being at the Gilman lecture with Ellen and Hester but when Mrs. Henry Clay Frick summoned, one had little choice but to attend. Mrs. Frick was an ardent patroness of the Yorkville Social Center, which sponsored a dancing club, a civics forum, and amusements for girls four evenings a week at a public school on East 88th Street. However, tonight's benefit would be in one of the ballrooms at the Plaza.

The attendees were senators' daughters, fashionable young married women and their husbands, some of the city's eligible bachelors, and a host of society matrons, decked out in their finest. Tea tables scattered around the room left the center open for dancing. Louisa planted herself at one of the tables with her notebook. She noted that several girls sold cigarettes and flowers. Mrs. Frick — a handsome, buxom woman wearing a fashionable gown with sheer sleeves and sapphires dangling from a chain around her neck — stopped by her table to ask how she was doing. Like any empress acknowledging one of her subjects, she wasn't really interested; she was merely signaling her approval of Louisa's presence.

"Fine, thank you," Louisa said, but Mrs. Frick had already moved on.

In her notes, Louisa dutifully described the dances — the Boston waltz, the foxtrot demonstration, the tango exhibition, and so on. She could waltz with the best of them, but she did not know how to tango, and she wished she had more time for fun in her life. She was always working. As she sat there, the idea of the trip to Florida intruded. It did seem as if winter in New

York would never end. Was Florida really as warm as everyone claimed, and if she went, might she actually enjoy herself?

"Louisa Delafield, you must come bid on a hat," said a tall, handsome woman of about thirty.

"Alice!" Louisa said. "I thought you lived in Washington now."

"I take any opportunity I can to get away from you know who," Alice Longworth said. Louisa assumed Alice meant her husband, Congressman Longworth. Theirs had not been a happy marriage ever since the election of the previous year. "I am in New York, consoling Daddy after that disastrous election, which he should have won. Wilson is an absolute fool, you know. He despises colored people, which is unforgiveable. By the way, I read your column. Did an anarchist really try to shoot you?"

"I don't know," Louisa admitted. "My publisher wants me to go to Florida to get out of the way for a while."

"You must do it then!" Alice exclaimed. "Palm Beach is a delight."

"This trip would be to St. Augustine," Louisa said.

"That's one of Daddy's favorite places," Alice said. "The city is a bit past its prime, but he loves to go bird watching there. Now, come and choose a hat."

Louisa followed Theodore Roosevelt's eldest daughter to the long table where the hats were displayed. She bought a turban-style number with a glittering brooch on the front. She rationalized that the expense was for charity.

As she took one last look to see if she'd missed anyone whose name might need mentioning, Julia Markham, wife of attorney Herbert Markham, approached her. Julia always reminded Louisa of a Kewpie doll with her full lips and rouged cheeks.

"Mrs. Markham, what a lovely dress you're wearing," Louisa said, admiring the fashionable creamy silk tunic over the lace flounce skirt.

Julia Markham generally yearned to have her dresses mentioned in Louisa's columns, and for once Louisa thought she would oblige.

"Is it a Lucille?" Louisa asked, pen poised above her notepad.

To her surprise, Julia Markham didn't answer. She attempted a smile, but there was something brittle about her face. Wrinkles formed around her eyes as if she were fighting back a flood of tears.

"Mrs. Markham? Julia? Are you quite all right?" Louisa asked.

The woman nodded vigorously, but her eyes betrayed her.

"I'm sorry. I'm... I'm not feeling well, Miss Delafield," she said. "I should probably go home." She abruptly exited the ballroom, leaving Louisa mystified. Julia's husband had been the attorney who handled Louisa's father's legal affairs, and he'd been the one to break the news to her more than a year ago that her family was effectively broke. She knew it wasn't his fault, but she'd harbored an intractable sliver of ill will toward him ever since, which made her less inclined to mention his wife in her columns. Now she regretted her pettiness and hoped that the couple wasn't experiencing some sort of distress.

In the cab on the way home she looked at the hat she had purchased. It wasn't her style at all and she realized for whom she had purchased the hat. It would be perfect for Suzie to wear on the train to Florida. Somehow, the matter had been decided.

When she got out in front of her house, she saw Forrest's Packard parked across the street with Mr. Kimura dozing at the wheel. For heaven's sake, she thought. Forrest would not stop pestering her about getting out of town. What would Suzie think of him coming to her house at night like this?

She opened the front door, prepared to chide him, but a somber look from Suzie halted her.

"What is it?" Louisa asked.

"Mr. Calloway is here with some news," Suzie said.

Louisa found him on the sofa in the parlor. He rose as soon as she entered.

"All right. I'll go to Florida," she said. "That is why you're here, isn't it?"

"No," he said. He put his hands on her arms and said, gently, "Dottie took a turn for the worse today. After the surgery, there was a blood clot. It traveled to her heart. She died tonight."

A loud pounding filled Louisa's head, and she slid out of Forrest's hands to her knees. She put her hands over her face. Sobs shook her relentlessly. *This is my fault,* she thought. *That bullet was meant for me.*

Chapter 6

Ellen

Ellen typed Louisa's notes from the Yorkville Dance and occasionally glanced at the editor's office. After a bit, Louisa came out of Thorn's office. She'd worn black today and her eyes looked swollen and puffy. She'd taken Dottie Parson's death hard, Ellen thought.

"So, are you going?" Ellen asked when Louisa sat down at her desk.

"I am," Louisa said. She smiled wanly. "I told Mr. Thorn that Florida weddings are all the rage and that even though the family of the bride's money is so new the ink is still wet, the newlyweds intend to move to New York and the groom is some sort of French nobility."

"There's that and the attempt on your life," Ellen said. "If we publish articles from St. Augustine, I worry about the anarchists even knowing you're down there."

Louisa waved a hand.

"You don't honestly think they'd go all the way to Florida to get me," she said. "They're a bunch of sad little rabblerousers."

"I wouldn't underestimate anyone with a gun," Ellen said.

Louisa's eyebrows pinched together and her lips quivered. Ellen immediately regretted bringing up the shooting, but it was imperative that Louisa understand the danger.

"I'm sure there will be entertainments to write about," Louisa said, changing the subject. "And sports. Tennis, most likely."

"Before I forget, this came for you," Ellen said and handed over a small package. "From Theodore Roosevelt."

"Roosevelt? What on Earth?" Louisa said.

She tore the brown paper and found a book: Chapman's *Bird Life* along with a note she read and showed to Ellen.

> *"Dear Miss Delafield, My daughter tells me you will be going to Florida. I hope you can find time to write a story about the beautiful birds in that state. If we don't save them from the ladies' hat makers and pass a bill protecting the migrating birds, there will be no more. Please take this old book along with you with my compliments. Yours very truly, T.R."*

"Will you take it?" Ellen asked.

"Of course," Louisa said and put the book into her bag. "Roosevelt has long been an advocate for saving migratory birds from extinction. Did you know that in Florida hunters killed as many as five million birds a year in their heyday? It's not much better now. I've written several columns supporting regulation against such wanton killing for fashion. I even referred to the ridiculous *Aigrette* hat as 'white badge of cruelty.' That got me in hot water with a few of the ladies, but I don't care. It's time for a national law to protect the snowy egrets and wood ducks and so many others."

Ellen had no idea what an *Aigrette* hat was, but it was good to see the fire in Louisa's eyes and even better to know that she was leaving New York for a while. Ellen would have to work quickly to find her would-be assassin.

"Will you be wanting a camera to take with you?" Ellen asked. "They just purchased some new Kodak vest pocket cameras. They're small enough to fit in your handbag and use film rather than plates."

"That's a marvelous idea," Louisa said.

"By the way," Ellen said. "I met this L. Byron fellow at the lecture last night."

Louisa looked concerned.

"What was he like?" she asked.

"Hard to tell," she said. She didn't want to give away the fact that she had made plans to meet with him. "It's not him so much I'm worried about as it's them that read his words."

Louisa suddenly looked at her suspiciously.

"You're not going to involve yourself in anything dangerous while I'm away, are you?" she asked.

"I wouldn't dream of it," Ellen said.

"Because it would be just like you," Louisa said.

"The only dangerous assignment I have is looking out for that mother of yours," Ellen said and looked into Louisa's keen gray eyes.

She went to the storage room and checked out one of the new cameras, which came in its own leather case. Together they opened the case and figured out how to work it.

“Each cartridge of film takes eight pictures,” Ellen explained.

“I think I’ve got it,” Louisa said. “All right. I’m off. I’ll wire you my stories as I write them or send them by post.”

“Speaking of the post, don’t forget your mail,” Ellen said, handing her a stack of letters.

“Thank you,” Louisa said and walked through the maze of desks to the elevator.

“Now, all I’ve got to do is find an anarchist shooter before she gets back,” Ellen muttered. She thought of L. Byron and his invitation to lunch and wondered how she would convince him to let her into their circle.

Chapter 7

Louisa

Buckets of rain fell on the street as the cab driver removed the trunks in front of Grand Central Terminal. Louisa shook out her umbrella before entering the station and then realized she didn't want to cart it all the way to Florida and back, so she simply handed it to an older man standing just inside the door, who was obviously not relishing the idea of getting wet.

"Thank you!" he called after her.

Suzie had never been to Grand Central before, and she stood in awe of the enormous turquoise ceiling with its constellations, the marble floors, and the crowds zipping around each other with the precision of ants. She stopped to look at the oval-glassed clock above the information booth and circled it to look at all four faces telling the time to travelers in all directions.

"It's accurate to within one second every twenty billion years," Louisa said.

Suzie turned to Louisa, "Then we better get going. Our train leaves in thirty minutes." The older woman's excitement was palpable. Her hands fluttered as they walked. She hadn't traveled anywhere outside of the northeast since 1866 when a white woman had brought her from a burned-to-the-ground plantation in South Carolina and deposited her on the doorstep of Louisa's grandmother.

A porter followed them with their trunks on a cart. They'd be in Florida for two weeks and Louisa needed clothes to wear to various social functions and to the wedding itself. Suzie needed less. She was posing as Louisa's lady's maid, but they'd purchased a couple of new dresses for her to meet her family, and she was proudly wearing her new hat.

They boarded their train and got settled in a first class car, courtesy of tickets purchased by Forrest Calloway. Once they were in their seats and the train had chugged out of the station, Louisa took the stack of letters from her purse, mostly invitations to second- and third-tier events as the social season was effectively over, but among the invitations, she found a personal note.

Dear Louisa,

Please forgive me for my hasty departure from the Yorkville Benefit last night. You may as well know I have learned that Herbert has been seeing a woman (a showgirl!) and I am utterly distraught. I plan to divorce him as soon as possible.

I also wanted to let you know that I may have some rather delicate information that pertains to your family. Could we meet this afternoon?

I'm taking a ship to visit friends in London tomorrow and will be gone for several weeks.

Yours truly,

Julia Markham

Louisa stared at the note, stunned. What could Julia possibly know that pertained to her family? Did this have to do with her and Forrest? No, she was sure it couldn't be that. Then what else could this be about? She rubbed the top of her nose and pondered. Julia's husband, Herbert Markham, had been her father's attorney. Did he know something about her father's murder? She wanted to jump off the train and go straightaway to Julia's house, but the landscape was rushing past. Talking to Julia Markham would have to wait. Whatever she knew had kept this long; it could wait a few weeks. She found herself clenching her hands into fists, so she exhaled and slowly released them.

"What is it, Louisa?" Suzie said.

Louisa showed the letter from Julia to Suzie.

"What do you think it means?" Suzie asked, reading the contents of the letter.

"I believe she knows something about Father's murder," Louisa said.

"Can you write to her?"

"I suppose I could, but this sounds like something she needs to say in person," Louisa said.

"Hmm, and she's taking a trip to London. Well then, I suppose you'll have to wait," Suzie said. "I know that your father's murder still weighs on you, child, and I do wish you could get some peace of mind."

"Thank you," Louisa said, grateful that Suzie was on this trip with her.

They sat quietly, watching the landscape pass as if they were in the cinema with the constantly changing picture within the window frame. Small blue and yellow wildflowers bloomed along the tracks.

Louisa thought of the day she had stood by her father's fresh grave when she twelve — the dirt on her white gloves, the smell of the lilies, and the granite grave marker. She had promised herself she would someday find out why he was gone, why he was in that grave and not standing next to her, his arm around her shoulder, but she had learned little in the intervening years.

She sighed. Now, she had the death of Dottie Parsons on her conscience, and she couldn't investigate that because she was on her way to cover a Florida wedding. What good was being a reporter when you were confined to such pointless trivialities?

Chapter 8

Ellen

Ellen drank a cup of strong Irish tea as she sat at the kitchen table of Detective Paddy O'Neil. Paddy's wife Paula moved around the kitchen in a blur, snatching the 18-month-old from the floor before he touched the hot stove, slinging a plate of toast in front of the four-year-old, setting the littler one back down on a blanket in the corner, wiping strands of hair from her face with an arm, moving the kettle from the heat, and all the while complaining about Paddy's long hours since he'd joined the bomb squad.

"Give it a rest, woman," Paddy said.

"Jam?" Sean asked, waving his toast in the air.

Paula reached for the jam just as the baby discovered a pot in the cupboard and began beating it with a spoon that he'd somehow managed to get his chubby hands on. Ellen's shoulders jerked with every bang of the pot. Paula wheeled around and stared at Paddy.

"I think I'll take the little one for a stroll in his carriage," Paddy piped up. "Ellen, care to join?"

"Sure," Ellen said, picking up the small boy and gently prying the pot from his hand. "Will you come with us, Sean? Let your ma have a moment or two of peace?"

Sean jumped up from the table and ran to put on his jacket.

"You're a saint, Ellen," Paula said.

"And what about me?" Paddy asked.

"You're the devil incarnate." She smiled as he bent to kiss her.

They found a spot in a nearby park and sat on a bench while the baby played in the grass and Sean tossed pebbles into the pond.

"What's on yer mind, Ellen?" Paddy asked. "I can tell yer up to no good."

"It's that anarchist that shot at Louisa," she said.

"Ay, they're a sorry lot," he said. "The squad's got our hands full, trying to figure out what or who they plan to blow up next. Between the Italians and the Jews, I'm not sure who's the worst of the lot."

"I don't approve of their means," Ellen said, "but if the robber barons and the government would play fair, there'd be no cause for them in the first place."

"Ellen, we're in America now," Paddy said. "You're still warring with the Sassenachs. It's all us against them. Yet look at your life. You've got a good job, and from what I can tell you're pretty chummy with at least one member of the upper classes."

Ellen glanced over at him. He knew about Hester. He'd known Ellen from childhood in Galway. She'd always been a tomboy and never cared a hoot about the things other girls cared about. He'd even met Hester once.

"Hester is one of the good ones," Ellen said.

"I believe it. The question is, whose side are you on?"

"Right now, I'm on Louisa's side. I want to find out who this shooter is, so you can arrest her, and Louisa can come back and do her job without fearing for her very life." Ellen balled her hands into fists.

"And how do you plan to do that?" he asked.

"I'm after infiltrating their organization. That's what you do, isn't it?"

"But I'm a trained detective with the full weight of the New York Police Department behind me. You're just a woman," he said.

"And that's exactly why I can find out information that you can't," she said, straightening the collar on her dress.

"Yer playing with fire, girleen," he said in a low voice.

He was no doubt right, but she never could resist the flame.

"The thing is, Paddy, I've already made contact with them," she said. The little one had rolled over on his back and kicked at the sky, working his legs so that he could be up and running soon with his big brother.

Paddy placed his elbows on his knees and cradled his chin.

"Which ones are ya talking about?" he asked. "The Italians? The Bresci Circle?"

"No, I know that's where your boys are concentrating. I'm talking about the ones that publish that magazine *Mother Earth*."

"Woman! What are you thinking?" he said when he raised his head.

"I've told them I work at *The Gaelic American*," she said. "I couldn't say I worked at *The Ledger*."

"No, they would not trust ya. But what happens if they check to see if you're working for *The Gaelic*?"

"That's what I'm after you about," she said. "You know Devoy, don't you? The owner?"

"Every New York Irishman knows Devoy," he said.

"Think you could put in a word? Tell 'em I'm one of those police matrons on an investigation?"

Paddy rolled his eyes before dropping his gaze on her.

"Paddy," she said, "I know you have no one in with the *Mother Earth* anarchists."

"We do not," he confessed. After a long moment, he said, "All right. I'll talk to Devoy."

She smiled and called out to Sean, who had climbed atop a boulder and was flapping his arms. "Eh, boy-o, careful now."

***

For the second day in a row, freezing rain blanketed Manhattan Island. Ellen huddled under a black umbrella as she searched the side street where supposedly the restaurant was hidden in a basement. Finally, she found a small sign that said THE BOHEMIAN above a stairwell. She descended the steps and walked down a narrow hallway, shaking rain off her umbrella. She'd never been to one of these Greenwich Village restaurants before but had heard that artists frequented them. Perhaps that's why the place was so obscure. Perhaps ordinary folk weren't welcome.

The head waiter, a gaunt fellow with a crooked nose, greeted her effusively. As he led her through the room, she examined the surroundings — brick walls, round tables, a man playing "The Boatman's Song" on an upright piano while a boy played the fiddle. Curious types populated the room. The men had long hair and wore flowing ties. The women had kohl-rimmed eyes and seemed above caring about fashion as if such petty concerns were beneath them. The smell of grilled meat wafted in the air. The head waiter led her to a table in the corner where L. Byron sat, smoking a thin brown cigarette.

"Good day, Mr. Byron," she said as she sat down. A cigarette pack lay on the table, and she noticed the label was written in what looked like Russian.

"Good day to you, Miss Malloy," he said.

"What does the L. stand for?" she asked.

"Nothing," he said, flicking ashes on to the floor. "L. Byron is my *nom de plume*, a reference to a certain 19th-century aristocrat, but I admire his causes and his poetry. He couldn't help the circumstances of his birth. My friends call me Karl."

"Nice to meet you, Karl," she said. Louisa had been right. The man was a phony. Then again Louisa used a "*nom de plume,*" too, so it could be he had his reasons.

"Likewise, Ellen," he said.

The waiter came over, wearing a stained apron. His thick hands rested on his hips as he looked from one to the other. Karl asked for the veal paté with minced macaroni. Ellen said she'd have the same.

The food arrived quickly, hot and filling with bread and grated cheese. As they ate, they spoke in generalities. He mentioned he was born in Germany, but had lived in Paris for much of his life. He'd moved to New York when he was eighteen. She estimated he must be around thirty. She told him that she'd come to America two years earlier and worked for a wealthy family as a domestic until they accused her of theft.

"A lie, of course," Ellen said. "I knew too much about the man of the house. He'd gotten one of the maids in the family way and she died on an abortionist's table right in front of my eyes."

Karl grimaced.

"These plutocrats haven't a shred of conscience. They'll lie, steal, and even murder if they have to," he said, smoke curling in front of his squinted eyes.

He wasn't wrong, she thought. Yet that didn't give him an excuse to incite someone to murder her friend, who wasn't a plutocrat or any other kind of "crat." When the waiter cleared away their plates, Karl ordered a Turkish coffee for both of them and lit another cigarette.

"Mr. Byron, I mean Karl, I believe in the anarchist cause. I'd like to help."

"We'll see," he responded. His eyes brightened as he looked beyond her. "Ah, there she is."

Ellen turned to look toward the door. A young woman in a black raincoat had stopped to talk to some men at a table at the other end of the restaurant. She lifted her eyes and waved vaguely in their direction. A moment later she shed her raincoat, handed it to the head waiter, and joined them. Tendrils of blond hair dangled along the sides of her narrow face. Her dark eyes examined Ellen.

"Hello," she said and took Ellen's hand in her own. "You must be Miss Malloy. I'm Lulu." Her voice was husky and rich as the Turkish coffee, her face pale, her cheekbones prominent. She smiled, showing perfect white teeth, and Ellen felt a magnetic pull.

"Lulu is an editor for *Mother Earth*," Karl said.

"Call me Ellen. Pleased to meet you."

"So are you an anarchist?" Lulu asked. Ellen hadn't expected such a forthright question. She hesitated before answering. Lulu glanced at Karl.

"I don't know yet," Ellen said. "All I know is that the rich have always enjoyed crushing the common man — and woman — under their thumbs, and I am sick of it. I've seen both sides, and I know it's not fair. It doesn't have to be this way." As she spoke her conviction grew. "If Rockefeller and Frick and Carnegie and all the rest of the petty barons simply paid workers their due, there would be no need for revolutions. Instead they buy houses and yachts and blood diamonds for their wives and mistresses. I worked for them, and I know all about how they spend their money. My mistress had forty pairs of shoes. Expensive ones that I had to brush or polish and keep clean."

Lulu nodded.

"That's all well and good, Ellen, but what do you even know about us?" she asked.

"I've been reading *Mother Earth* for the past year," Ellen said. "And the ideas creep into your head. Your piece about the Ludlow Massacre kept me up at night, Karl."

"Karl told me you work at *The Gaelic American*. A weekly isn't it? Like our *Mother Earth*?" Lulu asked, taking a cigarette from Karl's pack.

"Yes. Our main focus is Irish independence. I'm all for the cause, but I happen to live in America now, and what I see here isn't pretty either. Before the paper, I worked for one of the wealthiest families in the city. And it left a right bitter taste in my mouth. What with all their society galas and balls, the money those women spent on their hats and dresses could feed a family for a month. They all pretend to care for the poor, but if a servant falls sick, they're out on their ear. And if the lord of the manor takes a liking to one of the maids . . . ."

Ellen shook her head and went quiet for a moment.

"Where in Ireland are you from?" Karl asked, twirling his cigarette between his thumb and index finger.

"I grew up in the Claddagh and then moved in with my aunt in Galway City when I turned sixteen," she said. "I worked at the Salt Hill Resort in the summers and helped with my aunt's used bookshop the rest of the year. That old bookshop is what got me to be a reader."

"Did you do any work with the Irish Brotherhood?" he asked.

"I was too young, but my *da* was an outspoken member. He was a guest of the Crown more than once," she said with a laugh.

"Do you write?" Lulu asked.

"No," Ellen said. "I'm a good typist though."

Lulu shrugged and looked at Karl.

"I don't see what good she can be to us," she said. "We don't need a typist."

Ellen worried that they were losing interest in her and she would find out nothing about the attempt on Louisa's life.

"I'm still connected to the servants' network. I can find out things. And I...well, I have a friend...who has money."

"We can always use money," Lulu said with a grin.

"I don't know about asking for money. I just meant...." Ellen stopped. She didn't know what she meant. She'd never ask Hester for money. Why did she even bring it up? She also shouldn't look too desperate.

"Maybe you're right. I don't know how I can help you. I'm sure not going to shoot anyone."

Karl grinned and said, "We've got all the shooters we need. Still, we don't turn anyone away. If you want to help out, we'll find something for you to do."

Ellen wanted to ask him how many of those shooters were women, but there was no need to show her cards. She turned to Lulu.

"You're an immigrant, too, aren't you?" Ellen asked. "Where are you from?"

"Latvia," Lulu said. "Like your father, mine was also a revolutionary. He died in a Russian prison."

Ellen felt a stirring in her soul as her gaze met Lulu's. Eyes so dark, thin lips that looked a little cruel and incredibly enticing.

"Deeper and deeper grows the ancient grief. Blackest of all intolerable things," Ellen said.

"One of your Irish poets?" Lulu asked.

"It's called 'The Eternal Rebel,'" Ellen said. "We published it in *The Gaelic American.* A rallying cry to all rebels, everywhere."

They were quiet for a few minutes, drinking their coffee. Ellen felt Karl watching the two of them curiously.

"I love poetry. Let's go out sometime, Ellen," Lulu finally said. She reached over and ran a finger over the back of Ellen's hand. Her skin tingled at the woman's touch. She thought of Hester and guilt rushed through her veins. Lulu might as well have been made of dynamite.

"When?"

"Tomorrow night," Lulu answered. "Where do you live?"

Ellen hesitated. She was supposed to stay with Louisa's mother. Then again the old woman usually went to bed early and no one would know if Ellen slipped away for a few hours.

"Why don't I meet you somewhere? Say Times Square?" Ellen suggested.

"I'll be there at 9:00," Lulu said.

Lulu rose, ruffled Karl's hair and strode away. Ellen watched her receding back and cursed the desire that flared inside her.

Chapter 9

Louisa

Suzie opened a bag on her lap and handed Louisa a packet of Graham crackers and an apple. When Louisa bit into one of the crackers, childhood memories swam to the surface of her mind.

"You used to give these to me every afternoon up in the nursery. You pretended like it was our little secret," Louisa said with a smile.

"It was our little secret. You weren't supposed to eat in the nursery," Suzie said.

"Miss Lane always had to have her afternoon nap," Louisa said. She shook her head, remembering the woman who was her governess for six years. "All those Latin conjugations wore her out, I suppose."

Suzie nodded.

"She wasn't too bad," Suzie said. "She was terrified when your father was killed."

"Of course, she was. She thought she had a secure job until I was eighteen," Louisa said.

"They all thought their jobs were secure," Suzie said. "I remember watching them leave one by one. Each with their suitcase in hand. They wouldn't even look at me."

They were silent for a bit, rocking with the train, caught up in memories. After her father's murder, Louisa's mother, who hadn't been particularly maternal to begin with, simply handed the childrearing reins over to Suzie. It had been Suzie who comforted Louisa in her grief, Suzie who explained to her about a woman's monthly, and Suzie who had encouraged her to go to college. Suzie's child-bearing years were spent taking care of someone else's child. She had never had a chance for a family of her own.

"You were eleven when you came to New York, weren't you? Do you remember any of your family? " Louisa asked.

"Of course, I remember them," Suzie said. "I remember Granny the most. She was the cook for the big house. Up before dawn every day, making breads and jellies. Her peach jam was famous all over the county. She taught me how to garden so I could help her in the kitchen and not be sent off to work in the cotton fields. I also learned how to sew, and I had to make the fires in the morning."

"They'd make a child work in the fields?" Louisa asked.

"Of course. The little ones just helped out, toting water to the field hands or picking weeds. When they got a little older, they'd get their own rows during the cotton pickin' season," Suzie said. "Kids' hands would be red with blood from picking that cotton. Granny made a special ointment to heal the skin. Smelled something awful but it worked."

The image of bloodied little hands horrified Louisa. When she was young, her grandmother had given her a copy of *Uncle Tom's Cabin*, and Louisa had never been able to forget the horror of learning what men were capable of doing to one another.

"What about school?" Louisa asked.

"School? Louisa, honey, there was no schooling for us. The only reason I learned how to read was because Granny had figured out how to read a receipt book and she taught me. I s'pose someone taught her the ABCs and then she figured out the rest by herself."

The train pulled up to a station with a great screeching of wheels. Passengers got off. Others came on, and soon the train was lapping up the miles again.

"But what about your brothers?" Louisa asked. "You mentioned brothers."

"I had two, George and Lloyd. Both of them younger. After Mama was sold off, I didn't see much of them. One of the other women took them in with her. My mother might have had more children after she was sold. I'll never know."

"Do you remember your mother?" Louisa asked.

"Honey, you never forget your Mama. She was so pretty she could get away with things that other slaves couldn't. There was something dreamy about her. She loved to tell stories. All the children and even some of the grown-ups would gather around her on a Sunday afternoon, the only time we didn't have to work. Except Granny. Granny never had a day off because the white people had to eat. I guess Mama's dreaminess is why they sent her off. That and she was pretty so the mistress hated her."

"Do you have any photographs of your mother? Or any of your family?"

"Nope," Suzie said. "But I do have a picture of Granny in my head. Her father was white so she was light-skinned. And she worked hard so she had muscles in her arms. But it was her smile that I remember, a smile that filled her whole face."

Louisa thought of her own grandmother, a kind and affectionate woman who had died of heart failure when Louisa was quite young

"How did your grandmother die?" Louisa asked.

"Influenza," Suzie said.

For all the suffering Louisa had endured when her father was murdered, she could not imagine what it would be like to have her family torn apart so cruelly. These weren't topics that Louisa and Suzie had ever talked about. Louisa had always been leery of asking questions that might be painful to answer, but now here they were going to search for Suzie's family and she wanted to know more of Suzie's history. Besides, the conversation kept her from thinking about Dottie, lying in the hospital, so cheerful when Louisa had visited her, with no idea she would not live to see the next day.

"Did you know your father? Where was he?"

Suzie shook her head. "My mother didn't get to choose the father of her children. They bred her like she was a horse. Some slaves did marry, but not my mama. My daddy was a carpenter from a neighboring plantation. I saw him one time when he came over to make some cabinets for the Missus. He was one of the lucky ones. He had skills and so he could earn his own money. He eventually bought his freedom."

"Why didn't he buy yours?" Louisa asked.

Suzie shrugged.

"It's not as if he loved us kids or my mother. He was told to 'mate' with her until his seed took root. I don't think it took long," Suzie said. "The masters must have thought they were a good match because he also fathered my two brothers."

"Oh, Suzie," Louisa said. "Your poor mother."

Louisa reached over and squeezed Suzie's hand. The train whistled long and low.

***

Louisa woke to Suzie shaking her by the shoulder.

"Louisa, wake up," Suzie said.

She opened her eyes.

"What's happening?"

"I got to move to another car," Suzie said, standing in the aisle, a porter behind her.

"I apologize," the porter said, "but we're in the South now, and your maid here will have to go to the Jim Crow car at the front of the train."

"But...but why? I don't want her to go," Louisa said.

"Miss, there'll be trouble if she don't go," he said.

"It's all right, Louisa," Suzie said. "I think we better get used to this."

Suzie already had her valise in hand.

"Let me take that for you, Ma'am," the porter said. "I can't tell you how sorry I am, but this is the way it is here."

"I see things haven't changed much then," Suzie said.

"No, ma'am, they haven't."

Louisa stood up.

"Then I'll go with her," Louisa said.

Suzie turned and looked at her with a steady gaze. "Sit down, Louisa. I'll see you when we get to St. Augustine."

Louisa was immediately an obedient child again and sat down on the soft cloth seat. She stared outside at the blur of landscape but nothing registered. Finally, she opened Chapman's *Bird Life* and looked at the chapter on water birds. The pictures of the birds were beautiful. She was particularly entranced by a large pink bird called a roseate spoonbill. The bird's feathers were the same color as the dress Dottie wore to Hugh Garrett's wedding. Oh, Dottie, she thought, will I ever be able to forgive myself?

Chapter 10

Ellen

Hester giggled at the sign outside the tea house: "Men allowed, but not welcome." They rarely came to the Village because Hester was usually busy with women's suffrage meetings and charitable work while Ellen had her job, but she had left work early that day, and the two decided to go back to the tea house where they first met.

The proprietress was an elegant silver-haired woman named Lillian, who served Ceylon black tea and delicious cookies. As they sat drinking tea near the window, Ellen looked up and saw Lulu on the sidewalk, staring at her. Hester was talking about the debate among the suffragists as to whether they should focus on the states or the federal government and didn't notice. Lulu looked at Hester curiously, then smiled at Ellen and blew her a kiss before walking away.

"You seem distracted," Hester said.

"I'm thinking I better get back to Louisa's house," Ellen said. "Her mother'll be after some dinner."

"I'll come with you," Hester said with a smile.

"There's no need," Ellen said. Hester didn't argue, but she looked perplexed. "I'm just tired." Ellen had no intention of telling Hester about her plans for later.

***

"Where are we going?" Ellen asked. She and Lulu strode along Christopher Street at a clip, Lulu's long, dark coat fanning out behind her. Evening had settled into an azure glaze over the brick tenements with their fire escapes and the businesses on the first floors.

"East Thirteenth Street. I'm taking you to meet her," Lulu said.

"Her?" Ellen asked.

"Emma Goldman. The Great!" Lulu said and turned to her with eyes shining. "There's a small gathering at her place tonight. Let's see if you meet with her approval."

Ellen's breath caught and she stopped short. *The* Emma Goldman? The firebrand anarchist who traveled around the country giving speeches about any number of social causes, and whose wit and intelligence matched any thinker of the day? Even Hester, who didn't approve of anarchism, spoke highly of Emma Goldman for her stance on issues relating to equality for women.

For a brief moment, Ellen wondered if this was a trap. Perhaps someone had learned that she actually worked with Louisa at *The Ledger* and not at *The Gaelic American,* as she'd told Karl. But Lulu's eyes shone with excitement, not malice.

"Where does she live?" Ellen asked.

"In an apartment nearby."

"Who will be there?"

"Karl and Sasha, certainly.

"Sasha?"

"You may know him as Alexander Berkman, the lead editor of *Mother Earth,* and my boss. He and Emma were lovers, then he tried to kill Henry Frick – he failed and went to prison for fourteen years."

"Did Emma wait for him all those years?" Ellen asked. She knew the name Frick from Louisa's column. Lots of money and lots of art and a wife who had her hands in everything. Hester had mentioned this same assassination attempt just a few days ago.

"No, now they are just friends. I won't go into detail about her current lover, but let me say, he takes the idea of 'free love' very seriously and it breaks poor Emma's heart, though she tries to pretend otherwise. Fortunately, he's out of town."

They hurried past an apothecary, a cigar store, a laundry, a lunch room, and a saloon. A trolley rolled by them, clanging its bell.

"Who else will be there?"

"Frank Tennenbaum from the International Workers of the World, and Becky, of course," Lulu continued.

"Becky?"

"Sasha Berkman's lover. Young, pretty, ready and willing to die for the cause."

Lulu put a hand on Ellen's coat sleeve. "Emma's a champion of people like us. I never heard any one speak on the topic of 'inverts' so passionately."

"Inverts?" Ellen asked.

"You know, women who like women and men who like men," Lulu said. "But Emma says love is love. Too bad not all the anarchists feel that way."

Ellen had not yet admitted to Lulu she was *that* way, but Lulu knew. She'd known the minute their eyes met.

"You hold her in high esteem, I take it," Ellen said, running her woolen-gloved hand over a wrought iron fence as they passed.

"The highest," Lulu answered.

Ellen wondered if that esteem was enough to cause Lulu to do something stupid for the cause, such as try to shoot a society columnist.

"Lulu, do you believe the ends justify the means?" Ellen asked. "For instance, killing Henry Frick. Would that have done any good?"

"Sasha says the point of violence is to rouse others to the cause. It's called propaganda of the deed," she said. "But Emma is against violence. Me, I think violence should be used...judiciously."

Shooting at someone in public didn't seem very judicious, Ellen thought. She tried, but couldn't picture Lulu dressed all in black with a gun pointing toward Louisa.

"Here we are," Lulu said, gesturing to a door framed by two dark brown, stone pillars.

They stood in front of a six-story tenement. An iron fire escape clung to the front of the building. Ellen took a deep breath. She wanted to find out who had tried to kill Louisa, but she also thrilled at the idea of meeting Emma Goldman. She hesitated for a moment. What if she fell under Goldman's spell? What if she forgot all about her original motivation for this adventure? If she joined these mad people, would she ever want to leave?

"Are you coming?" Lulu stood at the top of the stoop.

Ellen smiled and said, "Does it rain in Ireland?"

They climbed the gaslit stairwell to the top floor and then walked a narrow hallway to the door. Beyond the door she heard laughter and loud conversation. Lulu knocked twice. After a moment the door opened, and a bespectacled woman in her forties wearing a faded dress, her hair neatly pinned on the back of her head, stared at them. Then her face broke into a wide smile. She hugged Lulu first. Then appraised Ellen and to Ellen's surprise, she hugged her, too.

"Welcome, my little chicks, welcome," she said in a throaty voice with a hint of an accent. "You must be the Irish rebel, Miss Malloy. Karl mentioned you might be joining us."

Ellen felt dizzy for a moment. Had Emma Goldman just called her a rebel? She didn't have time to soak it in. Lulu pulled her by the hand into the living room where they stepped into a stream of talking, cigarette smoke, and laughter. Stacks of magazines and books filled every corner. Ellen scanned the room. Six men. Three women. She recognized Karl, alias L. Byron. Then Lulu pointed to a balding man.

"That's Alex Berkman, or Sasha, as we call him. He's the one I was telling you about earlier," Lulu whispered.

Ellen stared, fascinated.

"Who's that?" Ellen asked, nodding at a pale, blond-haired woman who stood silently in the corner, smiling at the scene like some beneficent angel.

"That's Sweet Sal," Lulu said. "She's the all-around errand girl. No education. Started working when she was ten years old and once started a riot when she turned over a pushcart." Then she leaned in and whispered, "She's terribly fond of Frank Tennenbaum over there. He's with the International Workers movement. Charlie, the handsome one next to him, might be dressed like a dandy but he's one tough foot soldier. His buddy, Artie, is the burly one."

"So many names to remember," Ellen said.

At that moment, Miss Goldman handed her a glass of ale and said, "Now tell me all about yourself, Miss Malloy. What brings you into our world?"

Ellen decided to tell truth. The fewer lies, the less chance to get tangled in them.

"It's simple. People are hungry, out of work, living on the streets, and I'm angry about it," she said, and she felt the heat of it in her throat. "I don't think charity is the answer. So I'm ready to do what I can to change things."

Miss Goldman's eyes were warm and sympathetic.

"I'm afraid the wealthy think the rest of us are little more than commodities to be used up and discarded. Not all of them, of course, but enough that they cause great misery," she said. "Don't worry. We'll find a way to make you useful. We always need organizers. By the way, call me Emma."

"I will if you'll call me Ellen. What does an organizer do?"

"You'll learn," Emma smiled and said. "Break bread with us, Ellen." Then she turned to the group. "Everyone, this is Miss Ellen Malloy. A friend of Lulu's. She's one of us! Now, let's eat."

Karl stood and patted Ellen on the shoulder.

"Nice to see you again. I knew you and Lulu would become friendly." His smile had something lurid about it.

The others glanced at Ellen and acknowledged her with a nod as they rose and filled their plates. The table was laden with food — beef stew, fried potatoes, greens, an apple pie and a chocolate cake. Emma bade her grab a plate and find somewhere to sit. Ellen and Lulu shared a settee.

After a few minutes while everyone ate in silence, Berkman cleared his throat and gazed out the window. He had heavy features and a lantern-jaw, a hairline that had abandoned his forehead, and hooded, reptilian eyes that made Ellen feel squeamish.

"The day is coming," Berkman said, looking directly at her. "When blood will flow in the streets of this city."

The handsome man that Lulu had identified as Charlie raised a glass and said, "Here. Here."

"We must live for that day, work for that day, and sacrifice for that day," Berkman intoned. "Damn the socialists and their incrementalism. To participate in government is to legitimize it," he continued. "The miners at Ludlow had legitimate grievances, but when they went on strike, Rockefeller sent in his goons to kill them. Women and children, too."

His voice cracked, and a young woman beside him reached for his hand. She had dark hair, parted in the middle, a pug nose, and enormous eyes.

"That's Becky, his lover. She's a firecracker," Lulu said.

"Next time I go to jail I'm going on a hunger strike," Becky announced. Her red-stockinged legs were crossed at the ankle.

"Next time?" Ellen asked.

"I've been getting arrested ever since I left the orphanage. They take one look at me and say, 'That girl's dangerous. Send her to Blackwell!'" she said and laughed.

"But you are dangerous, my own sweet spitter," Berkman said and pecked her on the cheek. The rest of the guests laughed.

Lulu said, "They're laughing because once during a march, Becky opened the door of a limousine and spit at the man inside."

"Down with the parasites!" Becky said, holding up her glass of ale.

Ellen marveled at how young and fierce she was. She easily pictured *her* firing a weapon at a crowd of wedding guests.

Lulu whispered, "She was fifteen when she and Berkman got together. She's a real hot one, huh?"

Ellen couldn't imagine the attraction between Berkman and the pretty girl. Of course she'd known many a girl back home to marry young and have a house full of children before they were twenty, but Berkman seemed so much older. And he'd been in prison!

She studied Becky and thought, *If she's brave enough to spit in the face of a rich capitalist, she's brave enough to shoot at Louisa.* Ellen would have to keep an eye on her and try to get close. It was one thing to have a suspect and quite another to have proof.

A quiet fellow, Ellen had forgotten his name, sat in a chair next to her. His left hand was mangled and missing two fingers.

"Hello, Miss Malloy. My name's Frank Tannenbaum," he said, holding out his right hand. She pulled her eyes away from his mangled hand and took the other.

"Pleased to meet you," Ellen said. "Please call me Ellen."

He looked down at the mangled hand and said, "It's all right. Everyone looks at it. I don't mind telling you the story. This happened seventeen-and-a-half hours into an eighteen-hour shift at a wallpaper factory. I fell asleep at the machine and woke up screaming."

"An eighteen-hour shift?" Ellen asked. "'Tis no wonder you fell asleep."

"I was sixteen years old," he said. "They patched me up, and I went back to work."

"It's a crying shame the way the workers are treated," Ellen said, shaking her head.

"Have you known poverty, Ellen?"

"I grew up in the Claddagh, and we were poor as dirt," she said.

"Did you ever go hungry?"

"My *da* worked on the water and Ma had a few chickens. So we always had some dried saltfish, eggs, and a couple of mealy potatoes if nothing else," she said. "The Great Hunger was over by the time I was born, thankfully. But the memory of it lingered."

Becky leaned forward and grinned, showing crooked teeth.

"Lulu, you should take Miss Malloy down to the Municipal Lodging House to see what the poverty in this city is really like."

Ellen eyed her and wondered what she was up to with this suggestion.

"I'll do it," Frank said. "I'll show you hunger right here in rich America like you ain't never imagined."

"I'd like to go with you, Mr. Tannenbaum, but I'm not sure how I can help," Ellen said.

"If you want to fight alongside us, you have to know what you're fighting for," Becky said.

"Are you with the Workers of the World like Frank, Becky?" Ellen asked.

"I'm not a member, no, but I'm there at every march right next to Frank," she said proudly. "He's the man of the hour."

"Here, here," the handsome man called Charlie said again, raising his glass. Next to him a portly fellow, named Artie, also raised a glass. She thought of them as "Thick and Thin." Charlie had a thin body, thin nose, thin lips, and squinty eyes. Artie, on the other hand, was thick with broad shoulders and temperamental eyebrows. Artie glowered while Charlie smirked.

The blond woman who had been standing on the sidelines came over and interjected, "Frank, can I get you another ale?"

"Sure, Sal," he said, smiling up at the woman. She went to the kitchen.

"Aren't you a writer?" he said to Ellen. "I saw you here with Lulu and thought that's what you were."

"Well, I do work for *The Gaelic American*. I s'pose I could take some notes," she said, hesitantly. "Maybe one of the columnists will take up the cause."

"*The Gaelic*!" Berkman exclaimed. "I know them. They're not far — on William Street. I support their efforts to overthrow the British overlords."

"Tyranny is tyranny," Ellen said.

"The bescumbers!" Sal said, handing Frank a glass of ale.

Lulu giggled and Ellen looked at her, perplexed.

"An old-fashioned insult. Means they spray others with their dung," she whispered to Ellen.

Sal's dirty mouth was a contrast to her soft, sweet voice, a round face with a bulb-like nose, and eyes that had known a lifetime of hurt.

Frank held up the glass with his mangled hand and said, "Down with tyrants everywhere." He turned to Ellen. "*Sláinte*."

Ellen looked around at the crowd of faces, trying to imbed their names in her memory. She felt an odd mixture of guilt and camaraderie. Could she be one of them and not be one at the same time?

Chapter 11

Louisa

Louisa stepped onto a metal footstool and then onto a concrete platform into a cloud of hissing steam as she disembarked from the train. She looked down the line of cars for Suzie. As soon as they found each other, they commandeered a porter to get their trunks and headed toward the line of waiting cars and carriages.

Large pots of bright pink flowers dotted the platform. Dottie would have loved this place, she thought. Before them was a wide, bright green field with grazing cows, and just beyond it the red tile roof of a sprawling building and the spire of a church next to it.

"It's like paradise," Louisa said. "I can't remember ever seeing light so pure."

"It smells just like what I imagine Heaven smells like," Suzie said with a wondrous look on her face. "I remember this smell from my childhood. It's honeysuckle." She pointed to a shrub with tiny white flowers.

"Miss Delafield?" asked a stalwart young Negro in a blue and gold uniform.

"Yes," Louisa said.

"I'm here to take you to the hotel." He pointed to a horse-drawn carriage between a couple of Ford Model T's with gilt letters on the side: THE FLORIDA HOUSE.

"The Florida House?" Louisa said, confused. "I thought we were staying at The Ponce."

"They're all full up," the young man said.

Louisa glanced over at Suzie with a raised eyebrow.

"It's probably fine," Suzie said and chuckled. "Just as fine as your Fifth Avenue Mansion." Suzie was poking fun at her for putting on airs. Their Harlem townhouse was a far cry from Fifth Avenue.

"It's just that I was looking forward to a little bit of luxury," Louisa said with a hint of a pout.

"Don't worry, Miss," the driver said. "Our hotel has plenty of luxury. We got a steam elevator, and each room has a private bath and electric lights. You'll like it. Your maid here will be in an adjoining suite. At the Ponce servants stay on the top floor and it's not so convenient."

"I'm sure it will be fine, Leon," Louisa said, reading the name embroidered on his uniform. She glanced at Suzie, who with her regal bearing looked like anything but a typical "servant," but it was a fiction they had to play if Suzie were to be allowed to stay in the hotel with Louisa.

Leon smiled and took her traveling case from her while the porter followed with the two trunks. Suzie carried a portmanteau, and they walked toward a carriage with two glossy black-maned horses in gilded harnesses. Louisa wondered that the hotel didn't have a motorcar, but supposed they were trying to achieve a quaint effect. The clip clop of horses' hooves undoubtedly was more pleasant than the chugging and sputtering of an engine.

"Madame, let me take your bag for you," a voice said. Louisa looked around to see a dark-haired man in a light gray suit and stylish straw hat, smoothly taking Suzie's bag from her hand. For a moment, Louisa was alarmed, and Suzie looked dumbfounded.

The man bowed slightly and said, "I am also staying at the Florida House, ladies. I hope you will not mind if I share the carriage with you." A French accent threaded through his words, softening the consonants.

Louisa stared at the man, opening her mouth as if to say something, but instead she lost herself in his dark eyes, surrounded by a thicket of black lashes. Maybe it was the warmth of the air, but she felt blood rushing to her face as he placed Suzie's suitcase in the back of the carriage, and then proceeded to help her inside.

"Why, thank you," Suzie said.

In New York, Suzie would have been invisible to a man of his obvious refinement. His kindness toward the older woman pierced Louisa's heart as surely as one of Cupid's proverbial arrows.

He sat across from the two of them in the carriage as they rode down a narrow street lined with one- and two-storey buildings, made of stone and brick. The place did indeed have the look of an ancient city. Louisa stole glances at the man across from her. She surmised he was not yet thirty years old, but he had the air of a world traveler. And there was something else, something aristocratic in his jawline and the set of his shoulders — an odd mixture of hauteur and exquisite manners. He caught her looking at him, and she blushed.

"I believe I heard the driver call you Miss Delafield," he said, his eyes locking onto hers.

"Yes, I am Louisa Delafield," she said.

"That is a French name, is it not?"

"Norman English," she said. Her grandmother never let her forget that her paternal forebears had conquered England in 1066.

"And your lovely companion?" he said, looking at Suzie.

"Su...Miz Blake," Suzie said.

"*Enchanté*. I am Monsieur Simon Bassett," he said.

"Bassett? Are you related to the groom? Henri Bassett?" Louisa asked.

"*Oui,* he is my brother," he said and smiled. He had lovely white teeth — all straight except for one charmingly crooked canine tooth.

"Why aren't you staying in the Ponce with the wedding party?" she asked.

"The Florida House is less expensive. The bride's family is happy to pay for Henri's suite, but I must pay for my own," he said.

Louisa liked his candor. She wondered, however, at his impecunity. He certainly had the air of a wealthy aristocrat.

"Are you friends of the bride?" he asked.

"I'm the society writer for *The Ledger* in New York," Louisa said. "My publisher thought this would be a wedding worth covering."

"A society writer?" he said. "Then you should have much to keep you busy."

"Oh, she does more than write about society," Suzie interjected. "She does investigating, too."

"*Vraiment*?" he asked, looking curiously at Louisa.

"Truly. But only occasionally," Louisa said and glanced at Suzie. She certainly didn't want to mention that she also wrote under a pen name. "It's nothing at all. Tell me, are you from Paris?"

"I grew up in Burgundy, but I have lived in Paris, yes," he said.

"I've only been once when I was much younger," Louisa said. "All I remember is museum after museum and cathedral after cathedral. My father loved art."

"Then you must see it again. Museums and cathedrals are nice, but there is so much more," he said, his eyes lingering on hers a moment before turning to look out the window. "Ah, we are here."

The carriage pulled up to a pink, four-storey wooden structure with balconies jutting out from the sides of the building and Victorian garlands along the carved panels atop a sprawling veranda.

"It's L-shaped so that all the rooms have a view of the bay," Leon boasted as he unloaded their bags and trunks.

The lobby was grand enough with a stately oak staircase and potted palms gracing the corners. A large cage filled with noisy, colorful birds occupied one end of the lobby. Rattan fans rotated from the ceiling and ladies sat at round tables, playing cards and board games and eyeing the newcomers to see if anyone of note had arrived. Louisa recognized a few ladies, including Lady Rutherford, a member of the British aristocracy, who frequented society entertainments whenever she was in New York. When their eyes met, Lady Rutherford rose and advanced toward her like a general surveying the new troops.

"Louisa Delafield, what a surprise," she said. Lady Rutherford's thick silver hair was coiled on her head like a crown, and she had a backbone as straight as a steel rod. "What are you doing in dear old St. Augustine?"

"I'm here to cover a wedding," Louisa answered.

"The Griffin wedding? How charming. I'm sure Daphne's mother is thrilled that a New York society writer is here. Expect to be treated like royalty."

"You know the Griffins?" Louisa asked.

"Of course, I do. Randall's sister married my cousin. Her fortune saved his estate."

"Ah, a dollar princess?" Louisa asked, *sotto voce.*

"Indeed. Is that woman your servant?" Lady Rutherford said curiously, looking at Suzie who was waiting at the front desk. "She seems a bit old to be a lady's maid."

"She's passing as my servant. She's actually my guardian angel," Louisa said.

"I see. Do come down after you've gotten settled and play with us, dear. Do you know Rook? It's great fun, and I promise the wagers are not prohibitive," she said with a mischievous smile. "Or we can play hearts."

Louisa exhaled and thought she might as well relax and enjoy this trip, after all. Anything to keep her mind off Dottie Parson's horrible death and the anarchists who might still want to kill her. She went back to the clerk and was given two room keys, one for her room and one for Suzie's, which adjoined hers as Leon had said it would.

"I am also on the third floor," M. Bassett said, looking at his key. "In the shorter wing."

"I believe you'll have a lovely view from there," Louisa said, hoping she didn't sound like a simpering fool. Something about this man robbed her of all composure.

"I have a lovely view right now," he said, looking at her. Then he bowed to the two of them and said, "*Au revoir*, Miss Delafield and Miss Blake. I hope to see you again soon. I'm off to check on my brother."

He strode off with a confident swagger, and Louisa felt her knees weaken.

***

Louisa's room had a large four-poster bed, a writing table, a chaise longue, and a bureau. White lace curtains covered the window and fluttered in the breeze. Suzie's room was similarly furnished. Their trunks had already been brought up by the bellman.

"Monsieur Bassett is a charming man, isn't he?" Louisa said, opening one of her trunks.

"So are cobras," Suzie said. "Or so I've read."

"Cobras? What are you saying, Suzie?" Louisa asked, shocked and a little annoyed.

"I'm only saying you need to remember who you are, even if we are far from home. You are a Delafield," Suzie said.

Suzie obviously sensed the attraction that Louisa felt toward the handsome French man, though attraction seemed too tame a word for the fluttering she felt inside.

"I'm a grown woman," Louisa said. "This is 1914, not 1850."

"I know you're grown, and I also know about you and Mr. Calloway," she said.

A lump formed in Louisa's throat.

"What about Mr. Calloway?" she asked.

"I'm not judging you, Louisa. I understand why you refuse to marry. I wouldn't want to give up my independence either if I were you," Suzie said. "And he is a good deal older than you."

Louisa was astounded. She and Suzie had never broached a topic so personal.

"But this is different," Suzie said with a warning tone in her voice.

"How?"

"It just is," she said.

Suzie turned to leave Louisa to finish unpacking.

"If I had a real lady's maid, she'd unpack for me," Louisa muttered.

"Well, you don't have a lady's maid, do you?" Suzie said as she walked into her room.

"No," Louisa said. She felt bad for being disrespectful to Suzie, but she was also annoyed for the implication about Monsieur Bassett. Louisa was not some floozy with no self control. She pulled a green day dress with a wide lace collar and black sash from the trunk and hung it in the wardrobe, thinking how flattering it would look on her. On second thought, she took it back out of the wardrobe and laid it on the bed. She would wear it this afternoon just in case she saw him again. Forrest Calloway had utterly disappeared from her mind.

She looked out the window. A large white bird, its neck curved like the letter *S*, flapped slowly past. She pulled her bird book from the bag and looked it up. A great American egret. She'd certainly seen feathers like those adorning hats in the most fashionable settings. She'd even had one herself. No more, she said. No more birds would die for her sake.

She closed the book. She would try to save birds, she thought but that would not assuage her guilt. In her mind's eye, she saw Dottie with her big smile. She imagined Dottie's loud laughter and the heavy scent of her floral perfume. A gloom darkened her heart in spite of the bright day.

Chapter 12

Ellen

The next morning Louisa's mother sat up in her bed and glared at Ellen, who had just entered the room with a cup of coffee on a tray.

"You were out awfully late last night," she said. "You are supposed to be taking care of me."

"I'm sorry, Mrs. Delafield," Ellen said, setting the tray down and then searching through the woman's wardrobe for a dress. "But I'm trying to find out who took a shot at Louisa. You want her to be safe, don't you? This violet dress is pretty."

"Give me the red one," Mrs. Delafield snapped.

Ellen pulled out the red dress and helped Anna onto the side of the bed so she could dress her. She wasn't such an old woman, but she had the lazy habits of the very rich and she'd never lost those habits even when she lost her fortune. How did Suzie put up with it, Ellen wondered. She'd be well within her rights never to return.

"What if Suzie doesn't come back?" Mrs. Delafield said, as if reading Ellen's thoughts.

"If she doesn't, then Louisa will hire someone else," Ellen said.

"No one is like Suzie. I've known her since I was nine years old. She's more like a friend," Anna said.

Except a friend doesn't have to wait on you hand and foot, Ellen thought.

"Maybe you should try to take care of your own self a bit more," Ellen said. "Suzie's not getting any younger."

"You're quite impertinent," she said and glowered at Ellen.

Ellen got her downstairs and into her invalid chair. It wasn't that she couldn't walk. She managed the stairs as long as there was someone at her side, but she claimed to have a bad heart and she didn't like to exert herself. Louisa had said she thought her mother just needed an excuse to never show her face in society again. Next, Ellen made sure Mrs. Delafield had a bowl of Post Toasties and her second cup of coffee.

It was Sunday so Ellen didn't have the excuse of work. She usually spent her Sundays helping Hester with charitable projects. Sometimes they'd spend an afternoon in the Metropolitan Museum, where it was cool and peaceful and no one paid any attention to them. Ellen had never been in a museum in her life until she met Hester. She relished wandering through the large well lit rooms, filled with glorious paintings and sculptures. It was the perfect substitute for church. As she washed Mrs. Delafield's dishes, she thought of her new anarchist friends. They would surely look down on museums as meaningless pursuits for the bourgeoisie.

"Why don't you read something to me?" the older woman suggested, settling into the parlor at her place by the window.

"Let me go out and get a newspaper," Ellen said, grabbing her coat. "I'll read the news to you."

"You better come back!" Mrs. Delafield said as Ellen flew out the front door.

Ellen could have picked up a newspaper a few blocks away, but as soon as she was outside, she had a compulsion to keep going. The old woman wouldn't die if she were left alone for a while. It might do her some good. A few minutes later, Ellen found herself gazing up at the platform of the elevated train, and she thought of Hester, who was probably just waking up. She heard the roar of the approaching train and hurried up the steps to catch it.

As the train rattled south toward Central Park, Ellen watched the city stretching and waking. As they passed by an apartment building, a woman glanced out her window to look at the sky. Below, street vendors moved carts onto the sidewalks. She imagined Hester's look of happy surprise when she showed up at her door.

But when the train slowed for the stop to Hester's apartment, Ellen didn't move. The doors opened, and Ellen didn't get up. Central Park disappeared, replaced by buildings standing shoulder to shoulder. She wasn't sure why she hadn't gotten off at Hester's stop. She could be tumbling into Hester's bed or at least having toast and jam together, but neither of those things drew her. Instead she thought of the Village and of Lulu's low laughter. The pull was like a steel cable.

Lulu had said that the offices of *Mother Earth* were next door to Emma's tenement, so she searched the cafes nearby and found Lulu in a basement dive, smoking a thin Turkish cigarette, at a table with Becky Edelsohn. This was a bit of good luck. Ellen needed to get to know Becky and find out why she shot at Louisa — if she had. Mainly, she needed to find out if she planned to do it again. And if she did, then what? The thought of turning her in to the police made Ellen feel unsettled, but she couldn't allow the anarchists to kill Louisa.

"I thought I might find you mad radicals here," Ellen said and sat down with them. "Where are Karl and Sasha?"

"They're with Emma, trying to get next week's issue done before deadline," Lulu said, smoothing the ash off her cigarette into an ashtray. "It's not easy stirring up the masses every week."

"I think there's a problem with Emma," Becky said. She pushed a thick lock of hair off her face.

Ellen looked with alarm from Becky to Lulu, who shrugged.

"Emma? I thought she was the leader," Ellen said.

"She's gone soft," Becky said in a low voice, leaning toward her. Her wide eyes roved over the room as if to make sure no one was listening. "She's against any sort of violent action. But I'm telling you that the bullet and the bomb are the only weapons we've got."

"Emma believes in the power of the word, as do I," Lulu said.

"The word is not enough and you know it," Becky said, leaning back in her chair as if she'd made an irrefutable point.

"The problem with violence," Ellen said, carefully, "is that you alienate those who might help you in your cause."

"Are you referring to your lady friend?" Lulu asked. She blew a plume of smoke in Ellen's direction and aimed a steady gaze at her. At first Ellen thought with a sense of panic that she meant Louisa, but then remembered that Lulu had seen her with Hester at the tea house. Ellen felt the magnet pull of Lulu's dark eyes. She wondered if Becky noticed it, but Becky was looking down at her own ankles, admiring her signature red stockings.

"Some of them are reformers," Ellen said.

Lulu stubbed out her cigarette and said, "Who is she?"

"Her name is Hester, and she's a suffragist," Ellen said. "Surely, you're not against suffrage for women?"

Becky shrugged. "The rich women will vote like the rich men. What good will it do?"

Ellen had no answer. She'd assumed any woman would want the right to vote. The suffragists in England were willing to die for it.

Becky straightened up and stretched.

"I'm off, girls. Ellen, will you be joining me and Frank when we march on the churches?" she asked. "Or are you too religious?"

"Religious?" Ellen asked.

"You are Irish, ain't you?" Becky asked.

Ellen glanced at Lulu and said, "What I worship isn't in a church." She immediately wished she could reel the words back in. She had openly flirted with Lulu and Lulu knew it, a grin spreading across her thin face. Ellen turned back to Becky, "Sure. I'll march on the churches. Those priests sit on their piles of gold like the hypocrites they are. Just let me know where and when."

"I will," Becky said and rose to leave.

***

Ellen and Lulu walked through the Village. The aroma of baking bread filled the air, and dirty snow lay on the ground in clumps. They sat on a bench near the great marble arch, pigeons circling their feet. A couple of squirrels played a game of chase up a tree, and bird song heralded springtime. Sunlight cut through the chill air.

"What about Hester?" Lulu asked. "Why aren't you with her today?"

Ellen shrugged. She didn't feel guilty. Something about being with Lulu made guilt seem like a waste of time – until a newsie on the corner began hawking copies of *The Tribune.*

"Mother Mary," Ellen said sharply. "I forgot all about Mrs. Del...the old woman and her newspaper." She had almost blurted out Louisa's last name which might have been a fatal mistake. Fatal for her mission at any rate. If Lulu knew she was working for the enemy, that would end their budding friendship. Then she thought of Louisa, who had trusted her to take care of her mother. She must have lost her mind to come here.

"Who?" Lulu asked.

"I got a side job, taking care of an old woman in Harlem. I only left to go get a paper," Ellen said, standing and searching for the newsie.

"You're a million miles from Harlem," Lulu said with a laugh.

Ellen saw the kid waving the paper and headed toward him.

"Gem theft foiled! Two arrested!" he yelled out.

"Why don't you read *Mother Earth* to her?" Lulu said, pulling a copy out of her bag.

Ellen shook her head, gave the boy a nickel and took a copy of *The Tribune*.

"She's not the type," she said. "I better go."

"You're not really taking care of some old woman," Lulu said. "You're going to see your lady love, aren't you?"

"Maybe," Ellen teased. "What of it?"

"Nothing. I hope the two of you have a delicious afternoon," Lulu said with a lascivious look.

Ellen stopped and looked Lulu in the eyes.

"I'm not going to her," Ellen said. She knew even as she said the words she was committing some kind of betrayal and it felt terrible, but she couldn't help herself.

Lulu suppressed a smile.

"Then I'll see you around? We have a meeting Wednesday night. Karl and some others are planning something big. You might want to be in on it."

"Big?"

"Explosive," Lulu said. Then she turned and walked quickly away, disappearing into the crowd.

On her way back to Harlem, Ellen found herself so engrossed in the front-page story of a gem theft she almost missed her stop. Old Anna Delafield would be fit to be tied by now.

Ellen hurried up the steps of Louisa's brownstone and entered the foyer. She heard voices coming from the parlor as she hung her coat on the coat rack. She recognized Mrs. Delafield's voice and then realized the other voice belonged to...

"Hester?" she said as she stood in the doorway to the parlor.

Hester looked up from a book and said, "Hello, Ellen. I was just reading to Mrs. Delafield."

"Call me Anna," Louisa's mother insisted.

"Of course, Anna," Hester said in her soft lilting voice. Guilt rampaged through every blood vessel in Ellen's body. How could she have implied to Lulu that Hester meant nothing to her? She felt a wave of disgust with herself.

"I brought you the paper," Ellen said.

"It only took you three hours," Mrs. Delafield grumbled and took the paper from her. "I can read it myself, by the way."

"I should be going," Hester said. "I'm taking a cart of milk to the tenements this afternoon. The hunger in those poor children's eyes is truly heart breaking."

"It's a mark of true class to help the unfortunate," Mrs. Delafield said. "Here, take this old blanket with you. Someone can probably use it. We have so many."

"How gracious of you, Anna," Hester said.

Ellen wanted to roll her eyes but kept them still. Rich people thought these pittances made a difference. Not that Hester's milk contributions wouldn't help some poor kids, but it was like using a tea spoon to bail out a leaky boat.

Ellen walked Hester to the door while Mrs. Delafield perused the paper.

"Thank you for coming by, Hester," Ellen said. She hoped she sounded sincere enough. Something was happening inside her. She wanted to be with Lulu, but she didn't want to lose Hester either. A battle raged inside her ribcage like two boxers in a ring.

Hester put on her tailored coat and kid gloves so different from the shabby black coat and woolen gloves Lulu wore.

"Where were you last night? Anna said you were gone until quite late," Hester said. "And then again today...."

"She was sleeping when I left last night," Ellen said.

Hester looked at her. The tips of her eyebrows squinted together, forming a set of wrinkles between them.

"That doesn't answer my question," Hester said.

"I was with L. Byron and some of the anarchists, trying to learn what I can about them — not just about the shooting, but other things I can tell Paddy to help with his investigations," Ellen said. "Why did you come over?"

"I thought you might enjoy the company," Hester said. "It's a good thing I did come. Anna shouldn't be left alone for so long."

Ellen caught the disapproval in Hester's voice.

"I didn't intend to be gone so long," Ellen said.

"Ellen..." Hester hesitated and then asked, "is there something you aren't telling me?"

Ellen thought of Lulu and felt sick to her stomach.

"No," Ellen said. "Why?"

"I worry that you find their ideology too appealing," Hester said.

"What if I do think it makes some sense?" Ellen said, suddenly defensive and even irritated. Perhaps her flirtations with Lulu were indefensible, but her beliefs were another matter altogether.

"Their way is unlawful and dangerous," Hester said.

"And yet when a wealthy man allows dozens of miners to be shot like mad dogs, that is perfectly legal," Ellen said, her jaw suddenly gone tight. "Can't you see how hypocritical it is?"

"I do. But your anarchist friends are just as hypocritical," Hester said. "Killing people isn't the answer. Their 'deeds of propaganda' are not noble. They're barbaric."

With that, she turned and walked out of the house. Ellen watched her. She didn't know whether she wanted to turn away and never speak to Hester again or run out into the street after her, begging for forgiveness. She shut the door.

That night after she put Anna to bed, she went to sleep in Louisa's room and remembered she had promised Frank she would visit the Municipal Lodging House with him. She'd need to ask the hired girl to stay and look after Louisa's mother. She wondered if Becky would be there with Frank.

When she closed her eyes, she had a vision of a veiled woman in a black dress and red stockings raising a gun and pulling the trigger.

Chapter 13

Louisa

After Louisa unpacked and refreshed herself, she went downstairs to the parlor where Lady Rutherford and several other ladies were playing cards. She knew she could get the lowdown on the St. Augustine social scene and any important gossip from Lady Rutherford, but first she had to pay the piper.

"Louisa, dear, how are you? I read about your kerfuffle with the anarchists," Lady Rutherford said after dealing a hand to Louisa. "How dreadful."

"It was, and it is," Louisa said, fanning out her cards and searching for high hearts. Apparently she'd have to learn to play Rook on another day.

"They should take them all to the gallows," the older woman continued and laid down a two of hearts to flush out the high cards. "Murderers. Poor Dottie Parsons. Was she a friend of yours?"

"We worked at rival papers, but Dottie didn't have a competitive bone in her body. She was always happy to share news. And she was enamored with society, but she also loved to laugh at their foibles," she said. There was a catch in her voice, which Lady Rutherford did not miss.

"I am so sorry, dear. We will speak no more of it."

Louisa laid down a five of hearts, hanging onto her king until the ace made its appearance, but the queen of hearts took the round. Lady Rutherford had laid a trap for her.

"Tell me about the Griffins," Louisa said. "I haven't met them yet."

"First, I must say, I have no quarrel with new money as some of you New Yorkers do," Lady Rutherford said, dropping the ace on the table and grinning when Louisa lost her king. "In fact, new money shows initiative. To get to the point, Randall Griffin is a hard-working, hard-driving industrialist, and if he wants to purchase a French baron for his daughter, then why shouldn't he?"

"Do they still have barons in France?" Louisa asked. "I thought they lopped off all their heads in the Revolution."

"That was then," Lady Rutherford said. "Nowadays, if you can prove you are descended from nobility, you can apply to the Department of Justice in France to regain your family's title." She made a rubbing motion with her fingers to indicate a payoff.

"French nobility is so confusing," one of the other ladies said. "However, I'd bet my last dollar that man comes from the aristocracy. Look at his bearing." She nodded toward the windows.

Louisa looked through the large parlor windows and saw the profile of Simon Bassett and immediately understood what she meant. He stood in the courtyard *contrapposta* as if posing for an Italian sculptor, while talking to a tall, blond woman with a narrow face and one of those long noses suited to haughty women. She wore a black dress with yellow panels, and an elegant yellow hat in an asymmetrical style that Louisa had never seen before.

"I've met him. That is Monsieur Simon Bassett, brother to the groom," Louisa said, "But who is the elegant woman?"

"Madame Veronique Ribault," Lady Rutherford said, peering at the window. "She's the wedding dress designer. From Paris. A bit *avante garde* for my tastes. Your readers would love to read an interview with her, I'm quite certain. It would confirm all their prejudices about the French."

"Which are?" Louisa asked.

"That they are vain, self-important, and somewhat ridiculous."

Louisa thought the aforementioned prejudices were most likely Lady Rutherford's and not necessarily those of the average American. She watched the exchange between Simon Bassett and the woman with curiosity. It was a bit like watching a movie but without organ music to provide the emotional context. Monsieur Bassett had his hands behind his back, leaning forward, and Madame Ribault seemed almost purposefully nonchalant, as she brought a cigarette in a silver holder to her lips, inhaled, and then blew smoke toward the sky.

The game was interrupted when a bellman brought her a note — a summons to meet with Randall Griffin, the father of the bride, in the courtyard of the Ponce near the fountain the following morning.

She scribbled an affirmative reply. When she looked up, Simon Bassett and Madame Ribault were gone.

***

The next morning the concierge informed her it was a short walk to the Ponce, and the weather was delightful. So with directions in hand, she ventured out onto the brick streets of the oldest city in the country. She'd never been to Spain, but she imagined some of its old cities looked similar to this one. A large cathedral stood opposite the hotel on Treasury Street. She turned right, and in a few minutes saw Flagler's extravagant beacon to wealth, the Ponce de Leon Hotel.

The Ponce was a massive gray building with red tile roofs, balconies, turrets, and outdoor corridors with brick arches that made her think of a Moorish castle. A bellman took her along a path lined with palm trees to the courtyard where Randall Griffin waited on a stone bench by a pond. He was a stout figure with pale, watery blue eyes in a rumpled-looking face. She wondered why he wanted to meet with her, and why his wife wasn't with him. Certainly, it was the mother of the bride who cared about publicity for her daughter's wedding.

Mr. Griffin stood, took her hand and said earnestly, "My dear Miss Delafield, thank you for coming to St. Augustine before the wedding. My good friend Mr. Calloway sings your praises."

Louisa lowered herself onto the bench and he sat beside her. Women with parasols strolled past, and children scooped water out of a fountain to fling at each other.

"My readers will be delighted to read about your daughter's wedding," Louisa said. "Florida weddings are all the rage now."

"There's another reason I've asked you here," Mr. Griffin said.

"What is that?"

He cleared his throat and said, "Forrest mentioned you also do investigative work."

Louisa drew a quick breath but said nothing.

"You see," he explained, "I'm not sure my daughter's fiancé, Henri Bassett, is entirely on the up and up. I'm worried that he may be some sort of...." He searched for the right word and finally came up with, "scoundrel."

He looked despondent.

"Mr. Griffin, what makes you think Henri Bassett is not a good match for your daughter? Do you know anything about his family?" she asked.

"All I know is that he was orphaned when he was twelve, and he has one older brother, Simon. After their parents' death, they went to live with an uncle in Burgundy. His grandfather was some sort of aristocrat who lost his head in the Revolution — a baron. Both he and his brother have the supercilious attitude of aristocrats. He acts as if he's doing my daughter a favor by marrying her. Apparently, he needs money to claim his title."

"Wouldn't his older brother be the one entitled?" she asked.

"I don't believe Simon cares about such things."

She thought of Simon Bassett. No, he didn't seem to be the type to care about something as superficial as a title, which only made him more intriguing.

"Well, Mr. Griffin, being a poor snob does not necessarily make Henri a scoundrel," she said.

"Perhaps not. But I don't understand why this wedding had to happen in such a hurry. They only got engaged at Christmas."

"That does sound sudden," Louisa said. She hoped that Mr. Griffin's daughter wasn't compromised.

"It was the brother who insisted upon it. He says Europe will be in a war soon, and I suppose he wanted Henri out of harm's way. He may be right, for all I know," he said. "I've hired a Pinkerton detective in France to find out more about both of them. They work in the uncle's wine business. It's not a particularly lucrative business and their uncle apparently does not like them much. That doesn't stop them from living a lavish lifestyle. Henri gave Daphne an absurdly expensive diamond pendant. How did he afford that?"

"He may have borrowed money and be in some debt," Louisa said.

"Or maybe he's a thief! I've heard unsavory rumors about his brother," he said, wringing his hands.

"One can never trust rumors," Louisa said.

"That's why I'm hoping you'll help me. Come to dinner tonight. We'll seat you next to the groom. Calloway said people trust you. They tell you things. Maybe this blasted interloper will let something slip. My daughter means everything to me, and I couldn't bear it if she made a mistake in marriage."

Louisa looked at Mr. Griffin. Her father would be about his age if he'd lived. And he would have been just as protective. She patted the older man's hand.

"I'll do my best," she said. "It will help if I can see the report from the Pinkertons when you get it."

"Of course. Please, keep this a secret. My wife and my daughter would have me hanged if they thought I was doing anything that would interfere with the wedding."

What a spot he's in, Louisa thought. As a good father he would want to make his daughter happy, but he would also want to prevent her from making a ruinous mistake. She hoped she could find out something to reassure him.

***

After lunch at the hotel, Louisa spent the rest of the afternoon with Suzie, exploring the historic city, winding their way along a narrow thoroughfare shaded by overhanging balconies, passing by gift store windows displaying stuffed alligators, boxes of citrus, and feathered fans. Tourists strolled along the street, stopping at vendors' stalls to buy fruit or flowers. Occasionally men wearing fancy silver spurs rode by on elegant horses.

"What a gay tableau," Louisa said as they crossed a plaza filled with tall palm trees, carefree tourists, and even nuns in black-and-white garb. They walked down a narrow lane to the bay, which lay flat and blue as a baby blanket. An octagonal building advertising hot baths jutted over the water. White sails glided by, and gulls whirled above the water. The great bell of the old cathedral struck 5:00.

"Let's go look at that castle," Suzie said and pointed to a huge gray fortress on the bank of the river.

"That's the Castillo de San Marcos. I read that it's made out of something called coquina," Louisa said.

"It's magnificent," Suzie said.

Louisa agreed. She could imagine Spanish soldiers standing in the turrets, ready to defend their city from invaders.

They headed toward the fortress, which was surrounded by an expanse of grass. Near the water a crowd had gathered. Curious, Louisa and Suzie wandered over to see what they were watching. When they came to the edge of the circle, they saw two men wearing white jackets and helmets, brandishing long thin swords.

"It's a fencing contest," Louisa whispered to Suzie.

"Fencing?"

"Like sword fighting, but a sport. They call the swords 'foils' or '*epees*'," Louisa explained. Suzie snorted, but crossed her arms to watch.

The man on the right crooked his arm, his foil pointed to sky, and yelled, "*En garde*!" and then immediately they engaged in a fierce dual, first one advancing and jabbing and then the other. After several parries, they retreated and stood, their foils pointing up, as they caught their breaths. Then the battle resumed. It was quite exciting with the crowd gasping and giggling when one or the other of the opponents had the advantage. The two men seemed evenly matched to Louisa, until all of a sudden the man on the left attacked his opponent with a fierce burst of energy. His foil sliced through the air with a swooshing sound. He had clearly overpowered the other man, and they froze with the stronger man's foil touching the other's breast bone. The vanquished man lowered his foil in surrender. The small crowd burst into applause.

The two men removed their helmets. Both of their faces were drenched in sweat. She recognized the winner immediately as Simon Bassett. The other man had thick golden hair and a face of exquisite perfection.

"That must be the groom, Henri Bassett," Louisa said to Suzie.

She studied the fleeting expressions on the faces of the two men. Simon had the look of a warrior intent on victory and Henri's slight pout was the look of a resentful younger brother. Then the older brother smiled and wrapped an arm around Henri's neck. Henri also smiled. He may not have liked being beaten by his brother, but he seemed to understand the way his world worked. She supposed he could put up with being beaten because he would be the one to marry a millionaire's daughter and buy his family title back.

The crowd parted as the two men strode off the field of battle, their helmets tucked under their arms, foils clasped loosely in their hands. Simon's gaze swept over Louisa, and he stopped. He came to her immediately, took her hand and kissed it, saying "*Bon jour*, Mademoiselle Delafield." Then to everyone's surprise, he took up Suzie's hand and kissed it as well. Then he turned and followed his brother to a waiting motorcar. Louisa felt momentarily giddy, but pulled herself together, and taking Suzie's arm in hers walked toward the fort.

They explored the ramparts of the fort with its thick walls and turrets. A guide pointed out the places where cannon balls had bounced off the soft coquina rock, made from millions of crushed shells. They went downstairs to look at the storerooms and peer into the dungeons. Louisa gazed up at the tiny window in the damp room where a sign said Chief Osceola had been held after being captured ignominiously by a general who tricked him with the white flag of surrender. Day after day, week after week, the great Seminole chief and his warriors lived in this dank room.

"Starved himself so he could crawl out that window," a guide noted, pointing to a narrow, impossibly high window.

Louisa thought this might be a bit of hyperbole.

"Was he successful?" she asked.

"Nope. About twenty of his warriors scaled the walls and escaped, but Osceola was too weak by then. They transferred him to Fort Moultrie where he died."

For a moment, Louisa imagined the great warrior, wasting away in this horrid little place.

"Dreadful," she said.

"There's no bringing him back from the dead," Suzie said sympathetically, and Louisa knew she wasn't only talking about Osceola.

After they left the fort, they walked through the city gates and then along St. George Street heading back to the hotel. They passed a newspaper stand where newspapers from all over the country were sold so the tourists could keep up with the happenings in their hometowns.

She purchased a copy of *The Ledger* from a wizened old man who was missing most of his bottom teeth. She always liked to check her column and make sure there'd been no mistakes in the printing. One time the typesetter had managed to leave off the entire last paragraph.

"Yer the second person to buy this paper today," he said, pocketing her coin.

Louisa looked at Suzie.

"Plenty of New Yorkers here," Suzie said.

"I suppose," Louisa said. "Let's get back to the hotel. I need a nap before dinner with the Griffins tonight. And tomorrow we need to set about finding out if your family is here."

"That we do," Suzie said. "I'm a little bit nervous."

Back at the hotel, Louisa saw that her column on the Yorkville Benefit looked fine, but it reminded her of the strange encounter with Julia Markham, and she wondered again what Mrs. Markham had meant in her cryptic letter.

***

A few friends and family members of the Griffins were seated around a large round table in the middle of the elegant dining room of the Ponce. The arched ceiling loomed overhead with painted winged seraphs looking down upon the diners. Palm trees decorated the corners, and the upper windows were made of stained glass.

Louisa had been seated, as promised, next to Henri Bassett. His bride sat on the other side of him. A Lord Wickham sat to Louisa's right and next to him was Madame Ribault, Daphne's wedding dress designer. Across the table sat the groom's brother, Simon, Mr. and Mrs. Griffin, and an old woman dripping in diamonds who must have been the grandmother.

The dinner was a sumptuous feast with *consommé tapioca, caviar à la Russe*, boiled snapper, stuffed capon, and mountain oysters *sautés aux champignon*. Louisa declined the last item, knowing exactly what they were in spite of the fancy French appellation — bull testicles.

Henri Bassett was devastatingly handsome with blue eyes peering out from a forest of lashes, full lips in a clean-shaven face, and golden-brown hair. Louisa felt a bit unnerved by his beauty, as if she'd suddenly been seated next to Adonis. His future wife, Daphne Griffin, sat on the other side of him. Unlike her fiancé, she was no beauty. She had a pixie face with a snub nose and an insignificant chin. A large, gleaming diamond pendant dangled from a gold chain around her neck.

Henri passed Louisa a plate of rolls and said, "Tell me all about New York society, Miss Delafield. Do you know the Rockefellers, the Vanderbilts, the...uh," he snapped his fingers and turned to Daphne, "Who else is in New York, *chérie*?"

"Oh, who cares about New York society?" she said and waved a hand. "They all think New York is the center of the universe, but it's nothing compared to Paris, *chéri*." She leaned over and pecked him on the cheek. Highly inappropriate, Louisa thought. Mr. Griffin turned a bright shade of red. Mrs. Griffin, a tiny wren-like woman, studiously examined the food on her plate while a teenage girl, presumably Daphne's sister, sat on the other side of her mother and glanced surreptitiously at her future brother-in-law.

"What a lovely idea to have a wedding in Florida, Miss Griffin," Louisa said. "How did you choose St. Augustine?"

"We vacation here regularly," Daphne said and looked pointedly at Louisa. "At least with our wedding so far from New York, no one will try to shoot you."

"You were shot?" Henri asked, and covered his mouth with his long elegant fingers, but his azure eyes twinkled in amusement.

"I was not shot," Louisa said. "Unfortunately, someone else was."

"But they were aiming for you, were they not?" Daphne asked, leaning across Henri with a curious expression. "You said so yourself in your column."

As she looked at Louisa, she twirled the chain holding her diamond pendant. Louisa felt a seedling of dislike for Daphne sprout in her heart.

"It may have been an anarchist," Louisa said. "They're all a bit deranged from what I can tell. You might want to watch out for them if you come to New York. They hate the wealthy even more than they hate society writers."

Louisa didn't care for the bride or the groom, and she wasn't above imagining just how condescending she might be when describing this impertinent young woman. Then she looked over at Daphne's adoring father and knew she couldn't write anything that would hurt him. She thought of his concerns about the groom. Henri did come across as arrogant. She doubted she could get any information from him at all. Then she caught Simon Bassett looking at her. If there were anything to learn about Henri, perhaps she might learn it from his intriguing brother. She wouldn't mind having a reason to spend some time with him. She should have been ashamed to harbor such thoughts, but she wasn't. Anything was a welcome distraction from worrying about anarchists and the weight of guilt every time she thought of Dottie Parsons.

She turned to discuss the weather with Lord Wickham. He looked to be in his mid-thirties. His nails were manicured, and his outfit fashionable. There was something impish and pleasant about him. He agreed with her that the temperature in St. Augustine was splendid.

"Daphne doesn't know what she's talking about when she describes Paris as incomparable. It's bloody dreary this time of year," he said, casting his eyes upward. He seemed to share Louisa's dislike of the wealthy young woman.

"And are you related to the bride or the groom?" she asked him.

"I'm not related to either," he said. "I'm a friend of Henri and Simon. In fact, I introduced Henri to Daphne at a party." He lowered his voice and added, "They say she was planning to marry some Wall Street financier, but Henri swept her off her feet. He's quite handsome, wouldn't you agree? I helped him find that diamond for her."

Louisa glanced at Daphne's pear-shaped diamond pendant as it caught the light from the chandelier. She remembered Mr. Griffin mentioning an expensive diamond.

"It's beautiful. It must have cost a fortune," she said. "How many carats is it?"

"Nine and a half," Lord Wickham said with a flash of his eyebrows. "But it's not just the weight that makes it so valuable, it's the brilliance. Look at how it sparkles. The clarity and the cut are exquisite."

"Forgive me," Louisa said, "but I was under the impression that Monsieur Bassett was not particularly well off."

"He's not, but we promised the seller there would be many more purchases in the future and so he sold it for a song," Wickham said, spearing a piece of fish with his fork.

Louisa looked at the white flesh dangling from the tines of his fork and thought this story about the diamond was also fishy. Perhaps, Mr. Griffin was onto something with his suspicions.

"You must know a lot about precious gems," she said.

"I'm an archaeologist," he said. "I have a nose for treasure."

"Tell me all about it," Louisa said, instantly intrigued. "This city seems quite ancient to me, but we're such a young country. To you St. Augustine must seem like modern history. You've seen actual pyramids, haven't you?"

For the rest of the meal, they talked at great length about his finds in Egypt. Every once in a while, Louisa glanced across the table at Simon, who had been seated next to Daphne's grandmother. When he flashed his smile, Louisa's heart skipped a beat. He was not as handsome as his younger brother, but he had something that Henri did not. He exuded an aura of mystery and adventure.

A plethora of desserts arrived including something absolutely delicious called sago pudding with fruit sauce. When the dinner was over, she hoped she might have a conversation with Simon or that he might walk back to the hotel with her, but he was nowhere to be found, so she walked back with Lord Wickham, who entertained her with his droll descriptions of British aristocracy.

"Old Lady Rutherford once had a party for everyone to meet a certain Russian prince. Once the guests arrived, they found she'd dressed up a monkey as a prince! It was the talk of London for weeks," he said.

"She is quite the character," Louisa said. Then she leaned in close to him. "Tell me, Lord Wickham, is our groom terribly in debt?"

"No more so than any young rake," Lord Wickham said with a jolly laugh.

He wasn't being particularly helpful, she thought. Being in debt proved nothing. Impoverished European nobility had been marrying wealthy American women for decades now. Even the Vanderbilts had foisted their daughter onto a duke.

They reached the hotel and were waiting for the elevator when Simon Bassett appeared in his dark suit and top hat.

"*Bonsoir*, Monsieur Bassett," Louisa said.

"*Bonsoir*, Mademoiselle Delafield," Monsieur Bassett said. He turned to Lord Wickham. "Hello, Percival."

"Hello, old chap," Lord Wickham said. "You disappeared after dinner."

"Henri needed some brotherly advice."

"He is fortunate to have you then, isn't he?" Lord Wickham said. Louisa sensed some tension between the two men and wondered what was being unsaid.

The elevator door opened, and they entered.

"Three, please," Louisa told the elevator operator.

"Four," Monsieur Bassett and Lord Wickham said in unison.

"I thought your room was on the third floor," Louisa said to M. Bassett and then blushed. She didn't want him to think she had remembered that detail.

"It is," Monsieur Bassett said.

"I am on the fourth floor," Lord Wickham said. "My room is next to Madame Ribault's atelier. Convenient in case I need a fitting. Thank you for calling out the floor for me, Simon."

Interesting, she thought, wondering why Lord Wickham mentioned Madame Ribault.

Steam hissed as the elevator ascended past the second floor. The operator opened the doors on the third floor. Louisa stepped out, and Simon Bassett followed her. The doors closed again.

"I hope my brother did not bore you at dinner," Monsieur Bassett said.

"Not at all," she answered. "I must confess, however, I was more interested in Lord Wickham's stories about Egypt."

A curious look crossed his face and he stroked his chin.

"Lord Wickham has many stories," he said. "Some are even true."

Louisa laughed. Then an awkward silence ensued. She looked at his inscrutable face. What was it that made him so intriguing?

"I bought a copy of *The Ledger* today and read your column," he said.

Louisa was stunned. Men didn't read the society page.

"You did?"

"*Oui.* I wanted to learn what interests you," he said.

"It was merely a recap of the Yorkville Benefit," she said. "Not interesting at all."

"I disagree. Your words are so descriptive. You made me feel I was there, observing the dancing and purchasing hats. I wish I had been there to buy a hat. *Une petit cloche, peut-être*?" He pretended to put a hat on his head in a ladylike manner.

"Perhaps," she said and giggled, imagining him with a bell-shaped hat on his head.

His eyes twinkled as he took her other hand, kissed the backs of her fingers, and said, "*Bonne nuit*, Mademoiselle Delafield."

"*Bonne nuit*," she said. They turned and walked down their respective hallways. When she reached her room, she sighed in relief that Suzie was not waiting up for her. Then she fell on her bed and covered her face with her hands. He had read her article. The column that day was nothing special, but she couldn't help it. She was flattered. *Stop,* she told herself. She shouldn't be mooning over some man she didn't even know. What about Forrest? Forrest made her feel secure, but he had never made her feel giddy like this. He had been her rescuer, she realized, more of a father figure who had become her lover.

Sleep did not come quickly, and when it did, she dreamt of neither Simon Bassett nor Forrest Calloway. She dreamt of Dottie Parsons, falling down an endless well into the dark, and woke up sobbing. It was hours before she could fall asleep again.

Chapter 14
Ellen

Frank met Ellen at Union Square. It was late March, and winter hadn't loosened its grip around the throat of the city. She had on several layers of clothing under her wool coat but the cold managed to burrow its way next to her skin. Frank had advised her not to look too comfortable.

"These people have so little," he said. "Best not to stir up resentment."

Ellen marveled at the idea that she, of all people, might stir up resentment.

"Is Becky joining us?" she asked as they walked through the square.

"Nope. She's busy helping Berkman write pamphlets," he said. "Besides, she's seen her share of the city's misery. Do you think you could get an article in that paper of yours?"

"I'm not a reporter," she explained. "I answer the phone, take notes from the reporters, file their stories and that sort of thing. Besides, isn't this what *Mother Earth* does?"

"Sure, but the readers of *Mother Earth* are already on our side. We need to convince other readers."

"Frank, if you can prove that poverty in America is somehow the fault of the British, *The Gaelic American* would take up this story and wave it like a flag," she said, ruefully. "Otherwise, I'm not sure they'd care. I do know a woman writer, though, who sometimes does features."

Most of the city newspapers were not sympathetic to the unemployed. One had recently featured a cartoon showing Frank and the higher-ups in the I.W.W. drinking Champagne and gleefully laughing above a caption that said, "The worst is yet to come!"

"I'm thinking you might want to write it yourself," he said.

"I'm not a writer," she said.

"Well, then talk to that woman writer, won't ya?"

"I will," she said. She thought of Louisa's muckraking alter-ego. Beatrice Milton was one of the few voices that actually spoke truth to the powerful. Sometimes she worried, though, that Louisa was no longer interested in Beatrice Milton. She was so busy with her syndicated column, doling out advice to women in the Midwest who wanted to live like the hoity-toity Manhattanites.

It was a fairly short walk from Union Square to the Municipal Lodging House on East 25th Street. When they got within sight of the building, Ellen was impressed. It looked like a public school. It was five storeys, built of brick and stone with decorative brick work on the top floor. Hester or Louisa would know the architectural style, but all she knew was that it had an attractive look.

"They opened this place up five years ago," Frank said. "At first, just a few hundred people used it. But lookee now."

She had been staring at the top of the building but now lowered her gaze to the street.

"Holy Mother of God."

Clogging the sidewalk were hundreds of men, fists jammed into their pockets, quietly stirring around to keep warm.

"In a few more hours, there'll be a couple thousand of them. Hungry and cold with nowhere to sleep."

"Aren't there flophouses where they can get a bed?" she asked.

"If you got a dime, you can get a room in one of the cheap flops in the Bowery," he said. "But most of them don't have a dime. For a penny, you can sleep in a back room of a saloon. That is if there's any space. Usually there ain't none."

Ellen scanned the crowd of men. She'd read newspaper reports about them: "derelicts," "flotsam and jetsam," "rounders," or "drunks." They portrayed them as lazy, unwilling to work. A local minister had been quoted as saying, "It is a piece of impertinence for a hungry man to dictate the terms and demand union wages and union hours." As if they should settle for whatever crumbs might fall to them.

The majority of these men did not look like drunks. They wore shabby suits, but they were not dirty. With her practiced eye, she saw that many of their suits had been mended here and there. They'd been presentable at one point in their lives.

Pure laziness couldn't account for this.

"Why are they here, Frank?" she asked.

"Why don't you ask them?"

She screwed up the courage to tap one of the men on his shoulder. He turned to face her. He had a wide, honest face.

"Evening, Miss," he said. He tipped his hat.

"Evening, Sir," Ellen said. "I hope I'm not intruding...."

"No intrusion at all," he said.

"Might I ask what it is you do — or did — for a living?" she said.

"I built the Woolworth Building," he said with evident pride.

"And why are you not working now, then?" she asked.

"Construction has dried up. There's a recession on, you know," he said.

"I was a baker," the man behind him piped up. "Lost m' job last November. Can't find anything. Not even street sweeping. My wife left. Went back home to her folks in Ohio with the kids. Can't blame her."

Another man said, "I was a barber. Had to sell all my gear just for food. Sold my coat, and now I'll freeze to death if I can't get a bed tonight."

"They only got 800 beds for the men," one of the men said.

"They reserve the top floor for the women and their tykes. Don't worry. You'll get one," the first man reassured her.

"Oh, I'm not...." Ellen said and then stopped talking. She didn't see how she could go back to Louisa's comfortable bed tonight, not after looking into the eyes of these men, and she had an urgent desire to share their experience. She saw a few women keeping to themselves.

She turned to Frank. "I'm going to stay here tonight."

"It's not fit for a dog, you know."

She nodded and realized this had been his plan all along. Fortunately, she'd asked the hired girl to stay and look after Anna until she got back. The girl would be happy for the extra money for staying the night though Anna was sure to complain to Louisa when she returned.

Frank continued, "They wake you up at four in the morning and make you work in the stoneyard. At least that's what they do to the men. You might have it easier on the women's floor."

"But, Frank, will I be taking a bed needed by one of these women?" she asked.

"They've enough beds to spare on the women's floor. It's the men who have the worst of it," he said. "There's just too many of 'em."

After another hour, the doors opened. It was 6:00 p.m. By that time, just as Frank had predicted, the crowd had swelled to more than a thousand desperate people. The crowd surged forward, but a giant of a policeman in his big warm coat ordered them in line. Once inside, the queue narrowed to a single line between a brick wall and a white railing. One by one, they walked up to a window and signed in.

After she'd signed in, Ellen was hustled off to a side room with several other women. They were taken to a large tiled room and told to strip so the matrons could look over their bodies and through their clothes for lice. The women didn't complain. They were used to having no control over their lives, she supposed. Wearily, silently, they took off their clothes. Ellen did the same. The older women's skin looked like parchment. They were bony and their hands trembled with fatigue. She was on the thin side herself but next to these women she looked positively plump. At least the room was warm.

While two attendants checked their hair, their underarms, and along their necks and backs, two others went through the clothing. Ellen saw one of them pocket the nickel she'd brought for the train home.

"Hey," Ellen shouted. "Give that back!"

"Findings is keepings," the attendant said with a smirk.

Ah, Christ, she thought. This meant she'd be walking a hundred blocks to get back to Louisa's house in the morning. Maybe Frank could spare her a nickel.

Dinner in the small dining room for women and children was watery soup and a piece of bread. She took a few bites, but couldn't muster up the appetite for it. There was a moldy smell about the place.

"Can I have it?" asked a little girl with a face as thin as a ruler. She had scraped her own bowl clean.

Ellen pushed the bowl over to the child and handed over the piece of bread. She'd never felt like one of the privileged before. And yet she was, wasn't she?

She followed the other women to a large dormitory, filled with iron bunk beds. It was clean enough, Ellen thought. She saw no roaches nor any rat droppings. A couple of bruised women argued over who got the corner bunk, and a gray-haired old crone huddled under a wool blanket, scratching her scalp and moaning. A girl who looked barely fifteen nursed a baby with a blank expression on her sallow face.

A child whimpered somewhere in the room, its ma shushing it. For a brief moment she thought about Hester, sleeping in her grand bed in her room overlooking Central Park. What would Hester think of this escapade? Hester cared deeply for the poor but she would never know what it felt like to be one of them. Finally, late into the night the women were settled and sleeping. At least they were warm for a few hours, Ellen thought, but what about all those men who had been turned away. Where had they slept?

Ellen realized she'd forgotten all about her mission to identify Louisa's would-be shooter. Her heart was with the International Workers of the World and the anarchists at *Mother Earth*.

Chapter 15

Louisa

Louisa rose groggily from her bed. She had tossed and turned all night. She wondered if the guilt and grief might cause her to have a breakdown.

After she washed her face, she stared at herself in the mirror. She had dark rings under her eyes, and the blush of youth had fled her cheeks. She would have to come to terms with what had happened to Dottie, she decided. Suzie was right. She couldn't bring anyone back from the dead. Not Dottie. Not her father. She must focus on her work and on Mr. Griffin's request. She might not like Daphne much, but no woman should be married to a man who didn't love her, a man who might even be a criminal. Of course, if Henri was some sort of criminal — how did he get the money for that diamond? — was his brother involved? That would be unfortunate, but perhaps her job was not to prove that Henri was up to no good, but to exonerate him.

She went back into the room and found Suzie already dressed for the day.

"I called downstairs for coffee and toast," Suzie said.

"Perfect," Louisa said. "We have a busy day, don't we?"

Suzie nodded as she cleared off the table for their breakfast. Louisa could tell she was excited and nervous about looking for her family.

Louisa put on her gray daydress. She hadn't realized how warm it would be in Florida and didn't have enough suitable clothes.

"I need to buy a few light-weight dresses while I'm here," Louisa said.

"Can you afford it?" Suzie asked.

"I won't be extravagant," Louisa said.

The coffee and toast arrived. They would not have been able to breakfast together in the dining room of the Florida House, but they sat at the table in Louisa's room just as if they were in the kitchen back home in Harlem.

"Have you any idea where to look for your family?" Louisa asked.

"No," Suzie said. "I'm not even sure they're in St. Augustine. I heard of a place called Lincolnville?"

"Let's go to the library and look in the city directory. Is their last name Blake, too?"

"Maybe. That was the master's name at the plantation. We didn't get our own last names," Suzie said.

"Well, let's see what we can learn," Louisa said.

It was another bright and balmy day. They walked down narrow streets past gift shops among meandering tourists and found the library on Charlotte Street in between two coquina houses. They opened the large wooden door and entered a courtyard. Louisa opened another door and poked her head inside.

"Is this the library?" she asked a bespectacled man in his thirties.

"It is," he said. "Come in."

Louisa stepped inside with Suzie behind her.

"Oh, I'm sorry," he said, looking at Suzie. "Colored people aren't permitted in the library."

"Excuse me?" Louisa said.

"It's the law," he said with a shrug. "The library is for Whites only."

Louisa's jaw dropped.

"What an absurd rule. We need to look in the city directory for her family members," Louisa insisted.

"I don't make the rules," he said and tilted his owl-like head. "You're more than welcome to come in. She can wait outside in the courtyard for you."

Louisa looked at Suzie, whose face had turned hard, her expression inscrutable.

"Let's go," Louisa said. The palms of Louisa's hands tingled. She wanted to slap the soft white cheek of the librarian, to knock his glasses to the floor. New Yorkers could be snobbish and inconsiderate; the city was certainly no open society, but this sort of outright prejudice was infuriating.

"No, you go ahead and look for them, Louisa," Suzie said. "I'll be outside." Louisa remembered the shame and anger she'd felt when she'd been excluded from the debutante balls when she was eighteen. How much worse this was.

"Tell me the names to look for," Louisa said.

"Blake was our name, but the master of the plantation where my father lived was called Jenkins, so they might be going by that," she said. Then she turned like a dignified swan and strode into the sunshine.

The librarian pulled a slim volume from a row of shelved books and handed it to Louisa.

"You'll know the person is Colored because there will be an asterisk by their name," he said, beaming as if proud of himself for being so helpful.

"Thank you," Louisa said through tight lips.

She flipped through the pages and noticed the street names attached to the asterisks. Washington, Central, Bridge, and Oneida.

"These include families who live in Lincolnville, correct? It's not a separate city?" she asked.

"Yes, they're included. Lincolnville is a neighborhood just a few blocks from here. Quite a charming community. The Colored have their own businesses and restaurants. Some of them are prosperous. They're a very happy people if not particularly ambitious," he said.

"Businesses and restaurants sound ambitious to me," Louisa responded.

She turned her back on the man and perused the names on the pages. She didn't find a single Blake though there were several Jenkinses. She jotted down the names along with their street addresses. Would they have to go door to door, she wondered?

She returned the directory to the man and went outside to find Suzie sitting on a concrete bench beside an azalea bush heavy with blooms. She handed her the sheet of paper with the addresses.

"No Blakes," Louisa said. "But several Jenkinses."

"That's a start," Suzie said. "I'll go out and check the addresses this afternoon."

"Would you like me to come with you?"

"No, you better start writing some articles. Don't want you to lose your job," Suzie said, ever mindful of the wolf at the door.

They left the library and came upon the town plaza populated by middle-class tourists passing the time of day. In the middle stood an open-air pavilion with a cupola on top and a sign: ST. AUGUSTINE OLD SLAVE MARKET. They hesitated for a moment before walking onto the brick flooring inside. Pillars lined the sides of the structure.

As Louisa walked through the old market, the air felt heavy as if she were walking through cotton. She tried to imagine what it must have been like fifty years earlier when men and women and even children were bought and sold here. What agony to know you had no control over your life or your children's lives — to have a child torn from your arms. She felt a tightening in her throat and a chill along her arms though it was warm even in the shade of the market building.

Neither of them said anything until they had passed through the market and crossed the street. Louisa leaned against a stone wall and stared out at the wide blue Matanzas Bay. Noon bells tolled from a nearby cathedral.

"Do you remember what it was like? On the plantation?" Louisa asked.

"Oh, yes, I remember," Suzie said. "I was fortunate, you know, because my grandmother raised me and they valued her. That didn't take away the pain of losing my mother, of not knowing what happened to her."

For a few minutes they stood silently looking down at the brown water sloshing against the embankment.

They spent the rest of the morning looking for gifts for Anna and Ellen in the shops on St. George Street, including a place called Ye Olde Curiosity Shoppe. Fortunately, the shop owners did not seem to care about the skin color of their patrons. Or they might have assumed Suzie was Louisa's maid, who simply came along to carry packages.

They had just exited the last gift shop with their purchases — a decorative fan for Anna and an alligator handbag for Ellen — when Louisa saw Henri and Simon Bassett walking along the street with their heads bent toward each other in conversation.

"*Bonjour, Messieurs,*" she said.

They looked up, startled. Henri seemed annoyed, but Simon's face brightened.

"Miss Delafield and Miss Blake, how charming to run into the two of you. Have you been seeing sights?" he asked.

"We have," Louisa answered. "This is a fascinating city."

"I wonder if you two ladies would like to see the Lighthouse tomorrow?" he asked. "It's supposed to have a spectacular view."

"Heavens no, I'm not going to climb up a lighthouse, not with these old knees," Suzie said.

Simon looked at Louisa with an inquisitive smile.

"I'm not sure it would be," Louisa hesitated, "exactly proper."

"You Americans," Simon said. "I promise you will be safe. We will be surrounded by tourists."

Louisa chafed at his insinuation that Americans were prudish. He was right, however. A French woman probably wouldn't have had a second thought. She thought of Henry James' *Portrait of a Lady*. In it, the Americans were hopelessly provincial.

"I'll meet you in the morning in the lobby of the hotel," Simon said.

As they walked away, Louisa heard Henri say, "*Tu es fou*?" which she believed meant, Are you crazy?

***

After lunch Suzie took the names of the Jenkinses in Lincolnville and set out on her mission.

Louisa found Lady Rutherford fanning herself in a deck chair outside The Florida House.

"Ah, Louisa," Lady Rutherford said. "How are you finding the social scene?"

"I don't know much about it yet," Louisa said, "but I get the sense it is more egalitarian and also more exciting than the tired system regulated by the grand dames of Old New York."

"I know who you mean, the Astors, the Morgans, the Fishes, and so on," Lady Rutherford said. "Those women have been so busy turning up their noses at new money they haven't realized that throughout most of the rest of the world, no one cares. These up-and-coming society women are elegant and sophisticated. Like the old guard, they buy dresses in Paris and have seasons in London, but they also eschew many of the traditions. Quite a few don't even bother having ladies' maids. Some of them, like you, my dear, have been to college, and they aren't all signing over their futures to a husband before they turn twenty. The most refreshing thing about them is that they know how to have fun. Go over to the Alcazar, Louisa, and look around. You'll see what I mean."

Louisa took her advice and walked toward the Ponce, which had the feeling of a king's court, and then across the street to its younger brother, the Alcazar Hotel, also built by Flagler and designed by the same architects with the same Spanish and Arabian influences — red tiles roofs, terra cotta belvederes and great arched windows. It did indeed look like a castle.

Louisa strode between two six-storey towers through a stone archway and into a lovely courtyard with a fountain and a charming wooden bridge over a pond where frogs croaked in a rambunctious chorus. Inside the grand lobby of the hotel, Louisa asked for a tour from the concierge, who was more than happy to show a New York City society writer around. So many New Yorkers bypassed St. Augustine for Palm Beach, the old hoteliers could only dream of a return to their golden era.

"This building houses the hotel rooms," he said, leading her up a set of stone stairs, "and back here is the main attraction. The casino."

"Casino? Is there gambling?" Louisa asked.

"No, that's simply what we call the entertainment center." He led her down a hallway and through another archway into a cavernous room. She heard laughter and splashing and looked down into the largest swimming pool she'd ever seen. Above her, she saw large glass windows and through them clouds.

"What's up there?" she asked, pointing to the balustrade above.

"That's the ballroom."

"Ingenious."

"There's more," he said. "If you take that hallway on the other side of the pool, it will lead you outside.

Around the corner, you'll find an arched doorway with wooden doors. Behind those doors is the bowling alley."

"Bowling alley?" Louisa exclaimed.

"Only at night. During the day, it's an archery range," he said with a pleased expression.

Louisa thanked the man for his time and found a table on the terrace overlooking the lush gardens of the courtyard so she could write her story, in which she would quote Lady Rutherford at length.

Her concentration was broken when someone sat down beside her and held out a glass filled with bright red liquid.

"Fruit punch?" Lord Wickham asked.

"Why, thank you," she said. She took the drink from his hand, sipped, and sputtered. "That's not fruit punch." She gave him a scandalized look. He grinned.

"No, it's a rum cocktail," he said.

Louisa took another sip and giggled.

"And a delicious one at that," she said. She was not one to drink alcohol during the day, but she was away from home and the strictures of her life seemed to loosen in the sea breezes. Perhaps, the horror of Dottie's death would also ease.

"Tell me, Lord Wickham, how long do you plan to stay in America?" she asked.

"Percival," he said.

"Percival?" she asked.

"That's my name. Please call me Percival. I don't find titles particularly meaningful," he said. "They tell you nothing about a person's character."

"Then please call me Louisa," she said. She'd only had a few sips of the alcoholic concoction but already she felt a little giddy. "Well then, Percival, will you go home to England after the wedding or do you have other adventures to pursue?"

"After the wedding, I plan to go to New York for some business."

"You'll have to let me show you around the city while you're there. I'll also be going back after the wedding," she said. Regardless of whether the police found Dottie's killer or not, she would have to go home sometime.

She leaned back, feeling quite relaxed indeed. The sun laid a gentle hand over the scene before her. A large grayish-blue bird descended from the sky and dropped gracefully into the pond in front of them.

"That is a blue heron," she said, proud of her new-found knowledge.

"I believe I've seen those feathers before," he said. "On some woman's head."

"You probably have. Women's rapacious taste for fashion has decimated their numbers," Louisa said. "I'm livid that the courts have ruled the Migratory Bird Act unconstitutional. Although I'll admit until recently I was as ignorant as anyone else. Theodore Roosevelt helped open my eyes."

"Didn't he kill animals in Africa?" he asked. "Big animals?"

"Well, yes, but he's also a conservationist," she said, pulling the book from her bag. "He gave me this book so I could identify the birds."

Lord Wickham opened the book and glanced through it.

"Wait here," he said. He went inside and a few minutes later, he came out with a drawing pad and pencil he had purchased from the gift store. He sat down and studied the heron, which stood still as a statue with one leg bent, and began to draw.

"You're an artist?" Louisa asked.

"It's just a hobby," he said, continuing to sketch.

A waiter brought them each another cocktail, and she remembered her mission to learn about Daphne's prospective husband. She sipped slowly to see what she might glean from her new friend as the alcohol loosened his tongue. If Henri were a scoundrel, then she might find out just what kind of scoundrel.

"How long have you known Henri and Simon Bassett?" she asked.

He stopped drawing for a moment, put the pencil to his chin, and seemed to be thinking about her question.

"Let's see. I moved to Paris in 1908, and I met Henri in the summer of 1909. He was practically still a boy, completely at loose ends. He and his brother had a small inheritance but they'd been cut out of the family business by their uncle, a loathsome man. And Simon, well, Simon had begun associating with the most disreputable sort. Have you heard of *La Bande à Bonnot*?"

"No," Louisa said, hanging on his every word.

"They were anarchists, bank robbers, killers, in fact. They went on a terrible crime spree!"

Louisa gasped. She could not imagine the urbane Simon Bassett consorting with men like that, but this must be the source of those rumors that Mr. Griffin had heard.

"We have quite a few problems with those anarchists in New York," she said and thought of the last time she'd seen Dottie in the hospital. She took a gulp of the alcohol in hopes of quelling the grief that leapt at the opportunity to squeeze her heart and reminded herself to stay focused on her mission.

Lord Wickham leaned forward and made quick strokes with the pencil.

"Fortunately, before the gangsters went on said crime spree, I persuaded Simon that as the grandson of a baron, he was far better than that. I told him to go to his uncle on bended knee if he had to and ask to be allowed into the family wine business. If he didn't, he would surely ruin both himself and his brother," Lord Wickham said in a confiding tone.

"And did he?" she asked.

"Yes. In the meanwhile, three members of *La Bande à Bonnot* were executed."

Louisa clapped a hand over her mouth.

"How awful. And what about Henri?" she asked.

"Henri, fortunately, was not involved in any of it," Lord Wickham said. Then he turned wistful. "I want nothing but happiness for Henri. Happiness and a fortune, of course."

She remembered he had mentioned that he had been the one to introduce Daphne and Henri.

"Lord Wickham, please don't take offense, but I want to know the truth about Daphne's diamond. I can't believe a reputable merchant would sell it without a hefty price tag," she said.

Wickham grimaced.

"You are a shrewd one, aren't you?" he said. "I loaned him the money. I wanted him to be able to impress her. He can easily pay me back after they're married."

"Is Daphne your Isabel Archer?" she asked, thinking of Henry James' unwitting American protagonist who was bamboozled into marrying a rogue who only wanted her money.

"Are you implying that I am Madame Merle, scheming to insinuate myself into their lives?"

"Are you?"

"I do want Henri to be rich, true. And I would hope as a small token of appreciation the wealthy young couple might invest in my next expedition," he said. Then he yawned and said, "Of course, I'll be financing most of it with my inheritance."

"Inheritance?" she asked. The only inheritance she had ever gotten was a hole in her heart where her father had once been, and a mystery that was yet to be solved.

"Indeed. That's the reason I need to go to New York after the wedding. To collect. My grandfather had many investments in America, and his attorney in New York will draw up a check for me, but I have to collect it in person," he said. "Not that I mind."

She sighed. She'd solved the mystery. Henri had come by the diamond pendant honestly enough though he may yet be a scoundrel.

"May I see your drawing?" she asked.

"Not yet," he said. "I have to put some finishing touches on it. You can see it in a day or so."

The cathedral bell tolled 3:00.

"Oh my," Louisa said. "I'm afraid I must go. I have an appointment to interview Madame Ribault."

Lord Wickham gave her a side-eyed glance and said, "Watch out for Veronique."

"What do you mean?" she asked.

"She'll have you dressing like a Parisian courtesan if you let her," he said. "You know her mother was one."

"One?"

"A courtesan. Famous and popular."

"How fascinating," Louisa said. Lord Wickham was a fountain of gossip. Louisa was still trying to absorb the idea of Simon Bassett as some sort of gangster.

"That's why she wants to move to America. Fresh start and all that," he said and sipped his drink.

Chapter 16

Ellen

Ellen persuaded Mrs. Delafield to go to bed early and hurried out of the house as soon as she heard her snoring. She hated to spend money on a taxi but she'd never get all the way downtown in time if she took the train so she scraped together some change and hailed a cab. Her money got her as far as 22nd Street and she walked the rest of the way. It was ten o'clock by the time she got to the Bohemian restaurant. She ran down the steps and strode through the dark hallway to the small, crowded restaurant. A man with rolled-up shirt sleeves played a tinny piano in the center of the room. She could see why this would be a good spot for a clandestine meeting. The noise level covered up any secret conversations.

Lulu and Karl, alias L. Byron, sat at a corner table with two men she recognized from the party at Emma Goldman's apartment. The three men hunched forward, sunk deep into their conversation. None of them noticed her until she was standing at the table and then immediately the men leaned back and quit talking.

"Ellen, have a seat," Lulu invited. "You remember Artie and Charlie, don't you?" Ellen did remember them – "Thick and Thin." Charlie was thin and dapper, and Artie, thick and slovenly.

"I don't mean to interrupt," Ellen said, hesitantly. Lulu reached out and grabbed her arm.

"Sit down," she said.

Ellen sat.

Charlie snarled, "Did you invite her?"

"Yes," Lulu said. "We can trust her."

"What makes you so sure?" Charlie asked, squinting at Ellen.

"Her papa is an Irish Republican," Lulu said with a shrug. "She works at *The Gaelic American.*"

Karl blew a trail of smoke from his nostrils.

"Is this your head talking or some other part of your anatomy?" he asked. "What if she says something to Emma?"

"I won't," Ellen said. "I hardly know her. You're the ones who work with her."

"Ellen," Lulu said. "Are you afraid of a little danger?"

"No, why?"

"Karl and I write editorials all day long and nothing happens. We're ready for action. Are you?"

Ellen felt her heart falter. What were they planning? Another shooting? Or a bombing?

"Jesus, woman!" Charlie hissed. "You talk too much."

Artie had said nothing at all, glowering at the pint of beer in front of him.

Karl stood up.

"Let's go to my place," he said as he tossed some cash onto the table. The men got up and followed him as he wound around the small round tables, dodging waiters with trays balancing on one hand.

Lulu took Ellen by the arm, and they trailed the men outside. They'd walked several blocks in silence when Karl turned to Ellen and said, "It's not that we don't trust you, Ellen, but you haven't proven yourself to me or to anyone else here that you're actually committed to our cause."

"And how do I do that?"

"That's for you to figure out," he said. He looked pointedly at Lulu who sighed and unhooked Ellen's arm.

"Sorry," she said to Ellen.

The four of them walked away and left her standing on the street by herself. She wasn't sure she wanted them to trust her with their secrets, but she saw no other way to make sure it was safe for Louisa to return.

Chapter 17

Louisa

The wedding dress designer, Veronique Ribault, had slightly bulging eyes in a narrow, alabaster-white face. She kept her thin lips tightly closed as if they were gripping a row of straight pins. She seemed utterly absorbed in her project. On a platform in the center of the room stood a dress form draped with ivory satin moiré, silk, and Limerick lace.

Louisa stood in the doorway and waited for an acknowledgment of her presence. When none was forthcoming, she said, "Thank you for agreeing to meet with me, Madame Ribault. I know New York society will be excited to hear about your design for Daphne's dress. They're always looking for something new and fresh so that they can out-do each other."

Madame Ribault did not respond. She held a pair of scissors in her left hand and snipped a long strip of lace, which she then wrapped around a sleeve. An assistant stood at her side holding a pin cushion as the designer pinned the lace. Then she stood back to assess her handiwork. The dress glittered in the sunlight. The designer had ingeniously incorporated glimmering crystal beads into the fabric where there might normally have been pearls.

"It's stunning," Louisa said.

"*Merci,*" Madame Ribault responded, still not looking at Louisa. "What do you think of the train?" She indicated a long white sheet of ivory satin with gold arabesques embroidered around the trim on a hanger nearby.

"It's exquisite."

"Four yards long," Madame Ribault said in her heavy French accent. "Mrs. Kermit Roosevelt had one that long, and Mademoiselle Daphne insisted on the same. I tried to explain to her the regulation court train is only three yards long, but she says she will not be going to court any time soon."

"Perhaps not," Louisa said. Many society brides kept their train for momentous occasions such as visiting the King of England, but Daphne Griffin was not in that exalted realm, for all her father's millions. She noticed a half veil resting on a dummy head. "That's original."

"*Oui*. A full veil is passé. This one just covers the eyes," Madame Ribault lifted the veil and put it on her own head, and smiled for the first time. Her teeth were small and yellowed from cigarettes, which might be why she so rarely smiled.

"*Trés chic,*" Louisa said.

"Would you like to see the bridesmaids' dresses? They are in the other room." Madame Ribault seemed to be warming up to her task.

The door opened and a man said, "Veronique?"

Madame Ribault looked up and Louisa turned to see Simon Bassett in the doorway. For a moment they stared at him and he stared back at them.

"*Pardonez moi,*" he said. "I did not know you were engaged. I wondered if you had finished my cravat." He looked at Louisa and said, "*Bonjour,* Mademoiselle Delafield."

Madame Ribault took a silk cravat from the neck of a male form and handed it to him.

"*Merci,*" he said with a little bow and then a glance at Louisa, a glance she could not read.

"*Au revoir,*" Madame Ribault said and dismissed him with a wave of her hand. He backed out of the room, shutting the door as he did so.

***

After dinner with Lady Rutherford and friends, Louisa went back to her room and was now at her writing table, writing her article about Madame Ribault and her creations. She would get it in the post tomorrow morning, and Ellen could type it up for the Saturday fashion section. When she was done, she glanced outside at the sparkling night sky. She wished this wedding were over so she could go back to New York. Someone had murdered Dottie Parsons and gotten away scot-free. She ought to go back and try to infiltrate those anarchists at *Mother Earth*, but of course, she would be recognized. Ellen could do it, but Louisa would never allow her friend to take such a risk. There was also the matter of Julia Markham's letter and the aching need to learn what the attorney's wife wanted to tell her.

A knock on the door startled her. She opened it to find Lord Wickham, wearing a mask and dressed like a bullfighter.

"You aren't dressed," he exclaimed.

"Dressed for what?" she asked.

"The masquerade ball at the Alcazar," he said and held out an elaborate red-and-gold mask and a tambourine. "You can be a Spanish tambourine girl. Do you have anything in red?"

Louisa hesitated for only a moment.

"I'll be right out," she said.

Dressed in a red taffeta gown and a sequined mask, carrying the tambourine in one hand and her camera case over her shoulder, Louisa accompanied Lord Wickham to the ball.

"In its heyday this was the most popular place on the East Coast," he said as they walked up the steps to the ballroom.

Louisa imagined her parents here. They must have danced and drunk the nights away, oblivious to their unhappy future.

The ballroom was gorgeous with pillars in every corner, elaborate moulding, and glowing chandeliers all surrounding an atrium that looked down onto the vast swimming pool. Masked dancers tangoed and foxtrotted around the room. Peals of laughter blended into the lively tunes played by a German orchestra.

While Lord Wickham danced a waltz with Daphne's mother, Louisa took photographs of the dancers and jotted notes in her notebook before putting away the tools of her trade so she might enjoy herself. She looked around for Simon Bassett, but did not see him. An older gentleman wearing a white wig and a blue-and-white mask asked her to join him for a waltz. Despite the wig and the mask, she knew exactly who it was and assented.

"Miss Delafield, have you found out anything about Henri Bassett?" Mr. Griffin asked as they danced.

"Only that the brothers had a small inheritance and were shut out of the family business, but they managed to persuade their uncle to relent," she said. "I did learn the source of the rumors regarding his brother. Youthful indiscretion, I believe. Henri was not involved."

"In my jacket pocket I have a report from my Pinkerton detective," he said. "When we round this pillar, please take it from my pocket," he said.

She smiled blandly and nodded and when he led her around the pillar, she slipped her hand in the jacket pocket and took out a folded sheet of paper. She tucked it inside the small purse dangling from her wrist.

"You haven't told anyone about this, have you? Daphne would be livid."

"No," she said. "I haven't."

"Well, don't. Especially Lord Wickham. I don't trust him at all," he said.

"Did you know that Lord Wickham loaned Henri the money for Daphne's pendant?" Louisa asked.

"And why would he do that?"

Why, indeed?

They joined the flow of dancers. When the song ended, Mr. Griffin bowed to her.

A few minutes later, his wife in a Marie Antoinette wig slipped her arm in Louisa's.

"Miss Delafield, I have a wonderful idea for a story for your column," she said. Mothers always had wonderful ideas for Louisa's column. "Why don't you join Daphne and her sister Margaret tomorrow at the pool? You can write about the two sisters having fun before the wedding. Daphne loves to swim."

She looked toward the balustrade, below which lay the pool.

"That is a wonderful idea," Louisa said, trying to keep the yawn out of her voice. "I'm afraid, however, I have plans for tomorrow."

"Then the next day," Mrs. Griffin insisted. "They'll be on the Alcazar Terrace by nine o'clock. I'll make sure they're on time."

At that moment, Daphne and Henri foxtrotted by them, dressed as Hansel and Gretel.

"Isn't she adorable?" Mrs. Griffin said, watching her plain-looking daughter in the arms of a Prince Charming.

"She certainly is," Louisa said.

***

The ball went on for hours, and it was two o'clock in the morning before she managed to get back to her room. She put an ear against Suzie's door and heard her snoring. She hadn't even had the chance to find out what Suzie had learned about her family.

She sat down at the table and read the Pinkerton report:

> *Simon and Henri Bassett left Paris in September 1913 for Alexandria Egypt where they were seeking business opportunities. According to our source, a cousin, they were to remain in Egypt until February. Instead they returned in November. They had little money before they left. When they returned they were accompanied by Lord Wickham. They paid off a sizeable debt at this time. How they did so is unknown.*

That was all the report said. The business with the debts was rather mysterious. Perhaps they found some business opportunities, which is why they returned early and were able to pay off their debt. Or if they'd been on an archaeological dig, perhaps they had sold some antiquities.

She put down the piece of paper and went out onto the balcony. The stars twinkled against the black sky. She thought again of Daphne's diamond. Had she been too quick to take Lord Wickham's word for how Henri could afford it? A nine-carat diamond would be worth nearly $20,000. Then there were the debts. Something had changed last fall, but what could it be? She decided she would cable Ellen and ask her to try to find any news items from Alexandria, a long shot, but she would be remiss if she didn't check it. Then she remembered she had agreed to go to the lighthouse with Simon Bassett the next day, perhaps a good opportunity to find out what, if anything, had happened in Egypt.

She looked across the bay and saw in the distance a stream of light moving across the sky, filtered through a thin layer of clouds, and she thought of Dottie.

Chapter 18

Ellen

When Ellen went into *The Ledger*, she found a cable from Louisa.

> *"Pls research Henri Bassett of France. Bride's father wants information. Look in New York Times index. Go to library, look in Le Matin. Check Alexandria, Egypt Oct. 1913."*

Le Matin was a French paper and Ellen didn't know French, so she didn't know how she was supposed to learn something there. This seemed like a silly errand, but she could make the trip in the afternoon.

In addition to the cable, she found an article from Louisa in the post to type. Her fingers made quick work of the column all about oysters and a lighthouse and its jewel-like lens. She thought of the lighthouse in Cork she'd visited once with some friends and her mind drifted to Ireland and the rumblings of war. No matter that she had sworn off the Catholic religion, her hand automatically made the sign of the cross, as she prayed her brothers would not get swept up in it if it happened.

With the column typed and delivered to the typesetter, she turned to the rest of the correspondence and opened up the invitations one after the other. Even though it wasn't the society season, minor events still happened. It was New York, after all. Ellen had worked for Louisa long enough to know which ones would matter. When Ellen opened the last invitation, her heart skipped a beat. It was from Mrs. John D. Rockefeller, Senior, father of the man responsible for the deaths of coal miners' families in Colorado, and a right old robber baron if ever there was one. She knew just the person who might know a thing or two about his wife.

***

Ellen rang the doorbell. She wasn't sure how Hester would receive her after their conversation — or was it a spat? — the other day. When the housekeeper opened the door, she said that Hester was in the parlor with her sister.

Hester smiled when she saw Ellen, but her sister, Mrs. Murphy, looked confused. Mrs. Murphy was a small powderkeg of a woman. She was not a member of high society but desperately wanted to be. Ellen's position as Louisa Delafield's assistant at *The Ledger* granted her some immunity from Mrs. Murphy's snobbishness.

"Ellen, how delightful to see you," Hester said.

Relief swept over her. Hester couldn't stay mad at her, and for that she was grateful because no one else could help her right now.

"Had a lull at work, so I thought I'd come and see if you need any help," Ellen responded.

"In fact, I do need help making signs for the suffrage parade," Hester said.

"Oh, Hester, you and your causes!" Mrs. Murphy exclaimed.

"Katherine, you know you want the right to vote as much as I do," Hester said.

"Mamie Fish thinks it's a foolish idea, and I do, too," Mrs. Murphy said, pursing her lips.

"But Alva Belmont is a proponent," Hester countered. Ellen only knew those names from Louisa's columns. They were the women who ruled New York society.

Mrs. Murphy grimaced. "Oh, I don't really care one way or the other. Mr. Murphy is perfectly capable of making those decisions for both of us."

"Well, we don't all have a husband as wise as John," Hester said, eyes twinkling as she looked at Ellen.

Mrs. Murphy nodded and said, "I suppose you're right. He is a dear. Well, I'll let the two of you get to your *important* work. I'm going shopping. We're only in Manhattan for the day so I should not waste it."

She rose and nodded peremptorily at Ellen as she left.

As soon as the door closed, Hester crossed the room and clasped Ellen's hands.

"I'm sorry I was cross with you the other day. I know that you're trying to find the woman who shot at Louisa," she said.

A blade of guilt twisted in Ellen's gut. Here was Hester apologizing when she was the one who was attracted to another woman. She comforted herself with the thought that she was only trying to save Louisa's life by finding the shooter.

"Do you really have signs to make for the parade?" Ellen asked.

"They're already done," Hester said. "Sit down and tell me everything that's going on. What do you hear from Louisa?"

Ellen sat.

"She's been having a grand old time, eating oysters on the beach, according to the article I received today," Ellen said. "Of course, there's some intrigue around the groom that I have to help her with."

"Sounds interesting."

"Hester, I have a question for you. What do you know of Mrs. John D. Rockefeller, Senior?" she asked.

"You mean Cettie? I don't really know her, but I do know she's a saint," Hester said.

Ellen was skeptical. It didn't seem believable that the wife of the founder of Standard Oil was a saint.

"How so?" she asked.

"She's the daughter of abolitionists and the apple didn't fall far from the tree. Can you imagine? Her father was part of the Underground Railroad. They saved countless fugitive slaves. I admire her a great deal. She's a teacher and a philanthropist. She's been most generous in terms of the education of Negro women. Spelman Seminary is named after her and her family."

Ellen pondered this information. She had assumed that anyone with the last name Rockefeller was a vapid capitalist who only cared about wealth.

"Why do you ask?" Hester asked.

"Louisa received an invitation to a charity luncheon in Tarrytown," Ellen said. Ellen pulled it from her bag and showed it to her.

"That's just like Cettie. She's an invalid now, but she's still hosting charity events," Hester said, perusing the invitation. She looked up at Ellen, eyes shining, and asked, "Are you going to go in Louisa's place?"

Ellen laughed.

"No, I've no plans to go there at all. I was just curious," she said. "Say, do you speak French.

"*Mais oui*," Hester said. "Our governess was French Canadian."

"I wonder if you'd like to go to the library with me? I need to look through some French newspapers for Louisa. She's looking for any dirt on the groom of this wedding she's covering. The bride's *da* has suspicions."

"Right now?"

"If you're free," Ellen said.

Thirty minutes later they had reached the corner of Fifth Avenue and 42nd Street. Ellen marveled at the massive marble building. It reminded her of their trips to the Metropolitan Museum. They hurried across the wide street. Motorcars puttered past. Two carved lions guarded the entrance. If they were meant to intimidate, Ellen thought they were doing a bad job of it. So many people of all stripes entered and left the building. Inside was another matter. When she saw the enormous room with its polished tables, tens of thousands of books lining the walls, and chandeliers hanging every few feet, she looked over at Hester and asked, "How does anyone find anything in here?"

"We'll ask a librarian for help," she said.

They found a librarian, who did know where the foreign newspapers were kept.

"We have a lot of immigrants in the city who want to read about home," the librarian said. "Of course, we keep copies of our own city papers, too."

She led the two into a smaller room and showed them where the various papers were located.

While Hester looked through *Le Matin* for mentions of Henri Bassett in the society pages, Ellen looked through the British papers for any mention of Alexandria, Egypt.

The afternoon disappeared while they perused the papers.

"I only found a few mentions of Henri Bassett," Hester said. "He was seen at the ballet with a Lord Wickham in the spring of 1912. And then a few months ago, there's a picture of him and an American girl. They're engaged. What did you find?"

"Not much," Ellen said. "The only mention of Alexandria, Egypt, is a diamond theft worth a half million. No suspects."

"I wonder what Louisa has gotten herself into," Hester said.

Ellen wondered as much herself. She thought of the invitation to Mrs. Rockefeller's party and wondered what she was getting herself into, as well.

Chapter 19
Louisa

"I found three of the addresses," Suzie said over their morning coffee. "Nobody was home at the first. The second was an elderly woman who had never heard of Lloyd or George. And the third was an abandoned house. I'm looking for a needle in a haystack."

"I'm sorry," Louisa said. "We can keep trying. In the meantime, let's go shopping for a parasol. If I'm going to the lighthouse with Monsieur Bassett today, I need some protection from the sun."

"You may need protection from more than the sun," Suzie said.

"I'm sure he's a perfect gentleman," Louisa said.

They found a pink-and-white parasol in a shop on St. George Street and then wandered further down the street, looking in windows. They reached the historic city gates and turned to go back when they passed a beauty shop. A pretty, brown-skinned woman in her thirties, wearing a high-collared white dress with a gold necklace, came out of the shop as they passed. She had deep brown eyes in an oval face and smiled pleasantly at them. They hadn't gone ten feet when Suzie put her hand on Louisa's arm.

"What is it?" Louisa asked.

"That woman we just passed. That woman had my mother's eyes. And her smile."

Louisa wheeled around and watched the receding back of the woman. Immediately she hurried after her, calling out, "Ma'am? Ma'am?"

The woman did not turn but continued to walk down the street, weaving through clumps of tourists. Louisa quickened her gait and was almost running by the time she caught up with the woman.

"Please! Wait!" Louisa called out.

Finally, the woman turned around with a confused look on her face.

"Do you mean me?" she asked.

"Yes," Louisa said, pausing to catch her breath. "My companion...." She began and pointed to Suzie who was walking toward them, staring intently. The woman glanced from Louisa to Suzie and back to Louisa. Louisa decided to let Suzie explain.

Suzie slowed down as she approached them, searching the younger woman's face.

"Are you...?" she began tentatively. "Are you related to George or Lloyd Blake? Or their last name might be Jenkins."

"My daddy was George Carpenter," the woman said. "He died three years ago."

Suzie clasped her hand to her chest.

"Carpenter? Of course. Our daddy was a carpenter. They wouldn't want to keep the name of the master," Suzie said. Louisa had forgotten about Suzie's father.

What a barbaric institution slavery was to deprive children of their most basic need, the love and guidance of their parents. For a fleeting moment, she thought of her own father and how much she missed him.

The younger woman stepped closer to Suzie and peered at her face.

"Why do you ask?" the woman asked.

"And what about Lloyd?" Suzie asked. "Do you know him?"

"Uncle Lloyd is just fine. He lives with me and my husband in the house my father built," the woman said.

Tears filled Suzie eyes, and a lump formed in Louisa's throat.

"I'm your Aunt Suzie," she said.

The younger woman brought her hands to her mouth. Louisa held her breath as she watched their interaction. How had she not understood the importance of finding Suzie's family? How had she ever been so selfish? The three women stood, a triangle in the flow of people passing them. Then the woman reached out and touched Suzie's arm as if making sure she was real.

"My name is Polly. Will you come home with me? There's some people who will want to see you," she said.

Suzie glanced at Louisa. Louisa clasped Suzie's arm and nodded.

"Go. I'll see you back at the hotel tonight," Louisa said. She released her grip and watched through the tears gathering in her eyes as the two women walked away.

The cathedral bells chimed. It was 11:00.

***

Louisa and Simon Bassett took a trolley down King Street under a canopy of magnolia trees and live oaks to the bay. There they found a terminal built out onto the water and another trolley car. This one would take them over the choppy waters of the bay across a long bridge built on wooden pilings. A guide told the passengers the bridge was the longest of its kind.

Louisa had her parasol, her bird book, and pair of binoculars. Monsieur Bassett carried a small carpetbag with a blanket for sitting on the beach.

She glanced back at the city and could see the tall Victorian tower of the Florida House. The whole place looked picture perfect.

The noise of the train limited their conversation, so Louisa leaned forward in her seat, her hat wrapped in tulle so it wouldn't fly off her head, and looked out at the fields of sawgrass as they rode along the coast. When the tracks went over the water, a pleasant breeze blew off the bay and in through the open windows. As they came to the island, billowing snow white dunes stretched to the west and a dark copse of pine trees and oaks stood to the south.

They exited the train and saw the lighthouse, a tall conical building with a black stripe spiraling up its white walls. Her skirt clung to her legs in the wind. Simon took her arm and helped her navigate over snaky vines traversing the low dunes to the platform, past the keeper's house. They entered through the open door to the lighthouse. A circular staircase wound up and up and up.

"Oh my," Louisa said, craning her neck to see the top. A sign said there were 240 steps to the top.

"We don't have to go up if you don't want to. Are you afraid of heights, Miss Delafield?" Simon asked.

"Not at all. When I was a child, my father and I went to the top of the Eiffel Tower, which has 1700 steps," she said. She paused and then added as she went up the steps, "If you prefer, Monsieur Bassett, you may call me Louisa."

"And I am Simon," he said.

They smiled at each other. Then she led the way up the steps, stopping briefly to look out the tall windows in the tower so they could catch their breath and admire the views.

Once they reached the top, they looked through a window inside the room where a giant jewel, taller than a man, shimmered.

"You have a Frenchman to thank for this lighthouse," he said.

"Oh?"

"The lens was designed by a man named Fresnel," Simon said. "Quite a feat of engineering. The lighthouse keeper climbs inside to light the kerosene. Ships can see the beam more than forty kilometers away."

Louisa stared, mesmerized, at a rippled glass cylinder, with a glass tower on top. As she gazed at the prismatic colors, she was reminded of the diamond pendant dangling from Daphne's neck.

"How do you know so much about the lens? Do they teach you about Fresnel lamps in French schools?"

He grinned and admitted, "I read a tourist pamphlet."

"I should have known," she said with a laugh. She turned and went through the door to the platform outside the lighthouse.

The wind had a heavy hand, so she held onto her hat. Simon followed her onto the platform with its thin rail the only thing keeping them from plunging to a certain death. Louisa held her breath as she gazed around. The wide blue ocean stretched out languorously as if opening its arms to the sky. So much blue to the east. So much green to the north and south. A line of large white birds with odd-looking beaks and black trim on their wings sailed past. Those must be pelicans, she thought.

She turned and gazed at the undulating ocean and imagined what it must be like to see that welcoming light far out in the dark. Simon stood so close she could smell the clean scent of his shaving lotion mixed with the salty sea smell. She felt a magnetic pull toward him. There were so many reasons she must not succumb to that pull, she thought, but for the life of her she couldn't remember them. She glanced at his face. He seemed to be brooding, but then he noticed her looking, and he smiled. She quickly turned away.

"Shall we go back down?" she said, eager to put some distance between their bodies.

"*D'accord*," he said. She rather liked that he seemed to assume she knew at least a smattering of French.

"Staying for the oyster roast?" a black-skinned man asked when they were outside the lighthouse. He spoke in a heavy, lilting accent unfamiliar to Louisa. Perhaps he was from the Caribbean.

"Oyster roast?" Simon asked.

"Every afternoon we have an oyster roast for the tourists but only in months with the letter 'r.' It's March so you're in luck," he said, flashing a brilliant white smile. "Go down to the beach. You gonna love them oysters."

They walked down to the beach where two men had dumped a pile of oysters on a steel plate over a fire. Smoke billowed from under a burlap bag on top of the palm-sized gray shells. The men gathered up the shells with a shovel, poured them onto a table, set with utensils and lemon wedges and then shucked them for the ten or so guests eagerly waiting.

"How do you eat them?" Simon asked.

"I'll show you," Louisa said. One of the oyster shuckers handed her a plate with five open-faced shells, each bearing a soft gray mound.

When the oysters had cooled enough to handle, she took one of the rough gray shells in her hand, squeezed some lemon on top of it, and then with a tiny fork, unloosed the oyster and tipped the shell over her mouth. The oyster slid down her throat as if it were hurrying home.

After they'd had their fill, they found a quiet spot on the sandy beach to sit. He unfolded the blanket, which flapped in the wind before landing softly on the ground. Louisa lowered herself to the blanket and took off her hat to feel the sun and wind on her face. Her mother would be aghast. It was important to keep one's skin as alabaster as a statue in a museum, but Louisa wanted to absorb the warmth of the day. The rhythm of the waves sloshing against the shore, the salty ocean smell, and the gentle rays of the sun could have lulled her to sleep. She reminded herself she had promised Mr. Griffin to learn what she could about his prospective son-in-law, so she turned to Simon.

"Tell me about your brother," Louisa said. "Is he marrying Daphne for her money?"

Simon looked out at the sea and shrugged.

"*Mais oui,*" he said. "Is there something wrong with that? Our uncle always said it's as easy to fall in love with a rich woman as it is with a poor woman."

"Is that your philosophy as well?" Louisa asked. "Are you also looking for a rich wife?"

He looked down at his hands and stretched out his fingers.

"No. I am not looking for a wife at all," he said and tilted his head toward her, squinting in the sunlight. "I think you are also not looking to be married or surely you would be by now. You are beautiful and intelligent, everything a man would want in a wife."

Louisa was taken aback and then annoyed with herself. She shouldn't be asking this man about his marriage plans. Stay focused, she told herself.

"I understand you were in Egypt last year," she said. "What was that like?"

"Hot and dry. Merciless," he said.

"Then why go?" she asked, attempting a light-hearted tone.

"We were in Alexandria on behalf of our uncle to find a market for his lesser wines."

"Lesser wines?" Louisa asked.

"Ones that even the Americans don't want," he said.

"Did you find a market?" Louisa asked, ignoring the dig at the provincial tastes of Americans.

"No," Simon shook his head. "The businessmen we spoke with are worried about a war in Europe. They wish to get into the arms business, not the wine business."

"War?" Louisa asked. She'd heard rumors, but there were always rumors of war among the Europeans.

"You know how you can smell the rain before it falls?" he asked. She nodded. "It is the same way with war. There is something in the air. War will come. I do not know when or exactly where, but it will come."

"If your trip was unsuccessful, how were you able to pay off your debts when you returned?" she asked.

He stared at her.

"Why do you want to know?" he asked. "Is this one of your investigations? How do you even know about our debts?"

She took a deep breath. She'd been stupid and obvious.

"I apologize. I shouldn't have brought it up. It's just that Mr. Griffin mentioned it to me. He's, of course, concerned about Daphne and wants to know more about the man she is marrying," she said.

"So you are investigating Henri?"

"No, not really," she said. "Why can't I simply be curious?"

He leaned back on his elbow and gazed up at her.

"*Bien*. My uncle paid our debts as soon as he knew Henri was going to ask Daphne to marry him. He wants to establish an import business in America and Henri's new connections will be useful. That's the answer to your mystery. Is your curiosity satisfied? Is that not why you came out with me today?"

His jaw had hardened and he gazed out at the sea.

"No," she admitted, softly. "I came out with you today because I wanted to."

He turned and looked at her. Her eyes traveled down the planes of his cheeks. His lips were full and inviting.

"May I ask you a personal question, one that has nothing to do with Henri?" she said.

"Yes, you may," he said.

"Veronique Ribault?" she asked. "Are you and she...friends?"

"I would not say we are friends," he said. "She and my brother were once close. She was his first."

That was not what she expected.

"Does Daphne know?" Louisa asked. Surely she wouldn't allow the woman to be here if she knew.

"No. Veronique will behave. She has promised me," he said.

"I see. You're always looking out for him then?" Louisa asked.

"Always," Simon said. He picked up her book which had slipped from her bag. "What is this book you have?"

"I'm writing a feature piece on birds. I hope to enlighten the ladies that feathers belong on birds' bodies, not on our hats." She felt a wave of relief that the subject had changed and that Simon had answered her questions.

He thumbed through the pages. "I see you have some of them marked."

"Yes," she said and leaned over. "These are all the birds I want to see while I'm here. I'm desperate to see a roseate spoonbill. Such a strange looking creature. Its bill really does have a spoon shape, but its feathers are the loveliest shade of pink."

"It is," he said. Their heads were only inches apart, both of them with their hands on the book, and it sounded as if her heart was beating as loud as cannon-fire in her ears.

"We should get back," she said, sitting up. "It will be time for dinner soon."

They strolled to the depot and waited for the train back to the mainland. He told her stories of his childhood in France. She found it fascinating how similar their stories were. They had both been born into privileged circumstances and both had lost their standing in society quite young in life, and through no fault of their own.

"My father died in some insane war in western Africa," he told her. "I was five and remember almost nothing of the man. *Maman* was always sickly. Henri and I were orphans when he was eight and I was ten."

Louisa placed her hand on his in sympathy. His hand felt warm and strong underneath hers.

When they returned to the Florida House, she found a cable from Ellen: "Nothing on Henri Bassett. Alexandria in news once in Oct. Half million dollar diamond theft. No one caught."

Louisa folded the cable and put it in her bag. She found Simon waiting for her at the elevator.

"News?" Simon asked as they boarded the elevator.

"Oh, nothing of any interest," she said.

"Will you be dining with the Griffins? Or going to another masquerade dance with Lord Wickham tonight?" he asked.

"How did you know about that?" she asked. "You weren't even there."

He touched his nose and said, "You are not the only one who knows how to ask questions."

"I'm planning to get caught up on my columns and go to bed early. Tomorrow I'm to traipse around after Daphne and her sister and show them having a grand time in dear old St. Augustine. We society writers must appease the brides' mothers now and again, and Mrs. Griffin will think she's died and gone to heaven when she sees her daughters on the society page of *The Ledger.*"

The elevator doors opened on the third floor. They stood at the intersection of the two halls.

"Then I hope you will consent to do more sight-seeing with me, Louisa," he said. "I enjoyed today. Or will you be too busy now that I have satisfied your curiosity?"

"I can find other things to be curious about," she said, amazed at her boldness.

He looked into her eyes long enough to cause her to blush. She turned away and hurried toward her room. She had flirted with Simon, she thought. She couldn't remember flirting with any man. She wasn't sure she even knew who she was any more.

She sat down at her writing table, ready to write about the lighthouse and the oyster roast while it was still fresh in her mind. She looked again at Ellen's cable. Stolen diamonds from Alexandria? Surely, that was just a coincidence. As she picked up her fountain pen, she remembered the giant jewel-like lens in the lighthouse tower. The image in her mind's eye transformed into a diamond on a gold chain dangling from a woman's neck.

Chapter 20

Ellen

Early in the morning Ellen came out of Louisa's house, down the steps, and headed toward the subway station when the sight of a familiar face startled her.

"Becky?" she asked. "What are you doing here?"

"Came to see where you lived," she said. She wore a black skirt with a ruffled white shirt and a longish jacket. "Is that your rooming house?"

"No," Ellen said. "I got a night job, looking after an old lady while her daughter is out of town. It's only temporary, but I need the extra money as my *da* is sick and hasn't been able to work."

"That's kind of you to help out your family back home," Becky said, squinting her eyes as she looked up at the house.

"How did you find me?" Ellen asked.

"Charlie followed you last night," Becky said.

"Why would he do that?" Ellen asked, squelching the tremor in her voice as she wondered what else they knew about her.

"Look, if you're going to be involved with us, we need to make sure you're on the up and up."

"Why wouldn't I be?" Ellen asked. "What would I have to gain?"

"Well, it is known you've been seen with one of those fancy ladies. She's the sister-in-law of John Murphy, isn't she? And isn't he the president of a company that makes weapons?"

Ellen's breath hunkered down in her lungs as if afraid to give her away. She'd no idea what Hester's brother-in-law made.

"I don't know about any of that. I met her at the Women's March in Washington last year. She took a fancy to me, and I to her. She's not like the others. She's a socialist. She's always going on about this Eugene Debs fellow."

"Socialists," Becky scoffed. "As if incremental reform ever got anyone anywhere. They have no backbone, and they aren't willing to fight for their beliefs. You're right to come to our side, Ellen."

Ellen decided not to argue the point. She needed to get rid of Becky somehow.

"It's been nice to see you, Becky, but I'm late to work," she said.

"That's fine. I'll go with you. Their office is downtown, isn't it? *The Gaelic American*?"

"Yes," Ellen said slowly, wondering how to play this as they walked down the street together.

She cursed herself for not having gone by *The Gaelic American* earlier to meet the editor and inform him of her subterfuge. She was a real *leathcheann,* her father would have said, an idiot. She had, of course, seen the building once or twice but she couldn't swear she knew how to get there.

They passed a newsstand and on an impulse, Ellen purchased a copy of *The Gaelic American*.

"Do you have to buy your own paper?" Becky asked. "I should think you'd get it for free."

"It's only a nickel, and I like to look over it on the train before I go in so I know what to expect," she said, quickly glancing on the inside page for an address. Then she saw it: 165-167 William Street. "For example, here's a story on Father Phelan's upcoming lecture. I'll have to follow up on that and get notes from his secretary."

They reached the subway station and bought their tickets, went down the stairs, and found two rattan-covered seats. They sat side by side as the train ricocheted through the city. Becky chatted cheerfully about how brilliant her "Sasha" was, how corrupt Rockefeller was, and how someday they'd live in a world where the workers controlled everything.

"You'll see. We'll have laws to prevent little children from working in the factories, and we'll have five-day work weeks. Workers will own the means of production."

Ellen didn't disagree with the sentiment, but it all seemed like a pipe dream to her. A beggar came on the train, but a cop ran him off at the next stop.

"Do you like your job?" Becky asked. "What exactly is it that you do?"

"I'm what they call a Girl Friday. I do errands, take notes for stories over the phone. That kind of thing. Like Sweet Sal does for *Mother Earth*."

"That's interesting because Charlie said he saw you coming out of *The Ledger*," Becky said. "The same newspaper where that society writer works."

Ellen's pulse raced.

"*The Ledger*? I thought the woman who was killed worked for *The Herald*," Ellen said.

"The bullet was intended for Louisa Delafield. At least that's what she seemed to think when she wrote that nasty article about us. *She* works for *The Ledger*," Becky said.

Ellen swallowed hard, and tried to stall for time.

"You mean that paper on 34th Street?" she asked.

"That's right."

"You know, I did go there recently. Sometimes our reporters have a story they want to reach a wider audience. The editor doesn't care as long as it's not something he wants to print. I went there to give some copy to their business writer from our newsroom," Ellen said. "Like I said, I do a lot of different things."

"I see," Becky said.

The train finally stopped at City Hall, and they walked toward William Street. When they reached William Street, Ellen turned left. Looking at the street numbers she immediately realized her error. She looked behind her.

"Don't you know where you're going?" Becky asked, suspicion lodged in her voice.

"Sure, I do. I'm after getting some tooth powder from the apothecary," she said, turning abruptly into an apothecary on the corner. Becky followed her as she purchased the tooth powder that she did not need. They went back outside, and Ellen turned in the right direction this time.

Becky interlocked her arm with Ellen's as they walked.

"I can't wait to see the inside of your newspaper office, Ellen," Becky said.

"Oh, you can't come inside. It's not so loosey-goosey as *Mother Earth*. You'd need a legitimate reason," Ellen said, trying to quell the panic in her chest.

They reached a stone entrance with the words The Reed Building at the top and glass doors leading to the lobby at street level. This was it, Ellen realized. Becky stuck out her lip.

"Not even if I'm your guest?" she asked.

"I'm not a reporter, girleen. I don't get to have guests. Besides, there's nothing to see but a bunch of men in shirt sleeves, smoking their cigarettes and yelling at the poor copy boy. I'll see you at the Worker's March," Ellen said and disentangled herself from Becky's clasp. A woman approached the door of the building, and Ellen smiled brightly and said, "I'll be up in a minute."

The woman smiled politely, and Ellen turned to Becky.

"Thank you for making my journey to work a little more interesting today," she said. "You can tell Charlie not to worry about me. And my connection with that socialist you disdain may actually be more useful than any of you realize."

She entered the building confidently, waving to the doorman as if they were old friends. "Top of the morning," she said.

He tipped his cap as any good Irishman would and said, "Top of the morning to you."

She felt Becky's eyes on her as she got on the elevator. When she turned around and faced outward, she saw Becky smile and saunter off. The elevator doors closed and Ellen sighed. She nearly collapsed from the tension and decided this was a good time to introduce herself to the editor of *The Gaelic American*.

Chapter 21

Louisa

Louisa and Suzie sat at the small table in her room as the waiter placed a silver coffee set and a basket of muffins on the table. He was an older man and looked at the two of them curiously.

"You two don't seem like a mistress and servant," he said. "Wouldn't any maid I know of sit at the table with her employer."

"You have a point," Suzie said to the man. "Even white servants in New York wouldn't be caught dead sitting at table with their employers. But what the rest of the world doesn't know won't hurt them."

"Suzie has been my family's housekeeper since I was a baby," Louisa said. "After my father died, we were more like partners in survival."

"Word of advice, don't let anyone in this town see you two being chummy. They make a mighty fine show of accepting us 'darkies,' but it's only a show," he said. He left them to their breakfast.

Louisa and Suzie shared a glance. They were both remembering the humiliation of the library. And yet, Louisa knew it wasn't only in the South where the old ways held sway. Louisa thought of all the years when Suzie had run the household and managed their budget, but it was only last year that Louisa had insisted that she sit at the dining table with her and her mother for dinner. *If you say she's like family, then you must treat her like family,* Louisa had told her mother. Now Suzie had found her true family.

"Tell me all about them," Louisa said as she buttered one of the muffins.

Suzie beamed.

"Polly is George's oldest daughter. He's got two others who live just a block away. Polly has a daughter named Pansy, who is sixteen going on thirty. Her sister, Irene, has a ten year old and a two year old. That two-year-old child is *too much,"* she said with a grin. "Lloyd, for some reason, never married."

"What was it like to see him?" Louisa asked.

"I wept copiously. He did, too. I hadn't seen him since he was six. But I knew him. I knew his eyes, I even knew his voice."

"How did George die?"

"Heart attack. I'm sorry I didn't get to see him before he died, but his daughters are wonderful and there are so many grand-nephews and -nieces I haven't met yet. They'll be there today."

"I'm so happy you found them, and I'm sorry I was such a dunderhead when you first mentioned a family, Suzie," Louisa said.

"You were a dunderhead, but I forgive you," Suzie said. "What about you? You seem mighty distracted."

Louisa showed her the cable from Ellen.

"Lord Wickham claims he loaned Henri the money to buy Daphne's diamond, but that had to be close to $20,000. I like him very much, but I'm not sure I believe him," she said.

"So you think Daphne's diamond might be one of the stolen Egyptian diamonds?" Suzie asked, pointing to the cable.

"I don't know what to think," she said. "Perhaps I'm inventing a mystery where there is none so that I don't have to think about New York and ...."

The cathedral bells chimed for the half hour.

"Oh! I have to go," she said. "I'm supposed to meet Daphne and her sister this morning."

She quickly dressed in a pinstriped daydress, complaining that she still needed to go out and buy something more suitable for the weather.

At 9:00 a.m. sharp Louisa climbed a twin staircase to the terrace at the Alcazar. Daphne and her sister stood there, waiting in white linen dresses. Daphne's sash was gold, and her sister's was blue. They looked as if they belonged in a French painting. A maid behind them held onto a cloth valise.

"Did you bring a bathing costume?" Daphne's sister, Margaret, asked. She was about sixteen and plain like her older sister.

"I did not," she said. "I wasn't planning on swimming." Louisa had been in the ocean but she'd never swum in a swimming pool.

"Don't you know how to swim?" Margaret asked with a note of condescension in her voice. These Chicago heiresses seemed to look down on everyone.

"I've got a spare one you can use," Daphne said. This surprised Louisa but she accepted the offer.

She followed them inside and stared at the giant indoor cavern where the sparkling blue pool stretched the length. Natural light from the skylights above flooded the space. Arches soared to the height of the casino. She had seen it twice before, of course, but there was nothing like standing at one end and contemplating swimming in it.

"They say the water comes from an artesian well," Daphne said as they walked along the surrounding arcade to the dressing room, passing a row of concrete arches extending the full height of the casino from the bottom of the pool to the ballroom above.

The arcade provided access to dressing rooms where Louisa donned the bathing costume, a knee-length one piece that was actually quite comfortable, if more revealing than anything ladies wore out in public. Fortunately, only ladies were allowed in the pool until two in the afternoon. Then the men took over. Louisa stepped slowly into the silky delight of the water and then did an awkward breast stroke across the pool. It was much easier to swim in the gentle water of the pool than it ever had been in that rough beast, the Atlantic Ocean, where she had learned to dog paddle just well enough to keep from drowning if she accidentally got in over her head.

Daphne swam up next to her with long elegant strokes.

"Race you!" Daphne said.

Louisa couldn't possibly win, and she splashed about in an ungainly manner. Her hair, which had been carefully coiled into a pompadour that morning, held into place with pins and a barrette, spilled out of its confines and drooped into the water. Surprised, Louisa slipped under the surface for a moment, and her long hair swam freely only to wrap itself around her upper arms.

"Help!" she called out, batting at the water with her hands. Panic seized her and she sank under the surface again. Then she felt a hand under her chin.

"Roll over and stay still," Daphne commanded her.

Louisa complied, and with strong steady strokes, Daphne pulled her to the side of the pool where Louisa disentangled herself from her hair and then looked over at Daphne hanging onto the edge of the pool.

"Thank you," Louisa said, utterly mortified.

"You owe me, Miss Society Writer," Daphne said. "I saved your life, and you can repay me by leaving my wedding alone."

"Your what?" Louisa asked, but Daphne had already climbed out of the pool and was walking toward the dressing room.

Louisa made her way to the steps and climbed out of the pool. An attendant handed her a towel and asked, "Are you all right, Miss?"

Louisa took the towel but didn't answer. She went to the dressing room and found Daphne's maid helping her into her dress.

"What do you mean, leave your wedding alone?" Louisa asked.

"I overheard Father telling Mother that he hired you to investigate Henri," Daphne said and shot her an accusing look.

"He did not hire me. He merely asked me to make sure you weren't making a mistake."

"A mistake? You're the one who will be making a mistake if you try to stop me from marrying the man I want," Daphne said, stepping close to her, dragging her maid who was trying to tie her sash in the back. "I will not have my life ruined by a meddling old maid."

With that Daphne turned away from Louisa and walked out of the room with her sash untied and her maid and her sister hurrying after her.

Thoroughly dispirited, Louisa got dressed and found a ribbon to hold back her sopping hair. Maybe Daphne was right. Maybe she was a meddling old maid. She looked at herself in one of the gilt-framed mirrors. She was twenty-five years old, ancient compared to a debutante. As she studied her reflection, she remembered something the concierge had told her on her first visit to the Alcazar. There was an indoor archery range under the pool. She decided she could wait until later to write her article — after all, what could she say except that Daphne Griffin was an excellent swimmer with the skills of a life-guard.

With the help of a bellman, she found the archery range. No one else was there except for a bored attendant sitting on a stool next to a cabinet lined with lacquered wooden bows nearly as tall as she and leather quivers, filled with arrows.

It had been years since Louisa and her friends had practiced with bows and arrows in the backyard of the Breakers at Newport, but she'd been the champion back then. After all, her zodiac sign, Sagittarius, was the archer. She wondered if she'd lost her touch.

Louise stood on a platform at one end of the range and notched the bright yellow arrow to the bowstring. She raised the bow, pointing her arrow toward the ceiling and then lowered it until she had the target in her sights. She steadied her breath, and with the string just inches from her cheek, she sighted the bull's eye and opened her hand. The arrow flew straight and swift, landing just on the edge of the bull's eye. A triumphant feeling instantly replaced the mortification she'd felt earlier. She practiced her archery for nearly an hour, relishing the feel of the bow in her hand and the satisfying sound of unleashed speed when she released the string.

Afterwards she went to a hairdressing salon in the shopping arcade.

"Chop it off," she told the hairdresser.

"Are you sure?" the woman asked. "You've a gorgeous thicket of it."

"Off," Louisa insisted.

Then she went for a long bicycle ride. At least for today she would not be a meddling old maid.

***

"Don't you look daring, Darling? I love your hair," Lord Wickham said when he found Louisa having dinner in the dining room of the Florida House that evening.

She invited him to join her for dessert and a cup of coffee.

"How about a little fun tonight?" he suggested. "I noticed you didn't dance the tango at the masquerade party the other night."

"That's because I don't know how," Louisa said.

"They're offering lessons at the Ponce," he said. "Care to join me?"

"I don't think so," Louisa said. She wasn't looking forward to running into Daphne so soon after their dust up.

"Think what a great topic this would be for your syndicated column. I'm sure women all over this vast land would like to know more about the exotic tango," he said and held his arms out and snapped his fingers as if he were a dashing young *Milonguero*, instead of a pudgy Englishman.

"Have you been reading my columns?" she asked.

"I have. All the New York papers are sold here," he said with a Cheshire-cat grin. "I even read the one where you excoriated the anarchists. Good show, old girl. So how about it? Tango lessons."

"All right," Louisa gave in.

Louisa looked in Suzie's room, but she had not yet returned. The family reunion must be going well, she thought as she donned a drapey, satin, ivory dress with a red-and-gold overlay.

When she and Lord Wickham arrived at the ballroom of the Ponce, she looked around for Simon. He was nowhere to be seen.

As couples took to the dance floor, a man with a Spanish accent explained, "Men move your left foot forward and to the side, ladies move your right foot back and to the side."

Slowly but surely the dancers learned the steps. Lord Wickham was a natural. He scissored and cortezed like an adept. Louisa wasn't bad herself. Just a couple of years ago, many of New York's ladies had declared the dance "wicked." Now it was all the rage. Even Charlie Chaplin tried to dance it in one of his moving pictures.

"Percival, were you in Egypt when those diamonds were stolen?" Louisa asked when they went outside for some air.

"Diamonds?" he asked.

"Yes, I was just remembering that I'd read about it somewhere. It was such a vast amount that it made the international news," she said.

"No, I don't remember anything about it," he said.

"I thought given your interests . . ." she said.

"My interests are strictly in antiquities, dear girl," he said. "I need more Champagne. You?"

They strolled back into the ballroom and found a waiter with a tray of Champagne glasses.

As she sipped her drink, she followed Lord Wickham's gaze and saw him watching Daphne and Henri gliding through the room. His eyes were filled with longing. Was he in love with Daphne? Then why would he have given Henri the money to buy a diamond pendant for her?

Chapter 22

Ellen

According to the calendar, the day before was the first day of spring, but three inches of snow had fallen overnight and Ellen's toes were cold in her old shoes as she walked from the station to the newspaper office. Spring was nowhere in sight.

As she approached *The Ledger*, she glanced around to make sure Becky or Charlie weren't spying on her. She saw no one and so she walked inside and went to Louisa's desk. An envelope lay on the desk and inside she found it full of Louisa's stories — tango lessons, masquerade parties, street dances, and a bathing bride. The usual fluff but with a tropical flare.

She yawned. She'd had trouble sleeping, imagining that Becky or Charlie were onto her. Lulu believed in her, and Emma seemed to believe in everyone. Emma had an enormous heart, but the rest of them trusted no one — as well they shouldn't. She knew from her talks with Paddy that the police infiltrated any group they could, any way they could.

The less time she spent at *The Ledger* the better, so she typed the stories quickly and dropped them off with the typesetter. She found a back way out of the building by way of the presses. The noise was deafening and the huge rolls of paper smelled like dead leaves. The pressmen ignored her as she hurried past them to the open bays.

***

"Look who it is," Emma said when Ellen entered the offices of *Mother Earth*. The offices were located in a few rooms on the second floor of the building next to Emma's tenement — a far cry from the busy newsroom of *The Ledger*. "Does your editor know you're over here with the radicals?"

"As long as I get my typing and filing done, I'm free to do what I please. Besides, my supervisor is on vacation, and since the cat is away, the mouse would rather be here," Ellen smiled, taking off her coat and standing next to the radiator to capture its warmth.

"Someday we may be able to hire you, dear, but in the meantime, keep your job. We don't need another mouth to feed," she said. "Tell me, what do the editors of *The Gaelic* think of these war rumblings? Where will Ireland stand?"

"It won't be with Britain. That's all I know," Ellen said.

"We, of course, will oppose war in any form," Emma said. "So unnecessary, and yet generation after generation we send our young men to their deaths."

Ellen thought of her brothers. Michael had already joined the Irish Brigade. He'd been spoiling for a fight since the day he fell out of the cradle, but Martin was his father's son and there was only one fight he'd die for — Ireland's self-rule.

"Let's hope it doesn't come to that," Ellen said. She spied Lulu sitting behind a desk piled high with books and magazines, pecking out a story on a typewriter. Lulu looked up at her, eyes squinting in her cigarette smoke, and smiled that lopsided smile of hers. Ellen's heart lurched and the proverbial butterflies danced in her belly.

"I'm off to see the printer, my lovelies," Emma said. "If I can at least give him partial payment, we can enlighten the masses for another week."

She donned her coat and left them.

Ellen sat down on a battered old couch near the window. A pigeon marched along the windowsill.

"Are you going to the march of the unemployed with Frank and Becky tomorrow night?" Lulu asked, and tapped ash from her cigarette onto an overflowing ashtray.

"I am," Ellen answered. "Frank hopes I can convince one of the reporters at *The Gaelic American* to write about the conditions for the poor and the unemployed here. I don't think I can, but I'm taking notes anyway."

"Good girl," Lulu said. Lulu brushed her dark hair away from her face, lowered her eyelids and said in a dreamy voice, "Too bad you take care of that old lady at night."

"Why's that?" Ellen asked.

Lulu grinned at her. "Because I would like you to spend the night with me, Miss Malloy."

Ellen felt her knees go weak. She had no response, so she changed course.

"Becky walked me to work yesterday morning," she said. "Seems she and Charlie don't trust me."

"They wouldn't trust their own mothers if they said it was daylight outside. They'd have to go check for themselves," Lulu said and shrugged.

"Well, I think I may have found a way to earn their trust," Ellen said.

Lulu looked at her with raised eyebrows.

Ellen pulled out the invitation to Mrs. Rockefeller's benefit and tossed it across the desk to Lulu, who glanced at it and then chuckled.

"Aren't you a clever one?" Lulu said. "Karl should be here soon. Let's see what he thinks."

***

"An invitation to John D. Rockefeller's estate, Kykuit, in Tarrytown. Where did you get this?" Karl asked, handing the invitation back to Ellen.

"My wealthy friend," Ellen lied. "She received it yesterday."

She couldn't tell them she'd gotten it from the desk of his enemy, Louisa Delafield.

"What's the charity?" Lulu asked.

"Who cares?" Karl asked.

"I do," Lulu said.

Ellen read the invitation aloud, "Laura Spelman Rockefeller requests your attendance to a luncheon to help support the Spelman Seminary. The luncheon is to honor Mrs. Rockefeller's parents."

"What do you think?" Lulu asked Karl.

He leaned back in his chair, lit a cigarette, and shook the match to extinguish it.

"I think the time is ripe for a little propaganda of the deed," he said.

Ellen looked from one to the other. Had she finally earned Karl's trust?

Chapter 23

Louisa

"Louisa, you should leave well enough alone," Suzie said the next morning after Louisa relayed her suspicions. "Do not get involved in this."

"But Simon, Henri, and Lord Wickham were all in Egypt when that cache of diamonds was stolen," Louisa said. "And that diamond Henri gave Daphne is bright enough to blind a person."

"Your job is to write about these fancy people and how gay their lives are. It's a job you are good at," Suzie reminded her.

"You are the one who was bragging about my investigations to Simon Bassett," Louisa said.

"Well, I'm an old woman, and I ought not to open my mouth so often," she said. "Now, I'm going to visit with my family again, and I expect you to go do something frivolous and then write about it."

She impressively arched a single eyebrow as she glared at Louisa.

"Fine. Simon has invited me to go look at alligators with Henri and Daphne. Perhaps, I can somehow get in the girl's good graces. She seems to think I'm the enemy."

"Alligators? I'm sure that will excite your readers more than some would-be, may-be diamond thieves."

***

They piled into a brand-new, black Oldsmobile Phaeton, Daphne and Henri in the back and Louisa and Simon in front.

"Are you sure you know how to drive this motorcar, *mon frère*?" Henri called as Simon climbed behind the wheel and pushed the electric starter.

"We will find out," Simon said and put the car in gear.

The drive to the alligator farm took fifteen or so minutes. They didn't talk as it would have been impossible to hear each other over the wind and engine noise.

Once they reached the alligator farm, they walked around low-walled pens, filled with fat, gray monsters that lay unmoving or lumbered about on their small legs. There were ponds in each of the pens. The foursome stopped at a large concrete pen with almost a dozen of the prehistoric amphibians. Louisa shuddered looking at them. One was an albino alligator with horrid white, leathery skin.

"He would look nice on my feet," Simon said with a laugh.

Louisa had seen both bags and shoes made of alligator skin, highly prized because of its durability.

"I could never own a pair of alligator shoes after this," she said. "I'd never be able to get the image of those teeth out of my mind." She pointed to one of the long snouts with its teeth making a helter skelter fence around its jawline.

She had brought the camera with her, so she persuaded the betrothed couple to stand beside a giant stuffed alligator so she could take a picture. They looked solemnly at the camera and Louisa hoped the light hadn't been too bright. She was no expert at photography, but fortunately these new cameras required little knowledge of shutter speeds and all that.

Above them snowy egrets flitted in the trees.

"Do roseate spoonbills ever come here?" she asked one of the workers.

"Not often, Miss. They roost in the swamps," he said.

"The swamps?" she asked. "I suppose I'll never see one then."

"I will find you a roseate spoonbill, Louisa," Simon said. "It will be my duty as a recipient of the Legion of Honor to find the roosting spot for you."

Louisa looked at him in surprise. He grinned and she realized he was teasing. The Legion of Honor was given to deserving French citizens but only for remarkable achievements, and Monsieur Bassett was young yet.

Daphne waved a perfumed handkerchief in front of her nose to hide the pungent odor of the reptiles.

"They must be very slow," Daphne said. "Look at those little legs."

A young man with long, black hair pulled into a ponytail laughed. Louisa surmised that he was one of the Seminole Indians whom she'd heard about.

"They can run faster than you think," he said. "Faster than you."

Daphne shivered and backed into Henri's arms.

"I won't let them eat you, *chérie*," he said.

Simon leaned over the wall and observed one of the beasts, a creature about eight feet long with its eyes almost closed.

"Can they kill a human?" he asked the young man.

"Sure they can. And they do sometimes, but usually they go for something smaller. I've seen 'em snatch up a 'possum like it's a cupcake," he said and mimed eating a cupcake.

"Oh, dear," Louisa said. She wouldn't mention that detail in her column.

The young man pointed to a small amphitheater with wooden benches.

"Over there you can see the alligator wrestling," he said.

"*Magnifique!*" Henri exclaimed and squeezed a reluctant Daphne.

"Do they wrestle each other?" Daphne asked.

"No, we wrestle them. It's a Seminole tradition."

The men couldn't wait, and Louisa and Daphne followed.

A man missing his arm from the elbow down guided them to a sort of arena for the wrestling show. The most frightening aspect was when a young man pried the beast's jaws apart. The alligator then seemed to freeze, its enormous mouth wide open, a giant white tongue laid out between the teeth lining either side.

The young man reached in the mouth and flicked the back of the tongue, drawing out his hand just before the jaws snapped shut with a loud clap. Daphne and Louisa both let out a little yelp and then giggled in relief as the young man stood up and raised both arms.

Then he pointed at the man with the one arm and shook his head.

"The old man wasn't fast enough," he told the crowd.

"Your day will come," the old man rejoindered.

***

"That was fun," Henri said as they rode back to the hotel.

"I expect to have nightmares," Louisa said, and yet she was glad she had joined them on this excursion, for Daphne seemed to have warmed up to her. Of course, Louisa had found nothing to discredit her fiancé besides a vague suspicion about stolen diamonds. Could Henri have been involved? And if so, did that mean that Simon was also involved?

"I've been meaning to ask you about your beautiful diamond pendant, Daphne," Louisa said. "The cut is exquisite. Is it very old?"

"No," she answered. "I believe Henri purchased it from Boucheron in Paris. *N'est pas, chéri*?"

"*Oui*," he said. "Only the best for my future wife." He stroked her cheek and she blushed.

"I see," Louisa said. She had heard of Frederic Boucheron, whose designs were world famous. It would be easy enough to contact them and learn more.

When they got back to the hotel, Louisa asked Daphne if she could photograph her for her newspaper article.

"Let's meet in Madame Ribault's atelier. The light is excellent there. Don't forget to wear your diamond," Louisa said.

***

In the dressing room, Daphne stood on a small dais in an exquisite gown that Madame Ribault furnished for the occasion. Louisa looked at Daphne's reflection in the mirror. Her brown hair had been skillfully sculpted by her maid into a fluffy coiffure. Madame Ribault sat at her sewing machine, working on a gown.

"I see you've chopped off your locks," Daphne observed as Louisa set the Kodak camera on a table to keep it steady and unfolded it so the lens jutted forward like a Cyclops.

"I didn't want to take a chance on drowning again," Louisa said.

"You are a clever one," Daphne said. "Have you gotten the goods, so to speak, on Henri?"

"No, I haven't," she said. She steadied the camera and shot a picture. "I suppose you can explain where he got the money for that diamond," Louisa said, pointing to the glittering pendant. She took another photograph. The film cartridge only held eight shots so she wanted to make sure each one was good.

"I believe he borrowed it from Lord Wickham," Daphne said, and touched the jewel that rested on her breast bone. "He can pay him back after we're married."

"Why do you want to marry Henri?" Louisa asked. "I'm sure you could marry someone with a fortune to match your own."

Daphne pointed to her reflection. "That's why."

Louisa was confused.

"Look at me. I'm plain. All my life I've been plain. You have no idea how the pretty girls lord it over us ordinary-looking girls. The year I came out, Betsy Filmore and June Delaney and four other beauties also came out. It was so humiliating. Eligible men walked right past me as if I were one of the servants. Oh, a few of them danced with me out of pity, and they called on the family out of form's sake, but the only man who showed any real interest in me was a forty-year-old widowed banker with three brats I would have been expected to raise. I'm not being glib. Those were the worst behaved children you've ever seen. I'd happily feed them to those alligators."

Louisa was stunned. It had never occurred to her that being plain would hamper a young woman as wealthy as Daphne.

"You, for example,...." Daphne wheeled around and gazed at Louisa.

"I'm not beautiful," Louisa protested.

"Not beautiful, perhaps, but you are pretty and you have something else. Your intelligence and breeding gives you that superior demeanor, which beauty pales next to," Daphne said. "All you have to do is open your mouth and men lean forward, eager to hear your thoughts. Look at how Simon can't take his eyes off you."

Again Louisa was at a loss. Was this true?

"I'm clever enough," Daphne continued, returning her gaze to her own reflection, "but I'm not what you would call smart. Our family is new money so I don't have that *je ne sais quoi* of the blue bloods. But new money is still money, so I can buy beauty and breeding."

"But at what cost?" Louisa asked.

"Cost? Miss Delafield, think of the children I will have," Daphne said. She stood up a little straighter and raised her chin.

Louisa saw the logic of Daphne's move.

"They will be adorable little aristocrats, and they will be mine," she said. Her eyes already gleamed with pride for the attractive children she would one day bear. "And their behavior will be impeccable."

Louisa grudgingly admired Daphne, who had been raised to be a wife and a mother and had few other options. She would seize her role and she would excel at it.

***

That evening the bridesmaids arrived, and Louisa had to go to the bridesmaids' dinner. The six of them sounded like parakeets as they chattered and squealed and gossiped. They regarded Louisa with a sort of awe – a society writer from New York! And they took turns grilling her about luminaries such as Elsie Rockefeller and Edna Woolworth.

"I wish I lived in New York," one of them pined.

Another claimed that Chicago was a big enough pond for her, and said that the men in the Midwest were more manly than New York men.

"But none of them quite so dashing as Henri," a plump blonde said, and they all agreed that Daphne had captured Prince Charming.

"I hear he's a duke," one of them whispered.

"No, he's a count. Or a baron," another corrected.

Louisa thought the dinner would never end, but it finally did. She went to her room and knocked on Suzie's door. There was no answer. She leaned her ear against the door and heard nothing. She turned the doorknob quietly and looked inside the room. It was dark but enough moonlight streamed through the window that she could see no one was there. She turned on the light to be sure. Suzie's bed was empty.

What could have happened to her, she wondered. A wave of guilt washed over her. Perhaps something had happened to Suzie when she'd gone to see her family.

Louisa remembered the waiter's remark about attitudes towards Negroes here. She also remembered the many news stories over the years of lynchings. Just two years ago a mob had raped and hanged a Negro woman in Oklahoma, and apparently Florida, along with Georgia, was the worst place in country for the horrid practice. She should never have let Suzie go off alone.

She went to her room and paced the floor, wondering what she should do. A half hour passed but still Suzie had not come back. It was ten o'clock at night. Much too late for Suzie to be wandering the streets. Maybe she'd gotten lost? She'd said herself she was getting older.

Louisa couldn't pace around the hotel room another minute. She must go find her, but what risk would *she* be taking out alone at night?

She grabbed a wrap and went into the hallway. She remembered quite well seeing the number on Simon Bassett's key when they first checked in. It had been seared into her mind. She found room 314 and knocked tentatively. What would he think when he opened the door and saw her standing there? She didn't have to wait long to find out. The door opened and Simon stood, fully dressed, eyes wide, wiping sweat from his forehead.

"Louisa?" he asked.

"I'm so sorry to disturb you but Suzie is gone, and I need help finding her," she said.

"Suzie?" he asked, confused. He wiped his brow with his handkerchief.

"My companion, Miss Blake," Louisa said.

"But of course, I will help you find her," he said.

They left the Florida House, and Louisa took one last look up at her room to see if the light was on, if perhaps Suzie had come back while she'd gone to find

Simon. Her room and the adjoining one were dark, but above them on the fourth floor a man stood on one of the balconies, the lights in his room silhouetting him. He raised a hand and waved at her. It was Lord Wickham, she realized with chagrin. Would he be gossiping about her and Simon tomorrow? She couldn't worry about that. It was more important to find Suzie.

The night air was cool, but her wrap kept her comfortable. They went to the police station first. The officer there said they couldn't do anything till the morning and Louisa should come back then.

"Do you have a city directory?" she asked.

"What sort of police department would we be if we didn't have a city directory?" he said and brought out a volume from under the desk. She looked up the address for Lloyd Carpenter.

"It's on Oneida Street," she said. That couldn't be too far since Suzie had walked over there and back.

"That's in Lincolnville where the darkies live," the policeman said. "They don't cause much trouble. And the streets are lit." He gave them directions and they left.

They walked through the historic district and over to a bridge that led across a wide creek, shimmering like a cache of jewels in the moonlight. She heard the sound of Simon's breath as they walked.

After they crossed the bridge, they passed a butcher shop, a beauty salon, and a brick church. They crossed each street, checking the street signs, until they found Oneida Street where they turned onto a residential street of small tidy yards, and one- and two-storey houses with front porches and balconies. Through a window, they saw a woman pacing back and forth with a crying baby. At the next house, a man sat on a porch, playing a banjo, singing softly.

It was difficult to see the street numbers in the dark, but finally she was able to read one of them. She picked up her pace and in a moment she could smell roses. This was it, just as Suzie had described — a blue house with white trim, easy to see in the cascade of moonlight.

They climbed the couple of steps to a screen door, and she heard a gentle snoring. She opened the screen door quietly and entered the porch. There was Suzie, eyes closed, in a large chair with a sleeping child in her lap. Louisa's mouth dropped open, and she placed a hand over her heart. She felt Simon behind her. Quietly she turned and nudged him back out.

She gently shut the screen and then hurried down the street. They said nothing until they were a few houses away and then she burst out laughing from relief.

"So beautiful," Louisa said. "I wish I had a painting of it."

"Was that her grandchild?" Simon asked.

"No, she's never had children. I suppose it's her brother's grandchild or maybe great-grandchild." She stopped, took a breath and then wiped some tears away. She turned to Simon. "I'm sorry I got you out of bed. It was silly of me to worry so."

"I wasn't in bed. I was doing my nightly regimen of fifty push-ups," he said. "And I was glad to help you."

"Fifty push-ups?" she asked. "I didn't know the French were so conscientious about fitness."

"Most of them aren't, but I cannot afford weakness," he said.

"Really? Why is that?"

"We were always looked down upon. *Peut-être* because my father was the older brother, the one entitled to be called 'Baron.' So I had to look out for Henri."

"Once he is married, won't you be free of that burden?"

"An older brother is never free of his familial obligations," he said.

They walked back through the balmy, velvety night. Even in the summer, the air never felt like this in New York. She took his arm as they traversed the empty streets. The relief had left her feeling so light she felt she might levitate. They did not walk directly back to the hotel, but found themselves meandering alongside the creek.

"Look," he said, pointing towards the sky.

A long beam of light swept across the horizon.

"The Fresnel lamp," she whispered.

She turned and looked at him. He stood close to her, his eyes resting on her lips. Then they leaned toward each other and kissed — a kiss that set every nerve in her body afire.

She pulled back and gazed at his slender face; he had not shaved since the morning, and his chin and cheeks were covered with a dark stubble. His eyes searched hers. Then without a word, they continued walking, as if stopping for a kiss were the most natural thing in the world. Her lips tingled with pleasure.

They walked down Cordova Street past the Alcazar and then past the Ponce to the narrow cobblestone Treasury Street and turned right. She felt Simon's body close to hers as they walked down the darkened street and felt a fierce longing. It did not matter that she was the society writer and women's page editor for a prestigious newspaper. It did not matter that she was intimately involved with another man. This desire had a power all its own. The cathedral bells chimed 11:00.

Footsteps hurried toward them and Louisa looked up startled.

A man crossed the street to avoid them but in the light of the gas lamp she could see it was Henri.

Simon inhaled sharply.

"*Pardon,* Louisa," he said. He hurried over to his brother.

"Henri," he said. "*Arrête.*"

Henri turned and faced him.

"*Es fini*!" he said. "*Fini*!"

Simon drew close to his brother. She could not hear what they said, but she could tell Henri was upset. Something was apparently finished, but what?

Simon returned to her.

"Forgive me, Louisa. My brother has had...," he searched for a word, "*la dispute* with Veronique. I believe she wanted one more fling with him. I need to be with him now. We are only one block from the hotel. You will be safe, getting back, no?"

"I'll be fine," she said. "Take care of your brother."

She left him with a pang of disappointment mixed with relief. She had come close to doing something morally reprehensible. She was in a relationship with Forrest, and she'd almost invited another man to her bed. She was not so old fashioned to believe that sex should be confined to the marriage bed, but Forrest trusted her. Unlike Veronique Ribault, Louisa did not intend to be a duplicitous woman.

As she approached the hotel, she looked up at the fourth floor, wondering if Lord Wickham would be watching for her. Returning by herself should quell any suspicions he might have. Not that it was any of his business, but society women, as well as society writers were held to certain standards, and she did want to avoid any appearance of impropriety. But his room was dark.

When she got to her room, she sat down at her writing desk and composed a letter.

Dear Forrest,

I am deeply sorry for what I am about to say, but I wish to end our...

She couldn't think of what it was they had. A liaison? An affair? She finally resorted to "understanding." She continued.

There is nothing you have done, but we both know that our understanding is not appropriate. You are the publisher of the paper for which I work. I believe in the future we should confine our relationship to a professional one. Please do not think this is a reflection on you or in any way diminishes my deep respect for you. You have been a true gentleman and I will always think of you fondly.

Regretfully,

Louisa

She folded the letter, placed it in an envelope, and addressed it to Forrest Calloway. She would send it in the morning. Her heart was heavy when she lay down in bed, but she knew she had done the right thing. She did care deeply for Forrest, but she feared she had clung to him as a father figure, someone who would protect her, who offered security. And if there was even a chance she might be intimate with another man, she must do so with a clear conscience. Try as she might, she didn't think she could resist the advances of Simon Bassett. Even now, her body tingled with anticipation.

Chapter 24

Ellen

Hester showed up promptly at 5:00. As they stood in the foyer, Ellen could hardly look her in the eye.

"Thank you so much for coming over, Hester," Ellen said, slipping on her old wool coat, and pulling her felt hat over her hair.

"Why won't you look at me?" Hester asked, gently. "Ellen, where are you going?"

At first, Ellen evaded the question. Then she finally admitted she was going to one of Frank Tennenbaum's marches of the Army of the Unemployed. He had told her that the marches had been successful so far. The Church of the Messiah had provided dinner and shelter for the men just last week. But Frank worried that eventually blood would be shed. His blood. If he were hurt, she felt she had to be there. She finally understood the stories of Christ from all those Sunday school lessons. There was something utterly compelling about a person so selfless and so brave.

"I thought you were trying to infiltrate the anarchists," Hester said with obvious disapproval. "What does the I.W.W. have to do with finding Louisa's shooter?"

"The anarchists and the International Workers are closely connected. Becky will be there, and right now, she's my chief suspect," Ellen said. "And if you saw these poor men, Hester. I just feel I must bear witness. This is history in the making."

Ellen worried that following Frank was a distraction from her real mission, even if Becky would also be there. She was like Alice falling into a rabbit hole. The I.W.W. had nothing to do with the attempt on Louisa's life. The worst of it was that surely Paddy would want information from her. Then again, what was there to tell? Frank was an open book. He wasn't skulking around in alleys waiting to bomb a millionaire's mansion like Karl and Charlie and their ilk. He simply wanted the powerful forces in the country to take care of the workers.

"It's a way to gain trust," Ellen said. "If they see me marching with these downtrodden men and women, then they'll know I'm on the right side."

"Is it the right side?" Hester asked.

Ellen didn't answer. She stuck her head in the parlor and said good-bye to Anna, who was thrilled to have Hester stay with her for a while.

***

The lower realms of Manhattan always confused her — the streets that criss-crossed at strange angles and had names instead of numbers. She followed East Broadway past shops and businesses until she saw

Rutgers Square. Frank had told her to meet him at the Seward Park Library, which she found across the street.

He was inside at a table, reading the *Wall Street Journal,* turning the pages with his one good hand.

"It's important to keep abreast of the enemy," he said with a smile. He was always smiling, always unfailingly polite. She'd heard from Sweet Sal that he treated the ministers at the churches where the Army of the Unemployed had gone with great respect.

"I wish I could help," Ellen said.

"If you can somehow get us some positive press, that would be enormous," he said and held up the paper, tapping it with the back of his mangled hand. "See, the rich man needs to keep a supply of the desperate at the ready. And the papers like to keep the rich man happy, so if the poor or the unemployed man dare to show a little spine, then it's important to tell the masses that this is a great evil arising. Most of these newspapers are there to do the bidding of the rich. And they goad the police into doing their bidding. And the poor man gets crushed, time and again."

"Then why bother?" Ellen asked.

"Because we have no choice. Even if we lose, we must stand up. We must demand. Eventually we will win something. Then the rich man will find some other way to cheat us. And the battle begins all over again. It's an endless cycle," he said. "But I do think that progress — even if a little — is possible. The fight for justice is eternal."

"Today the rich man is Rockefeller," she said. "Tomorrow he'll be someone else. He's a black hole of greed and I s'pose he can't help himself."

As a servant, Ellen had seen ostentatious wealth. She'd heard her employer scoff at the poor. She knew they liked to toss bread crumbs to the needy. It made them feel magnanimous. But crumbs weren't enough to keep a body alive.

"Which church will you take your army to tonight?" she asked.

"St. Alphonsus," he said.

"I've seen it," she said. "The church has no shortage of money if that building is any proof." It was an amazing building to look upon with its gilt altar, said to cost $12,000, its numerous stained glass windows, and its green marble pillars.

The door to the library opened and in walked Charlie and Becky. Unlike the workers, Charlie always dressed like a swell. He seemed to think himself quite handsome. Becky and Charlie traveled in both circles – the anarchists and the I.W.W. Ellen got the sense that Charlie wasn't attracted so much by the ideals as he was by the promise of mayhem.

"Frank, they're gathering," he said in a low voice. "Looks like hundreds of 'em."

Frank looked pleased.

Becky sat next to her, her dress just short enough to show off her bright red stockings.

"You know you could get hurt, don't ya?" Becky asked Ellen.

"I've the meanest older brother to ever come out of the Claddagh," Ellen said. "I've had my share of bruises."

Becky nodded with approval. Ellen took that as a sign of progress.

Shortly after the sky darkened, Frank stood on the ledge of a fountain at Rutgers Square as the Army of the Unemployed gathered around him. Sweet Sal stood near Ellen, wearing an ungainly hat on her head topped with paper flowers. She gazed at Frank adoringly.

"You like him, do you?" Ellen said.

Sal grinned sheepishly.

"What brings you to this cause, Sal?" Ellen asked.

She twisted her mouth as she thought of her answer and then said, "I started work when I was but ten years old. And I been working ever since. I never thought nobody cared about people like me. But Frank cares."

She looked up at him and a light shone in her eyes.

Standing amongst the workers, Ellen heard so many different languages, so many accents. They were mostly immigrants, like her. They'd come to this country pursuing the dream of a better life, and the dream had failed them. Frank raised a hand and they quieted down.

"As a man, you have a right to eat," Frank said. "You have a right to shelter. If they cannot pay us thirty cents an hour for our labor, then the government must give us food. You have a right to share in the prosperity of this city. And if they will not share it with you, then you have a right to take it. Look at the churches. Large buildings, warm buildings, but will the priests share them with the poor? They will not. They ignore the teachings of the God they worship. They do not feed the hungry, they do not shelter the homeless. They lock their doors and say we are not wanted. Follow me. We will demand that these hypocrites do what their God tells them to do!"

With that he jumped off the ledge. The crowd parted for him. With Charlie, his right-hand man, at his side and Becky at his other, Frank led the throngs of men forward up Canal Street to the Bowery. Sweet Sal and Ellen fell in line behind the leaders. They stopped traffic as they crossed the streets.

"How many followers do you think are here?" Ellen asked Sweet Sal.

"We had two hundred a couple nights ago. Looks like three times as many," she said. "They've all come to follow Frank."

The motley crowd moved like a great caterpillar, singing songs as they marched. The swell of their voices touched Ellen, and she saw tears coursing down Sweet Sal's face.

When they reached the tall spires of St. Alphonsus, Ellen hesitated. With the exception of a couple of memorial services, she had stopped going to church the moment she got on the boat to leave Ireland, but that didn't mean the church didn't still have its hooks in her. The crowd pushed forward, and she allowed herself to be funneled toward the door. That is until a hand gripped her by the arm and pulled her out of the throng.

"What are ya thinking?" Paddy hissed in her ear. "Go in there, you won't be coming out unless it's in manacles." His face was grim and determined, blue eyes hard as stones.

He pulled her to the edge of the church steps before releasing his grip on her arm. She glanced around quickly to see if any of the others had seen them, but Becky, Charlie, and Sal had all followed Frank inside.

Ellen wanted to follow Frank. She wanted to be inside, to see how Frank handled the priests, but if Paddy were right that would mean jail. She'd been there once before when her employer had falsely accused her of theft, and she didn't plan on going back.

About 200 men and a few women made it inside, while the rest of the followers waited outside.

"What's going to happen?" she asked Paddy.

"Just you wait and see," he said. Paddy left Ellen standing on the margins of the crowd and went inside with the other detectives.

Ellen waited nervously. The workers no longer sang, but a defiant rumbling rose and fell. The wait seemed interminable. Then the rumbling turned into a roar. Ellen climbed onto a low wall, peered over the heads of the Army and saw Frank coming out of the church between two detectives. One of them was Paddy.

Frank smiled at the crowd. Becky and Sweet Sal were right behind him.

"It's all right," he said with a wave. "It's all right."

Then the police shoved him into the back of a patrol wagon. Sweet Sal, weeping and distraught, tried to follow him. Her devotion was that of Magdalene, thought Ellen. A policeman shoved her to the ground where she wailed like a banshee. Becky helped her up, and they managed to slip into the crowd.

The patrol wagon trundled off and another pulled in front. By tens, the rest of the marchers from inside the church were loaded up. Ellen saw Charlie's scowling face among the first lot. A thought crossed her mind: the police might regret tangling with that one.

She didn't wait for the rest of the men to be rounded up. She hurried directly to the offices of *Mother Earth* to report what had happened.

Lulu, Berkman, and Emma looked from one to the other when Ellen told them that Frank had been arrested. Berkman rose and immediately began to pace the floor.

"This is a moment we must seize," he said.

Emma nodded and thanked Ellen for the information. Lulu looked at her with admiration and Ellen felt she had finally crossed over. She could no longer deny which side she was on.

***

The next morning Ellen picked up a copy of *The Herald* on her way to work. She knew *The Ledger* would hardly mention the march. Their editorial policy was to ignore the poor and hope they would go away — except for the occasional Beatrice Milton column. But Louisa was off in Florida taking tango lessons! For all her complaints about the assignment, Louisa seemed to be enjoying the social scene in St. Augustine, judging by the stories she was sending in. Ellen felt a mixture of resentment and relief. Louisa had no idea what Ellen was doing with the anarchists. The more she thought about it, Ellen had no idea what she was doing with them either.

She took her place at Louisa's desk and read about what had happened inside that church. According to the reporter, detectives and policemen had been inside waiting for the men. The priest ordered them to leave, but the men refused, standing on the pews, yelling. A few frightened congregants were quoted in the paper. One woman had insisted that the fellow standing in her pew take off his cap out of respect. Which he did. Frank had asked the priest to let the men sleep in the church that night.

As Ellen read the story, outrage built a fire in her chest.

"You'll do nothing of the kind," Father Adrian replied. "The Catholic church is no place for you to sleep, and I strongly object to the way you entered here."

"Well, will you give us money to buy food?"

"No."

"Will you give us work?" Frank asked.

Again Father Adrian refused.

"But I tell you we're starving," Frank implored.

Of course, starving men and women were not Father Adrian's problem.

According to the account, Frank had finally given up but it was too late. The police were bound and determined to end the threat of Frank Tannenbaum.

"Hey, Malloy," a voice interrupted her reading. She looked up and saw Billy Stephens, the police reporter, leaning against his desk, a toothpick in the corner of his mouth. "Did I see you at that march last night?"

Ellen's jaw went slack. She had no idea what to say.

"I'm right then. I thought that was you," Billy said. "Taking notes for Beatrice Milton? Don't look so surprised. I know you and Louisa concocted that woman."

"I'm not at liberty to discuss it with you, Mr. Stephens," Ellen said.

"Suit yourself," Billy said and sat down at his own desk. "But when you wind up in the hoosegow — again — you better hope her ladyship, Miss Delafield, will come back and bail you out."

He rolled a sheet of paper into his Remington and his fingers pecked out a story.

If she went to the hoosegow again...it had certainly been a possibility.

After Ellen went through Louisa's correspondence, she typed up a column for the weekly syndicated column using notes that Louisa had sent last week. By noon she was done. She couldn't wait to get out of that cigar-smoke laden air, the smug laughter of the business reporters, and the insipid giggles of the secretaries.

The train took her to 14th street and she emerged into the Village, far away from the stuffiness of Midtown Manhattan. The temperatures had been steadily climbing all week and there hadn't been a drop of snow since that odd out-of-nowhere storm five days earlier. This day was positively balmy, sun shining like a long lost friend. She thought of poor Frank who would not be seeing the sun today except from the window of a jail cell at the Tombs.

She climbed the stairs to the *Mother Earth* offices, where she found Karl and Lulu busily putting together the articles for the next issue at one desk while Berkman and Emma conferred at another desk. On the broken down sofa, Sweet Sal sat, wearing black as if she were in mourning, her eyes red from crying.

"What's new?" Ellen asked Lulu.

"They set Frank's bail at $5,000. Can you believe it? An outrageous sum," Lulu said. "But the I.W.W. managed to get it. I went with them this morning to get him out."

"Then where is he?" Ellen asked.

At this, Sweet Sal sobbed loudly.

"He refused to leave," Lulu said, her eyes wide with disbelief and admiration. "Not unless the rest of the men got out, too."

"Hell no, he wouldn't leave," Sweet Sal said, her voice thick from weeping. "He's a martyr."

Frank was indeed a martyr, Ellen thought, and as an Irish woman, she knew a thing or two about the subject.

"When's the trial?" Ellen asked.

Emma Goldman stood up and said, "Day after tomorrow. They're wasting no time."

"We'll be there," Karl said as he ripped a story from his typewriter.

"Until then?" Ellen asked.

"We lay low," Berkman said. "Nothing can happen until we see how this trial plays out. If they convict him, there will be a very angry mob."

Berkman and Karl looked at each other as if nothing could be more desirable.

Chapter 25

Louisa

"Why, Suzie! Where have you been?" Louisa asked when Suzie appeared in her room the next morning, pretending she didn't already know.

"Fell asleep on Lloyd's porch," Suzie said and handed Louisa a cable. "I picked this up for you at the front desk."

Louisa opened the cable and read:

"Did not sell diamond to M. Bassett. Rough stone brought to us.

Lord Wickham paid our firm to cut and finish diamond.

L. Boucheron"

Interesting.

Suzie poured a cup of coffee and looked at Louisa expectantly.

"What's in the cable?" she asked.

"It's from a diamond merchant in Paris," Louisa said. "He says he only cut Daphne's diamond. He did not sell it."

"Louisa," Suzie said in a warning tone. "Don't get yourself into trouble over this."

"I hate to say it, but I believe Lord Wickham bought the diamond from thieves," Louisa said.

"Just how would you prove it? And what good would it do? Even if it is one of the stolen diamonds, that doesn't mean Henri knew it was stolen. Mr. Griffin told you to find out if he was some sort of ... what did he say...?"

"Scoundrel. You're right. Henri might not have known anything about it. I do think I should have a talk with Lord Wickham," Louisa said.

Suzie yawned and sat down in the wicker chair by the door to the balcony.

"I fell asleep on Polly's porch," she said, "with a baby on my lap. I slept like a baby myself, but I did wake up with a crick in my neck." She rubbed her shoulder.

"I've often wondered, why did you stay with Mother and me after all the money was gone?" Louisa asked.

"When your father was alive, I was a housekeeper in charge of twelve servants and a mansion, but no one else in New York uses colored housekeepers. I was too qualified and too dark-skinned. The only thing they wanted me to do was be a laundress."

"I thought it was because you didn't want to leave Mother and me," Louisa said.

"Well, where would I go? Besides, I felt responsible for your mother. Heaven knows she couldn't take care of herself."

"What about me?" Louisa asked.

Suzie laughed.

"Child, you never needed looking after. God saw your parents and said, 'I better give them a child with some common sense.'"

Suzie rose.

"I'm going to wash up and change my dress. What do you have planned for the day?"

"I'm going to the archery range this morning and then cards with Lady Rutherford and friends," Louisa said. "I have so many article topics that I'll be able to fill my column and my syndicated column for a month." She also decided she would find Lord Wickham and ask him where he got the raw diamond that Boucheron had cut and finished for Henri. She wasn't going to let him dodge the question. If he admitted the diamond was stolen, there wasn't anything she could do, but at least she could get him to tell her whether or not Henri was involved. Then she would have to decide what to tell Daphne's father.

She thought about Simon's revelation that Madame Ribault had some sort of sordid history with Henri. She could let Daphne's father know about that, but it seemed that Henri had put a stop to it the night before, and it hardly seemed fair to destroy a marriage over an affair that had happened in the past. On the other hand, if he were involved with a diamond theft and the police caught up to him, then that would be another matter altogether. The scandal would be ruinous for the Griffins.

"Any plans with that French fella?" Suzie asked.

To her chagrin, Louisa blushed.

"Not today," she said.

When Suzie left for her room, Louisa took her cup of coffee out to the balcony. She stared out at the bright, cloudless sky and watched as a line of large birds with long bills and enormous, out-stretched wings sailed by. More pelicans. She had to get to work on her bird story so women would understand the terrible price the birds had to pay to be placed on the heads of fashion-conscious ladies, for it wasn't just feathers the ladies loved. Sometimes they had the whole bird on their heads — smaller ones usually; nevertheless, Louisa hoped they might learn to be satisfied with bows and beads and other glittery objects.

As she stood on the balcony, enjoying the breeze from the ocean, her mind drifted back to the night before. She could still feel the pressure of Simon's lips against hers, as well as the weight of the letter she'd written to Forrest that sat on her writing desk, waiting to be sent. She hated to hurt him. Her feelings were a veritable stew of grief, longing, and pain. She hadn't forgotten about Dottie Parsons. She'd only temporarily suppressed the guilt she felt. She wished she could be one of those birds, lazily floating on currents of air.

As her eyes traveled from the horizon to the cup in her hand they caught on something gold below. She leaned over the railing and saw what looked like a brocaded robe spread like wings on the ground. Then her breath seized and her heart contracted like a fist in her chest. That wasn't just a robe.

"My God," she whispered.

She turned and ran from the room just as Suzie was coming back in.

"Louisa?" Suzie called after her, but Louisa didn't stop to explain. Instead of waiting for the elevator, she took the stairs, running down, clasping the banister to keep from falling. When she reached the first floor, she searched for the nearest exit.

"Can I help you, Miss?" asked an alarmed bellman.

"Someone's hurt," she said, her voice shaking. "Outside."

The bellman showed her to an exit and followed as she rushed along the walkway. She spied the gold brocade robe in the bushes and pushed through them. There on the dirt lay a man, his head bent at an impossible angle. She lowered herself to touch his neck. His skin was damp and cold. She looked closer at the face, now a mottled purple and blue. It was Lord Wickham.

She looked up at the bellman and whispered, "He's dead." The words were razors slicing her throat. She looked down at the body. Blood had seeped and crusted dry over a layer of dead leaves. His arms were outstretched, and his right hand was curled around a silk handkerchief. When she pulled the handkerchief from his hand, something fell out and glinted in the dirt. She held it up to the sunlight. A small glittering crystal.

As she stood there in the gleaming sunshine, her mind reeled. She told herself it couldn't be happening. Then she looked down at the body and knew that it had. Another death. Was she responsible for this one, too? She choked back tears. Stop it, she thought. She must curb her emotions. This time she would not run away. Instead, she would get to the bottom of this.

"I'll find a policeman while you get the manager," she said to the bellman, tucking the stone into her pocket. He nodded and hurried back inside. Louisa looked up and saw Suzie in the window, her hand over her mouth. Louisa ran to the street. She looked around but saw only a few tourists meandering down St. George Street. She had often seen mounted police in the plaza so she hurried there and found a few old and middle-aged men already sitting on the benches to watch the parade of pretty young women who promenaded past. At the far end of the plaza, she saw a roan horse with a policeman on his back. They seemed to be doing nothing more than enjoying a breeze ruffling the horse's black mane.

"Help," Louisa called to him. The man and horse trotted to her.

"What is it, Miss?" he asked.

"A body," she said. "At the Florida House."

"A body?"

"Yes, yes. It's Lord Wickham's body," she said, impatiently. "I'll have to show you."

"All right then," he said. "Climb on board."

With the help of his strong arm, Louisa managed to perch on the horse's rump and guide him back to Lord Wickham's corpse.

***

"Looks like a suicide," Detective Hagan said. He had a wide jaw and thin lips. His voice was deep and southern, his skin ruddy from constant sun exposure.

"Or an accident," the manager suggested. "Perhaps he had too much to drink...."

Louisa watched as police officers carted the body off on a stretcher.

"I found this in a handkerchief," she said to the detective as she handed over the small glittering rock. "I think it's a diamond that hasn't been cut yet."

He held it up to the light.

"Don't know nothing about diamonds," he said. "Where did you find it, Miss...."

"Delafield, Louisa Delafield," she said. "I believe it may be a stolen diamond."

"What makes you think that?" he asked.

"Lord Wickham was in Alexandria, Egypt, at the same time that a large cache of diamonds, about a half million dollars' worth, went missing from a broker. I hate to say it, but I wonder if he had something to do with the theft...."

The detective turned to the manager. "Make sure the victim's door is locked. We'll want to search his room after we get his body to the morgue."

He turned back to Louisa. "Anything else you want to tell me, Miss Delafield?"

"He was alive shortly after 10:00. I saw him standing on his balcony. He waved to me," she said.

"Were you alone?"

She hesitated and then said, "No, I wasn't. Simon Bassett was with me. We were going to look for my maid."

"I see," he said.

"When I came back at eleven, the light in his room was off," she said.

"From the looks of things, I'd say he died about twelve hours ago. The coroner will know better. But if I'm right, then he fell during that hour you were gone," he said.

The detective told her he had no further questions for her, and so she left with the manager. A crowd had formed around the garden area, craning their necks to see what was happening.

"I'll make sure Lord Wickham's door is locked if that helps you," she said to the manager.

"I would appreciate that greatly, Miss Delafield," he said with a look of relief. Then in a loud voice he called out to the gathering crowd. "Ladies, gentlemen. There's nothing more to see. An accident, nothing more. Please, let's leave the police to do their job."

As she rode up the elevator, she wondered why Lord Wickham would kill himself. Did it have something to do with the diamonds? What if he hadn't killed himself? What if someone had poisoned him and pushed him over? What if he himself was the one who stole the diamonds in Alexandria? And maybe, just maybe, he had an accomplice. Her imagination was running away with her, she realized. Facts and evidence mattered. She'd read enough Sherlock Holmes to know that.

The elevator doors opened and she walked down the hallway to Lord Wickham's room. She tried the door knob. It opened. If he had been by himself when he fell or jumped, the door would have been locked.

Chapter 26
Ellen

Even *The Ledger* announced the verdict in Frank's trial — one year in the penitentiary for leading his Army of the Unemployed into a church and demanding shelter. Berkman leapt into action, demanding a rally at Union Square of both the Anarchist Red Cross and the I.W.W. The clarion call was heard 'round the city.

On Saturday morning, Ellen left the hired girl with Mrs. Delafield and went to her room at Mrs. Cantor's house for a fresh dress and to pay her weekly rent. Then she headed out to get to the rally early, only to find Paddy O'Neil on the sidewalk in his rumpled brown suit, hands shoved in his pockets, his derby pushed back on his head. He was whistling a sea shanty she remembered from home.

"Hullo, Paddy, what's the story?" she asked.

"You can't go to Union Square today, Ellen," he said.

"It'll look suspicious if I'm not there," she said. "I'm very close to learning who shot at Louisa."

Paddy leaned close to her, his face inches from hers.

"You're close to getting your head stove in," he said. "Commissioner McKay has sent 400 men to the square, and he's got at least 200 plainclothesmen wandering through the crowd, ready to knock some heads the second trouble starts. Not only that, there's cops in every hotel basement between here and the Ladies' Mile, just waiting for the word. And a thousand reserves in the outlying precincts."

Ellen inhaled deeply.

"Today," Paddy continued, "the Anarchist Red Cross, the International Workers of the World, and all their followers will be going down."

"But if I'm arrested, I trust you'll get me out," Ellen said.

"That's misplaced trust, girleen. I'll be out doing my job, which may include cracking a few heads myself. We've got orders. I can't come get you out of jail, and I can't fix a broken skull."

Ellen looked down at the sidewalk, saw the steel-toed boots on his feet. She looked back at the rooming house. She did not have to go to the march, she supposed. She could drop the whole matter. Then she thought of Frank, just twenty-one years old, and his march to the church with that horde of hungry, desperate men who only wanted to be able to work for honest wages. She remembered their faces, drawn and gray, those eyes so devoid of hope.

"I must go to the march, Paddy," she said.

"This isn't just about finding the shooter, is it?" he asked.

Ellen shook her head.

"Ellen Malloy, I'm ordering you not to go," he said. "Your brothers aren't here to protect you, but I am. Mikey Malloy would never forgive me if I let you go into that fray."

"You must not remember Mikey too well then," she said. "He beat me and Martin regularly so we'd be tough enough for anything."

"He never beat you with a bully club, I'll wager," Paddy said. "What's it going to be, Ellen? It's either stay home or I'll have you taken to the hoosegow."

Ellen jerked back.

"You'd put me in jail?"

"To save your life I would." He crossed his arms and glared at her.

"You really think there will be bloodshed today?" she asked.

"I do," he said, gravely.

Her shoulders slumped. "I guess I do have some washing I could do."

"That's a girl. But just in case you change your mind, I'm leaving one of the boys here to make sure you stay put." He pointed to the corner where a uniformed cop stood, twirling his bully club like a cop in a cartoon.

"You drive a hard bargain," Ellen said, turning her back on Paddy and climbing the steps up to the door.

Upstairs she gathered her underthings, took them to the washroom, and dumped them in a basin full of water and Duz laundry soap. She squeezed the soft wet cloth and then pulled her hands, dripping from the water, dried them on a towel and went back to her room. She peeked out the window. Sure enough, that cop was meandering along the road. She went back to the washroom, rinsed out her underclothes, ran them through the wringer, and then took them back to her room to hang on the drying rack near the radiator.

Then she went downstairs, and glanced out the window again. Now the policeman was leaning on the wall of the house across the street, staring at the door of her rooming house.

"Paddy, you no good...." she muttered.

She went into the parlor and found a fellow roomer, a telephone operator, reading a magazine. It took her a moment to remember the woman's name, and by the time she did, she already had a plan.

"Good morning, Kate," Ellen said, cheerily.

"Good morning," Kate said without looking up from her magazine.

"Say, Kate," Ellen said as she sat down in one of Mrs. Cantor's sturdy arm chairs. "How'd you like to have an extra bath night this week?"

Kate lowered her magazine and stared at her, curious now.

"Go on," Kate said.

"See, there's a police officer outside. He's actually a friend of my former boyfriend, and he's watching the house to make sure I don't leave," Ellen said.

"Sounds fishy," Kate said.

"You know how these cops are. They're all corruption and vice. My former boyfriend was no better. So his friend is out there trying to stop me from going out to see a new fella," Ellen said.

"I never figured you for having a boyfriend," Kate said, laying the magazine on a table next to her. Ellen wondered what that meant!

"I guess you figured wrong," Ellen said. "Anyways, I'm only asking you to go out and talk to this officer, distract him for a bit so I can get out for a while."

"What night is your bath?" Kate asked.

"Tuesday."

Ellen could see Kate imagining two baths in one week. Then Kate stood up and fetched her shawl.

As soon as Kate had strolled across the street, Ellen ran upstairs and dug out her men's clothing. She shoved her hair up into a cap and put on men's trousers and a jacket. She'd worn the same clothes, which had once belonged to Louisa's father, the previous year when she and Louisa were on their first investigation together. The clothes weren't in style but the thousands of union members milling about in the north end of the square wouldn't be concerned. It was the perfect disguise. She slipped out of the house while Kate flirted with the cop across the street, hopped on the El, and soon she was joining the throngs heading to Union Square.

Once she was there, she looked out onto an ocean of hats — derbies, homburgs, caps — and wondered what Frank would think if he knew these members of the union had come to protest his sentence. She gazed around and saw a bookseller's shop, a union headquarters office, striped awnings, offices, and apartments. Union Square was the site of so many protests over the past few months and yet otherwise just another slice of New York City.

The sun shone in the sky, and a gentle breeze, unlike the harsh winter winds, blew across her face. It felt like a good omen. She heard a loud roar; the anarchists from the Anarchist Red Cross had arrived. They seemed to spring out of nowhere. Berkman strode defiantly, at the head of a column of cheering protestors, shoving their way through the crowd, passing out pamphlets, written by Becky Edelsohn, to the wide-eyed union workers.

Ellen looked up and saw windows filled with spectators as if they were in the Roman Coliseum.

Becky, wearing her red stockings, carried a sign with the simple words: "End Hunger Now." Becky was like a beacon of beauty for her cause — her skin glowing and her eyes bright. For all their militancy and espousals of blood-letting, Ellen believed that the demands of the anarchists and the I.W.W. were reasonable. Food. Jobs. Dignity. She understood their frustration. Hadn't her own people chafed under the thumb of oppression for hundreds of years? Sometimes rage was all that was left.

Lulu stood on the sidelines with her notepad, scrawling as fast as her hand could fly. Someone had to record the moment for their side. The "other" press was everywhere, press cards in their hats, photographers at the ready. She even passed a cameraman taking motion pictures.

Berkman leapt upon a makeshift stage and stood not six feet from a police outpost. He raised his arms exultantly and the crowd erupted. When he lowered his arms, the crowd noise subsided. The moment entangled her as the swell of emotion rose from the crowd, and the smell of humanity surrounded her.

"We, the Anarchist Red Cross, stand in solidarity with our working class brothers from the I.W.W. I want to share a poem with you, written by our beloved Voltairine de Cleyre, who died two years ago."

The crowd raptly listened as Berkman intoned the poem:

"What ye have sown ye shall reap :
Teardrops, and Blood, and Hate,
Gaunt gather before your Seat,
And knock at your palace gate!
There are murderers on your Thrones!
There are thieves in your Justice-halls!
White Leprosy cancers their stones,

And gnaws at their worm-eaten walls!
And the Hand of Belshazzar's Feast
Writes over, in flaming light,
Thought's Kingdom no more to the Priest;
Nor the Law of Right unto Might."

When he was done, Berkman leapt into the crowd. Like a great beast, the crowd murmured and soon began to roar. Signs waved above their heads: "Free Tannenbaum!" "Give us Work!" "Remember Ludlow!" Ludlow – the slaughter of innocent women and children in a Colorado mining town and the impetus for unrest across the country.

Ellen's head swiveled toward the police, her fists squeezed in anticipation and fear. For a moment the police stuck fast as if unsure what to do. Then a burly red-faced policeman grinned and waved his club.

"Come on, lads!" he bellowed. All hell let loose. She could see the clash coming. She remembered how as a child one time in her father's boat she'd seen a huge wave rise, and there'd been nothing to do but flatten herself on the bottom of the boat and pray it wouldn't capsize.

The protestors swung their signs at the police, and the police swung their clubs back at the protestors. The police tried rounding up the protestors, shoving them toward the paddy wagons at the edge of the square but a screaming mob followed them and most of the protestors escaped. The mob might have won the skirmish but suddenly a line of mounted police approached, swinging their clubs right and left. Marchers fell, and blood sprayed.

Becky ran up to her, wild-eyed, her hair falling from its pins.

"Nice disguise," she yelled over the din and grabbed Ellen's wrist. "Come on!"

The men made way for Becky and Ellen as they struggled to the front line where Arnie, the big man who had never said more than two words in Ellen's presence, boomed in a loud voice, "I say we march to Rutgers Square!" He held out an arm to Becky, and she hooked her arm in his and held up her sign. Together they led the way with hundreds of people cheering and following them. Ellen hesitated but a moment. She knew she should get out of this crowd. She heard Paddy's warnings in her head, but something pulled her forward. She had to see it through. Perhaps they'd be allowed to march to Rutgers Square. After all, they weren't harming anyone. Yet. She heard shouts: "Kill the Capitalists!" "Revenge for Tannenbaum!"

The mounted police slowly advanced toward them. A vague unease filled her. As they passed a hotel, officers streamed out of the doors and formed a line marching next to the crowd. Just as Paddy had forewarned her. As they reached 14th Street, a detective clambered on top of the hood of a police car. It was Paddy!

"Break it up, by order of the N.Y.P.D. You've no permit for protestin'!"

Ellen ducked into the crowd so he wouldn't see her.

"Shut your trap, you lackey!" yelled one of the protestors. Others followed suit. Ellen eyed the police on their horses. Hatred bloomed on their faces. At some invisible signal, they charged! Terror rose in Ellen's throat as she turned with the others to flee the mêlée. The blows came fast and furious. Screams punctuated the air as the horses trampled protestors, and police swung their clubs blindly. A man dropped in front of her, blood seeping from his skull. She could smell the horse sweat. One of the beasts jostled her, and she pushed to get free. She heard the whizz of a club as it sailed past her head and hit her shoulder with a *whack*.

She staggered forward and saw Arnie on the ground curled up like a snail as the clubs landed on him over and over. "For Christ's sake! Stop!" he screamed. Ellen watched with horror, holding her aching shoulder as Becky pushed through the pack of police and threw her body across the prone man.

"Save him!" she called out. "Save him from the oppressors."

Becky's courage astonished Ellen.

The police yanked her off Arnie and shoved him into the back of the paddy wagon.

"Get inside, you bastard," one of the cops yelled and punched the poor man once more in the face. Blood splattered off the policeman's fist and Arnie slumped down. The doors slammed shut, and the paddy wagon rolled away. Charlie stepped out of the crowd and stared at the back of the paddy wagon, his constant smirk replaced by a quivering rage. *This is how you turn mischief makers into murderers,* Ellen thought.

The discouraged, defeated protestors slowly dispersed.

Ellen found Becky weeping in anger, a clump of hair torn from her head, blood on her hands, face, and dress. Her famous red stockings ripped. Ellen helped her up and led her down the street. She flagged down a cab. The first three refused to stop but finally one of them let them in, and Ellen took the wounded warrior to Emma Goldman's apartment where Emma, who had trained as a nurse, had set up a triage station. Lulu was tending to a man who had a broken nose.

"You're dressed like a man," Karl stated, matter-of-factly, when he saw Ellen. "Are you deserting the female race?"

"To be honest, there's a peeler from Galway that knows my brothers. He thinks it's his business to keep me out of trouble. So he came by and warned me away from the march. I didn't want him to recognize me," she said. She knew it was dangerous to let them know she had any connection with the police, but too many lies would be hard to keep track of.

"Is that who pulled you away from us at the march when Frank was arrested?" Becky asked.

Ellen's breath stuttered. She hadn't realized Becky saw her.

"Yes," she said.

"I didn't know you were so chummy with the 'peelers' as you call them," he said.

Ellen didn't know what to say to this. She was afraid she'd lose all credibility.

"Oh, lay off her," Lulu said. "Just because she knows a cop from the old country doesn't mean anything."

Berkman set about washing the blood from Becky's face, checking for cuts, all the while she ranted about the police and the damned capitalists and how there'd been no provocation. All this was true, as far as Ellen could see. She wondered if she could somehow talk to Becky and convince her to leave Louisa out of her war. An idea occurred to her.

"Becky, would you like me to go to your place and get you some fresh clothes? Your dress is covered in blood and your stockings are torn," Ellen said.

"Not necessary," Becky said.

"A very good idea, Miss Malloy," Berkman said. Then to Becky, "You'll feel better, my love, with some clean clothes. We can't have you going out in public like this. They'll arrest you first and ask questions later."

He handed Ellen a key and told her the address, just a few blocks away.

Ellen reached the apartment — it was a two-room loft with little furniture except for a bed and some mattresses on the floor, books, and magazines scattered about. She found Becky's stockings in a box — five or six pairs, all red. She also pulled a dress out of the closet, set the dress and the stockings on the bed, and then proceeded to search as quickly as she could. She pawed through the boxes, looked under the mattresses, peered through the closet, opened cupboards. Being so small and so sparsely furnished, there weren't many places to hide something — something like a gun. The rooms had no heat, and she imagined it was freezing in the winter. Finally, she noticed a picture of a man with a goatee hanging on the wall. She lifted the picture and behind it saw that a hole had been punched through the plaster. She stuck her hand into the hole, felt around and came out with a gun. For a moment, she couldn't breathe. Was this it? Was this the gun that killed Dottie Parsons? Her pulse raced. If she took the gun, they would know she had done it. She stood on tip-toe and looked inside the hole and saw a small rectangular box. She picked it up and read the cover.

20 CALIBER .38 REVOLVER BALL CARTRIDGES
For COLT'S DOUBLE ACTION REVOLVER
Smokeless Powder

Inside the box, she found small brass bullets with rounded metal tips. Surely, the police would know if this was the same kind of bullet they found in Dottie. She pocketed one of the bullets. Then she put the box and the gun back and lowered the painting back in its place. The eyes of the man with the goatee gazed at her accusingly.

"You didn't see a thing," she told him, grabbed Becky's clothes, and left.

Chapter 27

Louisa

Louisa entered the dead man's room. It had the eeriness of a tomb, and she thought of her father's death in an anonymous hotel room in Greenwich Village, where he had been stabbed to death by a man who was never caught and for reasons no one seemed to know. She swallowed and took a deep breath. She needed to focus on the matter at hand. Percival Wickham had fallen or jumped or been pushed from the balcony of the fourth floor of the Florida House Hotel.

She gazed at the neatly made bed and wondered what was going through his mind in his last moments. There were no signs of a scuffle in the room, no signs that he had been robbed. Why hadn't anyone heard a scream when he fell? Unless it really was a suicide. She looked in his wardrobe and found nothing of interest. She checked the drawers of the dresser; everything looked in order. She peeked under the bed and saw nothing except a pair of button boots. His diamond stickpin lay in a silver tray on the dresser. Finally, she went to the doors leading to the balcony. They were shut. Had he shut them before leaping? How strange. She opened the doors and stepped out onto the balcony. Nothing was out of the ordinary. She let her eyes scour the floor for any more diamonds. She saw none but she did notice a dark spot about the size of a dime on the wood. She bent down to examine it. Was it blood?

"And just what are you doing in here?"

Detective Hagan stood in the doorway, staring at her.

"I... I thought it odd that Lord Wickham would kill himself. Look at this spot here. Is it blood?"

The detective walked over and examined the spot.

"Does look like blood. Makes sense."

"Why does it make sense?" she asked.

"His chest was pierced with some kind of sharp object," the detective said. "Your friend was probably dead before he hit the ground."

"Oh," Louisa said, and clasped her hand to her mouth. "Poor Percival."

"Who do you think would do that to him?" the detective asked.

"I don't know," she said.

He went back in the room with Louisa following, looked around, picked up the stickpin, and said, "Don't look like he was robbed."

"Detective Hagan, if Lord Wickham had something to do with the stolen diamonds in Egypt, someone might have believed he had them here," she said.

"Miss Delafield, this story of an international diamond theft sounds awful far-fetched," Detective

Hagan said. He had something lodged in his cheek, and he took a moment to walk over to the balcony and spit brown juice over the railing. "I understand you're some sort of newspaper writer?"

"Society writer," she said, trying to ignore the bulge in his cheek, which she realized must be tobacco.

"I see. Why don't you leave the investigating to us, little lady?" he said. He spit again.

"Of course," she said. Other than a single raw diamond and Daphne's pendant, what sort of proof was there to support her theory anyway?

"Now would you mind going about your business so me and my men can do a thorough search of this room. I don't need to search you, do I?" He crossed his arms and stared at her.

"Of course not," she said, and turned toward the door. Then she spotted a piece of paper on the nightstand. It was the sketch of the heron! While the detective looked through the chest of drawers, Louisa snatched up the sketch.

As she headed toward the door, the detective said, "One more thing." She froze. "Don't say anything about this being a possible murder. That's for the police to announce once we've gathered more information. Could still be an accident, for all we know."

An accident?

In the hallway, she looked at the sketch. It was lovely and somehow captured the bird's personality, that large, round eye looking out at the world with an amused gaze. Percival Wickham may have stolen diamonds, but he didn't deserve to die like this. She took the sketch to her room and placed it in her notebook.

"Louisa?"

She turned around and saw Suzie.

"What happened?" Suzie asked. "Did you know the...?"

"Yes, I'm sorry I didn't come back earlier. It was Lord Percival Wickham. I went to his room to make sure the door was locked and then spoke to the police again."

"Do you think this has something to do with those stolen diamonds?" Suzie asked.

"I do," Louisa said. "I think there's a connection. I found one of the raw diamonds in his hand." Nervousness roiled in her stomach and she twisted her handkerchief nearly in half as she paced the room.

"Why don't I stay here with you today?" Suzie suggested.

"No, you should go to your family," Louisa said. "I need to tell the Griffins what has happened."

"All right," Suzie said.

Louisa left the Florida House and strode over to the Ponce. She searched the courtyard and saw only the latest batch of tourists. In the lobby, she found the concierge and asked where the Griffins were.

"They're at a concert in the music parlor," he said. "I'll show you."

He took her through the hotel and quietly opened the door to the parlor. She slipped inside a vast room with gleaming chandeliers hanging from an elaborately carved ceiling. A marble fireplace graced one end of the room, and nearby sat a grand piano where a young man played one of Liszt's "Hungarian Rhapsodies." A collection of plush wingback chairs had been formed into a semi-circle. There sat the Griffins.

Louisa stood at the side of the room, trying to be inconspicuous until the piece ended. While the audience applauded, she circled around the chairs until she could catch Daphne's eye. Daphne looked at her with a curious expression on her face, so Louisa beckoned her. Daphne rose and followed her into a side room.

"Thank God you showed up. I was bored beyond belief," Daphne said.

"Something terrible has happened," Louisa said. "Lord Wickham was found dead this morning."

"Dead?" Daphne gasped. "What happened?"

"The police aren't sure," Louisa said, remembering Detective Hagan's admonition not to tell anyone he suspected murder. "Somehow he fell from his balcony."

"Oh no," Daphne said.

"Dead! And only a week before the wedding!" Mrs. Griffin exclaimed, palms on her cheeks. Louisa hadn't noticed that the older woman had followed them out of the room.

"Oh, Mother, we barely knew him. I'm not even sure why he was here," Daphne said.

"He was here because he's a lord and a friend of your future husband," her mother chided her. "I hope this doesn't cast a pall over the celebrations."

"We won't let it," Daphne said. "Thank you, Louisa, for informing us."

"Join us for dinner tonight, Miss Delafield," Mrs. Griffin said, placing a hand on her sleeve. "Seven o'clock at our table in the dining room." Mrs. Griffin was eager to have her daughter's wedding written up in a New York newspaper, especially *The Ledger,* and she didn't want an inconvenient murder to muck it up.

"Thank you. I'll see what I can learn about Lord Wickham's death in the meantime," Louisa said. "Daphne, where are Henri and Simon? We should tell them as soon as possible."

"Fishing," Daphne said. "Far out in the ocean."

Louisa sighed.

She wondered if Madame Ribault had heard anything. Her atelier was right next to Lord Wickham's room.

***

Louisa found Madame Ribault on the floor of her atelier surrounded by an eruption of coral-colored fabric. She was steadily ripping out the seams of one of the dresses.

"Madame Ribault?" Louisa said.

"The bridesmaids are too fat," she said, drily. "I have to alter the dresses."

"Did you hear about what happened to Lord Wickham?" Louisa asked.

Madame Ribault nodded. She looked up at Louisa with dull eyes and her face crinkled.

"He was a silly old *folle,* but I liked him," she said.

"A *folle*? I do not know the term," Louisa said.

"You know, he had a fondness for men," Madame Ribault said. "That is, of course, why he did it."

Louisa sank into a chair.

"He killed himself over a man? But who?" Louisa asked.

Madame Ribault tilted her head and looked at Louisa as if she wondered how anyone could be such a naif.

"Henri, of course. He was madly in love with him," she said and used her seam ripper to tear through the dress on her lap.

"But I thought that you and Henri...."

"*Quoi?* Don't be absurd," she said. "I heard the two of them arguing and then Henri left. I would have gone over to check on Percival but Mrs. Griffin was here, the old nuisance. I was up until midnight with her, changing the bridesmaids' hats. More lace, she says, more flowers. The woman has no taste at all."

Louisa was stunned, absorbing this information. Then she remembered the longing in Lord Wickham's eyes as he watched Henri and Daphne dancing. He wasn't longing for Daphne. How had she been so blind? And Henri had not been visiting Madame Ribault to say it was finished. He had gone to Percival Wickham's room. Had Lord Wickham been so heartbroken he threw himself off the balcony and somehow managed to puncture his heart? Or had Henri stabbed him and then pushed him over? If Henri and Lord Wickham were lovers, perhaps they were also accomplices in the diamond theft? Was Daphne about to marry a thief and a murderer?

***

Louisa arrived at the Ponce just as Detective Hagan was leaving.

"Have you told the Griffins it was murder?" she asked him.

He stuck his hands in his pockets and grimaced.

"Well, ma'am, the coroner says he's not sure it's murder, after all," he said.

Louisa inhaled sharply.

"But the wound...." Louisa objected.

"Could have happened on impact," Detective Hagan said. "He *was* facing down when you found him."

"You think he fell on something sharp? Did you find anything underneath the body?" she asked.

"We didn't know to look until after the autopsy, and by then the scene had been trampled," he said with a shrug.

"I don't understand...," Louisa said.

Detective Hagan leaned so close she could smell the tobacco on his breath.

"Miss Delafield, if the coroner says he doesn't know the exact cause of death, then I have nothing to go on."

"But you seemed so sure...," she began.

He shrugged and took a step in the other direction.

"I think I understand," she said. He turned to look at her and she continued, "This is a tourist town. Its lifeblood is the tourist dollar. If there's a murder, especially one that looks unsolvable, and the tourists decide they aren't safe in their own hotel rooms... Am I right?"

He turned his eyes to the carvings above them.

"Look, Miss Delafield, if we *knew* for a fact this was murder then I would launch a full investigation, but when there's a gray area like there is here, there are other considerations," he said.

She understood that a mayor or the chamber of commerce must have learned about the incident and decided to shut down any investigation. "You're going to let a murderer go scot-free?"

"The coroner's report will say Lord Wickham died on impact, nothing more," he said. "Wind your neck in, Miss Delafield."

"Excuse me?" she said and touched her neck.

He didn't bother to explain himself.

***

Dinner with the Griffins was a small, gloomy affair with no bridesmaids or groomsmen in attendance. Louisa sat between Mrs. Griffin and her younger daughter, Margaret, and eyed Henri surreptitiously. He picked at his food while Simon tried to cheer him up with talk of fencing duels. Daphne and her younger sister chattered about clothes, motion pictures, and various entertainments they wished to attend. Mrs. Griffin smiled occasionally and Mr. Griffin sat stony-faced beside her. Was Henri despondent or guilt-ridden, Louisa wondered.

After dinner, Mr. Griffin offered to escort Louisa back to her hotel. It was dark, but the tourists were out in full force and one of the streets had been cordoned off for a street dance.

"This is a nasty business, isn't it?" Mr. Griffin said in a low voice.

"Quite," Louisa agreed.

"Do you think someone killed him?"

"I have no idea," Louisa said. "There may have been a motive, however. I believe that Lord Wickham was involved in a diamond...heist, I believe is the term."

"Diamonds?"

"My assistant in New York learned that a half million dollars' worth of diamonds were stolen from a broker in Alexandria, Egypt, at the same time Lord Wickham was there," she explained. "Daphne's diamond may have been one of those. And he also was holding a raw diamond in his hand when I found his body."

"Henri and Simon were also in Alexandria last year," Randall Griffin said.

"And there's this," she said. She took the cable from Louis Boucheron from her purse and handed it to him. He stood under a paper lantern and read it.

"My God," he said. "If Henri knew that Wickham had a half million dollars' worth of diamonds, do you think he would have killed him for them?"

"He's marrying your daughter, and I don't wish to be crass, but she's worth more than that, isn't she?"

"Greed has no bounds," Mr. Griffin said.

She hesitated. Did she dare continue?

"Mr. Griffin, I learned something else."

"Yes," he prodded.

"Lord Wickham was an invert," she said.

"A what?"

"He preferred men to women," she said.

Mr. Griffin sputtered. "Disgusting!"

She thought of Ellen's love for Hester. There was nothing disgusting about it, but it would not help to disagree with him so she merely said, "I believe he was in love with Henri."

"I shall end this farce of a marriage this instant," Mr. Griffin said.

She put a hand on his arm.

"I have no reason to believe that Henri returned his affections," she said. "In fact, he went over that night to insist that Lord Wickham forget about him."

"What if Wickham was blackmailing Henri?" Mr. Griffin asked.

"It's possible," Louisa said. "But Lord Wickham had no need of money. He was to receive a sizable inheritance. Madame Ribault believes that he killed himself, despondent over Henri's rejection of him."

They had come within sight of the Florida House.

"Find out, Miss Delafield. I beg you. I cannot have my daughter marrying a murderer."

"I will do my best," she said.

Louisa had not mentioned the wound to Lord Wickham's chest or the fact his door was unlocked. If she could prove nothing then it would be better to let everyone think that Lord Wickham's death had been a suicide. She dreaded the idea of destroying Daphne's dream. She may not have liked the young woman at first, but she had grown to respect her. After all, Daphne had saved her life. And yet, Mr. Griffin was also right. They could not allow her to marry a murderer.

Then she wondered, why had Simon said that Henri and Madame Ribault had been an item when it was really Henri and Lord Wickham? Of course, Simon was protecting Henri, she realized. That's what he had done his whole life.

The parlor at the Florida House was abuzz with the news of Lord Wickham's death. Lady Rutherford insisted Louisa join them at the card table, for she needed to know everything that Louisa could tell her. Louisa hoped she might learn something as well.

"Louisa, you were the one who found him, weren't you?" Lady Rutherford asked as she dealt the cards.

"Unfortunately, yes," Louisa said.

"They say it's suicide," one of the other ladies noted.

Lady Rutherford said, "Poor Percival. I know his family quite well."

"I wonder why he would kill himself when he was so excited about his upcoming expedition to Egypt," Louisa said.

"How in blazes could he afford an expedition?" Lady Rutherford asked.

"I understood he was to receive a sizable inheritance. There was just a matter of some paperwork," Louisa said.

"A sizeable inheritance? Percival Wickham?" Lady Rutherford scoffed. "His grandfather disowned him before he died."

"Really? Why?" Louisa asked, laying down a trump card.

"His, er, peculiarities," Lady Rutherford said, glancing above her spectacles at Louisa.

"I see," Louisa said. If Lord Wickham wasn't to receive an inheritance, then why had he planned to go to New York on "financial business," she wondered.

"Excuse me, ladies," Louisa said. "I need to place a telephone call."

Chapter 28

Ellen

Ellen lifted the receiver of the telephone and asked the operator to place a long distance call to the Florida House Hotel in St. Augustine, Florida.

"You know this call will cost a king's ransom," Mrs. Delafield said, watching from her chair.

"I'm sure the paper will reimburse you," Ellen said. "It must be important for Louisa to have left a message for me to call her." She looked at the note that the girl had left, 8 a.m. sharp underlined. Louisa had probably been annoyed that Ellen hadn't been at the house when she called.

As she waited for the operator to make the connection, she drummed her fingers on the desk. Then she heard Louisa's voice on the line and couldn't help marveling that she was hearing the voice of someone at the other end of the country.

"We have to make this quick," Louisa said. "You need to find out where or to whom someone would sell raw diamonds in New York."

"The ones from Alexandria?"

"Yes. Lord Wickham was murdered here and he had a raw diamond in his hand."

"Murdered?" Ellen said. "Was he the thief?"

"I believe so, and I believe he was planning to sell them in the city. I need to find out if he had any accomplices."

"I did see something in the paper about a recent jewel theft. They nabbed a big-time thief," Ellen said. "Maybe Paddy can get me in to see him. By the way, I think I know who shot Dottie, and I may have the proof."

"Proof? What do you mean? Ellen, what have you been doing in my absence?" Louisa asked.

Ellen had completely forgotten that Louisa didn't know she was consorting with anarchists.

"I've been doing a little investigating..." she said.

"I should have known," Louisa said. "Be careful, please, Ellen."

"You, too."

Ellen replaced the receiver.

"Who was murdered?" Mrs. Delafield asked.

"A Lord Wickham," Ellen said.

"Never heard of him," Louisa's mother said with a dismissive wave of her hand. "Have Hester come over and read to me today."

"I'll ask her," Ellen said. She worried that one of these days Hester would be fed up with all the cloak-and-dagger business, but when she dialed Hester's number and asked, Hester hesitated only a moment before saying, yes, she would come and keep Mrs. Delafield company.

***

Ellen sat on a bench across from St. Peter's Catholic Church. When she saw Paddy and Paula coming out of the front door with the kids, she stood up, straightened her hat and hurried across the street. She had a newspaper tucked her under her arm.

"Paddy!" she called.

He looked at her in surprise.

"Missed mass, did you?" he asked with a smirk.

"Not at all," she answered. "I'm after talking to you about a couple of things. Can you walk with me?"

Sean ran up and wrapped his small arms around Ellen's legs. She ruffled the hair on his head.

"Oh, go on," Paula said. "I'll take the kids home and give them something to eat before they starve to death."

"Thank you, Paula," Ellen said. "I won't keep him long."

"Keep him as long as you like. He just gets in my hair on Sundays," Paula said with a teasing grin. He patted her bottom, and she pretended to be offended.

Ellen and Paddy walked along the street.

"How are things in that snakepit of anarchists down on East 13th Street after the riot?" he asked.

"The police started it, Paddy O'Neil," Ellen chided. "And you should know. You were there."

"So were you when you *shouldn't* have been," he said and turned a hard eye on her.

"You're just angry because I got past your watchdog," she said.

"I was only trying to keep you out of harm's way," he said, throwing up his hands.

"Never mind. I'm actually here on different business," she said. "You know Louisa is in St. Augustine, right?"

"Sure," he said. "After the attempt on her life, it's good she got away for a spell."

"She might have stepped out of the frying pan...," Ellen said.

"And into the fire?"

"Exactly. A Brit there — a Lord Wickham — was murdered. Louisa thinks he might be related to a diamond theft in Egypt and that he was planning to sell the stolen jewels here in New York."

Paddy arched his eyebrows in interest.

"Diamonds?"

Ellen pulled him over to a bench to sit down. She opened the newspaper she had tucked under her arm.

"I was reading about the arrest of a 'crackman' in Brooklyn. He specializes in safe cracking for diamonds, doesn't he?"

"Aye, Billy Burke's got a hell of a rep in the underworld," Paddy said.

"I'm thinking he might know where someone would sell stolen diamonds. You know the old adage, no secrets among thieves?"

"I believe it's no honor among thieves," Paddy said and leaned back with crossed arms. "What are ya asking for, Ellen?"

"A chance to ask him a few questions," she said. "Today if possible."

"And what will you give me in return?" he asked under beetled eyebrows. "I want some information about those anarchists and what they're up to."

She hesitated and then said, "I am thinking that it may have been Becky Edelsohn who took a shot at Louisa and killed Dottie. I hope I'm wrong. I don't mind saying I admire the girl's spirit."

"Careful, girleen. Don't be fooled by 'em. They're murderers," he said.

"Not all of them. Emma Goldman isn't, and neither is Lulu," she said.

"What makes you think this Becky is a suspect?" he asked.

Ellen watched a group of children playing hopscotch on the sidewalk before pulling the bullet out of her pocket and holding it out to Paddy.

"What's this?" he asked.

"It's for the gun that Berkman and Becky have in their apartment," she said. "I thought you might check if that's the same kind of bullet that killed Dottie Parsons."

He took the bullet in his fingers and glanced approvingly at Ellen, but she felt as low as a worm. If Becky had been the one to shoot Dottie, then she should pay for her crime, and yet Ellen felt like the worst sort of rat.

"I'll see if we can get into the tombs and interview your diamond thief," he said.

"Today?" Ellen asked.

"I'll try," he said and pocketed the bullet.

***

Mrs. Delafield's head drooped and she began to snore. Hester put down the book and looked over at Ellen, who was reading Berkman's prison memoirs. He had a way with words, no doubt about it: *"The People—the toilers of the world, the producers—comprise, to me, the universe. They alone count. The rest are parasites, who have no right to exist."*

Aye, there was the rub. He considered Louisa Delafield one of the parasites.

"May we talk?" Hester said.

"Sure," Ellen said. "Let's go to the kitchen so we don't wake Sleeping Beauty."

In the kitchen, Ellen heated water for tea and put cookies on a plate. Hester ignored the cookies, but drank the tea.

"Is there any cream?" Hester asked.

"We're all out," Ellen admitted. She hadn't done a great job of keeping the larder stocked.

"Ellen, I'm worried I may be losing you," she said.

"What makes you say that?" Ellen asked.

"These protests. They are so violent, and there you are in the thick of it," Hester said. "It's a wonder you weren't hurt."

Ellen had not shown her the purple bruise on her shoulder from the glancing Billy club.

"The police caused the violence, not the protestors," Ellen said.

"Is that so? I'm afraid that slogans such as 'kill the capitalists' do not come across as peaceful to me. Debs and the Socialists would never advocate for murder," Hester said, fiddling with her teaspoon.

"Emma Goldman does not advocate violence," Ellen said.

"What about Berkman? And your friend, L. Byron, or Karl as you call him," Hester said. "I read the most recent issue of *Mother Earth* and I was horrified."

Ellen drank her tea. She did not know how to answer Hester, who had no idea what it was like to live under the thumb of oppressors. The Irish knew, the Russian Jews knew, the Negroes knew, and poor American laborers knew.

"Emma says, and rightfully so, that capitalism is relentless, the state crushes every individual and social right, and the church is in league with them. We've a quarter million people in this city with no work. Of course, there will be violence," Ellen said, trying to get Hester to understand.

Hester set her cup in its saucer.

"If you involve yourself in any act that harms another human being, Ellen, I will not stand by you. We will be through." She frowned and stood up, straightening her navy skirt.

"Hester, please—" Ellen said. She stood up as well and reached for Hester's arm, but Hester was already walking out the door.

"I'll see myself out," Hester said as she marched down the hall to the front door.

"Hester!" Ellen felt a sudden boiling of the blood. Hester had no idea what it was like to be cold, to be hungry. What right had she to –

The front door banged shut, and Hester was gone.

Ellen turned back to the kitchen and stared at the empty teacup. Her anger dissipated and she felt as empty as the teacup.

***

True to his word, Paddy had arranged a meeting with the diamond thief.

"Will the old lady be okay?" Paddy asked as they made their way downtown to the City Prison on Centre Street.

"As long as I'm not gone too long," Ellen said. She had given Mrs. Delafield something to eat and her knitting and headed out with Paddy.

Ellen had been in the Tombs once before when the Garrett family falsely accused her of stealing a pair of earrings. That had been a harrowing few hours. Now as they approached, she looked up at the Bridge of Sighs connecting the prison to the courthouse across the street and thought about the poor souls, including Frank Tannenbaum, who every day faced the excessive and brutal punishments meted out by American justice.

Sure, some were violent criminals, but others were simply unwilling to starve.

They went in through a series of clanking doors and followed dark hallways that led into a small room with a narrow window that smelled of mildew. They sat at a scarred wooden table and waited until a middle-aged man in manacles was shown into the room and sat down opposite them with a quizzical look on his face.

"To what do I owe the pleasure?" he asked. He spoke in a lilting, polite voice, and smiled pleasantly.

"You are the famous diamond thief Billy Burke, are you not?" Paddy asked.

"I don't know how famous I am," Burke replied. "But yes, I am William Burke, at your service."

"I'm Detective O'Neil, and this is Miss Malloy. We have some questions for you," Paddy said.

"I am always happy to cooperate with law enforcement. By the way, have you seen my wife, Sophie? She's been trying to get a visit with me, poor girl. But they won't let her in," he said. Ellen could tell he had been handsome in his younger days as he was still a nice enough looking fellow.

"I'll see you get a visit with her this week," Paddy said. "Anything else?"

"A pack or two of Coupon cigarettes would be greatly appreciated," Burke said.

"Duly noted," Paddy said with a nod.

"Now, how can I help you, sir?" Burke asked.

"Know anything about a diamond theft in Alexandria, Egypt last year? Worth a half million dollars?" Ellen asked.

He looked at her.

"Irish girl, aren't you? My family is from County Cork," he said and grinned at her.

"Yeah, yeah, we're all from the old country," Paddy interjected. "She's a Galway girl, and you don't trouble her kind."

"I'll remember that," Burke said. "Why, yes, Miss Malloy, that particular escapade is quite well known in my circles. I was in London shortly after it happened, and Scotland Yard tried to pin it on me, but I had an alibi. Air tight."

"We're not accusing you of doing the stealing," Paddy growled.

"We only want to know, if someone were to try to sell the raw diamonds in New York from that heist, who would they go to?" Ellen asked.

Burke looked from one to the other.

"You're asking me to turn in one of my own clients?" he asked. "That's more than I bargained for."

"No one wants to arrest them," Ellen insisted. "I'm not with the police. My employer is a journalist and she believes she knows who stole the diamonds. She's trying to protect a young woman from getting herself involved with the wrong type."

"Wrong type?" he asked.

"You know exactly what I mean," she said, tapping the table with her forefinger.

"Then why's he here?" Burke asked, indicating Paddy with his chin.

Paddy stood up and went to the door.

"Guard!" he yelled. A guard came to the door. Paddy asked to be let out. He turned around and said to Burke, "Tell her what she wants to know. And you'll be seeing Sophie tomorrow."

He walked out of the room, leaving Ellen alone with the renowned thief.

Burke leaned over and said, "I'm going to trust you because you're Irish, but if you rat this guy out, there will be hell to pay, girl."

"I swear on my gran's grave, I won't give him away," she said.

He looked at her with eyes so blue she felt she had fallen into the sky and he proceeded to tell her what she had come to learn.

Chapter 29

Louisa

"If the police won't rule it as a murder, then there's nothing you can do," Suzie said as they walked out of the hotel together. "What did Ellen say on the phone?"

"She's going to try to find out who would buy stolen diamonds in New York. If anyone can find out, I'm sure it will be Ellen."

"If you accuse someone of murder, you must be able to prove it, Louisa," Suzie said.

"I know, and I would rather not be the one who dashes Daphne's dreams," Louisa said. "On the other hand, what if Henri is a murderer? And what if I say nothing about it? I must at least confront him."

"Does he know you suspect him?" Suzie asked.

"I don't think he does."

They reached the corner where Suzie turned to go to Lincolnville, and Louisa turned toward the Ponce Hotel when she saw Daphne and her mother approaching the Florida House.

"No swimming today?" Louisa asked.

"Madame Ribault is fitting our gowns for tonight's ball," Daphne said.

"And where is your betrothed?"

"He and his brother are taking one of the sails up to Cap's Beach."

"Weddings are women's work," Daphne's mother said.

"That they are," Louisa said. "Tell me, Mrs. Griffin, weren't you in Madame Ribault's atelier the night that Lord Wickham fell to his death? Did you not hear a scream?"

"I heard a quarrel of some sort. That's all. I didn't recognize the other voice. Now, if you'll excuse us, we're running a bit late," she said.

Why hadn't Lord Wickham screamed when he fell? She would think even suicide would be terrifying, unless that puncture in his chest happened before he fell.

***

Louisa had heard of the short cruises, taken by almost everyone who came to St. Augustine. The twenty-five-cent ride took tourists to a northern beach for lunch at one of the oyster restaurants and back in time for an afternoon siesta.

She hurried to the landing and got passage just as the boat was ready to leave. The brothers were not difficult to find. They stood on the deck side by side, leaning against the rail. She stopped and observed the two men for a moment. Henri's gold hair shined in the sunlight, but it was the dark-haired Simon who reminded her of a prince with his full lips and hooded eyes.

"Mademoiselle Delafield," Simon said, eyes widening with surprise when he saw her. "I did not know I would have the pleasure of your company today. Are you fully recovered from the shock of your find?"

"Yes," Louisa answered. "What a terrible tragedy. I didn't know him well, but I did like him."

"The detective said that he may have killed himself, but I do not believe it for a minute," Henri said.

"Were you close, Henri?" she asked. "I know he certainly admired you."

Henri looked down his long, aquiline nose at her.

"Close?"

"You were probably the last one to see him alive," she said.

He lowered his head to hers and said, "No one knows that."

"I understand your desire for discretion," she said. "I will not expose your relationship with him."

"Expose me? Percy was a silly poof. I cannot help the way he felt about me, but I am not that way," Henri said. "I am a ladies' man." He pushed his blond locks off his high forehead and gazed out at the sea. The vanity of the man knew no bounds.

"I understand there was a theft of diamonds from a broker in Alexandria at the same time you and Percival were there," she said. "Do you suppose Lord Wickham had something to do with the stolen diamonds?"

"Louisa," Simon interjected. "What do you mean?"

"I found a raw diamond in Lord Wickham's possession when he died," Louisa said. "Why would he have something like that? In his hand?"

"If our friend Lord Wickham had anything to do with any stolen diamonds, we know nothing about it," Simon said, shaking his head.

"But what about Daphne's pendant?" she asked.

"What about it?" Henri said. "Daphne deserves only the best."

Louisa looked at him curiously. For all his egotism, she thought she detected a shred of sincerity when he spoke of Daphne. Did he genuinely love her? Would he kill to protect his relationship with her?

"I know Lord Wickham gave a raw diamond to Louis Boucheron and that became Daphne's pendant," Louisa said. "That's why you could afford to buy it."

Henri's mouth gaped before it turned into a grin.

"Do you hear this, *mon frere*?" he asked Simon. "Our friend was a jewel thief! I did not know he was so... clever."

"Then you knew nothing about it?" Louisa asked.

"*Mais non,*" Henri said. "If it's true then I am even more sad about his death."

"You don't seem sad," Louisa quipped.

Henri's cheerful countenance disappeared, and his expression turned dark.

"You do not know how I feel," he muttered and walked to the other side of the boat.

"My apologies, Louisa," Simon said. "Percival's death is harder for him than he will allow to show. I know you write the investigations. However, to question my brother at a time like this, it is gauche, is it not?"

She felt as if he had slapped her in the face as he followed his brother, leaving her standing by the railing at the front of the ship. She gazed out to sea and saw a line of black clouds against the horizon.

***

Later that night, the rain fell in buckets and lightning intermittently flashed, but inside the ballroom of the Ponce, the jewels glittered in the light of the chandeliers. Laughter and music drowned out the thunder. Daphne's gown had elaborate silk sleeves that looked like wings as she danced with Henri. She was right. His beauty shined enough for both of them.

"I suppose Lord Wickham's tragedy is all but forgotten," Lady Rutherford said in a low voice.

"The wedding must go on," Louisa agreed. She looked around the room at the happy faces. Even Mr. Griffin and his wife were dancing. She couldn't help remembering dancing the tango with Lord Wickham only a few nights ago. Simon seemed to have been roped into a dance with Daphne's little sister. She glanced again at Henri, the carefree expression on his perfect face, and felt a surge of anger for what had happened to Lord Wickham. Then she looked at Daphne, whose face shined with happiness. If Henri murdered Lord Wickham, what would he do to Daphne when he grew tired of her?

"Excuse me," she said to Lady Rutherford. "I think I'll get some air."

She found the desk clerk taking surreptitious sips from a cocktail that had somehow made its way from the party to his station. He put the glass down quickly and smiled at her as she approached. She let her eyes drift down to the drink and then smiled warmly at him.

"Everyone should be allowed to celebrate," she said.

He smiled and nodded, reassured that she would not report him.

She leaned in.

"The bride, Miss Griffin, has asked me for a favor," she said. "She would like me to deliver a gift to the groom's room. But no one is to know about it. I won't tell if you don't."

She looked down at his drink and arched her eyebrows.

"What do you need?" he asked, nervously.

"I need his room key," Louisa said. She felt as nervous as the clerk but she was better at hiding it.

"Oh," he said. He glanced around. Then turned to the cubbyholes behind him and plucked out a key, which he handed to her. "This is it."

She headed upstairs. As she reached the third floor, a young woman who'd had too much to drink walked unsteadily down the hallway but took no notice of Louisa. Louisa waited for her to get on the elevator before she opened the door to Henri's room, slipped inside, and glanced around. It was an elegantly furnished room and smelled of shaving lotion and cigar smoke. The fencing helmet sat on the top of the bureau like a disembodied head, watching her. Next to the helmet were three bottles of wine. She looked under the bed, in the closet, in each of the drawers. The room was neat — the room of a man who did not have a valet and had learned to take care of himself. She peered into the closet, carefully examining the shoes. She'd once read a story about a smuggler who hid diamonds in shoes, but these appeared not to have been tampered with and now that she thought about it, that smuggler had been a woman and the shoes were high heels. She was running her hand over the various suits when a voice caused her to nearly jump out of her skin.

"What are you doing in here?"

The entire room went white as lightning flashed outside and thunder rumbled. She looked into the mirror and saw the reflection of Simon Bassett, his dark eyes with a thunder of their own. She turned and faced him but said nothing.

"You think my brother killed Wickham, don't you?" he asked, advancing toward her.

"I think it's possible."

She saw a flicker of anger on his face, but he suppressed it and assumed a mask of nonchalance.

"Then I'll help you search," he said. "What is it you're looking for?"

"Diamonds. Or a murder weapon," she said, gazing around the room.

"Murder weapon?"

"There was a wound on the body. Something sharp through the heart. Like a fencing foil, perhaps," she said.

"A foil? The tip is quite dull on purpose."

"It's sharp enough that it could puncture a man. That's why you wear the padded vest, isn't it?"

"Why would my brother murder Wickham?" Simon asked.

"I believe Lord Wickham stole those diamonds from a broker in Egypt," she said, standing her ground. "Your brother may have been his accomplice. Maybe he didn't want to share or maybe Wickham was blackmailing Henri for being his lover? Remember your brother said, *Il est fini*. Even I know that means 'it's finished.' Maybe it was finished because Lord Wickham was dead."

"Why do all this snooping when we can ask Henri himself?" Simon walked over to the bedside table, picked up the telephone, and spoke to the desk clerk, "This is Simon Bassett. I need you to find Henri Bassett in the ballroom and tell him that his brother wishes to see him. I'm in his room. Be discreet, please. Tell him I've stained my shirt and wish to borrow one of his."

Simon hung up the phone. He sat down in the arm chair in the corner of the room. Rain pattered against the windowpane, and fear fluttered in Louisa's chest.

"Simon, is it possible that Lord Wickham and Henri stole those diamonds? Were you with them all the time in Alexandria?" she asked.

He rolled his shoulders to loosen them and said, "No, I was not with them all the time. I had many meetings with potential buyers. Henri has no head for business."

"If he did take the diamonds, if he killed Lord Wickham, why would he admit it? Even to you?" she asked, lowering herself to the chaise longue.

"You are an only child, are you not?" Simon asked, his head tilted.

"Yes."

"If you had an older brother or sister, you would know it's the job of the eldest to torment the younger ones."

"Torment? You tormented your brother?" she asked.

"All older brothers do. I also protected, advised, and guided him, but when we were younger I beat him to make him a 'tough guy' as you say in America. Now, that we're older, *vraiment*, we do not engage in such childish behavior, but memory is long and I am the one person Henri fears," he said.

Louisa remembered the look on Henri's face after the fencing match. Simon was telling the truth. Henri worshipped and feared his older brother.

She clasped her hands in her lap nervously as they waited.

After a few minutes, she heard footsteps in the hallway. The door knob turned, and Henri entered, smiling and looking at his brother with a puzzled expression. Simon didn't say a word, but jumped up from the chair, crossed the room, and slapped his brother across the face.

"*Quoi?*" Henri yelled in surprise.

"Speak English," Simon demanded. "And tell the truth or I will beat you. Did you kill Wickham?"

"No!"

"Why did he provide the diamond you gave to Daphne?" Louisa asked.

"He wanted me to win Daphne. He wanted me to be happy. He wanted me to have a rich wife." He turned to his brother and asked, "Simon, what is this about?"

"Miss Delafield thinks you were his accomplice and you murdered him. Where is your foil?"

"My foil?" Henri said. He opened the wardrobe and pulled out his fencing foil. He tossed it on the bed.

Louisa looked at it closely. She saw no blood, but of course he could have cleaned it.

"Was Lord Wickham blackmailing you, Henri?" she asked.

"Blackmail?" Henri stared at her in confusion. "*Pourquoi?*"

"Why? Perhaps because he threatened to tell Daphne about you... and him?" Louisa said.

Henri looked down at the floor and said, "It's true. Percival and I were lovers at one time. But that was over. I told him that night."

"If you want to be with men, why are you marrying Daphne?" Louisa asked. "Is it only for her money?"

Henri stared at her.

"But I love Daphne. In every way," he said. "I've been with many women. And a few men. I can't help it if they all want me."

Louisa stared at him, the sharp cheekbones, the straight nose, and the azure eyes. Of course, women and men wanted him. She did not understand how a man could enjoy both women and other men, but she was no expert on these matters. Henri looked from Louisa to Simon, and his bottom lip quivered like a child's.

"Simon, *mon frère*, please."

"What's in those bottles?" Louisa asked, pointing to three wine bottles on top of the dresser.

"Wine," Henri said. "From our family's vineyard."

"Pour it out," Louisa said.

"No!" Henri said.

"Daphne's father has asked me to vouch for you. If you don't show me what's in those bottles, I won't do it, and there will be no wedding."

Simon took a corkscrew from a silver tray on the writing table and opened the first bottle. He went into the bathroom, held it over the bathtub, and poured. Louisa held the other two bottles and watched from the doorway.

"*Mon Dieu!*" Henri said. "At least save the wine."

Simon handed the empty bottle to Louisa. She looked inside. Nothing. She placed the bottle on the counter.

"The next one," she said, handing him the second bottle.

Simon opened the next bottle. Henri barged into the room, grabbed the empty bottle and held it under the second bottle. Once the liquid was all gone, Simon showed her the second bottle.

"No diamonds."

"Do the last one," she said and handed it to him.

Henri shoved the cork into the first bottle and likewise saved the wine from the third.

After Simon showed her the last empty bottle, he asked, "Are you satisfied?"

She looked at Henri. As handsome as he was, he did not seem like a clever man.

"I am," she said, gently. "And I am sorry for my suspicions, but you cannot blame me or Mr. Griffin. He only wants what is best for Daphne. And Lord Wickham's death is suspicious."

"I only want what is best for Daphne as well, Mademoiselle Delafield," Henri said.

She did not want Henri to be guilty. And yet, someone had to be. No matter what the coroner had ruled, Lord Wickham had been murdered. She was sure of it, and yet a sliver of doubt had crept into her mind. What if Lord Wickham had merely been despondent after Henri's visit? What if he'd managed to stab himself with something sharp before falling or fell on something sharp enough to pierce his heart. Stranger things had happened.

"After you," Simon said. Louisa walked out of the room, and the two brothers followed her. They got into the elevator. Surely, Simon must despise her now, she thought. His face was inscrutable as they made their way back to the party.

"Darling, where have you been?" Daphne asked and commandeered her fiancé from them. Mr. Griffin looked at Louisa with a questioning look. She shook her head quickly, and he understood her meaning. Henri had not murdered Lord Wickham.

The orchestra struck up the lively waltz "Nights of Gladness," and she felt Simon's warm breath on her neck as he whispered, "May I have this dance?" She looked up at him in surprise. He smiled and held out his hand.

Within moments, she was in his arms and he was twirling her around the dance floor. He gazed down into her eyes, but she couldn't bear the scrutiny and looked away.

"You must hate me," she said.

"*Non*," he said, his voice low. "You only wanted to protect Daphne."

She felt as though drums were beating inside her torso. Their hands clasped, their bodies melded together. She was flush with desire.

He whispered, "Come to my room tonight."

Her whole body screamed *yes*. She nodded and tore her gaze away from him, afraid that she would lose herself altogether if she looked into his eyes.

***

Everything about it was wrong, scandalous even. And yet here she was, standing at his door, willingly. She still hadn't sent the letter to Forrest, but in her heart she had released him. It was 1914, after all. She was a modern woman, she told herself. The truth was that her desire for Simon overwhelmed any sense of propriety or loyalty to Forrest.

The door opened. Simon looked at her with dark, hooded eyes. She stepped in the room, and he shut the door. His arms encircled her as he pulled her into him, kissing her feverishly, his mouth slightly sour with wine. His hands quickly worked at the buttons on her dress, and then he roughly pulled off her clothes and shoved her onto the bed. He unbuttoned his trousers and pounced on her. She whimpered as he thrust himself in her again and again. This was nothing like making love to Forrest. This was animal-like. When he was done, he collapsed on top of her. She stroked his sweat soaked back.

"Forgive me," he said. "I wanted you too much. I will be slower next time."

He kissed her face and then rolled off of her.

Next time? She was still trying to understand what had happened the first time. Perhaps because he was older, Forrest was gentler, and he made sure that Louisa felt pleasure. There had been something exhilarating about Simon's brute passion, but in the end she simply felt used. She turned to look at him. He was snoring. Sound asleep.

She slipped off the bed and put on her clothing. Then quietly she opened the door and glanced into the hallway to make sure it was empty. A few minutes later she was back in her room, cleaning herself. Forrest always used something to make sure she did not get pregnant, but there had been nothing between her womb and Simon's flesh. She must never let this happen again. She looked at the letter to Forrest still on her desk and felt a surge of regret. Had she been rash?

Chapter 30

Ellen

Ellen spent her lunch hour trying to find Mr. Van Mott, the man that Billy Burke had said would have the information she needed, but she'd had no luck. He owned an estate jewelry store on West 47th, according to Burke, but a young man behind the counter told her that Mr. Van Mott was out for the day. When she pressed him, he said in no uncertain terms that he had no idea where Mr. Van Mott was and that she would have to wait until morning to speak to him.

"Fine," she said and went back to work.

That evening, she left the paper through the back way, as had become her habit and made her way back to Louisa's house in Harlem. She was almost to the stoop when she heard a loud whistle. She looked across the street and saw Charlie, leaning against the wall of a brownstone. He wore a snappy suit and a velour hat aslant over his face.

She crossed the street and asked him what he wanted.

"I've got a little job for you," he said.

"I've already got a job, taking care of this old woman whilst her daughter is gone," Ellen said.

"You said you wanted us to trust you, well, here's your chance," he said.

"All right," she said. "Let me go in and tell the hired girl to stay for a while. She won't mind the extra money, but this better be worth it as I'm the one losing money."

Ellen went inside to beg the girl to stay longer. As she expected, the girl was more than willing as long as the pay was ten cents higher.

Ellen had begun to wonder if it hadn't actually been a man dressed as a woman who had shot at Louisa. Charlie certainly seemed capable of anything. He was handsome and lithe and could easily fool someone if he wore a dress and a hat with a veil. Ever since Frank's arrest and Arnie's beating, he'd been seething with menace.

"It's time to stop pussy-footing around," he said when she joined him.

"What do you plan to do?" she asked.

"You'll see," he said.

As they walked down Lexington Avenue, Charlie asked her if she knew how subways were built.

"No, but I've seen a few windows blown out from the explosions underground," she said.

"They tear up the streets with dynamite, clear away the rubble, build the tunnel, and then cover it back up."

"I see," she said, wondering what he was getting at.

At 59th Street a tall wooden fence ran along the sidewalk. On the other side she could see a crane.

Charlie stopped at the end of the fence, quickly glanced around, and then kicked the bottom of a wide board.

"Ever wonder where we get our dynamite?" he asked. "Most of it is home-picked. Wanna see how we do it?"

Was this some sort of test? Within minutes Charlie had slipped sideways through the gap in the fence.

"You coming?" he asked.

Ellen pulled her skirt up to her knees and put one leg through the hole. She dipped her torso and then she was in. Charlie let the board flap back down. She straightened up.

"Where are we?"

"Someday this'll be a subway station," he said. "In the meanwhile this is where they keep the dynamite."

He carefully walked the perimeter of the site, avoiding the large holes that would someday lead down to trains. Ellen followed him, peering at the machines, the barrels, the shovels, and pickaxes scattered around. Charlie took her by the wrist and pulled her along until they got to the very back of the lot. There stood a shed with a lock on the door. Charlie took a tool from his pocket and pried the entire lock off the door.

They went inside. It was dark, but he pulled a candle from his pocket and lit it. The feeble light showed a small room, filled with boxes. He opened a box and Ellen looked inside. Hundreds of sticks of dynamite. He handed her a few sticks.

"Put these in your pockets," he said. He jammed three sticks into each of his coat pockets.

"What if it explodes?" she asked.

"It won't. You have to light a fuse," he said.

She obeyed him, terrified. What if they were caught? How could she explain herself?

"We don't need much," he said. "We ain't building a subway. A few sticks at a time and we got a good stash."

"Where?" Ellen asked. "Where do you keep it?"

"At Lulu's place," he said "Didn't you know?"

She followed him out of the shed, around the work site and then back through the hole in the fence.

Then they walked up Lexington Avenue to the tenement where she assumed Lulu lived. She handed over the dynamite as soon as they got to the top of the hill.

"Ain't you coming up?" he said.

She shook her head. She kept hearing Hester's voice in her head, *if you do anything to hurt anyone...*

"I've got to get back to the old lady's," Ellen said. "I can't be raising suspicion."

He shrugged, went up the stoop and inside.

Ellen hurried back to Louisa's, paid off the girl, and slept fitfully that night.

In the morning she went back to the diamond district and got to the door of Van Mott's Estate Jewelers five minutes before it was supposed to open. Ten minutes later, the young man she'd spoken to the day before let her in.

"Mr. Van Mott is back in his office," he said.

The jeweler had white hair and a long face with large, rheumy eyes. He held a stunning necklace of diamonds and rubies in both hands.

"Mother Mary!" Ellen said, staring at the glimmering jewels.

"No, they belong to a woman who believes these jewels are all real," he said with a sad expression. "How may I help you?"

"It's a rather delicate matter," she said.

It took some doing, but Ellen finally got some information from the man. He told her a Frenchman had been to see him as recently as a couple of weeks ago with some story about a large cache of raw diamonds that would be available soon.

"What did he look like?" she asked.

"Like a Frenchman," he said. "I don't remember. He wasn't old. Dark hair, I think."

Ellen hoped it was enough. She would send a cable to Louisa from the paper.

Chapter 31

Louisa

The day after the ball, the wedding party gathered for Lord Wickham's funeral service in an airless chapel across from the Alcazar Hotel. Simon, Henri, Daphne and Daphne's younger sister, Mr. and Mrs. Griffin, Lady Rutherford, and Madame Ribault all attended. The sickly scent of lilies filled the air as a minister who'd never met Percival Wickham said some empty words. The women fanned themselves, and the men wiped their foreheads with their handkerchiefs.

As soon as it was over, everyone seemed eager to move on with life. Lord Wickham's body would be buried in a cemetery on the outskirts of town. His family had wired money for a headstone. That would be the end of it.

As she walked out of the chapel, Louisa exchanged a glance with Simon and felt a flush creep up her neck, remembering the night before. He smiled and came alongside her.

"I have something to show you," he said.

"Now?" she asked.

He nodded, taking her by the elbow.

"Where?"

"It's in my pocket," he said and glanced quickly around. She caught a whiff of his scent and suddenly she had no willpower. She allowed him to cut her out of the herd and led her away from the others.

"Here," he said, indicating the cathedral. They went inside. It was cool and cavernous and smelled of centuries-old stone.

"Simon, please, explain yourself," she said.

The cathedral was empty but for the two of them. He slid into a pew and she followed him. From his pocket, he pulled a letter and handed it to her.

"Henri received this before he went to see Percival. We cannot let anyone see it, but I show it to you so you will understand Percival's state of mind."

Curious, she opened the letter and read:

"My dear Henri,

I know I am a fool but I cannot bear it if you will not come to me. I beg you. I plead with you. After your wedding I will go away, but let me have one more night in your arms. My life is not worth living without you. You are my sun and my moon. Please, my love, one more night. I will never ask again if you grant me this. If not, I cannot say what I will do.

Your slave,

PW"

"You see, of course, why we cannot go to the police," Simon said.

Louisa nodded. Poor broken-hearted Percival. When Henri came to tell him it was over, he must have been so despondent.

"This is heart-breaking. But I still have questions. For one thing, why didn't he lock the door before throwing himself off the balcony? What about the puncture wound in his chest? And where are the other diamonds?"

Simon looked at her curiously.

"Why are you obsessed with these diamonds?" he asked.

"A half million dollars' worth of diamonds? Who wouldn't wonder what happened to them?" she responded.

He shrugged. Then he leaned close and whispered, "Will I see you again tonight?"

"*Impossible,*" she said in her questionable French.

He tilted his head forward and looked up hetr at through those thick eyelashes, while running his fingers over the back of her hand.

"I promise I will be slow this time," he said.

The feel of his fingertips sent a shiver up her arm. Temptation loomed. Then she looked at a stained glass window above and saw Jesus rebuffing Satan.

"Some other time," she said, rising. "I have some writing to do or else my editor will wonder what I'm doing with myself down here."

She spent the rest of the day in her room, catching up on her articles. Her letter to Forrest sat on her writing table like an accusation. When Suzie brought back barbecued chicken from Lincolnville for dinner, Louisa couldn't touch it. Instead she went to bed early, but sleep eluded her. She wasn't even thinking about Lord Wickham. Instead, guilt crawled into bed beside her and put its cold hand on her belly. She couldn't stop thinking about Simon's promise to go slower "this time." She should be through with him, but she wasn't and she knew it.

***

Louisa and Suzie sat at the little table in Louisa's room for their usual breakfast and coffee. The waiter who brought up the fresh-squeezed orange juice, hot muffins, and coffee felt like an old friend at this point, always asking after Suzie's family and who else she had met in the Lincolnville community. He liked to tease her, asking if she was looking for a husband and telling her how the men in town were already asking about her. Louisa hoped he wasn't serious. She didn't know what she'd do if Suzie didn't go back to New York with her.

After he left, Suzie looked at her curiously.

"What's wrong? Are you still worrying about those diamonds and who killed that English lord?" she asked.

"Everyone believes it was suicide. While it's plausible that Lord Wickham killed himself, I do wonder where the diamonds are — if there are any diamonds," Louisa said.

"Will there still be a wedding?"

"Yes. So far I have no reason to think that Henri isn't telling the truth. I made a fool of myself, demanding they pour out the wine because I thought there might be diamonds in the wine bottles."

Suzie set down her coffee cup.

"Then you should be happy. That poor girl doesn't need to be humiliated," Suzie said.

"I suppose someone else could have killed Wickham, but Daphne and her father were attending a play in town that evening and Mrs. Griffin was in Madame Ribault's atelier. So they both have an alibi."

"What about Simon?"

"The police determined it happened between 10 and 11 p.m. and Simon was with me, looking for you," Louisa said. "I was worried."

"Then what will you do now?" Suzie asked.

"My job," Louisa answered. "I'm not a detective. I'm a society writer. I plan to interview the bridesmaids today and write about what they're doing for fun while they're in St. Augustine. I don't want anyone getting hurt because of my interference, and I'm finally going to go shopping for myself."

"No day trips with Smooth Simon then?"

"No." She shook her head as a bolt of shame coursed through her. She couldn't let Suzie know that she had slept with the man. "And what are your plans?"

"I'm going to spend the day with my grandniece, Pansy, and show her how to cook sweet potato pie the way Granny taught me," Suzie said, a happy light shining in her eyes.

After they were dressed, Louisa walked with Suzie to the lobby.

"Any cables for me?" she asked the clerk.

"Not yet," he said. The machine behind the desk began clicking and clacking. "That might be for you."

"I'll wait," she said.

At that moment Simon showed up at her side. Her body tensed and then relaxed as he smiled at her.

"I have a surprise for you," he said. "Are you busy?"

"I'm going shopping," she said. "Then I have to interview the bridesmaids."

"They're all still sleeping," he said, leaning close to her. "You can see them this afternoon. I promise you won't regret this."

"What is it?" She wasn't sure she should go anywhere with him.

"Have you seen your roseate spoonbill yet?" he asked.

"No, I have not," she said.

"I promised I would find them for you, remember? I've learned where they nest," he said.

"Really?" She felt a swell of excitement. Just what she needed to finish the bird article. Certainly it couldn't hurt to just go look at some birds and take some pictures. They would be outside. Nothing untoward could happen. "Will it take long?"

"A couple of hours at the most," he said.

"This would only be to look at birds?" she asked.

"I promise," he said. "I'm sorry if I have made you feel uncomfortable. We can pretend the other night never happened." His voice was gentle and sincere.

She looked over at the clerk who was standing by the telegraph as the message came in. If it was for her, she preferred that Simon not see it. She wasn't sure why, but she didn't want him to know she had still been digging for information.

"I'll come," she said and held up her bag. "Fortunately, I've gotten into the habit of bringing my bird book and camera everywhere with me."

As she walked out of the lobby at Simon's side, she heard the desk clerk call her name, but she didn't turn back. She would get the cable when she returned.

They drove west of town along a road called King's Highway. Louisa let the wind wash over her as she gazed out at the endless palm trees and pine groves. Her feelings toward Simon softened. She certainly had been hasty going to bed with him, but maybe if they got to know each other better, the next time wouldn't be so awkward. She could not believe she had just thought that there might be a next time.

It wasn't long before they turned onto another road and then down a dirt road. They crossed a small bridge and continued down the bumpy dirt road until it ended at the edge of a creek. An old ramshackle shack huddled under the trees. Simon turned off the car, and they got out. A soft breeze rustled in the palm fronds, and the tea-colored water was crowded with lily pads.

"Where are we?" she asked.

"Turnbull Creek," he said. "It leads into the swamp where the rookery is."

Louisa gazed around. Spiky-leaved thickets crowded the road. Trees draped in long strands of gray moss looked like bearded old men watching silently. The clouds in the sky looked like stretched cotton with white streamers swirling over the blue.

"Is that for us?" Louisa asked, pointing to a rowboat tied to a short dock.

"Yes, I paid the owner for the use of it," he said. "I found this place while you were...what's the word? — sequestered? — in your room yesterday. I worried that you did not want to see me again."

"I admit I had second thoughts about our ... relationship," she said and found a bench seat at the front of the boat. She opened her parasol to keep the sun off her face, her Chapman's *Bird Life* in her bag and the camera hanging on her shoulder. Simon untied the boat and used one of the oars to push off into the creek. Soon the water spread out like a hand opening and they were in the swamp. Trees hung their heavy branches over the water.

"What changed your mind?" he asked.

"I'm not sure my mind is changed," she said. "However, I'm excited to see some of the local flora and fauna before I leave."

The water lay flat as a mirror, reflecting the trees and the clouds in the sky. Small bugs danced over the surface. A large heron with blue-gray wings rose from the water and slowly flapped away. Turtles sunned themselves on logs. She heard a splash and saw what looked like a half-submerged log — except it moved.

"Good heavens, Simon, is that...?"

"*Oui*, an alligator," he said, sounding excited.

"Turn around," she said. The local fauna had rapidly become less enticing. "Quickly."

"It won't hurt us as long as we're in the boat," Simon said.

"My God, it's big," she said, her eyes traveling from its snout over the lumpy spine to the tip of its tail, a good eight feet away from the head. "Are you sure this is safe?"

"Remember what the Seminole at the alligator farm said," Simon said. "They don't eat people."

"Often," Louisa corrected. "They don't eat people often. That's because people don't live in swamps. We live in cities. And this is why." She grew increasingly uneasy, but Simon continued to row while the large reptile stayed close to the bank. She thought of the older man at the alligator farm and his missing arm.

As they continued through the swamp, they passed a few smaller alligators sunning themselves on the banks; a larger one passed within four feet of the boat. Louisa held her breath as the creature slowly swayed through the water and swam by them.

"Simon, look!" she said and pointed toward a bank where a nest of small black snakes lay coiled. A larger one slipped silently through the water, its head raised as if it might spring out and fly toward the boat. Louisa shuddered, but Simon said nothing.

Louisa took the camera out of her bag and took a picture of two very small alligators asleep on a log. Then she twisted around and aimed the camera at Simon. He looked at the lens and once again his expression was inscrutable. She had no idea what was below the surface. She snapped the shot.

As they continued further and further into the swamp. Louisa gazed up at the treetops, hoping to catch a glimpse of a wood stork or a roseate spoonbill. She saw several more herons and quite a few lovely white egrets and an anhinga with its wings drying in the sun. Strange woody knobs protruded from the brown water. She'd seen some of them polished and made into lamps at a gift store. Cypress knee lamps, the sign had said.

"There's an island up ahead where I think the rookery is," Simon suggested.

A mound with a hammock of trees rose above the murky waters.

"What about the alligators?" she asked.

"Do you see any on the island?"

"No, but they could come up as soon as we land," she said.

"They won't come. They're more afraid of us than we are of them," he said.

"I don't see how that's possible," she said and shivered.

Simon pulled on the oars and aimed the prow directly toward the shore of the island. The boat landed against the sand with a scraping sound. Louisa looked around for alligators but didn't see any. She stood up and made her way out of the boat, stepping onto the sand. She walked up the small mound, still looking for alligators but also entranced by dozens of bright blue and green dragonflies. It seemed as if they were looking back at her with their big round eyes. The place was magical.

She looked up in the treetops, searching for the birds. An osprey launched itself from one of the limbs. She should have taken a picture, but realized she'd left the camera in the boat. She turned around to go back for it, but Simon was in her way. It took a moment for her to register what was happening. He stood before her, holding one of the oars aloft.

"Forgive me, Louisa. You left me no choice," he said.

Alarm thundered through her body as the oar came toward her head. She ducked and fell to the ground on her hands and knees. Scurrying across the sand, she looked back to see him, following her, the oar over his shoulder like a baseball bat. Then he swung it directly at the side of her head. This time he did not miss, and darkness descended.

Chapter 32

Ellen

Ellen sat at her typing table, finishing the last of her tasks. Louisa had sent her part of a long story about the birds of Florida with a note that she hoped there would be more to come. The birds sounded like mythical creatures. Back home they did not have wood storks and ospreys and pelicans at the shore. They had pesky seagulls and puffins, whose feathers no one wanted to wear. She pulled the paper from the carriage of the typewriter and slipped it into the box for unfinished stories. She looked over at Louisa's empty chair and wished she would come home, which made her realize she hadn't heard from Paddy. So she called the precinct and after she waited for an eternity an operator connected her to his office.

"Ellen, you caught me just in time. I was on my way out to visit one of our city's fine gambling establishments. Seems the proprietor didn't pay off City Hall, so we're allowed to shut him down," he said.

"What's the story on the bullet, Paddy?" she asked.

"Not good, I'm sorry to say. Not the same caliber," he answered.

Relief and frustration vied for her attention.

"I don't know who else it could have been besides Becky," Ellen said. "She's the only one crazy and brave enough to do such a thing."

"Then you'll have to get cozy with her and get her to talk. It's the only way," he said. "Not that I'm telling you to do that, mind you."

After they hung up, Ellen slipped out of the back of the building and headed downtown to the offices of *Mother Earth.* If she had to get chummy with Becky, then that's what she would do. There was another possibility, however. It was possible that Lulu knew who the shooter was, and perhaps in an unguarded moment would let it slip.

***

"Where's Emma?" Ellen asked, finding Lulu, Karl, and Berkman in the office, having drinks.

"Off touring the country. Have some gin, my Irish rebel," Karl said and held up a bottle of clear liquid.

"I think not. We Irish have a weakness, you know," she said.

"Just one," Lulu said, taking the bottle from Karl, and pouring some clear liquid into a tumbler. She added some Rose's lime cordial and handed it to Ellen. "This is called a gimlet. Try it."

Ellen tasted the liquor. It went down easier than she thought it would, too easy. She set the glass down.

"The luncheon is the day after tomorrow," Karl said.

"You mean the one in Tarrytown?" Ellen asked.

Berkman abruptly stood up.

"Karl," he said in a warning voice. "I cannot be privy to this conversation."

"My apologies, Sasha. We will wait until you're gone," Karl said.

Lulu and Karl exchanged glances. Berkman finished his drink and put on his coat.

"Becky is waiting for me," he said. "I hope you have a productive meeting."

He slapped Karl on the back and left the three of them.

"What was that about?" Ellen asked.

"He knows we're planning a surprise for the Rockefellers," Lulu said. "But he doesn't want to know anything else before the fact. He's already been to prison, and the less he knows the better."

"I'm not sure I want to know either," Ellen said.

"But you're the star of the day's activity," Karl said. "You and your lady friend will go to Mrs. Rockefeller's luncheon and deliver a little present to John D. from his admirers."

Ellen looked from one to the other. They can't possibly be expecting her to do this.

"Karl," Lulu said, taking a cigarette from his pack. "Why should Ellen have to deliver it?"

"She wants to be one of us. She has to prove herself," he said, settling back into his chair with a Cheshire cat smirk. He lit a cigarette and then leaned over and lit Lulu's.

"My lady friend can't go," Ellen lied. "She has a prior engagement."

"Go without her then," he said.

Ellen had thought that providing the information about the luncheon would have been enough.

"What sort of present?" she asked.

"A bomb," he said.

"Jesus! How many people will this gift kill?" Ellen asked, eyes wide with consternation.

"No one if you do it correctly. Property destruction is what we're after. Not murder. Sometimes there are casualties, but that can't be helped."

"How big is this bomb? How do I know it won't explode and blow me to smithereens before I get it there?"

"It will fit in a package the size of a tin can, and I promise it will not explode. A bomb is filled with certain substances. If you ignite it, then gigantic amounts of gas are released in less than a second. But it must be ignited to explode," he said. He was quite adamant, but Ellen was not comforted.

"And how will I get it in? Have you thought of that?" she asked.

"You'll have to go in as a worker," Karl said, tapping the ash from his cigarette into the tumbler Berkman left behind. "I can't see you passing as a fine lady by yourself. Show up early and say you're the florist or something. Leave the bomb somewhere inconspicuous."

"Like where?" she asked. "I've never been there. And if I'm seen skulking around, I'll surely be thrown out or arrested. This is a terrible plan. It's not even a plan."

"She's right," Lulu said.

The three of them sat in silence, Ellen with her hands in her lap as Lulu and Karl smoked.

Then Karl stubbed out his cigarette, went to his desk, and pulled a file from the top drawer.

"Here it is," he said, taking out a newspaper page. "I knew that Delafield woman's column would be useful."

Ellen sat up straight at the mention of Louisa's name.

In a mincing, hoity-toity voice, Karl began to read, "'The grand reopening of John D. Rockefeller's Kykuit home is a reason for celebration. The exquisite 40-room beaux art mansion graces a 250-acre plot of land overlooking the scenic Hudson River. The name 'Kykuit' comes from the Dutch word for Lookout Point.'"

Karl smacked his lips in derision.

"Such fawning makes me want to regurgitate," he said, perusing the article. "Ah, this is what I was looking for. 'Not only is the architecture dazzling, but the landscaping, based on Italian and Renaissance gardens, creates a feeling of clarity and serenity. Mr. Rockefeller himself has said that the views invite the soul.'" He held up a finger and continued. "'Commanding the forecourt, one finds the towering statue of Oceanus, replicated from Giambologna's Renaissance fountain in Florence. This magnificent Greek god greets visitors ...' and so on and so forth."

He lowered the paper.

"You will assassinate Oceanus," he said. "You don't even have to get inside the house."

"This is ridiculous. What kind of statement does that make?" Lulu asked.

"Lulu, this is our first bombing. The Italians do it all the time, but our people have always used guns," Karl said, leaning forward and speaking in a hushed tone as if the walls had ears. "However, I am not going to ask a first-timer to kill someone in cold blood, and she doesn't have to. If she sets off the explosion while the elites of New York society are innocently drinking their fancy Champagne and eating oysters, they will be terrorized. They will know that they are not safe around the Rockefellers. He and his wife will be shunned. They'll be pariahs. It's a different kind of death, but still a death. Besides, that statue is a colossus. It's worth a fortune."

Ellen gulped. Even if it were only a statue and Rockefeller's reputation, destroying a valuable work of art was as criminal an act as murder to some people. Louisa would certainly fire her if she found out. And Paddy! Paddy would send her back to Ireland on the first ship if he didn't throw her in the clink. If she did this thing, there was no going back to her old life. She looked over at Lulu's glittering brown eyes and wondered if it might be worth it.

"Sure, I'll figure out some way to get onto the estate," Ellen said with a tremble in her voice. She had no idea how she would get out of this.

Lulu reached over and squeezed her hand.

"We'll send Becky along to help you," she said.

Becky? This whole scheme was getting worse by the minute.

"Drink up," Karl said.

Ellen reached for the glass of gin and lime juice and drained it.

***

As they walked up the hill toward Lulu's apartment on Lexington Avenue, Lulu sang a song in a language that Ellen didn't recognize. Her voice was surprisingly beautiful, and Ellen felt her heart break a little. When the song was done, Ellen took her hand.

"Was that a song from your childhood?" she asked.

"We Latvians are known as a country of poets and singers," Lulu said, bumping against her shoulder.

"It sounded mournful," Ellen said.

"It was about people lost at sea," Lulu said.

Ellen could imagine the turbulent waves, the sense of drowning. She was afraid that she herself was drowning and she had no idea how to save herself. First, it would be a statue. Next...?

They reached the steps to the apartment building.

"You called the old lady's house, didn't you?" Lulu asked.

"I did. The hired girl put her to bed," Ellen said.

"And what if you don't get back till the morning?" Lulu leaned forward and whispered in her ear.

Ellen's knees grew weak and she heard herself say, "I don't s'pose she'll know."

They climbed the six flights to the apartment. Once inside, Lulu took Ellen by the hand and led her into a bedroom at the back. She lit a candle. The light flickered and danced. On the walls were posters from various anarchist marches. In moments the room smelled of bergamot and candle wax. Without a word, Lulu began to unbutton Ellen's dress. She knew she should stop her. She should turn around and walk out, but then Lulu's lips kissed along her neck while her hands cupped Ellen's breasts and then lightly pressed her nipples. Ellen's senses swam as if she were intoxicated. An ache, a need, a thirst overwhelmed her. She was Jericho, and her walls were collapsing. As her body responded to Lulu's touch, they moved to the bed, hands and tongues and hips and legs all touching, all desperate need amid the sweet oblivion of desire. She forgot about Hester, about Louisa, about Louisa's mother all alone in the house in Harlem. And she forgot to ask Lulu who shot Dottie Parsons.

Chapter 33

Louisa

Louisa's eyes opened to the night sky hovering over her. A gibbous moon hung like a cold white fist amongst the stars. A moan emerged from her throat. She rolled over and vomited. When her stomach was emptied of its contents, she slowly pushed herself off the sand. How long had she been unconscious? She raised a hand to her throbbing skull. It was damp. She felt woozy and lowered herself back to the ground. A high-pitched ringing sounded in her ears. Something swished near her head and she rose up again. She pushed herself to standing. She had to get out of this place. She remembered the snake they'd seen that day, its head raised above the water menacingly.

"Help!" she called out in a feeble voice. Useless. No one could hear her, and who would be out here in the dead of night? She had no idea how far out into the swamp she was. It seemed as though Simon had rowed for at least an hour. Simon. He was more poisonous than any of the snakes out here. Why hadn't he gone ahead and killed her? Perhaps he thought he had. Her head throbbed as she held onto a sapling for support.

She looked out across the inky water. What were those small red lights glinting on the surface? She took a tentative step forward and peered at the swamp. Then with a sudden horrifying clarity she realized she was looking at the eyes of alligators reflecting the moonlight. She screamed, turned back toward the hammock and dashed through the clawing, scratching palmettos and scrub trees. She stumbled over roots and slammed into a tree. Everything swirled around her.

"Help me! Please, God!" she yelled, flailing about in the dark until she finally reached an opening and saw before her more water, more glinting red eyes. A whimpering sound came from her throat.

She turned back, slower this time, using the moonlight to make her way back through the trees and palmettos. She found a large tree, looked up and saw the head of a pine tree — black against the midnight blue sky. She slowly lowered herself to the ground, pulled her knees close to her chest, and felt around the ground till she found a palm frond. She swept the area around her in the hopes of keeping bugs away. Then rested her head on her knees as sobs shook her.

When the sobs finally subsided, she wiped her face on her sleeve. Her mind wandered where she did not want it to go. To Simon. What had she missed? He'd been such a gentleman and so kind to Suzie. Then the kiss. The kiss that she foolishly thought meant something. The sex, on the other hand, had revealed his true nature. He was a brute. She'd set out to use him to learn about his brother, but instead she had fallen under his spell, and this was the result. She'd believed that because he was descended from nobility that he was somehow worthy of her trust. She'd never imagined him to be capable of such treachery.

She wished she were as wise as Ellen, who never trusted anyone based on their status or wealth. Ellen would never have been duped like this. What a fool she'd been.

This anger, even if it was directed mainly toward herself, revived her somewhat. She momentarily forgot about the pounding in her head. Then it came roaring back, and her eyelids slammed shut. She toppled over and slept, oblivious to the snakes and alligators slithering through the swamp, to the opossum that tiptoed over and sniffed her hair, and to the smattering of spring mosquitoes that came and drank their fill of her blood. She slept as if she were dead.

Chapter 34

Ellen

She woke early the next morning, light creeping in through the window like a burglar. The moment her eyes opened, Ellen felt an avalanche of guilt. Hester, she thought. What had she done? Not only that, Lulu was allowing men to build a bomb in her apartment. So much for the power of the word. Ellen felt sick. Hester had said that if she involved herself in the harm of others, they would be through. Blowing up a statue, bits of marble flying through the air, the chances were good that someone would indeed be hurt. Of course, after last night she surely could never face Hester again.

Lulu's arms reached around her.

"Morning," Lulu said in a sleepy voice.

"Morning," Ellen answered. She wanted, needed, to get away. "I should go. The old woman needs help getting out of bed and getting dressed. If she realizes I wasn't there, she'll be fit to be tied."

"You may leave if you must," Lulu said. "First I make coffee."

They rose and dressed quickly. Ellen's body felt raw and she had a headache from the gin, for she'd had two more drinks after the first one. Lulu's scent covered her face and her hands.

"Do you have a water closet?" Ellen asked.

Lulu pointed her to a doorway down the hall. After she relieved herself and washed her face and hands, she went to the parlor. Karl, Charlie, and Artie were already at work, sitting around a small card table. Artie's face was still bruised from his encounter with the police.

"Good morning, ready to take a trip to Tarrytown tomorrow?" Karl asked. For once, he had no cigarette in his mouth or hand, for which Ellen was supremely thankful as she eyed the sticks of dynamite and the various components spread across the table. She understood that this was not play-acting. They truly expected her to take a bomb to the Rockefeller residence the next day. She had foolishly agreed, but now she wanted no part of this scheme.

"Why should I take the bomb?" Ellen asked. "Why not Sweet Sal?"

"True. Sweet Sal is la-de-da over Frank," Lulu said. "She'll enjoy the chance for vengeance."

"She can't," Charlie said. "She's on her way to Florida."

Ellen's body involuntarily jerked.

"And why, might I ask, is Sweet Sal going to Florida?" she asked.

"She's got some unfinished business," Charlie said.

"I wish I could go to Florida," Lulu said. "I would like some time in the sun."

"You didn't try to kill some society writer dame like Sal did," Charlie asked. "So Ellen'll go to Tarrytown."

"I don't understand," Ellen said. "I know you had a feud with Louisa Delafield, Karl, but it seems like foolishness to harm a member of the press. She's not the enemy."

Karl lifted his head up from the work at hand and said, "Sweet Sal didn't shoot at the woman on my orders. Why would I want to kill another writer? Even if her work is insipid and cloying."

"But why would Sweet Sal do it?"

"She was tryin' to impress Frank. She's nuts for him," Charlie said as he hooked a wire delicately to a stick of dynamite.

"She told me she has a plan to get Frank out of jail, but first she had to get rid of Delafield," Lulu said. "She's not right in the head."

"She has a sponsor, someone who promised to help Frank and who doesn't like Louisa Delafield," Karl said. "But it's not one of us."

Ellen had been barking up the wrong tree! It wasn't Becky who shot at Louisa. And it wasn't the anarchists who were funding Sweet Sal's trip to Florida. Ellen realized she had to go. She would have to send Louisa a telegram immediately. No, she'd have to do more than that. She'd have to go to Florida. Louisa wouldn't even know what Sweet Sal looked like.

"All right. It's not a problem," Ellen said, trying not to appear too distracted. "When should I come back and get the bomb?"

"Early tomorrow morning. That way you can go straight to the train station. Tarrytown's about twenty miles north."

Charlie held up the device. Karl had been right. It was the size and shape of a tin can. A long fuse hung from the bottom.

"Come on. I'll walk with you," Lulu said. "I have got to get to the office."

As they left the building, Ellen's mind was churning. How would she get the money to go to Florida? She couldn't ask Hester. They passed a newsy hawking papers, and Ellen thought of the one person who would be more than willing to help her.

When they reached the corner where they would separate, Ellen said, "I'll be seeing you later, Lulu."

"Tell me. Did you enjoy last night?" Lulu asked.

"Does it rain in Ireland?" Ellen answered. She had more than enjoyed herself, much to her shame. What Lulu didn't know was that it would not happen again. Ellen would not return the next day to take the bomb to Tarrytown. She would be leaving as soon as she could to get to Florida. She might have felt passion for Lulu, and she might believe in the cause of the anarchists but her loyalty was to Louisa. She had already betrayed Hester. She couldn't betray her friend, too.

Lulu gave her an impish smile, but then, all of a sudden, her eyes went wide and she crumpled to the ground as a loud *boom!* buffeted the sky. Ellen reached for Lulu as her own knees buckled. Her head felt as if it were swathed in cotton. She looked up, dazed, as furniture and debris dropped from the sky. The top three floors of Lulu's apartment building were gone.

Chapter 35

Louisa

Louisa woke to a high-pitched whining sound in her ear. A dull ache emanated from the top of her head. She shivered in the dawn chill, looking at her blood-stained hand, and wondered how she was still alive. She rose and staggered through the hammock to the edge of the small mound. It could hardly be called an island. The sun pulled itself over the tree line to the east, its beams sharp as scythes. Shielding her eyes, she gazed over the swamp. It had been full of alligators the night before. Where were they now? Then she saw one, snoozing on the beach not twenty yards away. She crept back into the trees. She had to relieve herself. At least she didn't need to worry about her privacy.

When she was done, she eased back toward the small beach where the day before Simon had deposited her and conked her on the head. He was the only person who knew where she was. Would he return?

Stricken with remorse? Or to finish the job? Perhaps she should try to walk through the swamp. She didn't think it was very deep, at least not until the creek, but the six-foot alligator sunning itself on the beach might as well have been an armed guard. She could never out swim one of the beasts. At least on land, she could perhaps scramble up a tree.

A terrible thirst overcame her. She went to the water's edge and looked at it. Small bugs floated on the surface. She wet her fingers in the tea-colored water and then licked them, hoping that she wouldn't get sick. Her skull still felt as though a spike had been hammered into it.

As the sun rose higher, she wondered what had happened to her hat and her parasol. She looked around and found the hat on the ground near the water. He must have hit her so hard he had knocked it off her head. She saw that her parasol had floated downstream and was lodged in the crook of some branches. She couldn't reach it, and besides it was soaking wet. Her bag with her bird book was on the ground near where she had fallen. Where was the camera, she wondered. Still in the boat? She put the hat on her head, picked up her bag, and sat down on the sand, keeping an eye on the sleeping alligator.

She thought of Suzie and Ellen and Forrest. Would she ever see them again? How she longed for Forrest's steady presence right now, for the warmth of his mahogany eyes, and the strength of his arms around her. Then she remembered the letter she'd written to Forrest, telling him she no longer wanted to be in an intimate relationship with him. Thank God, she hadn't sent it.

Suzie must be worried by now. She would be the one who would have to go back to New York and tell

Louisa's mother that her daughter was gone, and they had no idea where.

As the sun crept up a ladder of low-lying clouds, her stomach churned with hunger, but at least she was warming up. What if she were here for days? Or weeks? She'd been poor and known scarcity before, but she'd never known real hunger.

A pair of dark wings circled above her. A buzzard! Well, it would have a while to wait for its meal if it was planning to eat her, she thought. The alligator continued to lurk on the beach nearby, as still as if it were carved in stone. Its eyes blinked, and she cringed. Another smaller alligator swam past her and crawled halfway onto the beach about ten yards away. Louisa held her breath and slowly inched backward. The smaller alligator opened its long mouth and let out a bellow. Louisa screamed and scuttled into the cover of the hammock. She peeked around one of the trees and watched as the larger alligator swam toward the smaller one. Was there going to be a battle? She bit her lip and watched as the larger alligator pulled itself on top of the smaller one. They lay like that, one on top of the other with their strange frozen smiles. Were they mating? After a short interval, they swam off in different directions. Her encounter with Simon Bassett had been nearly as romantic, she thought.

Chapter 36
Ellen

Ellen's ear still rang with the sound of the explosion, even hours later as she boarded the train with Forrest Calloway. She had gone to his house in Gramercy Park after leaving Lulu at the office of *Mother Earth.*

"Louisa's in trouble," she had told him. "I must go to Florida."

He had insisted on coming with her and sent his housekeeper to Harlem to look after Louisa's mother.

Before going to the train station they drove to Paddy's precinct. Ellen told him everything. He was angry with her, but her information would help them identify the victims. Apparently, besides the three men in the apartment, only one other person had died, a stroke of good luck. She thought of Karl and his foolish idealism. This tragedy would set the anarchists back decades. She felt sorry for Emma, even for Becky and Berkman, and she worried for Lulu, who could be in trouble for letting the anarchists build a bomb in her apartment.

"Take this with you," Paddy said, scrawling a note on New York Police Department stationery. "You'll need it."

As the train rocked along the tracks, Ellen thought of the long letter she'd written to Hester. She had told her the truth about all of it. She admitted to having had feelings for Lulu, to getting caught up in the revolutionary fervor, and to putting that fervor above all else — above her job, above Louisa, and worst of all above Hester — Hester, who had been so good to her; Hester, who spent her days helping others, caring about the poor and unfortunate. "I've been a fool," she wrote. She added that she had no right to ask for forgiveness. She only wanted Hester to know how deeply sorry she was.

"I will treasure the memory of my time with you for the rest of my life and forever regret hurting you."

Hester was probably reading it right now. Ellen wiped a tear. No business feeling sorry for herself. She'd made her bed, and Hester wasn't in it. Now, she must concentrate on making sure Sweet Sal didn't kill Louisa. Perhaps this time Ellen would take the bullet. God knows she deserved it, she thought. It wasn't that she no longer sympathized with the aims of Emma Goldman and the others. She would always believe in the principles of the anarchists and the International Workers of the World. But there must be another, a better, way. Hester had often talked up the Socialists and that Eugene Debs fellow. Maybe Lulu and Karl were wrong about the Socialists. Maybe it was better to work within the system that was already there.

Forrest Calloway sat in the seat across from her, staring out the window at the passing scenery. His temples were slightly graying, and he had deep lines on either side of his mouth. Perhaps it was just worry, but his age was starting to show. Even so, his eyes had a steady gaze that Ellen found reassuring. This wasn't the first time they had joined forces to come to Louisa's rescue. He turned his face toward her.

"This business has gone on long enough," he said. "She isn't safe. If it's not anarchists trying to kill her, it's gangsters kidnapping her. She should be married with nothing to worry about besides a child's skinned knee."

It was true that a lady gangster had kidnapped Louisa last year and tried to sell her off to the highest bidder, but not only had Louisa survived, she had exposed what could happen to women by writing about it. Yes, it was dangerous, but what Louisa did was important. Ellen had to believe that.

"She said you weren't interested in marriage," she said, leaning forward. "And neither is she."

"I've changed my mind," he said.

"But... I thought you were still married," Ellen said.

He glanced at her in surprise.

"Louisa told you?"

"She did," Ellen said.

"It's true. A month ago I hired a private detective, and he has found my wife. I'll serve her with divorce papers as soon as I return," he said. "I was deeply hurt by my first marriage, but I'm sure Louisa would never betray me. Not the way my wife did."

Ellen's own betrayal made her skin crawl. She imagined Hester tearing her letter into bits and tossing it into the trash.

Chapter 37

Louisa

As the sun set, the sky in the west purpled while shades of periwinkle blue coated the east. Another night in the swamp. She hadn't eaten since breakfast the day before. She felt faint, her head throbbed, and her skin itched, her legs covered with red welts. She had explored the mound of land on which she was marooned. It wasn't much. No bigger than a large parlor. Yet it contained a multitude of life forms — ants, millipedes, beetles, large yellow and black spiders strategically waiting in webs that stretched from tree to tree. Gorgeous iridescent blue damselflies flitted around her, and the occasional dragonfly circled her curiously. The hardwoods, cedars, and pines towered overhead while low to the ground, deep green palmettos spread their fan-shaped leaves in all directions. She tried to rip one out of the earth to fan herself, but its roots were stronger than she.

She had dismissed the idea of any supernatural intervention into her situation earlier, but she desperately needed solace, hope, and so turned to the idea of a benevolent deity that might come to her aid. Tomorrow or maybe the next day she would be desperate enough to wander into the swamp, to pray that the alligators and snakes, the sentries of this wet world, would let her pass unmolested. Even if they did, however, she wasn't sure which way was out.

When all the light had finally bled from the sky and night bloomed, she nestled next to a tree away from the bright, red gleaming eyes that would soon be gathering in the swamp, and she shut her eyes. She put a hand up to her skull and felt the clotted blood. If Simon's aim had been just an inch lower, he would have hit her in the temple and she would be dead. Perhaps a quick death would have been better.

The tree wasn't much of a pillow. The bark felt rough against her skin. Her thoughts traveled back in time and then circled above a moment when she was ten years old and in a forest with her father. Outings with him were rare and precious. They'd been visiting family friends in the Hudson Valley, and her father had left the festivities to show her the view from the cliffs overlooking the river. He didn't particularly enjoy socializing the way her mother did.

She remembered how he smelled of cherry pipe tobacco and the feel of his palm on her head as he stroked her hair. She had leaned against him as his hand rested on her shoulder, a cocoon of love and safety surrounding her. When the cocoon was ripped away from her two years later, the blood in her heart had gone cold. She would never trust that feeling again, she had told herself as she looked down at her white-gloved hand covered with the dirt she'd thrown on his coffin. She would rely on one person and one person only. Herself.

Was that why she was so willing to cast off Forrest Calloway, she wondered. He made her feel safe. He made her feel loved. And those were terrifying feelings. Simon Bassett, on the other hand, felt dangerous and exciting. Now she knew why.

The night grew cold and she thought once again of her father, his smiling gray eyes looking down at her. As she dozed off, it seemed as if arms had wrapped around her and the smell of cherry pipe tobacco wafted in her dreams. Was he there, waiting on the other side of the valley for her?

Chapter 38
Ellen

"Ellen, we're here," Forrest said, shaking her shoulder.

She woke up and heard the conductor announce they had arrived in St. Augustine. She gathered her things, stepped off the train, and gazed around. The air felt soft against her skin. Flowers bloomed in a riot of springtime. It was as if they'd stepped into another world — colorful and warm. No time to indulge, she told herself.

Forrest summoned a porter for the bags and found a cab for them. It was a short trip to the Florida House hotel, a big rambling wooden building. They entered, and turned their bags over to a bellman.

"Will you be needing rooms?" a concierge asked.

"Not now," Forrest said. "We're looking for someone, a Miss Delafield."

The concierge looked at the ceiling as he thought.

"Come to think of it, I haven't seen her in a day or so," he said.

Forrest turned to Ellen.

"Do you have her room number?" he asked.

"Yes. It's on the third floor," she said. "She should be expecting us, sir. I telegrammed."

"And I phoned earlier, but got no answer. That worries me, Ellen," he said.

They took an elevator to the third floor and hurried toward Louisa's room. The door was open a sliver. Ellen pushed it all the way open and saw Suzie, pacing the room. Suzie looked up at them with an expression of joy which within seconds turned to disappointment.

"I thought you were Louisa," Suzie said.

"Sorry to disappoint," Ellen said.

"Where is she, Suzie?" Forrest asked.

"I haven't seen her since the day before yesterday," Suzie said. "I've been staying with my family. I came back last night and she wasn't here. I thought maybe she was out covering a party or something. But this morning, no Louisa. And her bed hasn't been slept in."

"I tried to call you at Louisa's house, but no one answered," Suzie continued. "I've been worried sick."

"Suzie, I'm afraid I've some bad news. The woman who tried to kill her in New York is here in St. Augustine," Ellen said.

Suzie inhaled sharply and raised a hand to her mouth.

"Do you think Louisa knows?" she asked. "Maybe she's gone into hiding somewhere."

Ellen looked at Louisa's writing table and saw an unopened telegram. She opened it quickly and perused the contents.

"No, she doesn't know about Sal," Ellen said. "This is my telegram warning her."

"Then where is she?" Suzie said. "I went to the police last night, but they said it was too early to file a missing person's report."

"I'm going to get to the bottom of this," Forrest said, turning in a circle to survey the room.

"This looks like a letter to you," Ellen said and handed him the letter she found on the desk.

Forrest opened it and read. His face grew dark.

"What does it say?" Ellen asked.

"Nothing that will help us," he said and put the letter in his pocket. "I'll find Griffin and see what he knows. Ellen, you know what Sal looks like, don't you? Do you think she would trust you if she saw you? Perhaps, you could tell her that Emma Goldman sent you."

"Oh, sir, I don't think Miss Goldman has anything to do with this. She's not a proponent of murder," Ellen said. She couldn't help defending the woman she would always admire.

"Then whoever her co-conspirators are. Tell her she's needed back in New York this instant," he said. He headed for the door and left them standing in the room.

Suzie turned to Ellen and said, "I'm afraid we've got more to worry about than your anarchist assassin, Ellen."

At that moment a bird flew by the window, screeching, and a sense of dread filled Ellen.

"Tell me," she said.

"I'll tell you on the way," Suzie said.

"On the way? Where?"

"To see my brother," Suzie said.

Ellen followed Suzie down the stairs and out of the hotel into the bright light of day. She wished her hat had a wider brim to protect her watering eyes from the sharp rays of the sun.

"Why are we going to your brother's house?" she asked, hurrying to catch up with Suzie. "Shouldn't we stay here and look for Sweet Sal?" Ellen asked.

"Trust me when I tell you there's something else going on," Suzie said, walking faster than Ellen had ever known her to walk. They dashed down a cobblestone street, passing street vendors and shops, weaving through tourists.

"I didn't want to say anything in front of Mr. Calloway," Suzie said. "But Louisa has been keeping company with a French baron or some such thing. Name is Simon Bassett. Older brother of the groom. Louisa is smitten, I'm afraid. They've been going out just about every day to see the sights. And at night, she's learning to dance the tango!"

"That's part of her job," Ellen said. "She has to write about the social scene."

"It was more than work. It seemed like she was under his spell. And, to be honest, I've been so busy with my family that I wasn't paying much attention," Suzie said, her voice filled with guilt.

"I'm glad you found them."

"Oh, it's been wonderful until now," Suzie said.

"What makes you so sure she is in trouble?" Ellen asked her.

"Every morning, Louisa and I have coffee together in her room and catch up. I missed yesterday morning because I had stayed with my family. Like I said, I came back last night and she was gone. I finally went to sleep last night, thinking she might be out at a party or maybe... she was with him. When she didn't come back to her room this morning, I went out looking for her. I found that Simon playing tennis with his brother while the bride's dress designer — some skinny French woman — watched from the sidelines.

"Veronique Ribault. I typed up a story about her," Ellen said.

"I asked Monsieur Bassett if he'd seen Louisa and he said something about being sick yesterday and staying in bed. Then the woman pipes up and says she had to bring him soup. She said he was a '*pauvre bebe.*' That means poor baby. I learned French sitting right alongside Anna when we were girls. Then she winked at him. It all seemed very fishy to me. They don't seem at all concerned that I can't find Louisa."

"It sure sounds strange," Ellen agreed. "You think any of this has anything to do with Lord Wickham and the stolen diamonds?"

"Well, when Lord Wickham fell to his death, Louisa started fishing around for information. She didn't suspect Simon Bassett but maybe she should have," Suzie said.

"Why, Suzie? I don't understand," Ellen said.

Suzie didn't answer her right away. They walked over a bridge, crossing a large creek, and down a residential street lined with tidy wooden houses close to the sidewalk with flowering trees and bushes in the side yards. A few residents were outside, chatting on porches. They waved at Suzie.

"You've only been here a few days," Ellen said, "but everybody knows you."

"This is a tight-knit community, Ellen," Suzie said. "Like your Irish village, most likely. If a stranger showed up and turned out to be someone's family, wouldn't everyone in the village know it by sunset?"

Ellen nodded.

"Are you going to tell me why you suspect this Simon Bassett of something?"

Suzie stopped and turned to face her.

"Yesterday, my brother's daughter and I were in Butler's Market buying some greens for dinner when an old fellow by the name of Dewberry came in, crowing about how some Frenchman gave him ten dollars to rent his boat for one day. Dewberry was buying supplies, which mostly consisted of a lot of liquor. I thought it was odd that one of the Frenchmen would want the old man's boat, but we were in a hurry so I went back to Lloyd's house and we had dinner and I just didn't think anything more of it. Until this morning."

"You couldn't have known it was important. And maybe it's nothing."

"Simon Bassett rented a boat for the day two days ago, but he told me he was sick," she said. "He lied. I think he took Louisa out in that boat and she didn't come back." She pursed her lips.

Ellen's heart thudded chaotically in her chest.

Suzie turned and continued walking with Ellen silently following. A cloud passed overhead and Ellen felt an inexplicable chill. They arrived at a two-storey wooden house with a balcony and a porch swing. Leafy green potted plants framed the doorway.

They climbed the steps and entered the cool, elegantly furnished living room and walked through the house to the backyard where a wiry man a few years younger than Suzie yanked a handful of weeds from a garden bed. He looked up at them and then stood. His wide smile could have brightened the darkest night.

"Who's this red-headed queen of Sheba?" he asked.

"This is Ellen Malloy," Suzie said, tersely. "She's Miss Delafield's assistant. And we're here because Louisa Delafield is missing."

Lloyd cocked his head. "Missing?"

"Missing," Suzie said. "You know a fellow named Dewberry?"

"Sure. Has a shack out by Turnbull Creek. Hunts turtles and gators. Polly buys his turtles sometimes and makes a soup so good God asks her for the recipe."

"This Dewberry fella rented a boat to a French man, and I'm worried that French man might have done something with Louisa," Suzie said. Her voice caught and Ellen heard her clench back a sob.

Ellen put a hand on Suzie's arm.

"We know something's happened to her," Ellen said.

"She would never go off somewhere without telling me. Never," Suzie said. "Though she hasn't been right since poor Dottie Parsons died."

Lloyd rubbed his chin. Then he said, "Come on."

They followed him inside, through the long hallway of the house and out front to a truck. He cranked the engine and jumped in the driver's seat, and they took off.

Chapter 39

Louisa

It was April Fool's day, and Louisa was the fool.

She had seen every kind of insect known to man, she thought, as the day dragged on. She knew it probably wasn't safe to drink the swamp water, but she crept over and wet her lips occasionally. The swamp was noisier than she would have thought. A *caw caw caw* here and *whee whee whoot* there. Gray Spanish moss hung from branches overhead. Underneath the noise was a stillness, a sort of quiet thrumming. If she weren't stranded and starving, it would actually be beautiful.

The fear and horror of what had happened to her had subsided. The alligators hadn't attacked her. A snake hadn't launched its fangs into her in her sleep. She had quite a few red welts from mosquito bites and scratches from tree branches and bushes, not to mention a goose egg on her skull, but she was alive though her head still throbbed and the light hurt her eyes.

She gazed up at the sky and took stock. Someone would miss her. Suzie would miss her. She would alert the authorities. Someone would begin to search for her. Perhaps they would question Simon — although no one had seen her leave with him.

She wondered how long she could live out here. Was there anything edible? What about turtle eggs or bird eggs? She wandered around, searching through stumps sticking out of the sandy area and the palmettos clustered together. She didn't see any nests, but a beetle crawled across a fallen tree log. If she got hungry enough, she supposed she could eat a beetle. An earthy smell emanated from her body, and she craved her bathtub, her perfume, and her powders.

She walked to the end of her island and then stopped in surprise. There against a tree was the Kodak! She picked it up and examined the camera. Evidently he had thrown it out of the boat. The lens was cracked, the aluminum body dented, and the scissor mechanism broken. However, she managed to wind the film into the cartridge, pry open the back and remove the cannister. When they found her dead body, at least there would be proof of who had killed her.

A cloud passed over the sun, and as the shadow spread over the water, the morbid turn of her thoughts continued. If she died out here, who would take care of her mother? As a child, Louisa had enjoyed watching her mother dashing off to one event after another in her gorgeous gowns, her hair in the latest fashion. It had been like living with some sort of exotic bird until Richard Milton Delafield was found dead in a hotel room. Then the exotic bird lost her plumage. Anna didn't deserve what had happened to her, and she certainly didn't deserve the abject poverty that would ensue if her daughter did not return to support her.

Louisa sat on a fallen log and gazed up at the leaves slowly fluttering in a lazy breeze. Then she noticed just above her, a large black-and-yellow spider, seeming to float in the air. But as her eyes focused she saw it was in the midst of a huge, elaborate web. Strands of the web caught the sunlight and sparkled. Like diamonds in lace. She raised a hand to her mouth. The diamonds were in the wedding dress.

She could no longer wait to be saved. Who could possibly save her if they didn't know where she was? She sat down and took off her suede pumps. They had been cream-colored when she had put them on, but now they were dirty and the bow on the left shoe was gone. Then she took off her ripped stockings and tied her skirt up around her knees. She placed the film cartridge in her bag along with her book, then tied the bag so it would rest between her shoulder blades, and headed into the water.

Chapter 40

Ellen

They drove along a paved road out of St. Augustine and then turned down a wide sandy road and drove for several miles before they came to a small wooden bridge. Lloyd crossed the bridge and then turned the truck down a narrow dirt road. Dust billowed behind them as they followed the road through a landscape that boggled Ellen's mind. The trees seemed as if they might reach out and eat the truck along with its occupants. The air was dense and cloying. Perspiration trickled along her back.

Lloyd finally stopped the truck in a clearing of sorts. A shack stood built up on four-foot-high stilts. Next to it stood a wooden outhouse with its door wide open. Several chickens clucked and marched in the side yard. When they got out of the truck, the chickens burst into flight and found purchase on the branches of a nearby tree.

"I never in my life saw chickens in a tree," Suzie said.

"Well, Dewberry's too lazy to build a coop for them. And alligators love a chicken," Lloyd said. "So they figured out how to get up there."

A dark-skinned, wiry little man stepped out onto the porch of his house and looked them over.

"What are y'all wanting out here?" he asked, full of belligerence.

"What kind of way is that to talk to people, Dewberry?" Lloyd asked. "You must be hungover."

"So what if I am?" Dewberry asked.

"We want to know if a French man really gave you ten dollars to rent your boat, day before yesterday," Lloyd said.

"Who's we? What you got a white lady here for?" He eyed Ellen suspiciously.

Ellen stepped forward.

"Mr. Dewberry, my name is Ellen Malloy, and I'm looking for a friend of mine. She's gone missing, and I'm hoping very much you can offer some help," she said.

Dewberry's eyes squinted and he stared at her.

"You talk funny," he said.

"I'm Irish," she said. "And you sound pretty funny to me."

Dewberry stared for a good long minute before he burst out laughing and came down the steps. He was wearing overalls with only one shoulder strap clasped, the other flapping down his back.

"You want to know if that French man took my boat? He did," the man said.

"What did he look like?" Suzie asked. "Dark hair or light?"

"Dark hair," Dewberry said. "Not real tall, not short either."

"How do you know he was French?" Ellen asked.

"Same as I know you're Irish. I asked him why he talked funny," Dewberry said.

"Did you see him take the boat out yesterday?"

"No, ma'am. He told me to leave the boat at the head of the creek," he said. "But I know he took it out. He cracked one of my oars."

Suzie and Ellen looked at each other.

"Dewberry, let us borrow your boat," Lloyd said.

"The going rate is ten dollars," Dewberry said, smugly.

"I'll give you three," Ellen said. "That's all I got."

Dewberry frowned, but when she took three dollar bills from her purse and handed them over, he grinned and showed them down a path to the creek. The boat rested, half on the bank and half in the creek.

"You said he cracked the oar. Does it still work?" Suzie asked. She picked up the oar and looked at the crack in the paddling end. Ellen joined her and examined the crack.

"Look, a hair," Suzie said. She pulled a strand of hair from the crack. The two women exchanged a look.

"It'll work good enough," he said.

They thanked him and got into the boat. Lloyd took up the oars.

"Which way do you think?" Suzie said.

"Down into the swamp," Lloyd said and rowed the boat through the dark brown water.

"Holy Mother of God," Ellen said, as they passed what looked like some sort of prehistoric monster on the bank. "Is that ...?"

"A gator," Lloyd said. "You ever seen an alligator purse? That's about six purses worth right there."

Ellen shuddered. Poor Louisa, she thought. Poor, poor Louisa.

Chapter 41
Louisa

Her feet skimmed over the silty bottom as she trudged through the warm water, most of it reaching only to the tops of her knees although once she stepped into a hole and dropped up to her waist. Her skirt was drenched and heavy, slowing her pace. Constantly scanning the water for alligators and snakes, she froze when a five-foot alligator swam toward her curiously.

"Get away!" she shouted. "Go!"

It blinked its eyes and turned away from her.

She swallowed hard and continued through the water, glancing up at the sky to see where the sun was. Her best bet would be to travel north and east. She wished she'd thought to use a stick to test the depths of the water as she walked. To her right, she saw another island. She took a step forward, and her foot slid into some sort of crevice. She tried to pull it up, but it wouldn't budge. She glanced toward the spit of land. A large alligator lay like a log on the bank and watched her. She yanked her foot, but it was firmly lodged in something. She sank down on her hips and reached for her foot with both hands. It was stuck in a branch! Suddenly the alligator on the bank rose on its short legs, which weren't quite as short as she had thought they were. It lumbered into the water and with a sinuous motion came toward her. Fear surged through every cell in her body. She pushed on the branch with her other foot with all her strength and managed to free herself. Keeping her eyes on the creature, she bent down and pulled the branch out of the water. It was as long as she was tall. Screaming, she lifted the branch and pounded it on the surface of the water. The alligator stopped swimming. She stared at the alligator, and the alligator stared back.

Standing there, damp and dirty, her fear suddenly turned to rage. Simon Bassett had tricked her. He'd seduced her and then tried to kill her. Enough was enough.

"You will not have me," she said to the silent, implacable monster. She gripped the wet branch ready to wield it in her defense.

Then to her horror, the alligator rose up out of the water, its white mouth open and lunged to the side. She screamed, but a moment later she saw half of a long black snake hanging from the alligator's jaws as it swam away.

"Oh, dear God," she whimpered. She made her way to the spit of land and huddled close to a tree, her breath coming hard and fast. Fear electrified her body. She sat unmoving for what felt like hours but was probably only ten or fifteen minutes. It was hard to tell. The tempo of her heartbeat eventually slowed. She wiped perspiration from her neck with her sodden skirt. She had to think of her next step.

Then she heard a loud fluttering noise and looked up as a large set of bright pink wings flapped overhead. A roseate spoonbill! She stared in awe. The wing span was at least four feet; its neck long and white. The spoon-shaped bill should have looked silly, but it didn't. The whole effect was one of pure majesty.

She stood up and gazed around. Up in the trees, hundreds of the pink birds perched on branches and in nests, some large, some just babies. The large ones groomed each other and called out in loud squawks. The young ones lifted their heads and opened their mouths, begging for food.

She had found the rookery. She'd never seen anything quite so amazing in her life. Something on the ground caught her eye. A large pink feather. She picked it up and thought of Dottie Parsons in her pink dress. For the first time since the gunshot had exploded outside that Manhattan church, Louisa felt a sense of peace as if her friend's spirit had rested a hand on her shoulder to let her know that she was all right.

"Louisa! Louisa!"

She looked around in confusion.

"Louisa!"

From under the overhanging branches of an oak tree came a small row boat. Ellen and Suzie sat side by side, calling out her name. The boat moved forward as if of its own volition. Louisa wondered if she were dreaming.

"I'm here," she yelled and waved her arms.

The boat came closer and closer. They had come for her. Her friends, her dear friends, had found her. She saw someone else in the boat — strong dark-skinned arms and then the head of a man she didn't know. She didn't care who he was. Pure unadulterated joy burst out of her throat in sobs and laughter. The boat crunched against the sand. Ellen and Suzie stepped onto the spit of land.

"Aren't you a sight!" Suzie exclaimed.

"You poor wee thing," Ellen said. "You could pass for a Bowery urchin."

In the next moment, she was in their arms, and the three women huddled together, Suzie patting Louisa's back, whispering, "There, there."

"Ladies, we need to get moving while there's still a sip of light left," the man in the boat said.

"Yes, let's get you back to civilization," Suzie said.

The three women got into the boat, and the man, who looked a bit like Suzie, quietly pulled on the oars to take them home. They were silent as they slid across the brown waters. Louisa took one look back at the birds settling down into their nests.

Chapter 42

Ellen

Ellen waited until after Louisa had gotten her fill of food and water. Then they followed Suzie upstairs to the large, modern bathroom at the end of the hall. Suzie's brother, it seemed, had made quite a bit of money before he died, and the house had every convenience.

Ellen sat on the edge of the tub, washing Louisa's back. Louisa had told them the whole story in the truck on the way back, with Suzie "tsk, tsking" and saying she knew all along that the man was up to no good.

"I'm so glad you came down, Ellen," Louisa said. "You always seem to know when I need you."

"Look, Louisa," Ellen said. "This Simon fella isn't your only problem. I came here because I found out who shot at you. She's a woman likes to hang around the anarchists though they don't usually pay much attention to her. They call her Sweet Sal, but she's got some bats in the belfry, and someone sent her down to finish the job."

"Slow down," Louisa said. "Sweet Sal? Here? Who sent her?"

"That I don't know. Your friend L. Byron, whose real name is Karl, said it wasn't him. He told me that right before he blew himself up in an apartment on Lexington," Ellen said, and the image of bits of furniture and building material scattered over the ground flashed in her mind.

"L. Byron is dead?" Louisa asked. "In an explosion?"

Ellen nodded. She got up and held out a towel for Louisa as she stepped out of the tub.

"It's a long story for another day. As soon as I realized it was Sweet Sal who killed your friend Dottie, I went to Mr. Calloway's house and told him she was down here looking for you," she said. "So we got on the first train and came down."

"We?" Louisa asked.

"Aye," Ellen said. "I thought I told you already. Mr. Calloway's worried sick after you, and he doesn't even know the half of it. He sure doesn't know about this murderous Simon Bassett."

Louisa looked as if she'd taken a bite out of lemon.

"What's wrong?" Ellen asked.

"I feel so ashamed," Louisa said. "I don't deserve someone as good as Forrest. You wouldn't understand. You and Hester are so perfect together. It's probably easier when you're both women."

"Ha, if only t'were so. But we've got bigger problems than our love lives."

Louisa nodded.

"I'm going to go to the Florida House, get my bag, and get you some clean clothes," Ellen said. "I can tell Mr. Calloway that you're safe now. It's better that we stay here with Suzie's family until we find out where Sweet Sal is."

Louisa nodded again. She slid into a borrowed nightgown. It was obvious she was exhausted.

"You get some rest and we'll figure out what to do tomorrow," Ellen said.

Louisa stumbled down the hall and fell into the nearest bed.

"Ellen?" she asked, sleepily. "Who's looking after Mother?"

"Mr. Calloway's housekeeper," Ellen said. But Louisa didn't hear her. She'd already fallen asleep.

***

Ellen stepped onto the porch. Lloyd sat in the swing, softly playing a stringed instrument.

"What kind of instrument is that?" she asked.

"Banjo," he answered. "Folks brought it over from Africa."

"I like the sound," she said and smiled. "Tell Suzie I'm off to get some clean clothes for Louisa. I'll be back soon."

"You know where you're going?" he asked.

Ellen thought she remembered the way back to the hotel, but she wasn't sure.

"Hold on," he said, putting down his banjo. "I'll get Pansy to walk with you. I'd take you myself, but the white folks over there wouldn't take kindly to a colored man escorting a white lady."

"They wouldn't care if they knew I was Irish," she said.

"That may be true where you come from," he said, "but here we got only two kinds of people — White and Colored."

She leaned against the porch railing, and he went inside calling for Pansy. She heard a car engine and turned to see a cab pull up in front of the house. Forrest Calloway stepped out of the car.

"Mr. Calloway," she said in surprise. "How did you know where to find us?"

"A waiter at the hotel told me. Is Louisa all right? Did you find her?" he asked.

"I was just on my way to find you and tell you she was safe and sound," she said.

"Do you know what happened to her?" he asked.

She wasn't sure how much to tell him.

"Well..." Ellen began, "she went out into the swamp to look for birds and got lost."

Calloway looked down at his empty hands.

"Birds? Who was with her, Ellen?"

Ellen shook her head.

"I can't say," she said. "I'm going to go get our things now. We're both staying with Suzie's family. Sweet Sal won't be able to find her here."

Forrest frowned, hands on his hips.

"You better get the police involved, Ellen. I want this anarchist woman arrested. I can't have one of my employees' lives threatened," he said.

"I plan to, Sir," Ellen said, noting that he called Louisa his employee as if there were nothing else between them.

"And tell Louisa ... tell her that I got her message. I'll be going back to New York on the first train tomorrow," he said. He looked tired and sad. "Come. I'll take you to the hotel."

***

The next morning Ellen and Louisa sat on the front porch of Lloyd's house. A sultry breeze blew the scent of jasmine their way. Suzie and Pansy had gone to the market.

"He said he was going back to New York?" Louisa asked.

"He did. He seemed sad," Ellen said. Louisa looked downcast. A black and yellow butterfly danced over the flower tops in the yard.

Louisa chewed the inside of her lip.

"When you first got here, did he go into my room? Did he see the letter I'd left for him?" she asked.

"I gave it to him. I thought it was all right since it was addressed to him," Ellen answered.

"Of course," Louisa said, shoulders slumping forward. "It's just that I foolishly told him that I wished to be friends and nothing more."

"You're not the only one who has been foolish," Ellen said after a moment. "I'm sure I've lost Hester forever."

"No!" Louisa said. "Why?"

"I fell for an anarchist," Ellen said.

"An anarchist? Really?" Louisa looked at her with wide eyes.

"She's an editor at *Mother Earth*. Poor like me. An immigrant like me. Her father a revolutionary like mine. She drew me like a moth to the flame. With Hester, I never feel like I can be enough. She's kind and good, but she has no idea what it means not to have everything you ever wanted."

"What happened?" Louisa asked, reaching over to take Ellen's hand in hers.

"Lulu's apartment blew up from the dynamite we'd stolen. Right in front of my eyes," Ellen said. "People died. That's when I realized Hester was right. The anarchists' beliefs may be justified but the means they use to achieve their ends can never be. I canna' be with someone like that. And now, Hester will never take me back."

She felt as if she'd just ripped open her chest and dropped her heart on the floor, exposed to the whole world.

"Hester may be more forgiving than you think," Louisa said. "Forrest, on the other hand, was deceived by his wife and he's never forgiven her. I am certain I have lost him forever."

Ellen took a deep breath. They could sit there all day feeling sorry for themselves.

"Louisa, I think you've got bigger problems than losing Forrest Calloway. Like I told you, it's not the anarchists sent Sweet Sal after you," she said.

"Who would want me dead?" Louisa asked.

"I don't know, but it's not them. Emma Goldman doesn't even believe in violence," Ellen said. "Sweet Sal went after you the first time on her own. She's soft in the head and I believe she was trying to impress a fella named Frank Tannenbaum. My guess is someone found out she was the shooter and they sent her after you, promising to help her get her man out of jail."

"But you told me from the beginning the anarchists were the ones who were after me," Louisa said.

"I thought so, but they're more strategic than that. Killing you would not be a deed of propaganda," Ellen said.

Louisa looked at her with a mystified expression.

"Please explain," she said.

"When an anarchist commits an act of violence, the purpose is to rouse the proletariat, to foment rebellion. Your death would incite no one. Secondly, they've no money to be sending her down here after you. They used every cent to get protestors out of jail. They can't even afford a good attorney."

"Then who?" Louisa asked.

"That I can't tell you," Ellen said.

Louisa's cheeks trembled and she looked so vulnerable, Ellen wanted to wrap her arms around her.

"It's not pleasant knowing someone wants you dead," she said. "Actually more than one person."

"What are we going to do about this Frenchman?" Ellen asked.

"I've got a plan. Do you think you could get some film developed?"

"I'm sure I could find a place in a tourist town," Ellen answered. She looked down and saw a small cannister on Louisa's palm.

Chapter 43

Louisa

While Ellen was gone to get the film developed, Suzie soothed Louisa's bug bites with ointment, and her grandniece, Pansy, a long-legged girl of sixteen, helped Louisa put on an ivory dress with a lovely lace bodice.

"This isn't one of mine," Louisa said.

"You kept saying you were going shopping for a new dress but you never got 'round to it, so I found one and charged it to your room at the hotel," Suzie said.

"It's perfect," Louisa said, feeling the soft cotton material under her fingers.

"Those are some bad scratches," Pansy said, looking at the long red welts as she pulled the dress over Louisa's arms. "They hurt?"

"I got scared and ran through the hammock," Louisa said. "Then I ran into a tree. Then the mosquitoes and ants got me. And finally, I got in a fight with an alligator."

Pansy squealed and put her hand over her mouth.

"You could get a job at the alligator farm," she said and giggled.

"I sure could," Louisa said. She liked this lanky girl with bright eyes and a brilliant smile. In spite of everything, bringing Suzie here to meet her family was the best thing she could have done.

She looked in the mirror over the dresser in Pansy's room and saw a few bug bites on her face and a purple bruise on her forehead. She felt woozy, and the room seemed to slowly spin around her.

"I think I might lie down for a bit," she said.

"That's a nasty bump on your head," Suzie said. "You get all the rest you can."

Louisa lay down on the bed. The window was open and the white curtains rustled in the breeze. Within minutes she was asleep.

***

Ellen shook her awake.

"Dinner's ready," Ellen said.

"Did you get the pictures?" Louisa asked.

Ellen nodded.

"Do you want to see them?" she asked.

Louisa shook her head. She followed Ellen downstairs into the large formal dining room and saw a table laden with food. The aroma of ham made Louisa's eyes water. She hadn't had any appetite since her rescue, but now she was ravenous.

Polly's husband and two sons sat at the table. Lloyd sat at the head.

"Please sit down, Miss Louisa," Polly said. "You too, Miss Ellen."

They sat. After Suzie brought in a big bowl of steaming potatoes, and Pansy brought in another bowl of greens, the family all sat together and clasped hands while Lloyd said grace.

"Thank you, Lord, for bringing Miss Louisa safely out of the valley of the shadow of death and into our home. Thank you, Lord, for the hands that made this meal for our sustenance. Thank you, Lord, for bringing my sister back into my life." He had several more things to thank the Lord for, and by the end Louisa's eyes were tearing. She wasn't sure if it was from the poignancy of the moment or sheer hunger.

"We usually only have a big dinner like this on Sunday after church," Pansy said.

"You didn't do all this for me?" Louisa asked, gazing at the feast.

"And why not?" Polly said with a smile full of sunshine. "This family loves any excuse to eat."

The food was better than anything Louisa had ever had at Delmonico's or any of the fine restaurants where she had dined. Every mouthful sent waves of pleasure through her body. Even more gratifying was the laughter and joy at the table. She marveled to see Suzie interacting with her family as if she'd never been away from them. Lloyd teased Louisa by telling her the greens were "swamp cabbage."

"This is such a nice house, Polly," Louisa said. "It's so modern."

"My late father was a doctor," Polly explained. "He only wanted the best. Maybe that's from being a slave as a child."

"I do wish I could have seen him," Suzie said. "It's my one regret."

"He told me about you," Polly said. "I imagine he's here with us right now, smiling from Heaven."

As the eating wound down, Polly's baby girl — a chubby, messy, wiggly little thing with adorable dimples — got passed from lap to lap, even landing on Louisa's at one point and placing a sticky hand on the lace bodice of her new dress.

"Oh, my goodness," Polly said, taking the child from Louisa and handing her over to Suzie, who kissed the little girl's fat cheeks while Pansy got a wet cloth to wipe off the dress.

"No harm has been done," Louisa said.

She had been terribly hungry when she first sat down, but found that her eyes had been bigger than her stomach. It was impossible to finish.

"You have to have some pie, Miss Louisa," Polly said. "Pansy made it special for you."

"Please call me Louisa," she said. "There's no need for such formality."

Polly agreed to call her Louisa, but was adamant that Pansy would refer to her as Miss Louisa. "I raised my children to respect grown ups."

Louisa made room for a tiny slice of Pansy's sweet potato pie, and then looked over at Ellen and Suzie and said, "We need to talk."

They thanked Polly for a delicious dinner. Louisa thanked Lloyd once again for saving her, but he waved her off.

"Just don't be getting in any more trouble, now," he said.

But that was a promise she could not make.

***

The grandfather clock in the hallway chimed nine times. She knew from the schedule, which Mrs. Griffin had given her days ago, the rehearsal dinner for the wedding would begin at 9:00. Dinner would go on until at least 10:30. Then the men would retire to one of the parlors or the terrace for cigars and brandy and the women would drink sherry and play cards. The festivities would end by midnight so everyone could get a good night's sleep before the wedding.

She found Suzie and Ellen in the parlor.

"It's time," she said.

Louisa, Ellen, and Suzie left the house and walked down the gaslit streets past Victorian homes with flower gardens in the yards, the lights glowing inside.

"Are you sure about this?" Ellen asked.

"Yes," Louisa said, who was not sure at all. "You will go find Detective Hagan at the St. Augustine Police Department. Tell him to come with some men to the Alcazar pool. There's a back way through the bowling alley. Tell him I've found Lord Wickham's murderer."

"What if he isn't there?"

"If he isn't, they'll know where to find him," Louisa said.

"Why don't we both go to the police and then storm the rehearsal dinner? The police can arrest Simon right there and then," Ellen asked. "At the very least, they can charge him with assault. You've got the injuries to prove it!"

"Ellen, we need to expose Simon's accomplice and Lord Wickham's murderer. Simon did not kill Lord Wickham. That much I know. If we time it right, you and the police will get there a little before Simon does," Louisa said. "I'll make sure the door to the bowling alley is unlocked."

Suzie sucked her teeth in disapproval, stopping and placing her hands on her hips.

"I don't like it, Louisa. You've been lost in the swamp for two nights because that man took you out there and left you for dead. He's dangerous!"

"Trust me," Louisa said, taking the older woman's hands in hers. "He will not hurt me again."

"How do you know that?" Suzie asked.

"I won't be unarmed," Louisa said. Suzie's eyebrows rose in surprise.

"I should go with you," Ellen said. "Suzie can go to the police."

"Ellen, you don't know how it is here. As a Negro woman, Suzie might not even be let into the building," Louisa said. "Besides, the police didn't even want to admit Lord Wickham's death was a murder. But if I can get Simon to admit what he did and flush out his accomplice, then they'll have to take action," she said.

"If this peeler doesn't believe there's been a murder, why will he come with me?"

"Tell him about finding me in the swamp and show him the picture of Simon in the boat. That should do it," Louisa said.

"What do you want me to do?" Suzie asked.

"You can deliver a message to Simon from me. Then go back to our hotel room and pack the rest of our things. We'll go home tomorrow."

"You're not going to stay for the wedding?"

"If Simon goes free tonight, then it won't be safe, and if he doesn't, then I will not be welcome at the wedding," Louisa said.

***

They went to the back side of the Alcazar first, and Louisa showed Ellen the door to the bowling alley and archery range.

"There's a passageway to the pool from there," Louisa said. "It will be closed by then, but I'll make sure it's unlocked."

"Why there?" Ellen asked.

"The acoustics," Louisa said, "and there are plenty of pillars to hide behind."

Ellen left to go to the police station and find Detective Hagan while Louisa found a bellman at the Alcatraz and gave him a dollar to leave the archery range door unlocked.

Louisa and Suzie parked themselves on a bench in the courtyard of the Ponce and waited.

"It's getting awfully late," Suzie said as the bells chimed midnight.

"They must be having quite the party," Louisa said. "Remember to give him the picture of the baby alligators and tell him that I am willing to sell the other one, the one that proves he was with me in the swamp."

"You think he'll believe me?"

"Greedy people think everyone else is like them. He will certainly believe I can be bought off," Louisa said.

"How much?" Suzie asked.

"Tell him I want diamonds. As many as he can fit into the palm of his hand."

"That's a lot of diamonds," Suzie said.

"They have plenty."

"All right. And tell him you'll be at the Alcazar pool, right?"

"Right. He has thirty minutes. No more."

They continued to wait in silence. Louisa tried to still her racing mind and slow her breath. Would Simon take the bait? Would his accomplices? Was this the night she would destroy Daphne's happiness? She knew Veronique was in on the plot. The only one in question was Henri.

"There he is," she whispered.

Three people emerged from the portico of the building — Henri, Simon, and Veronique Ribault.

"Do it now," Louisa said to Suzie. "While Henri is with them. Make sure Simon sees the book." Louisa handed over Chapman's *Bird Life* along with the picture.

Louisa watched from the shadows as Suzie approached the three. Suzie said something and Simon turned to her. He bent forward, listening. He took the book, opened it, and looked at the picture of the two baby alligators. She could see the shock registering on his face as he looked around. Henri appeared to ask him something. Simon shook his head and then kissed Henri on both his cheeks. Henri returned to the Ponce with his hands in his pockets. He seemed not to have a care in the world. Perhaps he really was as innocent as he professed to be. Simon gave the book back to Suzie. She walked quickly away.

Now Louisa watched Simon and Veronique. They were agitated. Finally, Simon and Veronique walked down Treasury Street toward the Florida House — either for the diamonds or for a weapon. It didn't matter. She would be ready for him.

Louisa went around to the back of the Alcazar Casino and into the indoor archery range. She walked over to the cabinet and took out a glossy bow made of black locust wood and a quiver of arrows.

Chapter 44

Ellen

“We don’t like murders in this town,” Detective Hagan said, before shooting a brown glob of tobacco juice out of his mouth. “It ain’t good for business.”

“Then I suggest we get over to the Alcazar before there’s another one,” Ellen said. “This man already tried once to kill Miss Delafield. He’ll stop at nothing.”

“Why the hell didn’t she come to me before embarking on this foolhardy scheme?” he asked.

“Perhaps because you denied that Lord Wickham was murdered at all,” Ellen said.

“All right, all right,” he said. He placed his hat on his head and they hurried down the street. “Talk.”

“Louisa believes Simon Bassett and an accomplice killed Lord Wickham. They are in possession of a half million dollars’ worth of stolen diamonds,” she said.

“Who’s the accomplice?”

“She isn’t sure. It might be his brother,” she said.

He began jogging through the tourists, calling, "Out of the way."

Ellen jogged after him.

"Detective, there's something else," she said.

He slowed down and glanced over at her.

"I believe a female anarchist has arrived here from New York, intent on shooting Miss Delafield."

"For crying out loud, you Yankees come down bringing nothing but murder and mayhem," he said, puffing as he continued weaving through the crowd.

"I'm Irish," she said. "Not a Yankee."

"Why would an anarchist want to kill Miss Delafield?" he asked.

"It's a long story," she said.

A half moon lingered in the sky, illuminating the city below. Ellen saw the imposing twin turrets of the Alcazar Hotel, then noticed a subtle scent in the air — not of flowers, but of something old and primal. Smoke?

"Detective Hagan!"

The detective stopped in mid-stride and turned. Ellen followed his gaze. A young patrolman was running toward them.

"What is it, Officer McCormick?" Hagan asked.

"Fire! The Florida House is aflame!"

The Florida House? Ellen looked toward the Alcazar and then in the direction from which the patrolman had come. A tendril of smoke wafted toward the sky.

"Hell's bells," the detective said.

"Detective, what about Louisa?" Ellen said.

"She's on her own," the detective said. "I've got to get the fire truck!" He turned and ran down the cobblestone street, his footsteps echoing against the squat stone buildings, the patrolman close behind him.

Ellen stood on the sidewalk of the old city, looking first toward the Alcazar where Louisa was meeting with a murderer and then toward the Florida House, where Suzie had gone to wait for them.

Chapter 45

Louisa

Moonlight shone through the glass ceiling and electric light leaked in through the doors to the lobby but otherwise the casino – so lively during the day when the pool was filled with swimmers or on a night when the ballroom was in use – was a place of ghostly shadows. Louisa climbed the steps to the mezzanine and circled around the canvas barriers until she could see the doorway that led to the hotel lobby. She stopped in an alcove and watched the double doors, her bow and arrow at the ready.

She waited, steadying her breath. Finally the doors opened, and Simon Bassett stood silhouetted in the light. He entered slowly, looking first one way and then the other.

"Louisa?" he called out. "Louisa, please forgive me. I didn't mean to..."

"Didn't mean to leave me for dead in the middle of a swamp, surrounded by alligators?" she asked.

She watched as he turned his head this way and that, confused. Then he slowly circumnavigated the pool. As he did so, she circled the other way, gliding from one pillar to the next.

"I couldn't let you expose us," he said. He had stopped on the other side of the pool. She stopped, too, raised the bow, pulled the string taut and pointed the arrow at him.

"Tell me the truth or I'll shoot you in the heart. Who murdered Lord Wickham? Was it Henri?" she asked, her eyes locked on his chest.

Simon finally saw her. He gazed at her as if he thought he could somehow charm her, as if she would come rushing into his arms. What a conceited boor.

"Henri knew nothing about any of this," he said. "I promise you, Louisa. Leave him be and let him have his heiress."

"Does he know about the diamonds?" she asked.

"No, Wickham and I met the broker by accident, and we saw an opportunity." He clasped the rail above the pool and leaned forward. "We persuaded Henri to take him to a brothel in Alexandria for the night. That's when we took the diamonds."

"How did Veronique Ribault figure in the scheme?"

"She smuggled the diamonds here," he said.

"On Daphne's dress?" Louisa asked, hoping the detective was waiting in the wings, hearing all of this.

"Yes," he said. "Louisa, listen to me. I have a buyer in New York. We can share the money with you. Where is the picture?"

"It's with the police," she said.

"The police? What have you done, Louisa?" His voice rose in pitch.

"Whose idea was it to kill Lord Wickham?" Louisa asked.

"Not mine. It was Veronique's," he said. "It was she who insisted I take you out to the swamp. I didn't want to do it. Louisa, I...."

"You said you had killed her," Veronique's voice rang out in the cavernous room.

Louisa looked around, every nerve on high alert. How did Veronique get in? No one had come into the pool through the lobby. She noticed Simon looking up. *Veronique must be in the ballroom overlooking the balustrade.*

"Veronique, *ma chèrie*, I swear — " he was silenced by a loud, echoing *bang*. He looked down at a hole in his chest, looked back up in surprise, then tumbled over the edge of the railing, into the pool.

Louisa's breath caught in her throat. Simon's body floated in the pool. This was happening too fast. Where were the police?

"Come out, *putain!*" Veronique's voice echoed. Louisa did not know any French obscenities, but she surmised that *putain* was no compliment.

"I know where the diamonds are, Veronique!" Louisa called out.

"You cannot tell anyone if you are dead," Veronique said.

"They'll find Simon's body, and they'll know it was you," Louisa said.

"*Moi?* No," Veronique said. "No one would blame you for murdering him after what he did to you."

Louisa couldn't understand why Ellen and the police hadn't shown up. She slipped from pillar to pillar, trying to spot Veronique on the balcony above.

"Veronique, may I call you that?" Louisa asked. "After all, we've shared a man, haven't we?"

Silence. Louisa peered up at the arches above, but saw no movement. Minutes passed.

"Veronique?" Louisa called again.

"Are you looking for me?" Veronique said, her voice much too close. Louisa wheeled around and saw the elegant figure on the other side of the pool, her shoes dangling from one hand, the gun in her other hand. She must have come down the steps from the ballroom. Louisa dove behind a pillar as a shot fired. Her hands shook as she tried to fit the arrow onto the string.

"Out of time," Veronique said as she stepped out and pointed the gun directly at Louisa. In the time it took her to cock back the hammer, Louisa leapt over the railing, still clutching the bow and arrow, and dropped into the pool. She held her breath and swam under Simon's body. A shot exploded into the water as Louisa clambered back out of the pool. Veronique fired again, grazing Louisa's calf as she slid behind a pillar.

Louisa hunkered behind it, trying to catch her breath. At least she still had the bow and arrow.

"This is such a fun game, Louisa," Veronique called out. "A gun against a bow and arrow. Who do you think will win?"

Veronique's voice moved around the side of the pool to the end of the room.

"I think it will be me," Veronique said. "What a mystery for the police to solve. Two dead bodies. I will tell all your friends in New York how enchanting you were. So sad you died at the hand of your wicked lover."

Louisa fumbled with the arrow, notching it, pulling the string taut again. She inhaled and then stepped out from behind the pillar and saw the shadowy figure at the other end of the mezzanine. Veronique saw her at the same time. Veronique raised her arm and pointed the gun.

A terrible clanging sound startled both of them. Veronique looked around in confusion. Ignoring the sound, Louisa aimed, released the bow string, and let her arrow fly. She dropped to the ground as a bullet whizzed above her.

Veronique grunted. The gun clattered to the floor firing off another shot.

Louisa rose slowly. She walked along the arcade and found Veronique on her knees, clasping the arrow lodged in her chest just above her heart.

"Don't try to pull it out," Louisa said. "That only makes it worse."

"Simon belonged to me," Veronique said, panting. She groaned and glared up at Louisa with hatred shining in her eyes.

Louisa felt an overwhelming sense of fatigue. She kicked the gun into the pool, then dropped the bow on the floor and turned toward the door. She heard ragged breaths as Veronique lunged toward her, but she turned and shoved the weakened woman to the floor.

"Wait!" Veronique cried. "Kill me." She sobbed and gazed over at the dead man floating in the pool. "I want to be with Simon."

Looking down at the once elegant woman, Louisa felt her entire body constrict with rage. She thought of poor Percival Wickham's bloody body, lying among the bushes. She thought of Daphne and Henri, innocents caught up in a vicious scheme, and she thought of how she'd thrown away a good man and probably destroyed her chances of ever finding love.

"I'm not stopping you," she hissed. "Go. Be with him. You deserve each other."

The clanging sound continued outside. What could it possibly be? And why weren't the police here? Louisa turned and walked, soaking wet, out of the casino, through the lobby of the hotel, where a clerk stared at her, and outside to the courtyard.

She smelled smoke. To her right she saw great gray plumes. Horse-drawn fire trucks tore down the street and wheeled around the corner. Her walking turned into a trot as she approached Treasury Street. She heard the fire crackling before she turned the corner and saw one of the towers of the Florida House ablaze.

People scurried in all directions, shouting and crying. It took her a few seconds to register what was happening.

Suzie, she thought. Suzie is in the hotel. She ran toward the flames.

Chapter 46
Ellen

Ellen ran through the lobby. She stopped short and wondered if the elevator was safe. Should she take the stairs? That would take too long. The fire was at the other end of the building. An elevator operator slept at his post. Ellen shook his shoulder.

"Take me to the top floor," she demanded. "And then help me get these people out of here."

"Who are you?" He gazed up at her sleepily from his stool.

"Never mind! There's a fire at the other end of the building."

He stood up and looked around. He sniffed the air, and his eyes grew wide.

"Go!" Ellen shouted and shoved him in the elevator.

He shut the elevator door and pushed the button for the fourth floor. After an eternity the door opened again, and Ellen dashed out. The elevator operator followed her.

"You get this floor," she said. "I'll go down here."

She leapt down the steps, two at a time, clasping the railing. The smoke was still thin, but she knew it would grow fast. She reached the third floor and banged on doors, screaming "Fire!" "Fire!" "Fire!" Doors opened, startled guests stumbled out. A tendril of smoke crept along the ceiling. The guests gasped and looked at each other for confirmation. Most of them ran back in their rooms to grab a few possessions.

When she reached Louisa's room, she tried the handle. It opened easily. No one was in either her or Suzie's room, and Suzie's clothes were gone. She heaved a sigh of relief, but a second later a crackling noise caused her to look up. The ceiling glowed red and a chunk of plaster fell within inches of her head. She ran from the room.

Terrified guests clogged the hallway. One older woman with long gray braids and wearing a mink stole, dragged a trunk out of her room and pulled it along the hallway. Ellen tried to convince her to leave it behind but she refused and continued to drag the trunk with her.

"Quickly, go to the stairs," Ellen called out. "Don't try to use the elevator."

She found the elevator man in the stairwell ushering guests down the steps.

"Did you get everyone?" she asked.

"I don't know." Sweat pooled on his dark brow, and his voice shook. "I couldn't get to the end rooms. Smoke is too thick."

As she raced down the steps, she saw people coming out of second floor rooms.

"This way," she called, beckoning them to the stairs.

Underneath the sounds of people hurrying, calling to each other, there was another sound, a crackling and popping coming from the walls. As hundreds descended into the lobby, the manager stood by the doorway.

"Stay calm," he said in an authoritative voice. "Everyone will get out. Stay calm."

A bellman ran to pick up a little girl who had fallen. Ellen looked around at the people. So many of them. Their faces grim, eyes wide as they looked for the exits. Husbands and wives in their night clothes clinging to each other. The old woman dragging her trunk had persevered and had made it to the bottom floor. Above them large colorful birds swooped out of their cage and through the open doors to freedom.

The smoke thickened like gravy, and her eyes burned. A roar came from above as if hell had come to Earth.

She fled the hotel surrounded by frightened guests. Everyone was intent on getting outside where a loud bell clanged over and over, and horses pulling water and chemical trucks charged. The upper stories of the wing were ablaze. Another horse pulled a ladder truck and soon the firemen were climbing ladders and pulling guests from windows of the second and third floors. The voracious fire devoured the corners of the building, climbed over the roof, and reached for the sky.

Police and firemen corralled people away from the building, hurrying them along the paths to the street. The sky was bright orange. Smoke laced the air. She saw Louisa at the edge of the property, staring up at the conflagration.

"Louisa! Thank you, Mother Mary!"

Louisa glanced at her with a stricken expression.

"Where's Suzie?" Louisa yelled over the sounds of towering flames crackling and wood splintering.

"Safe," Ellen said. "Her room was empty. Clothes gone. She must be at her brother's house."

Louisa put her face in her hands and sobbed in relief while Ellen held onto her.

Someone nearby gasped in horror. Ellen looked up.

"Louisa," she said and pointed. Louisa's gaze followed the trajectory of her finger. On the top floor in an open window, a woman stood in a wedding dress.

"That's Madame Ribault's atelier. And that's ... Daphne's dress!" Louisa said. "Who is that woman?"

Ellen peered up at the figure, silhouetted against the flames.

"It's Sweet Sal," she said.

"What?" Louisa asked incredulously.

Ellen knew exactly what had happened as if she'd been there to see the whole thing. Poor Sweet Sal must have been wandering the hotel in search of Louisa and found the room with the wedding dress. And how could she resist? She would have put it on and admired herself in the full length mirror. She must have forgotten all about her mission to kill Louisa and imagined Frank next to her, swearing to love her for the rest of her life.

Smoke wrapped its arms around the would-be bride as curtains on either side of her ignited. Then the dress caught fire. Sweet Sal leapt from the window and fell like a blazing comet to the ground.

Chapter 47
Louisa

The firemen worked all night, trying to contain the blaze. They had managed to stop it at Hypolita Street; to the south, the bay had quenched the flames. The Ponce was untouched, but the courthouse had not survived. Neither had several wooden hotels by the bay. In all, 32 buildings were consumed by the blaze. According to the newspaper, the fire began in the kitchen boiler room and the damage would total more than $600,000. Miraculously, besides Sally Molansky, a wanted anarchist from New York City, there was only one other fatality reported.

The next day Louisa felt as though she were walking through a battlefield. The plaza was piled high with the personal belongings of the guests who had fled the fires with everything they could carry. The displaced guests had been put up in private homes and in every spare room of every inn and hotel in the area. Wherever she looked, Negro prisoners in striped uniforms worked, clearing debris.

Louisa went to the police station, but Detective Hagan was busy with the aftermath of the fire. A police sergeant at the desk told her they had found two bodies in the Alcazar pool. A man had been shot, and a woman had been wounded and then somehow drowned. Simon and Veronique's deaths were chalked up to a lover's quarrel. The police were still not inclined to record Lord Wickham's death as a murder.

"I suggest that when your men clean up the debris at the Florida House, they look for a burnt wedding dress. It will be covered in diamonds," she said. "They should be returned to a broker in Alexandria, Egypt."

The sergeant's eyes went wide.

"I'll send a message to Detective Hagan right away," he said.

***

Louisa found Daphne at the Alcazar pool, steadily swimming laps. Louisa examined the floor where she had left Veronique lying. Not a drop of blood remained.

Daphne swam to the edge of the pool and pulled herself out of the water.

"I should blame you for ruining everything," Daphne said, "but it seems the fire was even more destructive than you were. I know you are somehow responsible for the fact that my future brother-in-law and my dress designer are both dead, and I know all about your theories about diamonds and Lord Wickham. Father told us everything you found out."

"I'm sorry, Daphne," she asked.

Daphne's maid rushed over with a towel.

"Of course, I will still marry Henri. It will be a small, private affair back home in Chicago," she said. "Father managed to get us train tickets for this afternoon." Her expression softened. "I know you were only doing as my father asked, trying to protect me. I also know that you proved Henri innocent. For that I thank you. He's devastated by his brother's death, but between the two of us, I think he will be better off without Simon around. Simon was a dark force. I, for one, am glad he's gone."

Daphne was right. Without the influence of his brother, Henri might turn out to be a decent husband.

After leaving Daphne, Louisa walked across the street to the Ponce and found Mrs. Griffin in her room fluttering around the open trunks while her maids finished packing the clothes.

"What an utter disaster!" Mrs. Griffin said, throwing up her hands.

"Hello, Mrs. Griffin," Louisa said.

The woman whirled around and smiled weakly.

"How lovely of you to stop by, Miss Delafield. I'm sorry I don't have more time for a chat," she said. "Marie, please don't wrinkle my gowns!"

"I'll wait until you have a free minute," Louisa said. "I want to make sure my column has all the pertinent information for the new wedding. You do want Daphne's name in the paper, don't you?"

"Of course, of course."

Once the trunks were closed and the hotel's troupe of bellmen enlisted to take them downstairs, Mrs. Griffin began filling her traveling case with her toiletries and jewels while the two maids went to their rooms upstairs for their own belongings.

"What did you want to know, Miss Delafield?" Mrs. Griffin asked.

"Why did you give Madame Ribault an alibi?" Louisa asked.

Mrs. Griffin turned to her with a look of surprise.

"Were you really in her room the night of Lord Wickham's murder?" Louisa continued.

"I thought you wanted to ask about Daphne," she said, turning her back on Louisa, hiding her face.

"You may as well tell me the truth," Louisa said.

"Or what? You'll tell the world about Henri and that Lord Wickham?" Mrs. Griffin asked.

Louisa had no plans to tell anyone about Henri and Lord Wickham, but Mrs. Griffin didn't know that. She assumed everyone else was like her — duplicitous.

"I want the truth. And I promise I will never mention those two men. Ever," Louisa said.

Mrs. Griffin sighed and sat down in the nearest chair.

"I was with Veronique that night," Mrs. Griffin said. "For two hours."

"Two hours?" Louisa asked. "Did she kill Lord Wickham while you were there?"

Mrs. Griffin regarded her for a minute and then shrugged.

"It was her idea. Not mine," she said. Her face hardened. "It's not like you can do anything about it, can you? The police have already ruled Lord Wickham's death a suicide."

"But you went along with it?" she asked.

Mrs. Griffin nodded.

"I did," she said and looked at the ceiling as she seemed to recollect the night. "We were making some changes to the bridesmaids' hats when we heard a loud quarrel in the next room. The doors to the balcony were open and I heard Henri's voice quite plainly. That's when Veronique told me about the two of them and their disgusting past."

She shook her head in dismay and continued, "That horrid Lord Wickham wanted to destroy my daughter's happiness. You don't have children, Miss Delafield. You're something of an old maid, I take it?"

"My marital status is not important," Louisa said.

"My point is that a mother will do anything to protect her children, to ensure their happiness and well-being." Mrs. Griffin rose and packed a few more items into her travel case.

"Including aid and abet a murderess?" Louisa asked, circling around so she could look her in the eye. "We both know that's what it was. Madame Ribault left you alone in her atelier while she went next door, stabbed Lord Wickham with a seam ripper and pushed him off the balcony. Of course, she had motive enough. She and Simon could keep his share of the stolen diamonds while your motive for complicity was to get rid of a threat to your daughter's fiancé. Did you, by any chance, also offer an incentive to Madame Ribault? I trust you didn't know about the diamonds."

"Diamonds? I did wonder about the pendant Henri gave to Daphne," she said. "And, of course, Randall told me about your suspicions."

"Did you give her an incentive?" Louisa asked again.

"Well, certainly, I would have helped her get her business established in America. She was extremely talented, after all. It's really too bad," she said, closing her traveling case and locking it with a small key.

Then she lifted her chin and glared at Louisa. "Miss Delafield, I don't know what you're getting at with all these questions. I've done nothing wrong. I wasn't even in his room when it happened. For all I know Veronique went over there and tried to stop him from leaping to his death."

Louisa rubbed a hand across her eyes. She simply couldn't believe the nerve of this woman, but really she should not have been surprised. Ellen wouldn't be.

"Does your husband think you've done nothing wrong?"

"What husbands think doesn't matter. You'd know that if you had one," she said. "Now, if you'll excuse me. We have a train to catch."

Louisa stood aside as Mrs. Griffin picked up her traveling case and marched past her. She had a point. Legally, she had done nothing wrong — at least not that anyone could prove.

Louisa went to the window and looked toward the charred ruins of the Florida House. The air still smelled of smoke. She was glad Forrest had left for New York before the fire. One less thing to feel guilty about. Then she thought of that poor woman in the flaming wedding dress as she fell from the window of the burning hotel. They'd both been fools for a man.

***

The ruins smoldered for days. Louisa, Ellen, and Suzie stayed at Lloyd's house until they could get a train home. The kindness and concern of Suzie's extended family, especially her grandniece, Pansy, was touching.

Lloyd's house was crowded with guests who had been burned out of their homes. Suzie and Polly brought out plate after plate of food for people who were camped out in the living room. Ellen helped by washing dishes and even Louisa was put to work, finding enough bedding for the visitors. After all the horror of the past few days, she was glad to be occupied.

At night, she and Ellen shared a bed in Pansy's room. Pansy was sleeping at a friend's house. Louisa liked having the comfort of Ellen next to her.

"I am sorry I didn't come for you at the Alcazar," Ellen said.

"You were worried about Suzie. It's perfectly understandable," Louisa said.

"Standing in the street between you and the fire, I swear I had a knowing," Ellen said.

"A knowing?"

"I don't know how else to describe it. I knew you could take care of yourself and that there was a hotel full of people who had no idea their lives were in danger. Patrolman McCormick and Detective Hagan were off getting the fire trucks. Somebody had to get those people out," she said.

"You did the right thing," Louisa said.

Outside, insects made a constant buzzing sound.

"There's something else, Louisa," Ellen said. "I have a favor to ask of you. I want you to write a favorable article about Emma Goldman."

Louisa shot up in the bed, looked at her friend, and said, "You must be joking."

"I am not," Ellen said. "And you must talk about the Army of the Unemployed."

"Ellen," Louisa said with dismay. How could she ask such a thing?

"T'wasn't them that tried to kill you," Ellen said. "And I promised Frank I would try to get something favorable in the news for them. It's not right, Louisa. I've met these men, how desperate they are to work. They're not the lazy free-loaders that the newspapers make them out to be. If you could just tell the truth about them, then maybe your wealthy readers could see the other side."

Louisa sank back down in the bed. What an insane idea, but she knew the truth of the matter.

"I supposed I could write an article under Beatrice Milton," she said. "I'd have to frame it right, but it could be done."

"It must be under your own name," Ellen said. "It must be Louisa Delafield who sets things right."

Louisa thought about those days on the island in the swamp, how her stomach had gnawed at her. She'd realized that she would have done just about anything for food. Then she thought of all those people who appeared in her columns. Well fed, prosperous women who had never known a day of deprivation in their lives. Her editor might not be happy with her, but she could spare a column for those voiceless masses.

"I'll do it," she said.

"Thank you," Ellen said.

"After I finish my article about the birds." She shut her eyes then and willed herself into a dreamless sleep.

Chapter 48
Ellen

Louisa was scribbling away in one of her notebooks as the cab bounced down the road to the rail station.

"What are you writing?" Ellen asked.

"Do you remember the woman who came out of the hotel, fully dressed, dragging her trunk? That was Lady Rutherford. I interviewed her yesterday afternoon," Louisa said. "She's the epitome of a *grand dame.* She lets nothing fluster her, not even a raging fire."

Ellen sighed. Louisa Delafield might glorify the so-called elite, but that was her job, wasn't it — just as waiters, bricklayers, and automobile makers all did their part to stoke the fires of society's gluttonous maw. No one was innocent in this world, Ellen thought.

She wasn't sure she wanted to go back to New York. She had burned her bridges with the anarchists, but worse, Hester would not be waiting for her. She thought of Hester's scent, her large brown eyes, the softness of her skin. How could Ellen have thrown it all away?

The cab driver unloaded Louisa's trunks and Ellen's and Suzie's suitcases. Ellen glanced up at the deep blue sky. She felt she could swim in it if only the Earth would turn upside down.

"Well, all's well that ends well," Louisa said.

"Ends well? Half of St. Augustine is burnt to a cinder. You've lost Forrest. I've lost Hester. How is this ending well?" Ellen asked as they made their way to the platform to wait for the train.

"I didn't lose Suzie," Louisa said and looked over at Suzie in her black traveling dress and turban.

Suzie looked at Louisa with a quizzical expression and said, "New York is my home, Louisa. I enjoyed seeing my family, but I could never live here. Especially not after what I heard the summers are like. They say the mosquitoes will kill a grown dog in July. No, I can't live here."

"I suppose you could visit anytime you like," Louisa said, smoothing her gloves.

"I suppose I will. But what about your mother?"

Louisa shrugged and then said, "What if we hired a girl to help you around the house?"

Suzie pondered the idea. Ellen watched the interaction with curiosity.

"Depends on the girl, I guess," Suzie said.

"What if you were the one who hired her?" Louisa suggested.

Suzie thought about the idea a little longer.

"Pansy just turned sixteen. She's ready to fly from the nest."

"How would we get her to New York?" Louisa wondered. "She's much too young to travel unaccompanied."

The train heading south arrived in a flurry of steam and screeching wheels. The doors opened, and porters ran around quickly placing stepping stools so the passengers could disembark. The train heading north wasn't due for another fifteen minutes.

Ellen sighed and gazed across the tracks at the train on the southbound platform. Then her jaw dropped. Stepping off the train, wearing a pale green day dress and a straw hat was none other than Hester French. Hester looked around. Their eyes met.

A few minutes later Hester stood in front of her, eyes blinking in the light. Ellen nearly fainted, she was so surprised.

"I've never been to Florida before," Hester said. "It's quite warm, isn't it?"

Ellen searched for something to say, but the words were trapped in the depths of her heart. Tears filled her eyes.

"What are you doing here?" she asked in a faint voice. "I thought ..."

"You thought I would turn my back on you? I considered it, Ellen. I did not agree with the things you did. And I know I should hate you for your fling or whatever it was with that woman. For a short while, I did," she said.

"What changed your mind?" Ellen asked.

"I'm surrounded by people who are impressed by superficialities, people who are hypnotized by money and luxury. Even the most ardent reformer loves her satin and her silk. But you — you are nothing like that. You are the most honest person I know, and if you say that you regret what you did and that you would undo it if you could, I believe you," Hester said. She sighed, suddenly relaxing her upright posture, and continued, "Besides, my dear, I just couldn't imagine my life without you."

She reached out and squeezed Ellen's hands in her own.

"I swear on my gran's grave, Hester French, I'll never let you down again," Ellen said. Relief flooded through her body, and she smiled through her tears. She had almost lost this jewel.

"Ellen?" Louisa said. "Are you coming?"

Ellen looked at Hester, and Hester smiled at Louisa.

"I think we're due for a vacation," she said. "Where should we stay, Louisa?"

"Well ..." Louisa said.

Ellen answered for her, "Anywhere but the Florida House. It's gone."

"I believe the Ponce has some vacancies," Louisa said.

Ellen looked at Louisa and Suzie and said, "We'll bring Pansy back home with us in a couple of weeks."

She took Hester's arm, and the two of them strolled off into the sunlight.

Chapter 49
Louisa

The door opened and a harried looking Mrs. Kimura threw up her arms when she saw Louisa and Suzie.

"I thought you'd never get back," she said. "That is the most cantankerous old woman."

Louisa looked past Mrs. Kimura and saw her mother in her invalid chair, grinning like a mischievous little girl.

"I'm so sorry. I'll pay you right now for all your trouble. I can't tell you how much I appreciate it," Louisa said, hurrying into the parlor to write a check to the woman.

"No, no. Mr. Calloway already pay me," she said.

Meanwhile, Suzie instructed the cab driver where to put the trunks and suitcases.

"At least let me pay for the cab to take you home," Louisa said.

While Louisa gave instructions to the cab driver, Anna stood up from her chair.

"Suzie!" she called.

"Yes? What is it?" Suzie asked.

Tears stained Anna's cheeks and she held out her arms. Suzie looked confused and then stepped closer and allowed Anna to hold her. Anna sobbed.

"I was so worried you wouldn't come home," Anna whimpered.

"For heaven's sake, Mother," Louisa said, utterly baffled. For one thing, she'd never once seen her mother so emotional, at least not since her father died, and secondly, her mother had barely acknowledged her. "What about me, Mother? Were you worried about me?"

"Oh, I knew you'd come home," Anna said and lowered herself back to her chair.

"I almost didn't," Louisa muttered, but her mother didn't hear her.

Suzie had a stunned look on her face, but then smiled and said, "I missed you, too, Mrs. Delafield."

"After all these years, I think you can call me Anna," the old woman said. "Not in front of guests, of course."

Louisa suppressed a chuckle. Her mother would always believe in appearances. Fortunately, they never had guests besides Ellen. She and Suzie looked at each other for a moment, the memories of the past few weeks lingering somewhere in their gaze. Louisa had seen the disdain with which Negroes were treated, and now she could never forget. She had seen the mighty force of Suzie's dignity in the face of that disdain.

"Suzie saved my life, Mother," Louisa said.

"Of course, she did," Anna said. "She's been saving us all for years."

"Right now, I'm going to save my bones with a warm soak," Suzie said, and headed upstairs for a hot bath.

Louisa sat down on the sofa.

"Tell me about the wedding," Anna said. "Was anyone I know there?"

"There was no wedding, Mother," Louisa said. "Didn't you hear about the fire? It ate up half of St. Augustine."

"I didn't know it ate the wedding. What a voracious thing," she said.

"The bride and groom will go back to Chicago and have a small, quiet ceremony. I think destination weddings may be passé," Louisa said.

***

Louisa knocked on the door of the Markhams' Gramercy Park house. She looked around the street as she entered. Gramercy Park had once been one of the most exclusive neighborhoods, but the very wealthy had moved further north. The houses here were still lovely, and the residents had access to a private park. Forrest Calloway also lived in the neighborhood, but she pushed that thought out of her mind.

The housekeeper let her in and led her to the parlor where she perched on the edge of a chair. She looked up at the portrait of Julia Markham above the brocade couch — a rather lovely woman, who reminded Louisa of a Kewpie doll and fluttered around like a nervous butterfly. She remembered their last encounter at Mrs. Frick's benefit for the Yorkville Social Center — how distraught she had been. And she wondered if she had gone through with the divorce proceedings. The answer to that question came more quickly than she expected.

She heard a throat being cleared and looked up to see Herbert Markham, Esquire, in the doorway. He wore a vest with gold buttons and appeared to have just left his study. What was he doing here, she wondered. She had thought surely he would be at work.

"My dear Miss Delafield, how kind of you to visit," he said and sat down in a nearby armchair.

"I was hoping to see Mrs. Markham," she said.

"She'll be right down. How is your lovely mother?" he asked. "And you? Weren't you in Florida? I seem to remember a column about tango lessons."

"I was there for a wedding, which didn't happen," she said.

"That's right. The fire!" he said, leaning his elbows on his knees and studying her. "Fortunately you survived."

"I did. There was a casualty," she said. "A woman from New York."

"Oh, that's right, the anarchist?"

"Exactly," she said.

"Terrible," he said. "I can't imagine a more awful way to die. Here she is," he said with a bright smile. "Julia, look who's come to visit."

Julia Markham entered the room, in a blue ruffled lounge dress.

"Miss Delafield, what a pleasant surprise," she said. "Would you like some coffee or tea? Let me ring for Mrs. White. I haven't seen you in ages."

"Actually, we saw each other at the Yorkville benefit," Louisa said.

"Oh, that's right," Julia said. She lifted a finger to her cheek. "I don't believe you've ever called on me before."

"No," Louisa said. "I've been remiss."

Mrs. White brought in a tray with a silver coffee set, and Julia poured them both a cup of coffee.

"Sugar?"

"No, thank you," Louisa said.

"Darling, would you like some coffee?" she asked her husband. He shook his head.

There was a long awkward pause as the three of them sat there. Louisa looked around the room, observing the paintings on the walls — mostly 19th century landscapes.

"I loved the article you wrote about birds. I promise I'll never have another feather on my hat ever again," Julia said. "And that lovely drawing. It quite captured the essence of the bird. Who was the artist?"

"Lord Percival Wickham," Louisa said.

"A lord? How delightful," Julia said. She turned to her husband. "Isn't that delightful, dear?"

"Oh, yes," the attorney said.

"He's dead now," Louisa said. "Murdered."

"Oh my," Julia said, glancing in alarm at her husband.

"You certainly had your share of excitement, didn't you?" the lawyer said.

Louisa didn't understand why he was still sitting with them. Men usually left their wives to their own devices when other ladies paid a social visit. She turned and looked at him, her eyes wide and questioning. He finally seemed to get the hint, cleared his throat again, and pushed himself out of the chair.

"I'll let you ladies enjoy your coffee," he said.

"Would you ask Mrs. White to bring in something to nibble on, dear?" Julia said.

He agreed, bowed to them and left the room.

As soon as he was gone, Louisa leaned forward.

"I thought you were getting a divorce," she whispered.

Julia gazed down at her hands and said quietly, "It was all a misunderstanding. He explained everything."

Louisa exhaled loudly. She should be glad that the Markhams weren't divorcing. No woman should have to go through that, but she found herself oddly dissatisfied with Julia Markham's answer.

"What about the information you said you had. Something to do with me?" Louisa asked, setting her coffee cup down on its saucer.

Mrs. White entered at that moment with a plate of cookies. She set the plate down and left.

"Cookie?" Julia asked.

"No, thank you."

Louisa waited. Julia took a bite of one of the cookies and then put it back on the plate.

"They are rather stale," she said.

"Mrs. Markham," Louisa said.

"Julia. You must call me Julia."

Louisa sighed in frustration.

"Julia, please tell me," she said.

"There's nothing to tell, not really," she said.

"Not really? Is this about my father?" Louisa said, her fists clenched.

Julia coughed and looked around the room.

"I really shouldn't have said anything," she said, a miserable expression on her face. "He — " She didn't finish.

"Darling," her husband said in a loud, cheery voice as he came back in the room. "Don't you have an appointment coming up?"

"That's right," she said. "I promised Mrs. Bennet I would help her go over the menu for our party. I'm so sorry to cut our visit short, Louisa."

Julia rose and motioned toward the door.

Louisa stood up, mouth open as if to object, but Herbert Markham stepped in and took her by the arm.

"Let me see you out, Louisa," he said.

"Do come again," Julia called as he summarily ushered Louisa out of the parlor. He opened the door and swept his hand to indicate it was time for Louisa to go.

Once outside, she stood on the sidewalk, feeling as if she'd been hit by a truck. She stared at the closed door. What a strange encounter. Her stomach felt queasy and for some reason she remembered the alligator swimming toward her in the swamp and the horror she'd felt when it had leapt out of the water. She turned and hurried toward the subway.

Society Notes

By Louisa Delafield
New York
April 15, 1914

A few weeks ago I wrote about a shooting that occurred outside the wedding of Hugh and Cynthia Garrett. I believed that the bullet which struck Dottie Parsons was meant for me and had been fired from the gun belonging to an anarchist. I blamed an article in the magazine *Mother Earth* for inspiring the attack.

Since that time I've had the opportunity to speak to Emma Goldman, the publisher and founder of the magazine, and learn the truth of the matter. Although some of her adherents have a misguided belief that violence will advance their cause, Miss Goldman does not approve of violence as a means to an end.

"That every act of political violence should nowadays be attributed to anarchists is not at all surprising," Miss Goldman said. "Yet it is a fact known to almost everyone familiar with the anarchist movement that a great number of acts, for which anarchists had to suffer, either originated with the capitalist press or were instigated by the police."

I asked if she were suggesting that the police were responsible for the violence that resulted in the shooting outside the wedding.

"Of course not. I am simply acknowledging the fact that violent acts are often left on the doorstep of the anarchists."

Twenty years ago during the depression of 1893, Miss Goldman told unemployed workers that they must ask the rich for work; if the rich do not give them work, they must ask for bread; if they are not given bread, then they must take the bread. I asked if her views had changed since then.

"Today, once again we have thousands of men and women who are without food, without shelter, and most of all, without work. And yet when they ask for work, they are called lazy. When they ask for food and shelter, they are turned away. When they demand these basic necessities they are thrown in jail," she said.

Miss Goldman does not exaggerate. It is estimated that there may currently be as many as 100,000 unemployed in New York City, and winter this year was especially brutal.

"Is it too much to ask for decent wages? Is it too much to expect the industrialists who profit from the sweat and labor of these men and women to keep them afloat during hard times?"

Miss Goldman raises a fair question. Our foremost men of industry have uniformly opposed unionization. However, unions are a proven path to dignity and a living wage to our workers — both men and women.

"I am older and wiser than I was 21 years ago, but I am no less dismayed by the plight of the worker, who has no control over his destiny," she said. "Frank Tannenbaum is not the enemy of America. He is simply one who feels intensely the indignity of our social wrongs; whose very being must throb with the pain, the sorrow, the despair millions of people are daily made to endure."

As for Sally Molansky, the anarchist who fired the bullet which was intended for me but which killed Dottie Parsons instead, her motivations will forever be unknown as she died in the great fire of St. Augustine, where she had pursued me.

Like Miss Goldman, I believe we can do more to eradicate the injustices inherent in our economic system without giving in to chaos. I call on the readers of this paper to look to your consciences and ask yourselves if you are propagating a system that is fair and just to all members of society. If not, what are you willing to do to change?

Epilogue

Dusk had fallen when Louisa took a cab to Gramercy Park, paid the driver, and got out in front of Forrest Calloway's house. She carried a small, flat package, wrapped in white paper. Before climbing the steps, she inhaled deeply. At the top of the steps, she pushed the bronze doorbell and heard the chimes ring inside. Glancing across the street at the fenced-in park, she remembered the first time she ever looked out at the park from the windows of Forrest's bedroom.

The door opened.

"Miss Delafield," Mr. Kimura observed.

"Hello, Mr. Kimura. I wanted to give this to Mrs. Kimura as a thank you for taking care of my mother," Louisa said, holding out the white package.

"Please, come in. I will get her," Mr. Kimura said. Standing in the foyer of Forrest's home, she checked her reflection in the gilt-framed mirror above the credenza. She wore a day ensemble with a pleated hobble skirt, a stylish hat with a fan-like embellishment, and a dark blue choker necklace.

"Miss Delafield, you did not need to bring me anything," Mrs. Kimura said with a wide smile, her eyes pinned to the package in Louisa's hand. She was a short, energetic woman with a youthful face though Louisa was sure she was near sixty.

"Of course, I did not need to, Mrs. Kimura. I wanted to. You were so kind to look after my mother," Louisa said.

Mrs. Kimura eagerly took the package and tore off the wrapping.

"What have we here?" she said, opening the box and drawing out a glittering red scarf. "Oh, it's soft. Made of silk."

"I hope you like it," Louisa said.

"I love it," she said. "Thank you so much."

She bowed to Louisa, then wrapped the scarf around her neck and looked in the mirror. Mr. Kimura stood at her side, watching her and smiling.

"Very nice," he said.

Louisa glanced toward Forrest's study.

"Is Mr. Calloway in?" she ventured.

Mr. Kimura shook his head.

"He is traveling in Colorado, checking on his investments," he said.

"Oh," Louisa said. She didn't even know he had investments in Colorado. "Then I'll be going. Thank you again, Mrs. Kimura."

When Mr. Kimura opened the door for her, she gazed across the street to the wrought iron fence surrounding the park. Her feet felt like lead as she stepped outside. She had foolishly hoped that Forrest would be there, that he would take her in his arms and forgive her the way Hester had forgiven Ellen. She walked along the sidewalk as twilight, that interlude between the stark light of day and the ink-soaked night, slunk over the park and spread across the city.

The Markhams lived on the other side of the park, and as she passed by their house, a memory crept into her thoughts: Herbert Markham sitting across from her in his parlor, asking if it had been the anarchist who died in the fire. She stopped and clasped a wrought iron fleur de lis at the top of the fence poles. Her article had not yet been published, so how had he known that Sweet Sal was dead? She stared at the dark windows of the house as clouds passed overhead and the moon's reflection suddenly appeared in the upper window as white and round as if it had been painted on the glass, and a breeze tickled the back of her neck.

Author's Note and Acknowledgments

What a fascinating year 1914 was! I first discovered the anarchists and protesters of 1914 in the book *More Powerful Than Dynamite* by Thai Jones and quickly went down the rabbit hole, reading works by Emma Goldman and Alexander (Sasha) Berkman and learning about the Ludlow Massacre. I'm especially grateful to the Berkeley library for online access to Goldman's speeches. Of course, much of my information came from the *New York Times* archives, including the fact that Charlotte Perkins Gilman (of "The Yellow Wallpaper" fame) gave a speech in New York in the spring of that year.

While Karl (alias L. Byron) is a fictional character, most of the other anarchist characters are inspired by or based on real people, including the fiery activist Becky Edelman, who really did wear red stockings.

Sweet Sal is also a fictional character, her name inspired by an anarchist named Sweet Marie, who shot at and missed John D. Rockefeller, Jr.

I did make a few logistical changes for dramatic purposes. By 1914, Goldman and Berkman had moved the office of *Mother Earth* from East 13th Street to Harlem, and the explosion on Lexington Avenue, which killed three people, actually happened in July of 1914 not in April. I conflated Frank Tannenbaum with another Frank (of the mangled hand) who was described in Jones' book. Young Frank Tannenbaum led several marches of the Army of the Unemployed, during which the protestors asked for help from churches until the fateful day they were arrested.

When the Ludlow Massacre occurred in 1914, anarchists and many others, including Upton Sinclair, blamed the Rockefellers. Although John D. Rockefeller, Jr., was a magnanimous philanthropist, he and his father owned forty percent of the shares of Colorado Fuel and Iron Company. Unfortunately, Rockefeller denied that the Ludlow Massacre ever happened or that women or children were killed. However, according to a New York Times article, "The Ludlow camp is a mass of charred debris, and buried beneath it is a story of horror imparalleled [sic] in the history of industrial warfare. In the holes which had been dug for their protection against the rifles' fire the women and children died like trapped rats when the flames swept over them. One pit, uncovered [the day after the massacre] disclosed the bodies of 10 children and two women." For more information on the Ludlow Massacre, check out the primary sources on PBS' American Experience:
https://www.pbs.org/wgbh/americanexperience/features/rockefellers-ludlow/.

Once again, when it comes to New York History, the Bowery Boys were a tremendous help. Their tour of Greenwich Village is both entertaining and informative.

Louisa's story in this book is not based on real events except for the most important one: in St. Augustine a fire, which started in The Florida House, ravaged the city in April of 1914.

By then St. Augustine was no longer in its heyday but enough wealthy northerners came during the season to keep the grand old hotels afloat. The Ponce de Leon hotel is now Flagler College, where my good friend Kevin Murphy teaches creative writing. Kevin took me on tours of the college, explained much of the city's history, and went with me to the Lincolnville Museum where we learned so many fascinating aspects of Lincolnville's past. The St. Augustine Historical society was also font of information. Thanks so much to senior historian Charles Tingley for spending time with me and showing me the old maps of the city. The Alcatraz Hotel still stands and is now the gorgeous Lightner Museum. Much thanks to Lucy Perez, a docent at the museum, for her insights about how the hotel looked in 1914.

I learned much about the look and feel of St. Augustine in 1914 from the journal El Escribano, The St. Augustine Journal of History (1998), which published "A Confession of St. Augustine" by William Dean Howells.

As for the racial aspects of this story, in 1914 a Black American would have been excluded from the library, segregated into "Jim Crow" cars at the front of the train (according to The Smithsonian National Museum of American History), and generally looked down upon or ignored by St. Augustine's White locals and tourists. Lynchings were a terrifying reality at that time. Booker

T. Washington noted that "51 black Americans were lynched in 1913 — the smallest number since these grim records have been kept." I use the term "Negro" or "Colored" when referring to African Americans because those were the preferred (or polite) terms used by both races. Louisa, being the granddaughter of an abolitionist, would not have had the same prejudices as many people of her era, but she would have had the unconscious biases of her class.

In my blog I go into further detail about some of the fascinating historical tidbits I discovered in the course of my research: https://trishmacenulty.com/blog/

Thanks to the dear friends who read this book at various stages and helped make it better through their comments and encouragement: Tamara Titus, who read every bit of the book in first draft form; Pamela Ball and Kevin Murphy, who have helped me better my writing ever since graduate school; beta readers, Patti Wood, the body language expert who has such keen advice; Kathleen Laufenberg, always supportive and insightful, and Zannah Lyle, who saved me from several embarrassing anachronisms. Thanks to Amy Rogers for her meticulous proofreading. And always, so much gratitude for my husband, Joe, who makes it all possible.

Please visit my website trishmacenulty.com and sign up for my newsletter to learn more about my forthcoming books or to read my blog and get the deeper history. Speaking of upcoming books, you can pre-order *Secrets & Spies*, the next in the Delafield & Malloy Investigations series, here:

A preview of the book follows.

from *Secrets and Spies*

Chapter 1
Louisa

Louisa noticed the muffled laughter as she wended her way through the maze of desks, but didn't pay it much heed until she reached her own desk and saw that a bucket of oats had re-placed her trusty Remington typewriter. Hands on hips, she turned to look at the culprits, and that was when the muffled laughter turned to guffaws.

"Mr. Stephens, thank you so much for this delightful gift, but I'm not hungry at the moment," she said, looking over at the police reporter, who was surely the instigator of this juvenile joke. "Would it trouble you too much to return my typewriter?"

"Lovely piece you wrote, Miss Delafield," Mick Jones, the barely mediocre sports writer, called out. "Pure poetry."

"I'm so glad we're neighbors," Billy Stephens said, giggling like a school boy, as he brought her typewriter over to her.

"And please," Louisa said, indicating the bucket of oats, "find a better place for this."

The men continued to act foolish as they were wont to do, and Louisa sat down at her desk and ignored them as she was wont to do. She had gone out on a limb with that story, but she'd been so moved by the sight of the horses and especially that gorgeous roan mare with the black mane. She could still feel those velvety lips on her palm as the horse took the sugar cube from her hand. She'd always loved horses and remembered her own heartbreak when, after her father's death, they'd had to sell the pair of black geldings that pulled their carriage. Families all over the country must be feeling that same sense of loss as they gave up their horses for a senseless war.

"Where's your sidekick?" Billy asked, nodding at the empty chair where Ellen Malloy usually sat.

"She's off to Ireland to visit her sick father," Louisa said. "She leaves tomorrow so I gave her the day off to get ready."

Billy rubbed his chin and then asked, "What boat is she taking?"

"The Lusitania," Louisa said.

Billy went back to his desk and returned with yesterday's newspaper from his desk. He opened it to her column.

"Mr. Stephens, how long are you going to harangue me about this column? I know it's not my usual society fare. I may have gone a little — " she asked.

"Look at the advertisement," he interrupted.

She read the small print from the Cunard Ocean Steamships' advert aloud, "...vessels flying the flag of

Great Britain or any of her allies are liable to destruction…" She looked up at Billy.

"But the Lusitania is a passenger ship with mostly American citizens," she said. "I'm sure Germany would never provoke Wilson. This advertisement is just a bluff." And yet she felt extremely uneasy, thinking of Ellen crossing the Atlantic in the middle of a war, neutrality or no neutrality.

Suddenly the newsroom grew quiet.

"Oh, my," Billy said. He lowered the paper and whistled under his breath.

Louisa looked up. All the men were watching as a young woman zigzagged through the warren of news desks toward Louisa. She wore a stylish gray chenille hat with a black ribbon, a smart gray jacket trimmed in black velvet, and a flared skirt that landed a few inches above her ankles. Louisa surmised in a glance that the woman was perfect for the job, and her heart sank like a stone. The last thing she wanted was to actually hire a replacement for Ellen — even temporarily.

"Miss Delafield?" the woman asked, her voice light and lilting. "It's me, Phyllis Wolff."

She stood at Louisa's desk, dewy and glowing. Louisa was only 26, but she suddenly felt old and tarnished.

"I'm here about the position as your assistant," the young woman continued. "I sent you a let-ter."

Louisa patted her unruly hair and forced a smile to her lips, but it took another few seconds to wet her mouth enough that she could open it.

"Yes, I know. Please have a seat," she finally uttered.

"Miss, you don't want to work for her," Billy said, throwing a glance at Louisa. "We call her Bloody Delafield for all the murders she digs up. Sometimes literally."

Of all the impertinence. Louisa should be furious with him, but instead she suppressed a smile. Perhaps he would scare the young woman away.

"Don't listen to him, Mrs. Wolff," she said, emphasizing the "missus."

"Married, are you?" Billy asked in dismay.

"Widowed," she responded. Demurely, Louisa noted. Oh, she was good, this one.

"Mrs. Wolff was a debutante the last time I saw her," Louisa said and turned her gaze toward her. "Your coming out party took seven whole inches of my column."

"Seven inches?" Billy said, widening his eyes. Louisa decided ignoring him was the best course of action.

"A long time ago," Mrs. Wolff said in a world-weary tone and glanced down at her folded hands.

"Not that long ago. Four years, perhaps? You married that artist, Herman Wolff, soon after the party," Louisa said.

"Eloped," Mrs. Wolff corrected. "You may as well say the truth. It was quite the scandal. My family cut me off entirely. So we moved to Germany where Herman was from."

"Bad timing, that," Billy said with a grimace.

"It was unfair of your parents to cut you off," Louisa said. The belief of the older generation that they had the right to choose the spouses of their children had always struck Louisa as one of the pitfalls of being in the upper classes. Phyllis had married a destitute artist for love, and she'd paid a steep price.

"But widowhood has restored my respectability, which makes me a perfect fit for the job of assistant to the most respected society writer in America," Mrs. Wolff said.

Billy barked a laugh and noted, "She'll be great at this job."

"Mr. Stephens, isn't there a paddywagon somewhere you should be chasing?" Louisa asked, glaring at him.

"All right. I know when I'm not welcome." He wandered slowly back toward his own desk. Louisa had a mind to smack him with something but she had no weapon handy. Not to mention, she didn't want to confirm the "bloody Delafield" title. It was true she'd strayed off the society beat more than a few times over the past two years, but she was still first and foremost, "Louisa Delafield, syndicated society columnist for *The Ledger*."

"You know the position is only temporary," Louisa said. "I've promised Miss Malloy her job will be waiting for her as soon as she returns from her trip to Ireland."

"*If* her ship doesn't get torpedoed by the Krauts," Billy interjected from his desk where he had continued to eavesdrop on their conversation. "No offense, Mrs. Wolff."

"None taken. I'm not German. Besides, I saw that advertisement. It's German bluster. I came over from Liverpool on a cruise liner just last month," Mrs. Wolff said. "We made it without incident."

"There, you see," Louisa said. "Ellen will be fine." She didn't feel nearly as confident as she hoped she sounded.

The young woman leaned forward, her eyebrows pinched together.

"Ever since the war started, the Germans have taken to disliking us intensely. You'd be surprised how many Americans were on the boat with me — all leaving Germany. We're quite un-popular there. It was such a relief to step foot again on American soil."

"Their loss," Billy said.

Exasperated, Louisa tossed down her pencil.

"Mr. Stephens, please. I'm trying to conduct an interview here," she said.

With an exaggerated sigh, Billy rose from his chair, donned his hat and sauntered off. His broad shoulders moved with the swagger of a man who knows that he's attractive to a certain kind of woman. Louisa was not of that kind.

She turned to the unpleasant task at hand — unpleasant because she dreaded replacing Ellen, who was so much more than an assistant. Ellen was also her friend and confidante. And she was absolutely invaluable when it came to Louisa's darker stories, the one she wrote under her pseudonym, Beatrice Milton. On the other hand, this pert young thing would hardly need any training at all when it came to the society stories.

"If you don't mind my asking, Mrs. Wolff — why not move back in with your family and let them find you a new husband, one that meets with their approval? It's not easy for a woman to make it alone in this world," Louisa said.

Mrs. Wolff's eyes narrowed, her face tightened, and her breath sounded almost like a hiss.

"I'll never go back into that cage," she said.

"Cage? Your family?" Louisa was stupefied.

"Marriage," she responded. Again she leaned toward Louisa, this time her hands trembling with emotion as she clutched the bag on her lap. "He turned out to be horrid. I made a vow to myself that I won't be dependent on anyone ever again. And please call me Phyllis. I hate being burdened with his name."

Louisa blinked in surprise at the young woman's frankness, and her stone heart softened.

"Oh my dear. I'm so sorry."

"Thank you," Mrs. Wolff said, straightening her back and regaining her composure as she looked at Louisa with forthright, almond-shaped eyes.

Louisa sighed. There seemed to be no way out. Ellen would be leaving tomorrow, and Phyllis Wolff had all the necessary qualifications for the job — as long as it stayed within the confines of the society page.

"As you observed earlier, you are a perfect fit for the job of my assistant. You certainly know how to dress the part. You can even cover some of the events for me." Which, she had to admit, was not a function that Ellen with her working-class Irish background could have fulfilled. "Yes, I think you'll do quite nicely." Then she added, "Temporarily, of course."

"Of course." Then Phyllis Wolff smiled at her so warmly that the whole room lit up.

"I'll see you Monday morning," Louisa said. "Bright and early."

"How early?"

"Oh, by the crack of eleven," Louisa said. Then they both laughed. Completely against her will, Louisa had been won over.

After Mrs. Wolff left, Louisa returned to her correspondence. To her utter surprise, she saw an envelope from Forrest Calloway, publisher of the paper and her former lover. She glanced around to make sure no one was watching. Then she opened the note and read:

Dear Louisa,

Would you care to join me to go to a baseball game tomorrow afternoon? If so, please call my house tonight and let Mr. Kimura know. We'll pick you up at one.

Yours truly,

Forrest

She fought back the tears and told herself it meant nothing, but her heart told her she was lying. This meant everything.

To pre-order this book, please visit my series page: https://www.amazon.com/dp/B0BBDGKRKK?

About the Author

Trish MacEnulty is the author of the historical fiction series, Delafield & Malloy Investigations. She has written four other novels, two memoirs, a short story collection, and children's plays (some of these under the name Pat MacEnulty). She currently lives in Florida with her husband, two dogs, and one cat. She teaches journalism classes at Florida A&M University and writes reviews and features for the Historical Novel Society.

Made in the USA
Columbia, SC
10 April 2023